THE SEARCH
FOR THE
CRYSTAL KEY

A Continuation of Dark Escape

by

Eileen Sheehan

This book is dedicated to all the die hard romantics who enjoy a little mystery and a few thrills tossed in the mix.

Let's Do A Brief Catch Up...

On the cusp of her eighteenth birthday Tara O'Shea moved into the centuries old country estate she inherited from her grandmother. She wasn't long in the house before she started seeing an apparition of a man.

Tara's brother, Dennis, brought his friend -who was also Tara's ex-boyfriend- Mitch, for a weekend visit. The trio set out on an exploring excursion in the woods behind the house where Tara fell into an abandoned well. Fortunately, Tara's horse was with them and while waiting for Mitch to run back to the house to call 911, with the help of rope and the mare, Dennis pulled Tara from the well. Mitch returned with Dennis's jeep and the two men took her back to the house to await the ambulance.

While in recovery, Tara's spirit guide appeared and introduced himself as Liam. He spoke to her briefly and then disappeared.

Once recovered, she decided to drive into a nearby town for supplies. While enroute she met Maggie O'Shea. Maggie wasn't only her shirt tail relative, but her neighbor. Adept at metaphysical arts, Maggie took Tara under her wing to teach her spirituality and magic.

Maggie gifted Tara with an ancient text that was handed down in her family from generation to generation. Consumed by curiosity, Tara unwittingly read the wrong section of the book and unleashed the dark side. A threatening face of a demon appeared in a ball in front of her. Liam arrived and sent the demon on his way, before leaving just as fast as he came.

Taking a short cut through the fields to seek out Maggie to tell her about what occurred, Tara met a tall, dark, and handsome stranger, named Brandon, riding an enormous black gelding. They exchanged pleasantries and she continued on to find Maggie at the local country store. Maggie decided to stay with her for a few days to make sure all was well.

While eating at a local restaurant, Tara and Maggie met up

with Brandon. He slipped Tara a note asking her to meet him in the same field where they'd first met the following afternoon. When she arrived, she found him face down on the ground with a gash on his head. While debating how to handle the situation, an extremely handsome blonde, named Dominic, appeared. Claiming he was just traveling through the area and stopped to take in the view of the countryside, he offered to drive Brandon to the local hospital with Tara as his guide. Brandon was admitted to the hospital and Dominic drove Tara back to her home, where Maggie awaited.

Tara found Dominic absolutely gorgeous in a god-like way and completely missed the fact that he was more interested in the house than he was in her.

When Brandon was released from the hospital, he arrived at Tara's house late in the day to retrieve his gelding that she was kind enough to board during his hospital stay. While they're discussing what the safest route for him to ride his gelding back to the stable, they spotted a creature with the head of a wolf and the body of a cat stalking them. When Maggie grabbed a gun and shot it, the beast exploded into pieces.

They decided it was best for Brandon to stay the night. Maggie lured Brandon downstairs after everyone went to bed and drugged him so she could sample his blood to make sure he wasn't a demon. While Brandon was in his drug induced sleep and Tara was safely upstairs sleeping, Maggie shot a few more beasts lurking outside.

After that, some time passed without mishap before Dominic arrived unannounced at Tara's door while she was attempting to remodel. She accepted his offer to help. In the interim, he made a play for her that she couldn't resist. From that day forward he arrived at about the same time each day to romance Tara and help with the remodeling of the house.

Things moved quickly between Dominic and Tara. He soon offered his hand in marriage. This didn't sit well with Dennis, who argued vehemently with Dominic.

While taking a walk to cool off, Dennis was attacked by one of the demon beasts. He escaped death, but was badly injured and sought help from Maggie. While Dennis rested, she headed off to Tara's house to investigate the situation.

Maggie wasn't captivated by Dominic's looks like Tara was. Instead, she felt an evilness that she couldn't place. She was worried about the hold he had on Tara so she cast a spell asking for the person capable of separating Tara from Dominic to appear. Brandon arrived in response to Maggie's spell.

Panicked about possibly losing Tara to Brandon, Dominic decided to drug her and impregnate her so Dennis wouldn't fight the marriage. When Brandon and Maggie burst into the room to stop Dominic, he stormed from the house.

Full of denial, Tara refused to believe Dominic would do what Maggie and Brandon claimed he did, so she turned her frustrations on Brandon. Maggie took Brandon back to her house to let Tara cool off. En route, they fled from more demon creatures.

Tara finally came to her senses. While taking a shortcut on her mare through the woods to Maggie's house, she was chased by a dark figure. When she arrived, Maggie took her mare into her home with them because the fields were filled with the demon creatures and she had no other shelter for the horse.

The demon creatures turn out to be Dominic's pets.

They killed as many as they could until they ran out of ammunition, while Dominic insessently pounded on the door demanding Tara come to him. Maggie found a spell to counteract Dominic, but it required an herb from her garden outside. She wore her cloak of invisibility to sneak out amongst Dominic and his demon creatures. Dominic saw the ground flattening beneath her invisible feet. He tackled her and then let his creatures tear her apart.

With dawn rapidly approaching and, with it, the loss of his demonic creatures, Dominic set the house on fire to force them out. After much turmoil and expression of fear, Tara calmed down enough to gather her wits about her and called upon Liam for help. He immediately extinguished the fire and destroyed Dominic and his demon creatures...

...And so the story continues.

ONE

Flames engulfed the cottage and taunted the leaves of the old apple tree, forcing its sap to the surface to help ease the scattered damage to the charred bark. The hot, dry air seared her lungs. She'd never experienced heat of this nature. Her skin hurt to the touch. She could see the evilness in Dominic's eyes as he prowled the parameter of the dwelling. His bellowing pierced through the chaos, "I want to you Tara. If I can't have your body, I'll have your soul!"

Tara's firelight curls fell over her shoulders and down her back in wild abandonment as she shook free memories of that horrible, fateful night. Sliding her hands up the sleeves of her oversized lamb's wool sweater she hugged her tall, slender body against the chill both from the air and her thoughts.

Leaning her head against the window pane, her dark green eyes peered at the blanket of frantic white snowflakes as they billowed toward barely visible outbuildings. The howling gales of winter echoed throughout the rolling Pennsylvania valley with a resemblance of a collective of musical instruments paying homage to old man winter while they shook the one-hundred-eighty-year-old house; rattling its windows with such force that one might expect the antique dwelling to be swept into the Land of Oz.

The nor'easter had arrived with a vengeance, showing no mercy for the impuissant inhabitants of the land. She'd focused so hard on preparing the grand old house for the oncoming winter that the equally grand stable hadn't received the attention to insure its strength for a season of storms such as this.

The storm made it easy for her to come to terms with her decision to find a handyman to finish the needed repairs.

She filled her lungs with the crisp air that managed to find its way through her newly caulked windows and hoped the outbuildings were sturdy enough to make it to spring in one piece; after which she'd give them the attention they required.

Her daydream was so real, her lungs actually felt singed. She drew in as much cooling air as she could one more time and then released it slowly, focusing on the light mist that formed from the moist warmth of her breath on the cold window pane.

She was always active and outgoing. Finding herself snowed in with limited connection to the outside world for over a week took its toll on her mood. It gave her far too much time to think. It ripped at her soul to know that because of her and her stupidity in summoning the dark side -followed by her poor choice in men- many had suffered loss and heartache.

She walked over to the large, overstuffed horse-hair sofa she recently had restored and snuggled under the thick multi-colored afghan her Aunt Eva gifted her at Christmas. The roaring fire in the newly renovated fireplace illuminated the rustic red bricks that spoke of days gone by. She missed her aunt and was eager for her next visit. Her loneliness was accentuated not only by her missing Eva's vibrancy, but Dennis was on vacation down south and her father had called her last minute full of excitement about his archeological find and begged to be excused from the holidays because he didn't dare abandon the dig and risk vandalism. Tara understood, but was still saddened by his absence.

The warmth emanating from the dancing flames struggled to evade the draw of the chimney that permitted it to merely hover within feet of the open hearth, leaving the rest of the room prey to the icy air that crept steadily through the badly insulated walls and windows. The dilapidated steam radiators that were installed throughout the house soon after their invention provided little assistance. She stood up and pushed the sofa closer toward the fire, being careful not to get so close that a stray spark might damage its rich, newly applied tapestry upholstery. Resuming her spot under the afghan, she passed the dismal afternoon hours in cozy slumber.

The setting sun crept over the distant mountain top before Tara roused herself from her blissful snooze. The fire needed attention. She debated whether to add more wood and stoke it back to its former level or let it die out for the night. The house had eighteen fireplaces and, although she enjoyed the ambience of her downstairs study, surely she could find a room more protected from the outdoor elements and start a warming fire there. Deciding it was best to close the room off until its leaks were tended to, she pushed the glowing remnants of heat under a pile of thick, lifeless ashes and felt the last hint of warmth trickle away. Satisfied, she rubbed her upper arms against the impending cold of the night yet to come and left the room.

The antique grandfather clock that stood regally at the far end of the second floor hallway chimed six o'clock. It was time for Sugar's nightly feed.

She pulled on her heaviest hooded sweatshirt and thick insulated socks, followed by her goose down parka, insulated gloves, fur lined rubber boots, thick woolen neck scarf, and a pair of snowmobile goggles. True warmth spread through her chilled body for the first time all day. She was sorry to have to ruin it by going out into the cold, but she had responsibilities that were unavoidable.

Pushing the solid oak exterior door -that she was told was an original part of the house- open against the elements that were raising havoc wasn't an easy feat. Gusts of pelting ice mixed with snow still dominated the atmosphere. Pulling her woolen neck scarf over her nose, she plunged forward. It took all her strength to forge her way down the one-hundred-yard path to the stable. She could hear the crunch beneath her well protected feet as she broke through the mid-calf high seemingly endless sea of crusted snow.

Even with all the layers of warmth on her body, she felt the cold. Her moist breath left tiny frozen crystals along her lips and in her nostrils. She focused her flashlight in all directions while she checked for unwanted creatures lingering in the night, a habit she developed after her encounter with Dominic's demon beasts.

Time dragged as she plunged her way through the blinding blanket of white. When she finally reached the stable, she stared in breathless dismay at the amount of ice and snow that needed to be removed before she could slide the door far enough to pass her slender body through.

The sudden realization that she left the snow shovel on the opposite side of the door resulted in one of the loudest wails of frustration she could recall ever emitting. The urge to kick the door was overwhelming, but her legs were held hostage in the ever deepening heavy snow. The best she could do was lean her body against the side of the building and slam her heavily mitted fist against it. Sugar's whinny had a calming effect on her and she relaxed enough to think how to get into the stable.

Thin, icy tree branches lightly brushed her head as a gust of wind whisked a thin layer of the tree's burden off into the night. She would have found the spindly boughs of an ancient apple tree, that were laden with a thick coat of snow atop icicles that reached low to the ground, wonderfully marvelous to gaze upon under better circumstances. Wiping the excess snow from her face, she studied the tree and its position to the building. Its thick trunk indicated it was much older than the stable.

The thud of the branches scraping against the wooden door to the hay loft added percussion to the melodious whistling of the wind. She shone her flashlight to inspect the situation as best she could. Even laden with snow, the branches looked sturdy enough. If she was careful, she could climb up and enter through the loft. Under the best of circumstances Tara would have been hesitant to climb a tree, but she saw no other option. Once inside she'd be sure to grab that darn shovel and keep it in a place of easy access.

Tucking her trusty flashlight in the inside pocket of her coat, she wiped the melting snow from her goggles and gripped the lower branch of the ancient and gnarled apple tree.

"Here goes nothing!" she shouted into the night.

It took a moment for her eyes to adjust to the lack of the flashlight's helpful beam, but soon she was maneuvering with confidence. Although her slender frame was in prime physical condition, heaving her heavily clad body out of the deep snowy wells that sucked at her legs like quicksand felt almost unattainable. The exertion left her body wet and clammy with perspiration. She felt laden with damp, cumbersome, and smelly fabric. She was just about to give up when she found reserved strength to pull her out of the snow and make her way from one branch to the next.

Now that she was up the tree, the door was further from the branch than it looked when she was on the ground assessing things. She hadn't realized the actual extent of the ice on the branches either. She was higher than she thought she'd be when she first started this venture and, from her present position the branches felt dangerously feeble. The gnarled and rickety limb that she just hoisted her weight from threatened to rot away from the ancient, gnarled tree trunk. The new branch that she balanced carefully on felt like it might be a little too thin to hold her much longer. Looking closer, she realized that the old fruit tree was actually in need of serious TLC. She cursed the darkness. If she'd accessed the situation in the daylight, she wouldn't have climbed the tree to begin with.

As she stretched her body as much as she could, she caught a glimpse through the pelting snow into the endless darkness below. Climbing back down the prime candidate for the wood pile looked even more precarious than making her way to the loft door from her not-so-sturdy perch. She grabbed the frame of the loosely hinged door and from a crouched position, flung her body hard against it. It all happened as if she's performed a choreographed stunt in a movie. Her body hit its mark and the door flung open. She landed unceremoniously onto a pile of old, dusty hay.

Bits of sharp, dust riddled straw sent her into a fit of sneezing as her nose did its best to cleanse her nasal cavities, stopping only when it succeeded in flushing the majority of it out and leaving her sadly in need of a handkerchief. Rummaging through her pockets and coming up empty handed, she shrugged and used the sleeve of her down jacket; shuddering at her own actions. She grabbed a fist full of snow from the door frame and wiped her sleeve with it.

The ache on her rib cage reminded her of the location of her flashlight. Wincing, she reached in and pulled it out by its thick barrel and clicked on the beam. She'd been in this part of the loft only once and had never really taken the time to inspect it closely. Sugar's quarters were on the far end of the building. Shining the flash light's beam through swirling particles of dust and bits of hay that rode the occasional gusts of winter through the loft door, she was surprised to come upon a group of portraits leaning against the interior wall.

Looking closer, she saw they were of people dressed in eighteen and nineteen century attire. Interestingly, one man was in a confederate solder's uniform. She was no expert, but after a more in depth examination of the paintings, she was certain that they weren't recently painted. They were surprisingly well preserved, but clearly quite old. Tara felt certain the artist managed to portray a very strong likeness to the people in the paintings. She wasn't sure how she knew this. It was just something she felt.

The sound of her mare's stomping below brought Tara back to matters at hand. Making certain to securely latch the loft door, she searched for the ladder that would take her to the main floor and carefully picked her way down it. Once her footing found the concrete base of the stable she relaxed. She was on familiar ground now and, although the flashlight came in handy, she could actually accomplish what she needed to do without light if the situation called for it. Fortunately, the electricity hadn't been interrupted by the brutal storm and she was able to light up her surroundings with a flip of the switch.

Sugar's excitement in seeing her was barely contained. There had been no telepathic communication between them since the night of Maggie's brutal murder, but there was no need for Tara to understand her four legged friend's greeting. The mare was happy to see that her owner and care taker had arrived and her needs would be tended to.

The mare's part of the old stable was fairly well protected from the storm. Tara lowered the scarf from her face and removed her thick mittens so her hands could maneuver more comfortably. The heat of Sugar's breath as she nuzzled her affectionately was a welcome sensation. Working as quickly as she could, she refreshed the water bucket, put a wedge of hay in the hay rack, a scoop of grain in the feed bucket and made certain the mare's blanket was secure before she reached for the pitch fork to remove the soiled hay.

She thought nothing of the piercing cold on her cheeks and continued pitching hay, hoping to finished quickly and get back to the comfort of a hot bath and a snug blanket. When the cold grew bone chilling, she couldn't ignore it any longer. This part of the stable was too well protected for this type of cold to be assaulting her. She checked around for its source. Her breath caught in her throat and her chest constricted as she found herself staring into the large, brown eyes of the old man who hadn't appeared in months.

Unlike the other times when he was there and then gone almost as quickly, he stood zombie-like and as three-dimensionally opaque as any human would be. The only thing differentiating him from Tara was the hazy glow around his body. Every nerve stood at attention while she debated what to do. Running away was her first inclination, but a ghost could pop in and out whenever and wherever it desired, so running would be futile. Besides, how far could she possibly get in that blizzard? She longed for Maggie. Maggie would know what to do and Maggie wouldn't be so frightened.

With trembling hands, Tara moved the pitch fork in front of her and continued to clean Sugar's stall. Perhaps, if she ignored him, he'd go away. Sugar scraped her hoofs and snorted her disapproval. The air bursting from her nostrils created tiny clouds that floated into nothingness. The ghost wasn't going to go away, but it wasn't saying anything either. As if seeing a ghost wasn't frightening enough, his staring was creepy.

She was about to confront him when he uttered "Lucy", in an almost inaudible voice that held a distinct and thick brogue and then faded into nothingness.

Tara was dumbfounded. It took a stinging slap across her face by Sugar's coarse tail to bring her back to reality. Her body trembled, but at least the air warmed up to the point where her breath was barely visible. She recalled the book Maggie gave to her explained why the air got so cold when a ghost appeared, but she couldn't remember the details. She'd forgotten a lot of the teachings Maggie had worked so hard to instill within her along the way. They were locked up tight in the recesses of her mind; too painful to remember, for by remembering them she remembered Maggie. She shook her head. Did the reasons why the air got cold when a ghost appeared really matter after all was said and done? She thought not.

"It's for the best," she said aloud, "I don't need to know all of that mumbo jumbo. Look at what it got me. Not to mention what it got Maggie. It's just as well that I forget it all."

She hurried to complete her chores. The encounter with the ghost was quickly pushed into the back of her mind, along with the other memories she wanted to diminish and, hopefully, forget.

TWO

The storm ceased sometime during the early hours just before sunrise, leaving behind it mini mountains of icy snow to be removed before her home could run at its normal pace.

Tara sighed. Winters in Manhattan were so much easier. She couldn't have imagined such burdensome weather and was therefore not totally prepared for it. She was grateful for the good sense she exercised in following Maggie's suggestion to purchase the small tractor with a snow plow attachment. A cold reminder of her friend, the valuable piece of equipment was left dormant since the day it was delivered.

Today it would make its debut.

She'd programmed her coffee maker prior to going to bed and wafts of the dark liquid's rich aroma lured her out from beneath the warm security of her goose down comforter. She hated the cold and often wondered why her crazy ancestors settled in the north. Even if they had come from a cold climate, surely they could have acclimated to the warmth of the south had they given it a chance. She dreaded the air that awaited her outside her covers. She'd have stayed in it all day if she hadn't had duties and responsibilities. They forced her to brave the brisk air of the large, poorly insulated rooms of the great house.

She'd just reveled in her first sip of coffee when the telephone rang.

She rushed to answer it, hoping it was Dennis calling to tell her he was on his way. He'd urged her to join him on his vacation down south, but she neither felt the inclination to go, nor was she as free as she was when she boarded Sugar elsewhere. Now, if she wanted to go somewhere for any length of time she had to hire someone to look after her mare, her kittens, and her house. She wasn't up to entrusting people she didn't know with her most precious possessions. After her nightmare with Dominic, her trust level was exceedingly low.

Looking at the after effects of the horrendous storm, she wondered if leaving Manhattan was the wisest thing. She wasn't a farm girl and didn't profess to have any skill with something as formidable as a tractor and snow plow. The thought of having to sit on the mini-monster and maneuver it through the thick blanket of heavy, crystallized precipitation that went on for as far as the eye could see was horrifically intimidating. She fervently hoped that it was Dennis calling to tell her he'd returned early from his trip.

"So, how goes it out there in no man's land?" Mitch's sarcastic tone of voice that accompanied the equally sarcastic remark grated on her already frazzled nerves. "I understand you had a whopper of a storm last night. I just called to see how you survived it."

"I hoped you were Dennis," Tara grumbled.

"I see you're your usual sunny self in the morning. No coffee yet?" he sighed.

Having her rudeness so clearly pointed out startled Tara into realizing just how much she'd changed since she moved into her beautiful country estate.

As if reading her mind, Mitch continued, "You know, the Tara O'Shea that I knew and loved would have never been so curt and thoughtless, no matter how she felt inside. She was always the epitome of social etiquette. I'm not sure how I feel about the Tara you've become since you moved to the country. I think the hustle and bustle of Manhattan produced a much more amiable female."

"I'm sorry. I'm not feeling all that great today," she said earnestly. After a moment's silence she added, "I hear you're in love. Congrats."

"I am and thanks. I want you to meet her. I think you two will get along great. She has a lot of qualities you'd like. It's like you two could be sisters or something," Mitch said and then quickly added, "That's not why I'm with her. I love her for who she is. In fact, I asked her to marry me."

"I..." she started before he continued and interrupted her.

"I thought we'd pop out to your place this weekend," he said brightly. "Dennis should be back by then, right?"

Tara groaned inwardly. The last thing she wanted to do was entertain her former love and his new love, but things had smoothed out between them enough to make being around him tolerable and she didn't want them to revert back to the tenseness that dominated their interaction after they broke up. She regretted the fact that Dennis was good friends with him. She saw no way out of playing hostess to the new lovers.

"You're more than welcome," she lied.

Although the sun lit up the thick white blanket of endless crystallized sea, the air was still brutal. Mitch's voice faded into the background as she focused on the cold that consumed her room. There were some portions of the house that she hadn't yet managed to protect against the elements, but this particular room was one of the very first to be renovated. She watched the first flakes of snow fall with the illusion that she'd be warm and snug in this room at least.

The bitter cold she experienced now was disheartening. What could she have missed? What didn't get patched, insulated, caulked or weather-stripped? The tickling of the back of her neck as her hair stood at attention alerted her that she wasn't alone in the room. These feelings only happened when something not human appeared. It was an explanation for the cold, at least. She wasn't sure if she should be happy or unhappy about it.

Not up to facing whatever it was, she closed her eyes and prayed it would go away while Mitch continued with his recapitulation of the events leading up to his meeting and falling in love with Alana. He rambled on, completely unaware that his audience was only half listening. She finally let her eyes comb the room for the intruder. It was only a matter of seconds before she spotted him.

The old ghost was back.

She wasn't sure if ghosts were telepathic, but she sent him a message to leave anyway. Whether he heard her thoughts or simply felt it was time to go, she wasn't certain. Whatever the case, she gave a sigh of relief as she watched him fade away.

Just as his shape reached the point of being barely visible, she heard a faint "Lucy" in the same thick brogue that was spoken the night before. She had no idea why this ghost would be calling her Lucy and for the present she had no desire to find it out.

"Does that work for you?" Mitch's question brought her back to reality.

"Does what work for me?" she asked.

"I said," Mitch's impatience was clearly noted in his tone, "we can be there about five o'clock on Saturday."

"I'll make a pot roast," she said as she tried to reign in her focus.

"Sounds good," he replied.

Without seeing if Mitch had more to add to the conversation or even politely saying 'good-bye', Tara returned the receiver to its cradle and sat down to drink her coffee. Who was this ghost and why did he keep coming around? She didn't like it. She didn't like it one bit!

She missed Maggie.

Tara had only just started allowing herself brief glimpses into her memories of her time with Maggie. Little by little the shock of Maggie's brutal death at the hands of Dominic and his evil beasts was ebbing away and she was able to feel again. She could finally grieve properly. Now seemed like a good time to cry, so she did it with gusto. Since there was no one in the house with her except her rapidly growing kittens, there was no one to stop her; no one to comfort her; no one to care. Even though she knew this, she still imagined Maggie walking in her usual unannounced way through the door to linger in the recesses of her mind.

****

Tara fidgeted with her long firelight curls as she watched the tall, slender form of the future Mrs. Mitchell Longworth -better known as Alana- slide gracefully out of the late model Jaguar he'd miraculously maneuvered down the long, tree lined driveway she'd made a pathetic attempt to plow. The enormous fur hood hugging Alana's face and neck made it impossible to tell if she was a blonde, brunette, or redhead, but Tara lay dibs that Mitch's goddess was a blonde. Her breath caught in her throat as the woman looked in her direction. Mitch hadn't done his future wife justice. He'd declared her beauty over and over, but it always seemed that perhaps his vision was clouded by love. She could see now that it wasn't. Alana had to be the most beautiful woman Tara had ever laid eyes on.

Doing her best to arrange a few stray strands of hair with her suddenly clumsy fingers and wishing she'd chosen an outfit other than jeans and oversized hand knitted cotton sweater that hung loosely over her slender hips, she ran to the doorway to welcome her guests.

"Damn, it's cold!" Mitch said as he stomped the snow from his boots. He kissed Tara on the cheek and pulled his fiancé forward for a proper introduction. "I want you to meet Alana. Alana, this is Tara."

Alana was surprised when Tara showed no signs of recognition. Dominic had spoken truth. Alana could always tell when Lucy was lying. She'd clearly lost so much of her memory she actually thought herself to be Tara O'Shea. Well, at least she remembered the O'Shea.

"Welcome," Tara said with a little too much exuberance.

She hoped her words came across sincerer than she felt as she hustled her guests into the house and out of the bitter cold.

Mitch wasted no time in shedding his coat and scarf.

"I can't believe how fast this weather came upon us," he said. "One day I was enjoying a balmy fall day and then I woke up and there was snow everywhere!"

Tara furrowed her brows as she listened to Mitch ramble on. He seemed nervous. Was he worried she hadn't approved of his fiancé? What did her opinion matter anyway? Was there something about her that would make her not approve? She looked from Mitch to Alana for a clue.

"Your home is lovely," Alana said.

The words glided off Alana's tongue and past her perfectly aligned, pearly teeth just as gracefully as she'd glided out of the car. Tara was duly intimidated.

"It's a diamond in the rough," Tara managed to say, "but I'm excited about the end result. I have a vision in my mind of how it should be. I want to restore it as much as I can to its original condition."

"Really," Alana mused as she walked to the banister and caressed it admiringly. "I suppose that would be nice. Some people would take a fine structure like this and bring it up to date; modernize it. I think the old fashion is still beautiful." Alana flashed a smile that would melt a snowman in seconds, "Very beautiful."

Tara held her arms out to receive Alana's coat and hung it on the antique coat tree that came with the house. She only recently got it back from the furniture restorer she discovered while looking for a handyman. His work was excellent and his rates were surprisingly reasonable.

"I agree," Tara said awkwardly. "I put in a few new windows and an intercom system, but otherwise I'm doing my best to keep it as real as I can. Can I get you something hot to drink... coffee... tea... hot chocolate?"

"Brandy?" Mitch said with amusement.

"Can she drink?" Alana whispered to Mitch.

"Brandy it is," Tara replied, choosing to ignore Alana's question.

Tara suddenly regretted telling Dennis he didn't have to rush over. He'd sounded so exhausted from his fun in the sun that she insisted he relax and not rush coming to her house, but she really didn't want to be left entertaining his good friend -who was also her ex-boyfriend- and his gorgeous catty fiancé on her own. She was extremely uncomfortable.

At one time, Maggie would have been here with her; her bubbly personality dominating the room. The wave of sadness that consumed Tara didn't go unnoticed by her guests. Mitch and Alana exchanged looks with raised brows.

"Is everything okay? Are you okay? You seem sad," Mitch said with gentle concern; a factor that didn't pass by Alana.

He touched Tara's elbow lightly, adding to her sadness as it brought back memories of the good old days.

A dark cloud swept over Alana's brilliant blue eyes while she contemplated the exchange of emotional familiarity between Mitch and Tara. Their touch was too familiar for her not to question if there was more between these two than the good friends Mitch claimed they were.

Alana was gorgeous and she knew it, but Lucy was a beauty in her own right and could potentially pose a threat to her position with Mitch and her plans. Familiar feelings of rivalry surfaced. She wouldn't let Lucy beat her, memory loss or not. She needed to act quickly. Inching closer to Mitch, she touched his forearm seductively.

"Mitch, honey," she purred. "Perhaps our hostess is just tired. I mean... look at her, she looks worn out and it's no wonder. If what you tell me is true, she cares for this big place all by herself."

Mitch didn't catch Alana's undertone, but Tara certainly did. She would have been offended if Alana hadn't been so right. She was exhausted, but not from maintaining the place. She was tired from life. She felt like a bedraggled mop after what she went through. She probably did look as bad as she felt, but for a perfect stranger to say such a thing to her host was both appalling and insulting.

Tara locked eyes with Alana. Each woman did her best to relay her position with expression. Tara wanted Alana to know that she was on to her phoniness and Alana wanted it to be clear that Tara wouldn't beat her on anything.

Tara sighed. Leave it to Mitch to bring a viper into her home. Hadn't she been through enough?

Their silent exchange passed right past Mitch without notice.

"Well, hell Tara! Why don't you get some help out here?" Mitch asked as he twisted his head to look through the doorway of the parlor. "Where's that old woman who's always here? Dennis told me she's been good company for you. What's her name again?"

"Maggie," Tara said softly. Tears surprised everyone as they slid down Tara's cheeks while she choked out the words, "She's dead."

Mitch was horrified.

"Tara. I'm sorry," he said apologetically. "Dennis never said... I didn't know... Dead? When? How?"

"A few months ago," Tara said as she sniffed back the tears. She wiped at her moist cheeks with her sleeve, not caring about the impression such an unsophisticated action made on Alana and added, "I'm really not up to talking about it."

"Sure," Mitch replied. He put his arms around his former love and held her close; ignoring the jealous snorts emitted by his future wife, who remained close at his side. "I'm sorry I brought it up. I didn't know. I'm sorry. I just didn't know."

"It's okay," Tara assured him.

Her voice was muffled as she buried her face deep into Mitch's chest. It was some time since she felt the strong support of a human hug and she wasn't anxious to give it up. Knowing that his catty bitchy fiancé was standing nearby and wasn't happy with what she witnessed, Tara kept her eyes closed to avoid having to face the consequences of her actions for just a little longer.

Alana snarled inwardly. Mitch's display of concern for Lucy made her stomach turn. She smiled inwardly about the fact that she'd deliberately destroyed Dennis' letter telling Mitch what happened to Maggie. He told the whole sordid story of how Dominic tried to marry his sister in order to get possession of the house and find something. Fortunately, they never found out what that something was and poor, poor Lucy was far too traumatized to use her brain and think to look for it. She didn't doubt the whiny thing would tell the story to Mitch during their visit, but she planned on finding the crystal key and getting out of there before Lucy knew what happened.

Mitch interpreted Alana's thoughtful scowl as disapproval of his attempt to comfort Tara. He knew that in spite of her almost overwhelming beauty, Alana was a jealous female. Tara's beauty could easily rival Alana's. Hugging her was asking for trouble. He shrugged his shoulders and gave a look of chagrin, hoping to lighten the situation as much as he could as he gently pushed Tara away. To his surprise and relief, it worked and Alana's scowl gradually transformed into a broad smile.

Tara pulled herself together.

"Let me show you to your room so you can get comfortable," she said as she directed her attention to Alana. "Are you hungry? I made pot roast."

Alana sniffed the air and said in a sickly-sweet tone, "It smells wonderful."

Tara flashed one of the warmest smiles she could muster in Alana's direction, hoping to smooth over the tension. She had no idea why such a gorgeous woman would be jealous of her, but it was written all over her face; if only for a moment. As she guided them to their room, she was grateful her home was so large. She'd decided to put them in a room at the far end of the house that had only recently been furnished and prepared for guests rather than her normal guest rooms, which were closer to her own. She wanted to have Alana's negative jealousy as far away from her as possible while she was in the vulnerable state of sleep.

While passing the full-length mahogany trimmed mirror that was centered along the wide, elaborate landing that attached her quarters to the guest quarters, she caught a glimpse of herself. Alana was right. She looked worn out. There was nothing for her beautiful guest to be jealous about in this house, nothing at all.

Suddenly Tara regretted the bad start they'd had gotten off to. After all, it wasn't as if she wanted Mitch for herself. As for the woman's phoniness... well, it was probably standard in beautiful women. Beauty could be a powerful tool when dealing with men such as Mitch. Tara could hardly hold Alana's use of what nature bestowed against her.

Alana walked up behind Tara and stood looking at their reflection. Tara gasped as she realized how closely they resembled each other. Mitch was right. They could be sisters; with Alana being the prettier one. She watched as Alana adjusted a few stray hairs with the grace of a debutante and sighed. Tara craved female companionship and she wanted to get to know the future wife of her former love. Well, it wasn't too late. Perhaps, after everyone rested and dined she'd try to mend the fence between them before it got even worse.

****

Dinner went smoother than Tara imagined. After a hot shower and short nap, Alana's mood was more amiable.

She expressed a deep appreciation for the old house. Thrilled to have someone share her passion for everything vintage, Tara happily accommodated her with a tour. The two used their time alone to break through the icy chill that started their relationship and get to know each other a little better. Tara showed Alana every nook and cranny of her grand abode. Alana took in everything like she was burning it to memory.

Mitch, never an admirer of anything old, opted to relax in the den by the fireplace with a good scotch whiskey in his hand.

Tara found the amount she had in common with Alana

remarkable. They not only looked similar, but had similar tastes in just about everything, including men.

The hours passed quickly and before she knew it, it was time to say good-night. Mitch and Alana's trip over snowy and sometimes icy roads in a sports car was tedious and tense. The exhaustion from the trip combined with full bellies, alcohol, and a blazing fireplace, had practically put them to sleep in their chairs. Tara felt a little guilty for not considering their situation earlier and waiting until they could no longer disguise their yawns and droopy eyelids before suggesting they call it a night. Since she'd already shown them to their room and Alana now knew her way around the house almost as well as she did, Tara opted to remain downstairs to tidy up before retiring.

Feeling wonderfully cozy and satisfied with the way the evening went, she kissed the couple on their cheeks and bid them good-night. It was good to have life in the house again. She'd missed the companionship more than she realized.

Humming a non-descript tune, she picked up their glasses and the Mikasa snack dish that at one time sported an array of gourmet crackers and cheeses, but now, thanks to Mitch, had barely a crumb left thanks, and headed for the kitchen sink. She would wash them in the morning.

The cold chill down her back practically took her breath away. She didn't need to look around to know what was going on.

He was back.

Her exhaustion combined with the frustration over the appearing and disappearing of the resident ghost -mixed with the generous amount of brandy she'd consumed during the evening- gave her an abnormal sense of bravery.

"Who are you and what do you want!" she demanded while she continued to pick up the dishes. When she received no response, she continued, "If you aren't going to tell me, then just go away. I'm tired of your tedious visits. Speak or get out."

"Lucy," the ghost whispered.

"Who's Lucy?" she asked impatiently.

Tara set the glass she just rinsed off on the drain of the sink and turned to face the semi-transparent old man. As she did so, he faded away, but not before he issued a warning.

"Come home... danger," he said in a barely audible whisper.

Tara stood, motionless, as she stared at the spot where the old ghost had appeared. She had no clue what he could possibly be saying. She tried to remember the other times he'd shown up. What was occurring in her life when he'd appeared before?

The first time she saw him was after she fell into the well. Then, it was around the time she read from Maggie's book. These were all very different times, but they all revolved around danger. She wished Maggie was there to could confer with her. Maggie would have an explanation; she was certain of that.

She wondered if she should speak to Mitch about it. What would he say if she told him? Would he think she was crazy? She was sure he would. It would be better to hold off and talk to Dennis when they were alone.

She rubbed the chill from her arms. The wind had picked up outside and the house was cooling down. It was time to head upstairs to snuggle under her thick goose down comforter. She would get a good night's sleep and then decide if she would confide in Mitch or not in the morning.

As she flipped off the light switch it dawned on her that the first time she saw the ghost wasn't in her bedroom after the accident. It was while speaking with Mitch on the telephone. In fact, every time the ghost appeared, Mitch had either telephoned, was visiting, or was on his way to visit.

THREE

Tara was lightly dozing off when she heard the unmistakable padding of slippered feet on the wooden landing as they made their way past her bedroom door. Her bedroom was at the top of the first flight of stairs and centered between the guest quarters and the stairwell that led to the third floor. The creaking of the hardly used door at the base of that stairwell signaled to her that whoever was tip toeing around wasn't heading to the kitchen for a snack. There hadn't been enough time passed since she and Mitch were dating for her to forget the sound of his footsteps, which left only one other person; Alana.

Why would she be sneaking upstairs; especially after Tara specifically kept it out of their tour, explaining its disrepair as hazardous? In its days of glory, the third floor of the house was the residence for the servants. Since her grandmother neglected to maintain things for so many years, there was structural damage on the top floor where the leaky roof and broken windows left some of the rooms at the mercy of the elements. She'd declared it off limits to everyone, especially her guests. She boarded the windows and repaired the leaky roof almost immediately upon taking possession of the house, but there were still plenty of hazards for someone maneuvering around, particularly at night. Sliding out of bed she jammed her feet into her slippers, donned her well-worn robe, grabbed a flashlight from the drawer of her night stand and left the warmth of her renovated bedroom to brave the mercilessly fierce night air of the rest of the house. Stopping at the bottom of the narrow stairwell, she listened intently before cautiously making her way to the third floor. Fearful of it being a potential fire hazard in its present condition, she'd disconnected the electricity on the top floor; making the flashlight her only source of visibility. Stepping as lightly as she could, Tara felt as if she was the intruder instead of the other way around.

She wasn't sure why she wanted to keep her presence a secret. This was her house, after all. Even so, somehow she felt like she shouldn't be there.

She'd ventured onto the third floor three times since moving into the house. She took a tour with her father while awaiting the moving van, and shortly afterward when a repair company estimated the cost to bring it back to its original state of charm and glory. The number set Tara on her heels. She decided that until the main part of the house was finished she'd put the resurrection of the third floor on hold and just make it off limits to everyone for safety's sake. She ventured up there the third time to instruct the workers she hired to do the necessary repairs to the roof, disconnect the electricity and board the windows.

When she reached the top step, a thin beam of light moved near her. She ducked down to avoid being seen. The weak beam from Alana's undersized flashlight continued to comb the dusty great room that must have been the main room for the servants. Leading from this former great room that still harbored energy of time gone by was a long hallway with doorways that opened to smaller rooms that were humble in comparison to the spacious and grand rooms below.

Tara watched with amazed wonder as Alana rummaged through the enormous steamer trunks that were clustered in the center of the cluttered room. She acted intent on leaving disarray and mayhem behind her without a care of what Tara might think when she finally did venture upstairs. What is she looking for? Tara shifted to a more comfortable position. The scent of old dust swirled through the stale air at the disruption of fabric that hadn't been touched for possibly a century or more. She held her finger to her nose as she forced back a sneeze that threatened to burst forth.

Oddly enough Tara had no desire to interrupt her house guest. There was something intriguing about skulking about in the middle of the night watching this strange and beautiful woman rummaging through her dusty old unused rooms looking for heaven knows what. Alana's perfect face glowed in the dim light and cast shadows in multiple directions. It had a surreal mesmerizing effect.

Tara was certain that if her presence was known, Alana would cease her hunt. If she did, would she confess to the purpose of her search? She didn't know her well enough to have that answer, but she guessed she wouldn't. Not only was Mitch's new bride-to-be exceedingly beautiful, but she proved mysterious as well.

Alana's search uncovered a group of portraits. From what Tara was able to make out as the weak beam briefly illuminated them, they could be more of the same that were in the stable loft. If so, the artist was kept quite busy. Tara assumed they were portraits of her ancestors and wondered why her grandmother cared for them so poorly. She vowed to return to go through them more closely and perhaps put them in a friendlier environment for safe keeping. If they were in decent condition she would display them in the great room downstairs or along the hall like she saw in many grand ancestral estates.

"Drat!" Alana's muffled voice mixed with the clanking of metal as a tin type crashed to the ground.

Sensing her secret scavenger was about to abandon her search, Tara took advantage of the commotion and dashed back to her room. As she leaned against her bedroom door she was barely able to hear the padding of Alana's feet as she hurried back to her room above the crashing of her thunderous heart.

This unexpected event had adrenaline coursing through Tara's veins and there was no way she could go back to sleep. She stayed motionless against the door while she waited for her heartbeat to slow down and hearing to come back to normal.

Opening her door just far enough to hear better, she listed for sounds of activity. When she was satisfied no one else was up and wandering the house, Tara grabbed her large flashlight and made her way back up the stairwell to the third floor.

Her curiosity was peaked and she wouldn't be able to sleep until she investigated what the dusty and cluttered third floor could possibly offer a stranger visiting her home. The brilliancy of the beam from her large flashlight was in stark contrast to the faint eerie lighting that Alana's minuscule beam provided.

Standing at the top of the stairwell, she gasped as she took in the chaos that woman created. Of course, this floor was abandoned for a length of time that Tara could only guess at. Even so, it had been a neat kind of cluttered abandonment. What she witnessed now was indescribable chaos. Could it be that Alana thought Tara was so unfamiliar with its condition that she wouldn't notice it was ransacked? Or, perhaps she simply didn't care? Did she find what she was searching for?

The richness and glitter of the thick deep blue velvet adorned with tiny crystals that peeked out of an oversized trunk caught her eye. She lifted the trunk's lid, being careful not to disturb the thick layer of dust to the point where it would fall onto the remarkably well-preserved clothes within. Pulling the heavy gown to its full length, she held it out to admire it. Spotting a full-length mirror in the corner of the room, she wiped its surface with an old curtain that lay on the floor nearby and held the dress against her body.

The nineteenth century ball gown was her size, something she found interesting since she was taller than the average female of that era. Turning slowly from left to right gave her a better visual of how she might look in such a dress. Although the lighting was far more effective than before, she'd left the flashlight propped by the trunk and was now standing in the outer rings of its illumination. As a result, her image had a mysterious, hazy effect.

As she continued to admire the elegant dress of yesteryear, the room's reflection slowly changed. Her surroundings shifted from a dimly lit, dismal and dusty attic-like room to a brilliant, spotless quarterage. Startled, she dropped the gown and turned around only to find that the room was still dark, dreary and deserted.

Closing her eyes, she took a deep breath and braced herself to face the mirror once again. With her eyes still closed, she picked up the gown and rested it against her body. This time prepared for the vision that would follow, she slowly opened her eyes. Straining to view the room through the mirror's reflection, Tara marveled over its beauty. Even though this was clearly the residence of the help, it was still a fine room.

Behind her, the carved and gilded beech wood of the nineteenth century winged back armchair glistened from loving care and attention while the silk and its Beauvais tapestry cover sparkled with freshness. She longed to turn around and find such a chair behind her to relish and sit enveloped in its beauty.

Spotting a marble top commode off in the distance, Tara wondered how she missed its existence. Its finely polished, gilded mahogany was exquisite. The abundance of French influenced nineteenth century furniture brought many questions about her ancestors to Tara's mind. Clearly their Irish heritage didn't define their taste in décor.

Disappointed when the mirror once again reflected the dimly lit dusty decay of its former splendor, she turned to search for the marble topped commode. Although not all of the furniture she enjoyed in her vision was still in the room, she instinctively knew that if she searched for the commode she'd find it.

Carefully laying the dress over the now faded armchair, she took a moment to lament the chair's loss of its former splendor before picking up her flashlight and directing it to the part of the room where her she remembered the mahogany commode in her vision. She smiled with satisfied delight at the delicate marbled wisps of white and black stone peeking from beneath a pile of precariously stacked boxes.

She pulled at the stack of boxes, hoping the marble wasn't cracked and the wood was in restorable condition. The windows in this room hadn't needed boarding so perhaps the ravaging fingers of the elements hadn't stretched this far into the house.

She was standing back, catching her breath after removing the final box, when she heard a familiar male's whispered voice, "Lucy." Startled, she lost her balance and fell against the cool marble and was only able to catch a glimpse of her resident ghost as he faded into nothingness. Propping against the commode to support her shaky legs, she willed her body to relax and headed back to bed. She would return for the marble top commode and tidy up the place in the daylight.

Making a mental note to find a polite way to question Alana about her actions, she crept her way back to her room and immediately fell into bed. She was exhausted.

****

Alana's statuesque poise was in stark contrast to the dark circles under her eyes as she silently nibbled dry rye toast and sipped black coffee. Mitch questioned her apparent mood and was rewarded with a scowl accompanied by a reply of 'nothing's wrong'. Seeing his love like this for the first time was unsettling. He questioned his wisdom in introducing her to Tara. Could it be she figured out Tara had been more to him than just the younger sister of his good friend? If so, it might account for her sullen mood.

Mitch smiled to himself. How could his gorgeous fiancé possibly harbor jealousy over another woman? Grant it, Tara was a beauty in her own right and he could see her rivaling Alana for attention in certain circles, but by no means was she Alana's superior. She was her equal maybe, but not superior.

Women were an odd lot.

Even though Tara's return to the house from the stable was through the utility room off the kitchen, the cold air that rushed in behind her managed to find its way into the dining room. Mitch shivered in defense. He moved to the doorway of the kitchen and watched her finish stomping the snow off her knee high boots and then shake her coat free of the pesky white stuff before hanging it up on the hook above the boot rack.

Mitch marveled over how methodically she removed her boots and placed the boots carefully in their designated space on the rack before slipping on her sheepskin slippers with apparent little thought of her actions. It looked well-rehearsed.

Her rosy cheeks accentuated her rich green eyes as she smiled and made her way to the coffee pot for a hearty mug of the aromatic liquid. Caressing the steaming cup, she nodded to Mitch while she slid past him through the door and made her way to her favorite spot at the dining table. Looking at Tara in the morning light, Mitch could easily understand why his fiancé might harbor jealousy toward the woman. Although he would have liked to hang around to see Dennis, he thought it best they leave as soon as possible.

"I thought we'd head out today," Mitch stated as he cleared his throat.

"Why?" Alana and Tara responded simultaneously.

Surprised at his fiancé's reaction, Mitch stuttered, "Well, I noticed that you seemed tired and tense and I thought perhaps we were overdoing things, my love. I've been dragging you all over in my exuberance to show you off." He turned to Tara, "You have your hands full just surviving the winter without having us underfoot."

"Nonsense," Tara countered. She wasn't about to let Alana leave without the mystery of her rummaging excursion on the third floor being resolved first. "Besides, Dennis is coming today and he'll be disappointed if you're gone. I know he's looking forward to meeting Alana."

Tara eyed Alana warily. She knew all too well the reason behind the dark circles under the woman's eyes. She just didn't know the motive behind them. She thought about just bringing things out in the open and mention Alana's late-night wanderings, but decided it might be for the best if she didn't let on to Alana that she was even aware of her midnight ransacking until she found out her reason for it.

Alana watched her fiancé seat himself next to her in silence. After studying him for a brief moment, she reached across the table and caressed his forearm.

"Darling, I'm fine. Really, I am," she cooed. "I just didn't sleep well last night. The house is lovely, but it's old and full of noises that I was acutely aware of. An afternoon nap will correct everything. Please, let's not leave on my account." She leaned back and smiled over the rim of her coffee cup. "Besides, I'm eager to meet this Dennis I've heard so much about. If he's anything like his sister, I know I'll like him."

Tara eyed Alana with wary surprise, but said nothing. She had to give the woman credit. She was good.

Mitch was both relieved and confused by her last remark.

"Well, I guess I'm out voted," he said. Standing and stretching in a cat-like manner, he turned to Tara. "Since I'm here... ya got any chores for me ma'am?" he asked with an emphasis on his attempt at a southern drawl.

The two women chuckled.

Mitch may have regretted his statement, but he didn't show it as he listened to Tara's request for assistance with carrying in enough firewood for several of the fireplaces. Tara assumed he was grateful that she only asked him to carry it and not chop it. Fortunately for all concerned, Brandon chopped a considerable supply of firewood to keep himself occupied while awaiting her recovery from their traumatic ordeal at the hands of Dominic.

Alana took the afternoon to rest up. Dennis was expected for dinner and she wanted to be at her best for their introduction, which meant sleeping away those dark circles. She wondered who he was really and why he passed himself off as Lucy's brother. Oddly, Lucy didn't remember her. At first Alana thought she was putting on a show for Mitch, but as time wore on she realized it was true. Alana was warned that one's memory could be affected during the transport through time, but it was usually temporary. Is that what happened to Lucy? It didn't seem possible. She was a strong witch, after all. Her mind shouldn't have been affected at all. Alana's certainly wasn't. But then, Dominic said Lucy suffered memory loss in Shadow Land so perhaps that played a part in what was going on now.

Tara used this time to pull Mitch into the attic to retrieve the marble topped commode. Not a fan of anything older than a decade, Mitch groaned his distaste while he sneezed his way through the dust filled room. He heaved the ornate commode onto his shoulder and carried it down the stairwell as if it was nothing more than a box of feathers. Tara never ceased to admire the brute strength this man possessed and was never happier than now that he possessed it.

The commode was far lovelier than she imagined. She couldn't wait to see it cleaned up and displaying its rich, historic beauty. It fit perfectly beneath the large, antique mirror in the hallway. Standing back with her hands on her hips, she admired it briefly before rushing to the cleaning closet for the necessary supplies in hopes of returning the dry, dusty gilded mahogany to its original rich luster.

Since her inheritance of the estate house, Tara discovered an array of riches in the form of antiques. Much of the furnishings dated back far enough to have been considered an antique when first placed in the house. Surely they could have commanded a good price at an antique auction and helped in the maintenance of such an unusually grand estate, but then from the funds left by her grandmother there was no need to sell one stick of furniture. There was also no reason for the dilapidated condition of the house. She often questioned her grandmother's reasons for neglecting it.

After standing and admiring her handiwork, she suddenly remembered the portraits in the loft above Sugar. They weren't as safe from the elements as the ones on the third floor. Eager to rescue them, she rushed downstairs and donned her boots and coat, thankful the sun was brilliant enough to make visibility in the loft easy without a flashlight.

The brilliant rays coming through the open door she'd used to jump through during that horrific storm provided better than adequate lighting for a clear view of the portraits. As she slowly poked through the stack of various sized paintings of familiar feeling faces secured in beautiful antique frames resting against the interior wall of the old building's upper floor, she wondered why her grandmother left their family memories at risk of destruction by the elements. She questioned so much of her grandmother's actions. She would move them all back into the house and put them where they wouldn't be at risk by the elements until she could determine what to do with them. It might be fun to investigate the ancestry registries on the internet and discover who was who.

The framing was constructed of mahogany, cherry, or birch. Although making a beautiful outline around the portrait, lifting the larger ones was difficult. She'd need help. She selected the ones she was confident she could manage on her own and set them aside.

She was only a portrait or two away from the end of the stack when she froze in disbelief. There, standing tall behind an attractive woman seated in a beautiful nineteenth century cruelled tapestry winged back chair was her resident ghost. The hairs stood at attention on her neck as she studied the portrait more closely. She recognized the room in the portrait. It was the one she used as her formal sitting room. She was certain the chair was the one she saw in her vision in the mirror the night before.

This was all too eerie.

Taking a closer look at the woman seated in the chair, there was a familiarity about her that reached down into Tara's bones. Who were these people? Why was he haunting her?

She couldn't explain why, but she wasn't ready for others to view this portrait. She needed time to understand what was happening. If Maggie was alive, she'd ask her about it and would have gotten a logical explanation, but Maggie wasn't alive and she was more alone than she cared to be.

A brief thought of Liam passed through her mind before she pushed it away. She hadn't communicated with him since he gave her Maggie's message. He'd spoken of Maggie and said she was well and happy. Knowing that provided some semblance of comfort.

Thinking of Liam brought back memories of everything else that happened. The wounds were still too raw. After all, it happened only a few months ago. The type of healing she required would take much longer than that.

Although she was grateful to Liam for coming to their rescue, there was still so much she didn't understand. Why did a spirit guide have to wait to be called upon before he could help someone who was in perilous need of assistance? Why did Liam allow Dominic and his demon wolves to rip Maggie to shreds? If Liam was sent to guide and protect her, then why didn't he just step in and protect her and the ones she loved? Why? Why? Why? It was all very confusing and still too painful to think about.

She hadn't thought of Liam since he stood before her and she asked him if she could enter the shadows in time. He responded in turn that 'anything is possible if you believe'. Was that true? Would she find Maggie there?

Her life changed so drastically since she moved into this estate and she wasn't altogether happy with the changes. She loved and was bonded to her ancestral home and looked forward to the day when it was finally restored to its rightful beauty, but she was lying if she didn't admit regrets about the loss of innocence moving into it caused. The underworld, other worlds, and the worlds beyond were what she read about in novels or watched on the big screen or DVD. They weren't supposed to be part of her reality.

Picking up a stray burlap bag from the floor, she shook as much dust free as she could and secured it around the portrait of the old ghost with baling twine. The wood's density made the portrait extremely weighty and cumbersome as she tucked it away in the far recesses of the loft floor for safe keeping until she could return with help to retrieve it.

The sound of pacing below alerted her to the hour. She hurriedly gathered what she was able to carry and made her way down the stone stairway that led to the lower level. Carefully positioning her burden on the bottom step, she headed toward the feed room. She might as well feed and care for Sugar while she was there. Hopefully, by the time she went back to the house, Dennis would have arrived.

FOUR

Dennis pushed his chair away from the table and loosened his belt. He couldn't remember the last time he'd made such a glutton of himself at the dinner table. After a day of getting to know her future husband's friends and assured neither knew her, Alana decided to borrow the kitchen and cook them a meal. At first glance upon the Hot Bloody Mary soup, cod cobbler and blackberry and apple turnovers, Dennis doubted he'd survive, but much to his surprise and delight, the food was profoundly delectable. Completely taken by his friend's beautiful fiancé, Dennis praised her talent in the kitchen and questioned if she had more delicious recipes up her sleeve. She assured him she did and promised to prove it one day.

Tara wasn't as taken with the mix of textures and flavors. Perhaps it was the food, or perhaps it was because she was no longer taken with the chef.

After another night of inconspicuously following her mysterious house guest through the vacant and darkened parts of her house, the woman rapidly lost what little favor there was in Tara's eyes. Tara didn't appreciate her hospitality being violated in such a manner. Alana's behavior was nothing short of vandalism. What made it worse was the fact that the woman could care less about the fact that she left these areas in so much disarray it would take ages to clean them up again. The fact that Tara found even more disturbing was that she seemed unconcerned about being discovered. Tara decided she would confront Alana about it after dinner. It needed to stop and Alana needed to explain herself, not to mention the fact that Tara was feeling sleep deprived.

Their table talk eventually came to the topic of how Mitch met and fell in love with Alana. Tara couldn't have been less interested. She found their story lacking credibility and substance. There were far too many holes to fill in.

****

Alana waited for Tara, Mitch and Dennis to get comfortable in the den with a glass of brandy and a warm fire before she made her excuses. Her claimed a splitting headache and the desire for an early night. She hoped her hosts would forgive her.

After expressing their condolences, the men dove into a conversation about a new sports bar Dennis discovered. They barely noticed when Tara excused herself and followed Alana up the stairs.

As Tara had expected, Alana went directly to the third floor. It was barely nine o'clock and the entire house is still awake. Mitch mentioned they would be leaving the following day. Perhaps her brazenness had to do with the fact that she hadn't found what she was looking for.

"Is there something I can help you find?" Tara asked.

She illuminated the room with a battery operated lamp that she'd placed in it earlier that day.

Alana jumped, startled by Tara's unexpected intrusion.

"Tara! I wasn't expecting you," she said in a tone that actually sounded accusing.

Tara couldn't believe her ears. What type of response was this?

"I imagine you weren't," Tara said, indignantly.

"Get off your high horse!" Alana barked.

The woman's striking blue eyes turned dark with irritation, causing Tara to pause. There was something familiar about that look that took her aback. She suddenly wished she was anywhere, but there. She didn't like the mystery around what was happening. It felt wrong. It felt very wrong. She needed air.

Tara started back down the stairs.

"Where are you going?" Alana bellowed. "Do you think you can hide it from me? I'll find it. You can be certain of that."

Tara stopped in her tracks and shook her head to clear it. This was all so surreal. She had no idea what Alana was talking about.

"Lucy, leave us," barked the all too familiar voice.

"Pa!" Alana gasped with a mixture of surprise and delight.

Tara turned to face her resident ghost. This time the old man was as solid as the rest of them. She was sure if she dared to reach out and touch him, his flesh would be warm and supple.

The old man's eyes smiled warmly, but she didn't care. Her legs were wobbly as she moved as best she could across the room and down the stairs without bothering to look back.

"Pa, how are you here?" Alana asked meekly. Her words trailed down the stairwell as Tara made her way to her room.

Falling into the soft folds of her down filled comforter, she closed her eyes and urged her body to succumb to sleep. All those nights of stalking Alana had finally caught up with her. She was delusional. That had to be it. She couldn't face yet another creature from the underworld or other world or whatever world. It was too soon after Dominic.

It was probably in her mind, a kind of aftershock. She heard of people suffering post-traumatic stress syndrome for years. The nights of sleep deprivation had caught up with her. That was all. A good night's sleep would change things. A good night's sleep would bring normalcy and order back into her life.

As she lay in her bed with the escape into blissful nothingness almost upon her, the serene glowing a semi-opaque ball in the corner of the room caught her attention. She knew immediately Liam was making his presence known, but she wasn't up to communicating with him or any other spirit or creature from another realm or world. She was tired. She felt worn out and run down. She felt totally exhausted.

EILEEN SHEEHAN

"Go away," she groaned. Her words barely audible.

The golden ball obediently shrunk into nothingness while her body succumbed to a slumbering abyss.

****

Alana was overly eager to be up and on the road the following morning, barely allowing Mitch the opportunity to say good-bye to Tara and Dennis. Although he found her actions most unseemly, he said nothing. His romance with Alana was fast and furious and there would be many moments of surprise for each of them as their personalities and behaviors surfaced. He guessed his fiancé's unseemly rudeness was just one of many surprises to come. Making a mental note to speak to his love about her behavior when they were alone, he did his best to cover his embarrassment through smiles and hugs as he thanked Tara and Dennis for their hospitality and assured Dennis that he'd check out that sports bar real soon.

After experiencing Tara's storm induced plight first hand, Dennis decided to stay with his sister and help her get things back under control. The sun's intense rays mercifully melted a great deal of snow that accumulated during the storm so it was easy for Dennis to maneuver the small tractor effectively. Tara watched Mitch's Jaguar weave its way down the neatly plowed driveway and shook her head. She wondered if last night really happened. She was overly tired, after all. Alana certainly showed no signs of their encounter when she hugged her good-bye.

Tara sighed.

Alana managed to escape explaining her incessant rummaging through the house. The sly fox managed to avoid her right up to the point of their departure. She may be questioning her encounter last night, but she was certain Alana's rummaging was real. The mess that awaited her attested to it.

Misinterpreting Tara's scowl as a lover's scorned, Dennis stepped up behind his sister and wrapped his arms lovingly around her, pulling her back against him so that her head rested against his strong chest.

"Time marches on, sis," he said with a sigh.

"What's that supposed to mean?" she asked defensively.

"It means just what it means," he said. "Time marches on and things change... people change... we change."

Tara sighed. She had no clue what Dennis was referring to and wasn't in the mood to bother figuring it out. She patted him on the back of his hand and gently twisted free. She wanted to go back inside and rest a little more. Even thought it was in a part of the house that went unused and could stay as is indefinitely, just thinking about Alana's mess made her feel overwhelmingly exhausted.

"I think I'll feed Sugar," Dennis tossed the words over his shoulder as he made his way off the porch. "Maybe I'll do a little clean up while I'm there."

"Do you want my help?" Tara asked, secretly hoping he'd decline her offer.

"I lit a fire any man would be proud of in the study," he said. "Why don't you go inside and curl up in front of it?"

"I won't argue with you," Tara replied as she slowly shook her head. "I don't know why I'm so tired," she said, more to herself than to him.

"Entertaining can be exhausting. Plus, it's only been a little a couple of months since... you know. Of course you're tired. It will take a long time to heal. Don't rush it," Dennis said affectionately.

What they endured was so unfathomable that sometimes he had trouble believing it happened. He could only imagine the pain, guilt and denial his sister wrestled with after watching her close friend and mentor being ripped to pieces and knowing it was she who brought Dominic into their lives. He didn't blame her, but he knew she blamed herself.

He wondered if she would ever trust a man again. He hoped so. He knew for a fact that Brandon loved her and if his observations served him right, his sister was pretty keen on Brandon. Had Dominic not thrown himself into the mix Tara and Brandon would probably be a couple by now.

The thought of Brandon reminded him about the e-mail he'd received just that morning from the very man. His new friend and demon survival comrade was actually in the area. A visit from him might be just what Tara needed. He reached for his smart phone and shot off a reply, making sure he knew he was welcome to come that very day if he could.

He no sooner played cupid than he second guessed the wisdom in it. Tara was really looking poorly. Maybe Mitch's visit was too much for her. She might just need more rest instead of more company. He hadn't considered that in his desire to see her happy. He didn't know how to undo his invitation. There was nothing to do, but tough it out and hope that Tara wasn't overwhelmed when she saw Brandon at her door.

His shoulders felt heavy as he made his way toward the old building that housed his sister's prized equine friend. About half-way down the path, he squared his shoulders, shaking them as if he was shaking off an invisible weight, and then sucked in the cool air. There was nothing to do about it. Hopefully Tara would welcome Brandon with open arms and warmth and not hold him in distrust and disregard as she seemed to be holding all men except him these days. He had neither the heart nor the stomach for denying a man who was right next to him as they literally fought for their lives a visit. The ordeal bonded the men for life. Whether Tara liked it or not, she was bonded too.

&***

The majestic antique grandfather clock chimed three o'clock as Tara roused herself from slumber. She must have been more tired than she realized to sleep such a deep sleep in her favorite overstuffed chair. It was a cozy chair, but not that cozy. Her body was so stiff she could barely uncoil it. Groaning at the resistance her legs and lower back gave her, she slowly prodded her limbs into a standing position. She still had time to surprise Dennis with a nice meal. He'd made such a fuss over Alana's meal, perhaps it was time to show him she was just as adept in the kitchen.

As she grew more and more alert and took in her surrounds her brows knit together. Something was amiss. The fireplace was cold and it was dark outside. The only light on was the one on a timer set for seven pm. She felt the chill in the house as the feeling returned to her limbs. She wished she dared turn the thermostat up, but she didn't want to over tax the furnace that was still in need of repair.

Things were so different here than in Manhattan. There you could find what you needed day or night, seven days a week. Fortunately, with the help of a good fire in the fireplace, the room could easily be tolerable again. She walked to the window and pulled the draperies aside. The full moon hung high in a crisp, clear sky, providing just enough illumination for her to see Dennis' lone footprints leading to the stable. She gasped when it finally dawned on her that it was three o'clock in the morning.

How could this be?

After only a few short seconds of brooding, she decided to seek the cozy comforts of her bed and worry about how she managed to sleep so long and why her brother left her in such an uncomfortable position without tending the fire at another time. She found it amazing that she could even consider going back to sleep after such a long slumber, but her body longed to stretch out in the snug comfort of her cushy mattress and cuddle beneath the warmth of her down-filled comforter. The house felt incredibly cold. She jiggled the ancient thermostat and listened for the purr of the furnace. Satisfied that all was in working order, she headed up to bed.

Massaging the small of her back, she stretched it as far as she could to work out the knot in her lower back. She would have to have a serious discussion with Dennis in the morning. She was sure he felt not disturbing her was right, but she'd have preferred he sent her off to the comforts of her bed and would make that perfectly clear in the morning... nicely, of course.

As she made her way up the grand staircase, Tara saw the old ghost standing in her peripheral vision. Too tired to deal with anything except making her way to bed, she pretended not to notice him.

****

The sounds of winter birds communicating their delight in a new day outside her thick leaded glass window combined with the rainbow of light from the brilliant sun's rays that wove their way through the irregular glass added to the soothing ambience of her soft, warm bed. She stretched to her full length. With the exception of her brief ascent to her bedroom, Tara had almost twenty-four hours of uninterrupted sleep. She felt truly rested for the first time in months.

She slipped her feet into her plush sheepskin slippers. Her hand hovered near her worn out robe before bypassing it for the thick, lush robe her Aunt Eva had given her for Christmas and then headed toward the kitchen for her morning ritual of coffee and an English muffin smothered with organic blueberry jam.

The house was uncommonly quiet.

Tara was tempted to pop her head through Dennis' door to rouse him, but decided against it. He may not admit it, but he was also still recovering from the trauma of almost dying at the hands of Dominic. He refused to let her see it, but she knew. He needed his sleep just as much as she did.

Her brother had a penchant for aromatic foods. She'd make coffee and bacon. Perhaps the aroma would tickle his senses enough to prompt him to open his eyes and join her. If not, then she knew he was in need of recovery sleep and would leave him alone for the day. She smiled wryly as she contemplated the fact that his long hours of sleep would be achieved in the comforts of his bed and not split between his cozy mattress and an awkward overstuffed chair.

The sun's rays caressed the antique lace curtains as they lined the row of windows in the breakfast nook. The combination of sunshine and antique lace gave the house a cozy and inviting feel. The draperies that layered some of the windows were added as an afterthought to help insulate against the cold. Their days were numbered. As soon as the house was brought up to snuff and insulated correctly, she fully intended to remove them. They deterred from the charm of the old-world ambience she was working toward achieving.

While passing through the foyer, she glanced out the front door and saw a taxi slowly winding its way up the long drive to her front door. Wrestling with her irritation that someone would arrive at her home at such an early hour and her regrets at having to greet them in her robe and slippers instead of being properly groomed and dressed, she opened the door and stepped out onto the front porch. The cold winter air that assaulted her cheeks and bare ankles had a surprisingly soothing effect on her irritation.

The reprieve was short lived when she saw Brandon's tall, handsome figure ease out of the back seat of the cab. She stood frozen in total disbelief while he pulled a weekend bag from the seat next to him and closed the door. Her fickle heart beat wildly as it began its ascent from her chest to her ears.

This couldn't be!

The cab started back down the drive and Brandon reached the bottom step of her porch before she could find her tongue to speak.

"What are you doing?" she almost spat at him.

Tara no longer trusted men. She especially didn't trust herself around this man. The only other man who pulled on her in this way was Dominic and look how that turned out. The last thing she wanted was to expose herself to the possibility of losing her heart to another untrustworthy and possibly demonic stranger.

Brandon stopped in surprise. "What?" he asked in confusion.

"I suggest you call that cab back here on the double because it's mighty cold to be walking back to town!" Tara roared.

"Dennis... your brother invited me," Brandon replied. He was both startled and mortified by Tara's greeting.

Dennis warned him to be prepared for this type of a greeting. He stressed she was suffering post traumatic syndrome and developed a mistrust and hatred for all men, save Dennis. He'd assured him it would eventually pass and that they needed to be patient. While Dennis hoped that Brandon's visit would help heal Tara, Brandon hoped it would help spur her memories. If he could just get her to remember him then she'd remember everything else and her pain would go away.

His desire to see her, to be near her, was overwhelming, but he had no desire to hurt her or upset her like this. He never would have come if he'd known she was this bad. Even with Dennis warning him he never imagined it this severe. Unfortunately, the cab was long gone.

"I thought I was welcome. I'm sorry, I didn't realize. I didn't know," he apologized.

"Dennis invited you?" Tara was at a loss for words. "Oof!" escaped her lips as she indignantly expelled the reserve of air her lungs were rigidly hanging on to. The two stood awkwardly on the porch for a moment before Tara gave in and offered him entry to her home on the condition he would call the cab company to return right away. "There's coffee in the kitchen. You know the way. I'll get Dennis," she growled, "so he can explain himself to both of us."

Tara darted up the stairs to wake her brother. He had a lot to answer for. Why would he even think it was okay to invite Brandon into her home when he knew she wanted nothing to do with anyone or anything that reminded her of that night and especially didn't want a thing to do with men? What was going on in that mind of his? First he left her sleeping all crumpled up in a chair and then he invited the one person in the world who would bring to life the memories she so desperately wanted to forget into her home -as well a potentially raise havoc with her heart- as a guest. This was too much, just too much!

She flew into his room, fully prepared to rip into him about his thoughtless behavior. Only half a syllable escaped her lips when she saw the empty room and neatly made bed.

The room was a corner room. A row of oversized windows dominated the outer walls, offering an excellent panoramic view of the estate. Pulling back the heavy draperies, she scoped her snow covered property for signs of where her brother might have gone. The only tracks she saw were those that led to the stable. Could he have gotten up early and gone out to care for Sugar? If so, he was really going to spoil her.

Chagrined by her anger toward her brother when he was being so thoughtful about allowing her to sleep and helping her with her cumbersome chores, she ran to her room and quickly dressed in a pair of faded denim jeans and a thick woolen, light tan Irish wool sweater. She had no desire to face Brandon alone after the greeting she just gave him. She owed him an apology for her rudeness, but still wanted to speak with Dennis about it all. She would go out to the stable and discuss things in a calmer manner. There could be a very good reason for his invitation, although she couldn't imagine what. She should at least give Dennis an opportunity to explain himself. Tara was so engrossed in going over her future conversation with Dennis in her mind that she forgot about Brandon until she almost ploughed into him while rushing through the kitchen toward the coat room.

"I forgot about you," she stated flatly.

His closeness caused a stir in her that took her aback. She felt it when they first met. It was a type of school girl flutter. After all that happened she couldn't imagine why she'd still experience this reaction to him. It was unsettling.

"So quickly?" Brandon smirked teasingly.

Ignoring his comment while she struggled to regain control of her fickle emotions, Tara continued, "Dennis is out in the stable. I'll be right back."

She hoped she sounded cool and aloof instead of as twisted and confused as she actually felt. Eager to busy her shaking hands, she pulled on her boots and wrestled with her coat and scarf.

As an afterthought, she turned and said, "I made some bacon. Scramble some eggs for yourself if you want. You know your way around the kitchen."

Brandon grinned, remembering the first breakfast they'd cooked together.

"Thanks. I'll do just that," he said with gratitude.

Tara cursed herself for her inability to be a bad hostess and headed out the back door.

"Scramble your brains while you're at it," she mumbled viciously, more for her own benefit than for his. She was infuriated with her body for betraying her. "Better yet, scramble mine. Maybe then I'd forget about you and all the other nightmares in my life."

FIVE

Sugar whinnied in anticipation as Tara neared the old stable. The familiar sound of her mare's nose batting at an empty feed bucket concerned her. Sugar only did that when she was very, very hungry. Dennis helped tend to the mare since she was a small foal in training. It was improbable that he'd neglect to feed correctly after all of these years.

She slid through the partially opened door.

"Dennis!" she called out repeatedly, giving time in between for him to answer.

Her mare's persistence won out and Tara set to task feeding and caring for her equine companion. Completing her chores with still no sight of her brother, she climbed the stairs that led to the dusty loft. It was doubtful Dennis was up there. He could have easily heard her calling him and answered if he was. She felt compelled to look anyway.

All was quiet, just as she'd expected.

At the faint sound of Brandon calling her name, she scurried back to the house. She'd given him free rein of her kitchen and hoped she hadn't made a mistake.

****

It was early afternoon and there was still no sign of Dennis and no clue where he went. His SUV was parked in the driveway. There was nothing to indicate it had been used. Tara thought perhaps he'd decided to take a walk in the woods -something he did at times to clear his head and help him release some of the tension that built up during the week. The only footprints she or

Brandon could find stopped at the doorway to the stable.

When she called the police, they said Dennis hadn't been gone long enough to consider him missing, but if he didn't return by morning he'd be considered missing and they'd file a missing person's report on him. She hung up the phone disappointed.

The afternoon was endless. The sparks that flew whenever Brandon came near Tara were practically unbearable. When it finally reached a respectable hour to beg off and go to her room, she made her excuses, eager to put distance between them and to be alone with her thoughts. As she stretched out across the handmade quilt she'd discovered on a shelf in the wardrobe of one of the many bedrooms the house possessed, her mind raced with scenarios of what happened to her brother. She sensed the ghost of the old man standing in the corner of her room.

Too frustrated and worried to be fearful, she turned her head in his direction and whispered, "Where is he?"

"Lucy," the old man whispered.

"Who is Lucy?" she whispered.

"Aye, lass, ya are me Lucy," the old man replied with his thick Irish brogue and a smile.

"I don't know your Lucy, but I'm not her. You're mistaken," she grumbled.

Tara was feeling far too weary and far too worried about her brother to want to exchange pleasantries with the household ghost, but she didn't know how to avoid it.

"Yes ya are, lass. Now and before," the old ghost whispered.

"Now and before? What do you mean?" Tara asked with obvious agitation.

She had a feeling the old coot was talking about reincarnation, but, since she wasn't sure she even believed in such a thing, she wasn't going to be the one to suggest it.

"Ya went over the shadow line. Ya lived in this house with me in another time gone by. 'Twas your home. Try to remember, lass. Ya are me Lucy, me lovely, lovely, Lucy. Remember and come home, lass."

Maybe the old ghost wasn't referring to reincarnation? She was confused. What shadow line? Was it the same one Liam mentioned? Should she question the ghost about it, or just close her eyes and ignore him? What should she do? She decided to ignore him. Positioning herself on the bed with her back facing the spot where the semi-transparent man stood, she closed her eyes, hoping he'd take the hint and leave.

"Look at me, girl," he cooed.

Her eyes shot open at the familiarity of his tone. His words were like a warm, soothing caress. Even so, she had no idea who he was, where he came from, and why his voice was familiar. All she knew was that at this moment she wanted nothing to do with him.

"I'm your pa, girl. I'm your pa," insisted the ghost.

The certainty in his voice took her aback. The melody of his brogue reminded her of Maggie.

"Well, that's odd because I distinctly remember hearing Alana call you her pa, and since she and I have never met before..." Tara replied sarcastically.

"Ah, but ya have, lass. Ya grew up together," he replied steadily.

How should she answer this delusional dead man?

"They took your Dennis," he said.

The sadness that emanated from him permeated the room.

Adrenaline surged through her at his unexpected statement and she sat up with a start.

"Who took him?" she demanded.

"The shadow people," he replied.

She flew off the bed and moved closer, while maintaining a respectable distance between them. Even in her panicked state she could feel the tingling of the air around the entity from a few feet away.

"I can't stay. I'm not strong enough. I must go now," he said with regret. "Listen to the shadows in the wind, child. Ya can hear them. They carry the shadow people," he said as he faded away.

"What do they want with my brother? Where is he?" she asked as she watched him fade away.

Disappointed and panic stricken, she rushed to Brandon's room and barged in. Seeing his surprised look was like a bucket of cold water tossed at her face, bringing her quickly to her senses. Brandon was wearing a tee shirt that he filled out remarkably well. Memories of the afternoon she saw him with only a towel that barely covered his virility taunted her. Her blood pumped through her temples and her breathing grew labored. She couldn't believe her own insensitivity and lack of control. Her brother was kidnapped by shadow people and she stood there salivating over this man's hot body. She just wasn't herself because of the trauma she endured, that's it. That had to be it.

"Have you ever heard of the shadow people?" she asked, after gaining control of her breathing.

"The what?" he asked.

"Shadow people.... shadow people!" she roared impatiently.

As far as she was concerned, the fact that she barged, unannounced, into his room was no longer an issue. Dennis' abduction was once again in the forefront.

Brandon cocked his head to the side and knit his brows.

"They have Dennis," she said excitedly.

"What?" his eyes shot open wide, "Who has Dennis?"

"The shadow people!" she said in a way that made her impatience with him perfectly clear.

"We know this how?" he asked with a voice that was low and level.

"From the ghost," she said as she plopped herself onto the edge of his bed. Realizing how crazy she sounded, she added, "Oh, forget it."

Brandon cautiously eased himself down on the far edge of the mattress, being careful not to get so close that she felt threatened.

"Why don't you start from the beginning?" he said with firm gentleness.

The distraught beauty eyed Brandon long and hard. If he was any other person, she'd never consider telling the tale she was about to tell for fear of being labeled insane, but this was Brandon. This was a man who fought next to her against Dominic, his demon wolves, and finally the fire. After what he'd gone through, telling him about a ghost would probably seem like a bedtime story.

She drew a deep breath and began her tale.

****

Brandon sat behind the steering wheel of Dennis' SUV and honked the horn. What was taking so long? Tara told him she was ready fifteen minutes ago. Women!

"It's rude to honk like that," Tara clipped as she hopped into the passenger's seat.

He watched her struggle with the seat belt for as long as he could stand it before giving in and assisting her. She surprised him by accepting his help more graciously than he'd expected.

"I'm sorry. You're right, it's rude. I'm not myself lately," he offered humbly as he scowled at his own behavior.

He put the vehicle in gear and started down the drive toward their destination.

Tara was so busy being overwhelmed by the myriad of emotions she felt towards Brandon that she never took into consideration the fact that he too experienced a life altering, traumatic ordeal and he may have been holding back his true aftershock. From their conversations, she determined that he was alone in the world with no family to turn to for support while he healed. A spec of compassion trickled into her as she thought about how difficult it must be for him to just keep on with life as if nothing had happened. Although tempted to touch his arm and tell him she understood, she refrained. Until her emotions were under control where he was concerned, it was probably best if she held herself back. Pulling her thoughts back to the situation at hand, she decided to change the subject.

"The library isn't far from here," she offered.

"I know. I visit it quite a bit when I'm in town," Brandon said with a light laugh. "I even have my own library card."

"Are you serious? I didn't know they gave cards to people who weren't residents," she said.

He shrugged,

"I kill a lot of time there," he explained. "I guess the fact that I practically live there was enough."

"Now, I feel bad," she said lightly. "Not only am I not in possession a library card, but I've never stepped foot into the building and I'm a resident. You put me to shame."

"Hardly," he chuckled, "I have to do a lot of research for my assignments or, believe me, I wouldn't be there as much as I am; if ever."

"Well, I really should have at least checked it out by now," Tara said with a sigh. "Time's flown by. It seems like only yesterday I was a kid having ice cream with my grandmother at the local ice cream parlor."

"I thought the same thing," Brandon stated as he focused on a patch of precariously looking road.

"You ate ice cream with my grandmother?" she said with amusement.

He tossed his head back in a short laugh and said, "Funny. What I meant was it seems like the year has flown by for me and I'm not really sure what I've accomplished."

Tara smiled with admiration as she realized her companion's driving skills. She was certain she wouldn't be able to maneuver the patch of black ice as competently as he just had without stopping all conversation and focusing solely on the task at hand.

"Where did you learn to drive?" she asked.

"Why?" Brandon asked, puzzled. "Did I do something wrong?"

"On the contrary, your skills are quite impressive," she replied, "especially for a southern boy.

"Thanks, yank," he drawled.

Brandon's smile was full and genuine. Perhaps he was making headway with the beauty next to him. Having her distance herself from him at a time like this was excruciating. He needed her close. They needed to work together. He watched her from the corner of his eye -a skill he'd mastered as a youth. She looked amazingly identical to Lucy. Her personality was altered slightly, which was to be expected, but her looks were uncanny. Having only met one other who'd gone through the soul sharing process, Maggie -and having her be older than her doppelganger- Brandon was a little out of his element in dealing with the situation. He'd only just realized who Maggie was and shared information to open her memories when the fight with Dominic set in. He thought the only reason she hadn't developed full memory by her age was because she hadn't been exposed to someone like him who could prompt it to resurface from beneath the veil of forgetfulness. He was certain if she'd recognized him and remembered who she was and her purpose for being there earlier, things would have turned out differently.

Tara watched her companion with little side glances. There was something about him that she was only just noticing. His gentlemanly charm was outdated, as if he was from another era; a time gone by. She assumed it was the result of his worldly travels. Life in Manhattan exposed her to a variety of cultures that absorbed people into their own expression. This was probably the case with Brandon.

She had to admit his life certainly seemed far more interesting than hers. She'd traveled very little. It wasn't that she disliked travel. It was just that there weren't many opportunities. She lived through her father's wonderful tales of exploring and discovery.

In another time and under different circumstances when she wasn't worried about her brother and didn't struggle to hold herself back from the urge to swoon over his handsome, chiseled face and super-hot physique she would enjoy hearing about his travels.

****

Although the library's occult section was quite impressive, they were unsuccessful in their search for information on the shadow people. Saddened and disheartened, Tara asked Brandon if he'd consider extending his visit. She needed help and could hardly report a ghost appearing and telling her shadow people kidnapped her brother to the police. She may hate having the deal with her fickle body whenever he was around, but Brandon believed and understood what she was claiming happened to Dennis.

Brandon agreed.

Another storm was rearing its ugly head in the distance. Although still far away, they could feel its fury through the heaviness of the static filled air. Brandon listened carefully to Tara's instructions for securing the house against the forces of nature that were soon to come. The disappointment in her voice was obvious. Not only did they have to stop searching for a way to rescue Dennis, but they were forced to endure a storm the likes of which were rarely seen. It was unfair.

The two storms Tara already weathered were taxing to get through yet they were reported to be far milder than the one that was on its way. The storms carried with them an unbearable, never-ending battering of icy winds that taunted threats to lift her house from its foundation. If these storms were milder than the one making its way in their direction, she shuddered to think what was in store for them.

Thankful for modern technology and weather stations, Brandon took advantage of the calm before the storm and climbed the ladder to the top windows of the house to secure the shutters. This was something that wasn't done before. Although he wasn't thrilled with heights, hearing the weatherman's predictions gave him the incentive he needed to persevere. Covering as much of the old structure's vulnerability as possible should make a world of difference. The house was solidly built. Even in its disrepair the structure was strong and firm. Old man O'Shea knew how to build a fortress.

Tara was both grateful for and relieved by Brandon's help. For a brief time, she forgot about the tragedy they'd lived through together. She watched his strong physique stretch to its full length as he secured the last shutter and imagined what it would be like to be cradled in his strong arms while curled up in front of a roaring fire to ward off the cold. Her body froze as she realized her thoughts. What was wrong with her? How could her thoughts go in that direction when she needed to be focusing on saving Dennis? She scolded her wayward body and mind while she admired him as he cautiously picked his way down the ladder.

"Is something wrong?" he brushed at his pant legs after hopping off the ladder.

"Other than the fact that my brother's been kidnapped by shadow people?" she replied, a little more briskly than intended while she did her best to gather composure.

"Forgive my ignorant question," he stumbled.

"No," she smiled warmly, "forgive me. My abruptness was uncalled for. It's just that... well... I'm frightened and I wish Maggie was here."

She hated liars, but she saw no reason to go into detail and share her full thoughts with him. Since she actually thought of Maggie and really did whish the old woman was there to help them, she wasn't lying, but simply omitting facts.

"Well," he said as he lowered the ladder and pulled it away from the house, "I'm not Maggie, but I promise to do everything I can to help get Dennis back."

Tara smiled. The more she allowed herself to relax in Brandon's company, the easier it was to be with him. She was beginning to see why Dennis liked him so much. Although the two men suffered at the hands of Dominic together, their bond went deeper to a point she was only just starting to understand.

Feeling encouraged by Tara's warm countenance, but not wanting to ruin it by assuming too soon, Brandon heaved the ladder over his shoulder.

"I'll put this in the shed," he said as he started to walk to the small building not far from the barn. "Is there anything else that needs to be done?"

"I think that's it," she replied. "I'll tend to Sugar while you put the ladder away and I'll meet you in the house."

Brandon swelled with joy at the warm tone of her voice and the genuine smile she flashed before she scooted off to the stable. Could it be she was finally letting him in? Dare he hope?

****

Evening came and along with it the dreaded storm. Tara offered Brandon a dinner of hearty lamb stew from a batch she'd frozen, with warm cornbread on the side. It was a fitting meal for a cold winter's night and he devoured it with gusto.

The one thing he'd learned in the few times he'd spent alone with Tara was that food wasn't a priority. That part of her personality hadn't changed one bit. He found this fascinating, since she proved to be a wonderful cook -both now and then- when the mood struck. He quickly determined readily accept food whenever it was offered, for you never knew when she'd think to offer it again. As was the case today. This was the first she'd fed him since breakfast. Fortunately, he was comfortable enough to rummage the cupboards for a snack to hold him over while passing through the kitchen earlier in the day.

After his third helping of stew, he regretted his gluttonous ways. His stomach gave all of the warning signs of being abused. Excusing himself from the table, he made his way to the study in hopes that if he stretched his body out and relaxed he could avoid what seemed like it might be the inevitable. Tara chuckled to herself as she watched him leave the kitchen. She was amazed by the amount of food he'd consumed. It came as no surprise when he felt the negative effects of his incredulous actions. She always marveled at others abilities to pack away such an enormous amount of food in one sitting. She possessed a very limited ability and found one small serving more than enough work for her body to digest. This was probably the reason for her slender figure. That and a good metabolism. She'd never have to worry about excess pounds creeping on when she grew older. At least she hoped she wouldn't.

She took her time cleaning the kitchen, happy for the comforting knowledge that there was another person in the house during such a trying time, even if they were separated by a few rooms.

Preparing for the storm had temporarily taken their thoughts away from finding Dennis. Now that they were safe and secure, his abduction was once again heavy on their minds. They agreed to do their best to refrain from panic. They needed their thoughts clear to think of a way to rescue him. A peaceful and relaxed demeanor would give their minds the freedom necessary to brainstorm. Hopefully the solution to their dilemma would miraculously pop into one of their heads.

She knew little if anything about the shadow people, but their name alone stated so much. She had no idea why they kidnapped Dennis, but was grateful for the ghost telling her. So much had changed about and around her. If a ghost appeared to her a year ago and told her he was her father from another time and shadow people took her brother she'd have run to a psychiatrist.

She found Brandon stretched out on the fainting sofa next to the fireplace. The rhythm of his loud snores blended with the crackling of the roaring fire and the hammering of the winds. She couldn't blame him for dozing off. The exertion of securing the house and stress over Dennis's abduction, not to mention the horrible greeting she gave him when he arrived, all had to have taken its toll on the poor man.

She scowled. As much as she kept labeling the feelings she had for Brandon as physical, deep inside her she knew it was more than that. She just couldn't identify its exact nature. Even after all that happened, she had this nagging urge to trust him, cuddle him, and lay safe in his arms. It was a different type of attraction than what she felt for Dominic. It was softer, subtler, and very deep rooted. It felt like a combination of friend and lover, mixed with incredible physical sparks.

She wondered if he felt anything for her other than the bond created from surviving their war with Dominic together. It wasn't uncommon for soldiers who had nothing in common and who would never befriend each other under normal circumstances to bond after battling side by side. Was it this way for him? Maybe it was true with Brandon's feeling for her, but not with Dennis. She knew for a fact that Brandon and Dennis would have become friends no matter how they met. They had too much in common not to.

Deciding not to disturb him, she made her way to the den on the second floor. The day had been long and grueling. The necessity of preparing for the storm overshadowed her need to find a way to rescue Dennis. Now that the house was secure, delightfully cozy, and quiet, she could meditate and hope the information they weren't able to obtain at the public library would be provided to her by the spirit world.

She hadn't meditated since Maggie's death. In fact, she hadn't done much of anything except wander the house in a semi-daze while doing only what she absolutely had to do for survival over the winter months to come. The few times Liam tried to contact her, she insisted he leave her alone -which of course in his serene and respectful way he did. She wondered if he'd totally left or if he watched her from a distance. Perhaps he'd have the answers she sought.

Was it wrong to push him away like she did and then go to him because she needed help now? Would he even help her after the way she behaved? There was only one way to find out.

After lighting a candle, burning sage and to cleanse and balance the room's energy and sweetening it up with incense she positioned herself for meditation.

She almost instantly felt herself being swept away into another world with incredible intensity. It was both exciting and frightening. She did her best to maintain an overall balance to avoid hindering the experience. In the past, she'd get so overwhelmed that her balance was thrown off and she'd snap back into reality. This time it had to be different. She needed to learn how to find Dennis and bring him back. She needed to know who the shadow people were and why they took her brother like they did.

Flecks of colored light flitted around her. Instead of feeling cold, she was incredibly warm. Shifting to a more comfortable position, she kept her eyes closed and focused on her mission. It was only a brief moment longer when she found herself standing in a very familiar field of flowers stretching as far as the eye could see. Sensing she was safe, she slowly picked her way across the field, still feeling its familiarity, but not sure where such familiarity would lead her. Guilt nagged at her from deep within. This place was lovely, but she needed to find Dennis. With all of her might, she willed for the field to end and the answers to come to her.

Off in the distance appeared the very faint sky line of a small city. She eagerly headed toward it. As she got closer she was able to make out the rooftops amongst large, mature trees. The village looked historic. She was close enough to see activity and life within its streets and buildings when Liam appeared in front of her. Perhaps she was at one of those restored historic villages that catered to tourists, like Williamsburg, Virginia. That was a possibility.

"Greetings," he said warmly.

Tara hoped to find Liam, but she wasn't prepared for the blinding golden aura resonating around his flesh-like body. Prior to this, he'd appeared in a less life-like condition with a more subdued lighting around him. She squinted her eyes to ease the stress on them.

Noticing her discomfort, Liam dimmed his aura to a level

that was more tolerable for her.

"I apologize. I miscalculated your level of vibrational toler-ance," he said in a gentle, soothing manner.

"My level of... What are you talking about?" she asked.

Although she wasn't certain, she assumed that Liam re-ferred to the brilliant light around him, since it dimmed almost im-mediately upon his statement. Even so, she felt compelled to state she didn't understand. By doing so, she might receive a brief explanation in metaphysical terms which was something she suddenly realized she dearly missed. She hadn't had a lesson in the mystical arts since the last one she received from Maggie. Since then she pushed herself as far away from the world of the occult as she could.

"Everything in existence vibrates, dear one. The higher the vibrational frequency, the closer it is to the Source from which we all come," Liam stated softly. He allowed this bit of information a little time to sink in before continuing, "When I appear before you, I must adjust my vibration to one that you're able to tolerate through your human sensory system. There are very few humans who can with-stand the purity of the energy that comes from being so close to the Source of All That Is."

Tara creased her brows.

"I thought that the higher the vibration was, the less visible it became," she mused.

Liam smiled.

"Speed of vibration does indeed make visibility more diffi-cult, but speed of vibration is not the same as the level of vibration. A very low-level vibration can still have great speed and invisibility to the human senses," he explained.

"Oh," Tara replied. She mulled on Liam's answer, doing her best to digest its meaning to its fullest extent. "I think I understand."

"Very good," Liam smiled. He folded his arms across his chest and brought himself to his fullest height. "Now, how may I be of assistance?"

"Oh!" Tara said in surprise. "I don't know. I ... I mean, I do know. I looked for you. I hoped you could help me and then I saw that village and thought... I'm looking for the shadow people."

Although Liam's face was expressionless, she sensed his displeasure.

He cleared his throat before saying in a firm tone, "You seek the shadow people in the village beyond? May I ask why?"

"I sat down in meditation and asked for information on them and this is where I ended up" she explained.

"I see," he said in a flat tone.

"They took my brother," she added.

"I see," he said again in the same flat tone.

"I need to find them and get him back," she said with a bit of desperation in her voice.

"Indeed," he replied.

Tara was exasperated at the calm, almost detached demeanor Liam displayed. What kind of interaction was this? Wasn't he supposed to help her in times like this? From the way he was responding she expected very little assistance from him; if any.

Her patience ran out, "Are you going to help me?"

"Would you like me to help you?" he asked.

A loud gust of air burst from her lungs. Of course, she wanted him to help her. This was intolerable, and certainly not what she expected when she went into meditation. Maybe she should just stop and try something else.

"If you wish for my assistance, you will have it. You need only ask," Liam stated in a soft, but firm voice. "You must ask. I have stated this before. Unless you specifically request my aid and assistance, I must only stand-by, listen, and observe." Liam shook his head, "It can be a very disheartening position to be in, I can assure you."

Tara's words were controlled and deliberate as she said, "Will you please help me find the shadow people?"

"The people you seek will not be found in the village beyond. They are not of this realm. You will, however, find all that you need in the book of magic that was gifted to you by your dear friend. Look inside it and your questions will be answered."

"I forgot about that book," Tara said excitedly.

Liam bowed, "Is there anything more that I may assist you

with?"

"Can you find my brother and bring him back to me?" Tara asked, hopefully.

"Alas, dear one, I cannot," he replied. "This is a task that you must complete by your own volition. I can, however, be there for you as I have been in the past."

She didn't understand the ways of the spirit guide one bit. Sometimes they can help, sometimes they can't help. It was all too confusing.

"I really don't understand," she said with a scowl. "How come you can help me in times of peril, but you can't help me when my brother is in peril?"

"It does seem complicated, does it not?" Liam replied. He tapped his finger on his chin while the considered the best response. "I am the guide and the protector who has been assigned to you and you alone. Your brother also has a guide and protector assigned to him. We respond and protect only those who we are assigned to. Rarely, if ever, do we cross assignments." Liam watched Tara for signs of cognition before continuing.

"But," Tara replied, "you helped Dennis and Brandon when they were trapped in the fire."

"I came to your aid and assistance. Dennis and Brandon just happened to be able to reap the benefits of my assistance to you and escape the fate that awaited them had they not gotten out of the house," he explained. "I was able to assist your friend and her dog with a small amount of healing energy, but that was the extent of it. It was her duty to call upon her own guide which, alas, she did not." Liam watched Tara carefully for signs that she understood and accepted his explanation. When he saw puzzlement in her expression he continued, "Think of life as a school and the earth is one big classroom. I am your tutor and, in small ways your body guard. Now, I enjoy my responsibilities very much. This is good because I too am in school; but in a different kind of classroom, with a different form of advancement. By performing these responsibilities that I enjoy so much, I am actually progressing in my own school. Do you understand what has been said so far?"

She slowly nodded her head.

"Very good," he stated with satisfaction. "Now," he continued, "if another guide steps into my school and assumes my responsibilities, that guide deprives me of my progression, as well as my joy. Think of it like someone doing your homework for you in history class. How could you ever pass the course? Surely, the end result would be lack of progression and great sadness over it. For us it is similar. Therefore, we do not -to coin a human phrase- 'step on toes.'"

"Could you if you absolutely needed to?" she persisted.

"It is complicated," he said softly.

"Could you?" she almost screamed.

Liam closed his eyes and nodded.

"So, why don't you," she asked, exasperated.

"I am not your magical genie," he said gently, but firmly. "You're not in danger; nor, at the present, is he. The Spiritual Laws state that I must allow you and your brother to experience your lessons and provide you with guidance as needed and requested. Hence the term 'Spirit Guide.'"

Tara squared her shoulders and twisted a knot out of her neck. She wondered if she'd ever understand the world Liam lived in. There were so many unanswered questions.

"Well," she sighed, "can I ask why Dennis's guide hasn't helped him?"

"Alas," Liam hung his head, "too many humans are still closed to the connection of their guide and do not ask for help. If help is not asked for..."

"Help isn't given," she said flatly as she finished Liam's sentence. He smiled, but made no comment to the fact that her interruption was rude. "So," she continued, "are you saying that if Dennis was connected to his guide, his guide could save him?"

"Possibly," Liam's stated in a controlled, but gentle voice.

"Possibly?" she almost screeched with frustration.

Tara held her head. This was all too confusing.

"There are many factors involved in the relationship between a human and his or her designated guide," Liam explained. "There are rules that must be followed. These rules were put into place to prevent the guide from unintentionally stripping the human from the much-needed education and opportunity for progression that the privilege of life provides." He began to pace. "The joy of assisting is so great that if the rules hadn't been put into place, we could easily perform every task for our charges." He stopped pacing and turned to look Tara directly in the eye. "Although this would please us greatly, our charges wouldn't move forward on their journey, nor would we; for it is the lessons of life that are the prize of the experience."

He regarded her intently, as if waiting for her response.

"I still don't understand," Tara eventually admitted.

It sounded to her like Liam came up with some type of cop-out for not being able to, or maybe not wanting to help rescue her brother.

"We are forbidden to interfere with your lessons of life and aid you unless you ask and the assistance is justified," Liam said as he continued to pace. "We cannot take away your right to free-will and assume that our help is desired when, in fact, it may be just the opposite. We are also not allowed to perform miracles for you..."

"But, the fire..." Tara broke in.

"Unless your life is in danger or you're experiencing some other form of need extraordinaire when you call on us," Liam continued calmly. "We are allowed to instruct you on how to perform them yourself and we are allowed to assist you in performing them, but we do not perform them ourselves unless there is a dire need. We are allowed to rescue you in times of peril, providing it is not your soul's chosen time to leave your body."

"How would you know that?" she asked.

"We are able to see far more than a human can see," he explained. "When your time has come for your soul to shed your body, you're shadowed by Death."

"Death," Tara shuddered.

"Death is feared by man," Liam explained, "but in reality,

Death is a loving entity who is doing a great service to souls by assisting them in their journey and making it easy for them to shed the weight of their physical body and continue on."

"How long is Death shadowing you before you die?" Tara asked timidly, not certain she wanted to hear the answer.

"There is not an absolute response for that question. Each human life is reviewed by the board and Death is sent accordingly. Some humans are shadowed for months before they actually make their transition and others only seconds," he replied. "There was a time when Death didn't exist," Liam sighed, "but, the body of the human grew far too heavy and polluted for the soul to bear, so out of great love for his children the Source of All That Is assigned an angel he held dearest to become Death. It was at this time that reincarnation began. Now, instead of being burdened with a heavy and polluted physical body while one learns and progresses, one is given the opportunity to shed the worn out and polluted vessel in lieu of a newer and fresher vessel. This is indeed a gift."

"I hadn't thought of it in that way," Tara mused, "It does make sense."

Liam chuckled as he said, "It does indeed."

"So, what do I do now?" she asked in earnest.

"I suggest you consult with the book," Liam replied as he bowed his head and slowly backed away. "Always remember that I am near. You need only call my name."

"Three times, right?" Tara replied, hoping he'd confirm her statement.

He didn't.

She watched in wonderment as Liam was engulfed by a twirling funnel of rainbow colors while he rose into the sky and disappeared into nothingness. She took one last look at the charming little village in the distance. It was tempting to continue on and investigate it closer, but she needed to find her brother. Even though Liam said Dennis wasn't in any danger, he included "at the present time". This lead her to believe that this could change. There was no time to waste. She turned her back on the little village and *willed herself to return into her body. She was grateful she paid such close attention to Maggie's instructions. As the village faded she could have sworn she saw the ghost Alana called Papa walking down the street. She did her best to focus on him, but her surroundings were receding fast and she lost the vision.*

When she opened her eyes, the room was dark. Since she hadn't consulted a clock before meditating, she had no idea how much time had passed. Judging from the burned down candles and the coolness of the air, she guessed she'd been at it long enough for Brandon to go to bed.

The wind no longer threatened the house with its incessant battering. She used to love that sound. She used to feel snug and secure in her shelter while Mother Nature had her way before her ordeal with Dominic. Now when the winds beat and battered at her windows and walls, she sometimes trembled and waited for Dominic's terrifying voice to follow.

The thought of Dominic brought back visions of Maggie's final moments and the fact that Tara only narrowly escaped the same fate, if not worse. Chills permeated to the very marrow of her bones and the hair stood up along the back of her neck. Rubbing at her forearms, she decided to start a fire and grab a cup of herbal tea before settling down to search through the book. She did her best to push Dominic out of her mind and set about her tasks

SIX

Tara was so absorbed in her reading that she didn't hear Brandon climb the stairs. Assuming he was in bed she'd taken the servant's stairs to the kitchen and hadn't bothered to check the rest of the house before heading back to the den with tea in hand.

"You're up late," Brandon drawled lazily as he leaned his tall muscular body against the door frame.

"Did I wake you?" Tara asked in a voice just above a whisper as she gently closed the book and carefully set it on the antique side table next to her winged back chair.

"I'm a little big for that fainting sofa. I thought I'd try a bed instead," he said while rubbing and flexing his neck for emphasis. "What were you reading?" he nodded his head toward the book she'd just set down.

"I was seeing if I could find anything in this book about the shadow people," she replied hesitantly.

Although she knew he'd understand about the book and its contents, she remembered all too well Maggie's warning about allowing other people to handle it. After not heeding her warning about reading from the book haphazardly and calling forth the dark side, she had no intention of disregarding her words again.

"Really? What kind of book is it?" he asked.

He started toward the book, but stopped when she laid her hands possessively over it.

"I'm sorry, but this book was given to me by Maggie with the strictest instructions that no one was to read from it, but me. Not even Dennis," she explained.

Brandon's gasp was sincere while his hand flew to his mouth.

"You have the Book of Secrets," he whispered.

Tara was astonished.

"How did you know that?" she asked.

"It's a long story that I may tell you someday. For now, just look at chapter twenty-seven," he said eagerly. He positioned himself comfortably against the dark, freshly polished wainscoting covering the lower half of the wall. "I'll wait here."

Eyeing him suspiciously, Tara opened the book to chapter twenty-seven and started reading.

There are many dimensions belonging to the planet we live on. These dimensions contain various forms of life. Some are of a brilliancy that would blind the naked eye like the sun and others are of shadows that blow in the wind. It is of these shadows in the wind that we focus now, for they are of the shadow people in a land called Shadow Land. Knowledge is power over these people and protection against them as well. The shadow people live in a world very different to that of man, yet similar. At one time, they were the extension of man. Every human who walks the earth has a shadow side. These shadow sides do not always stay in synchronistic growth with their human counterpart, thus separating themselves from the brightness and taking on a persona of their own. Because they lack light, they prefer the presence of creatures that dwell within the darkness. Thus, the shadow people are a misguided lot who cannot be trusted and are often times of evil persuasion. On occasion, they find a portal into the human's world and steal away the unsuspecting, taking him back to Shadow Land to attach one of their own for the purpose of using that connection to assist evil with its quest of taking the world over completely. Many humans who have gone mad and committed heinous crimes for seemingly no reason have, in fact, been possessed by one, or more, of the shadow people.

Tara couldn't believe what she read. Here before her was the answer to Dennis' disappearance. She frowned at the time she wasted searching the library when it was in the book the entire time. Her mind snapped back to the realization that she directed to this information by Brandon and she scowled.

"If you knew of this why did we waste time in the library?" she demanded.

"I didn't know you possessed the book," he said.

His explanation seemed solid so Tara decided to let it drop.

"Well," she stood up and said, "I'll leave your explanation on how you knew about the book and its contents to later and focus on getting Dennis back. What do we do now?"

"Maggie told you not to allow others to handle to book, but did she say you couldn't tell me what it said?" Brandon asked as he pulled his body from its relaxed position in the door frame and straightened his shoulders. "If I know more, maybe we can put our heads together and think of something."

"You just pointed out to me where to look for the shadow people in this very book. Don't you know what it says?" she asked, duly confused and mildly suspicious.

"I only know bits and pieces of it," he said. "I promise I'll explain what, where, and why later, but for now can you just share with me a few things so that we can see about getting your brother away from these creatures?"

She replied sheepishly, "You're right."

It was daylight before they formulated a plan they felt was solid enough to execute. Both were exhausted and, since their plan would work better in the night than in the day, they filled their bellies with a rib-sticking breakfast and went to bed.

The sun was setting before either of them ventured out of their rooms, but when they did, they were ready for the night ahead.

Sipping on her coffee, Tara sat at her kitchen table and scribbled the incantation for crossing dimensions that she found in the book onto a sheet of yellow legal paper. Once she was finished she would go to her office on the second floor and make a copy of it for Brandon.

After writing the last word she set her pen down and looked across the fifties style enamel and steel table at Brandon, who was quietly studying her.

"You never told me how you knew about the book," she said as she stretched the small of her back.

"No, I didn't," he replied and then smiled softly as he raised his cup to his lips.

"And?" she said.

"Now?" he asked as he sat up straight, fidgeted his shoulders, and clasped his fingers together before stretching them out in front of him as if he was loosening himself in preparation for a fight.

"Now," she replied, unimpressed with his mock theatrics.

What they were about to do was risky and she wasn't comfortable going into such a situation alongside someone with as many secrets like Brandon seemed to have. He may have weathered Dominic's attack with her, but she needed to know just a little more about him before they ventured together into the unknown.

When he hesitated she continued, "Look around. This is me. You've pretty much seen all there is to know about me and my family, or at least enough to give you a fair idea of who I am and what I'm all about. We're going to embark on a very risky venture tonight. One which requires trust on both of our parts. Don't you think I deserve to know just a little more about you besides the fact that you ride an enormous black horse and take pictures for a living?"

"Wow," he said softly. "I've never heard my life simplified in such a way. There isn't much depth to it, is there?"

"I didn't mean it that way..." she stammered.

"No, it's okay," he said with sincerity as he shifted in his seat. "What do you want to know?"

"Well, for starters, how did you come to know about the shadow people? Why didn't you tell me you knew about them? How did you know they were referenced in Maggie's book?" She rambled before taking a deep breath to give him just the slightest opportunity to step into the conversation. When he didn't grasp the opportunity immediately she continued, "How do you even know about the book? I thought it was something handed down in Maggie's family..."

"Whoa!" he broke in, finally finding his tongue. "That's a lot of what, how, and why."

Tara frowned as they locked eyes across the table. She stayed silent. Her body language shouted much louder than words ever could. He saw no way around it.

Taking a deep breath and then pushing it out of his lungs with solid force, he began his story.

"In my line of work I'm required to travel to parts of the world that many only dream of. I've always considered it an honor and a privilege to do so. After all, that's how I met you, right?" he began.

She scowled and shifted in her chair. He was stalling. Why?

Brandon looked at her long and hard.

"Okay, okay," he sighed, "I didn't want to tell you this because I wasn't sure how you'd take it. You've had enough weird stuff going on around you without mine adding to it."

"What do you mean?" She questioned. "What weird stuff?"

Although it would be easiest to take the short route and explain away her questions and concerns, he felt that without the history of how and why, she may not accept his explanations in the manner he'd like, plus he needed time to formulate his story. So, focused on the book.

"When I was a young boy," he began, "my parents did a lot of traveling. My father was an assistant curator of a museum which required he travel to inspect and select artifacts. Whenever possible, he'd take my mother, sister, and me with him. On one trip in particular we spent almost two months in Ireland. My father selected this as his home base and placed us there while he made mini trips to various parts of Europe. Ireland was a lovely country and since my mother was Irish we were connected to it." He paused to see if she was going to comment on his Irish and

German heritage. When she didn't, he continued.

"We had some distant relatives that my mother managed to hunt down and I ended up spending quite a bit of time with them. One of them, Celia, -my aunt three times removed if I'm not mistaken- was into the supernatural. She had all kinds of herbs, bones and artifacts in her home. Maggie's kitchen was a lot like my aunt's kitchen as I recall. In the beginning, I was pretty frightened, but the more time I spent with her the more I grew to enjoy her company and ease up on the heebie jeebies when I went into her home. She got really sick," he whispered as he slowly shook his head. "I never did find out what she had. It was all so hush, hush."

There was a brief moment of silence while Tara waited for Brandon to continue. It was obvious this was still a sensitive subject and she wanted to allow him the time he needed to pull the story from the depths of painful memories.

"Before she died," he finally said, "she gave me an ancient book to look after. She told me the book was one of only a few left in the world and that I should guard it with my life. I tucked it under my bed and read through parts of it when I found a quiet moment. Eventually my mom discovered it. She knew enough about the book to be afraid of its contents so she tossed it out the window into the bushes below. I remember the fear in her face as she wrestled the book from my grip. She was afraid to even touch it," he said with a faraway look in his eyes. "She was adamant I wasn't to touch the book ever again." He sighed heavily, "So much fear, so much anger... I was about thirteen at the time. When my father returned that night, she told him about the book and he quickly ran to the bushes and collected it. I tried to explain to him that it was special, but he burned it," Brandon hung his head, "while I watched." He heaved another sigh, "Wow," he took a deep breath and forced the words out. "I couldn't believe he would do such a thing, especially when he was always on the lookout for old artifacts."

Realizing his emotions, Tara leaned forward and rested her hand on the table in front of him as a comforting gesture.

"That must have been hard," she said compassionately.

"I felt like I'd failed Aunt Celia," he poured forth. "I still feel like I failed her."

"Well, you shouldn't. You were just a young boy who was asked to do a grown man's job," she said with conviction. She twirled her cup as she stared at the swirling liquid contents for almost a minute before she continued, "Having possession of such a rare book... I know how difficult it can be. If Maggie hadn't prepared me, I've no idea what would have happened." She straightened her shoulders and leaned against the back of her chair. "As it is, I ended up summoning Dominic. You're lucky nothing came of your reading the book unsupervised." Tara contemplated her next words. "I have to question your Aunt Celia's reason for expecting such a young boy to watch over it."

"I sometimes wonder the same thing," he replied. He leaned against the back of his chair and allowed his body to relax while he smiled appreciatively across the table. "Anyway, that's how I knew about the shadow people."

Silence rang through the room while he waited for her response. She was certain he had more to tell, but for now she'd have to be content with what he was willing to share. It was enough to make her feel confident about moving forward with their plans.

The two listened with resolution as the clock struck eleven. Tara stood up.

"We'd better start preparing," she said.

"What room are we using?" Brandon asked as he pushed his chair back and stretched.

"I'd feel more comfortable in my upstairs den if that's alright with you," she said.

He smiled.

"Anywhere is fine," he replied.

Warmth spread over Tara's body while she basked in the rapture of Brandon's smile. The more time she spent with him, the more familiar he felt.

Since the upstairs den was where Tara and Maggie spent

much of their time with meditation and lessons of the craft there was very little that had to be added to the well-stocked corner cupboard. She and Brandon did a quick inventory, collected the few things they lacked from other parts of the house and were seated and ready to begin by eleven fifty-five. They would wait until the stroke of midnight on the antique grandfather clock in the hallway to begin.

Tara positioned herself on one end of the sofa and Brandon sat at the other end.

The room had an eerie feel to it as the clock struck twelve and the two closed their eyes, breathing in the sweet yet pungent aroma of burning incense as it mixed with the burning sage. Their objective was to be taken to the land of the shadow people. They filled their lungs and expelled the air in rhythmic unison for a full minute. Then, with incredible synchronicity they opened their eyes and each read the incantation Tara scribbled out earlier that night.

Nothing happened.

Waiting only a moment longer, Tara signaled for them to read the incantation again. With synchronicity they read the incantation in heartfelt earnest once more. Brandon watched Tara closely, making sure her eyes were focused on the words she read. Keeping pace with her, he slid his hand into his pocket and pulled out a small object that looked very much like a watch fob. Holding it low to his side, he flipped open the case. He stole a glance at the dial and moved it to the desired position with his thumb. After quickly closing the case, he pressed lightly on the crown and continued to recite the words.

As soon as they spoke the last sentence Tara felt her surroundings spin in a counter clockwise direction. The force was so powerful she was thrown toward Brandon, almost landing in his lap. He wrapped his arms around her protectively as the room spun faster and faster until it disappeared and they were spinning in a dark void. When the spinning slowed down she was able to see the colors of their new surroundings. Once stopped, they found themselves on a large cliff that overlooked a wide river at least one hundred feet below.

Tara pulled herself free from Brandon's embrace just in time to thrust her body forward while her stomach emptied its contents with full force. She wasn't a fan of amusement rides and this topped the wildest of the rides she knew to exist. Had she been aware of such a dramatic transition, she would have eaten a lighter meal.

Brandon was grateful Tara's stomach purge missed him, if only by a fraction of an inch. He reached in the back pocket of his jeans and produced a fresh folded handkerchief and handed it to her. His gentle hand stroked her back while she struggled to regain her composure.

"I'm sorry," she moaned and wiped at the corners of her mouth. "That's just gross!"

"I won't argue," he replied.

He wrinkled his nose, hoping the stench of her vomit wouldn't assault his body to the point he followed suit. It was difficult enough steadying himself after their whirlwind transition without having to worry about that as well.

He shook his head when she his handkerchief back.

"You keep it," he whispered. "Maybe we should move away from the cliff."

Feeling a little steadier, she nodded and allowed him the lead. They positioned themselves beneath to a nearby tree until they were steady enough to move on.

Visibility was poor as the two picked their way across a meadow of tall grass and boulders. Blades of emerald green grass caressed her thighs as they mixed with tall, wisps of goldenrod dancing to the rhythm of each step they took. The lighting resembled dusk during a winter storm, grey and hazy.

"Look at this place," she said in an awestruck voice barely above a whisper. Her head had cleared and her eyes finally adjusted to the lighting.

"I know," he responded in an equally hushed tone. "It's all

like this. I mean, do you think it's all like this?"

"I hope so," she replied.

He was grateful she didn't notice how he stumbled on his sentence.

"I've to say though, I question if we're really in Shadow Land," he mused. "This place seems pretty normal. It even has fog."

"Well... I..." she was at a loss for words. What did he mean? Where else could they be? "I can't imagine where else we could be. We were targeting Shadow Land."

"Did the incantation promise to take us into Shadow Land or to take to where we could find Shadow Land? There is a difference," he said.

"To Shadow Land," she insisted, "I'm certain of it."

"Does this look as foreboding as the book portrays Shadow Land to be?" he questioned cautiously.

He knew very well they weren't in Shadow Land, but he needed to allow her the opportunity to figure that out for herself or risk pushing her away with his explanation. The gap between them was steadily dissipating. He wasn't willing to risk bringing it back to full force. Not now. Not with the situation as it was.

Tara checked out her surroundings. Other than the fact that there was a hazy overcast from a heavy fog, it did seem quite normal. It was more like they'd stepped back in time than into a different world.

"I see what you're saying, but I could swear we were supposed to be taken directly to Shadow Land," she mused as she pulled the incantation from her back pocket.

After reading it carefully she dropped her hands to her sides in a dejected manner, letting the paper slip to the ground. Brandon watched it flitter to and fro as it made its way to the soft blanket of earth just inches away from his feet. He stooped quickly to pick it up and read the incantation carefully. It was easy to see why Tara looked as if the wind was knocked from her sail.

He cleared his throat and said, "Did you copy this exactly

as the book stated?"

Tara flashed a scowl that was enough to bring a dead man to his knees.

"I'm just being clear," he said quickly. "I meant nothing personal." After a few moments of silence, he continued, "I spoke it with you and never picked up on it either. The wording is very tricky."

How could he tell her that he knew how dangerous Shadow Land was and that he overrode the incantation and brought them there?

She heaved a sigh and allowed herself to calm down.

"What now?" she asked.

Brandon studied her carefully while he deliberated on his response. He could tell her that he knew the way to into Shadow Land and they were only a day's trip from its portal or he could suggest they return to their day and time and research the book for the correct incantation or he could take her to find Fiona. He opted for the third, but it had to be done the right way. He needed to wait until the right opportunity presented itself.

"It was an easy mistake to make. You have to be so darned precise with your words in these incantations," he soothed. Realizing he sounded far more experienced with incantations than he'd professed to be he added, "I would think."

"Yes, that's true," she replied.

Brandon expelled the air he'd been holding in and allowed his body to relax. Tara was so wrapped up in their dilemma of not being in Shadow Land she failed to notice his tense demeanor, for which he was grateful.

She turned and looked him long and hard in the eye.

"What do we do? I don't know what to do," she said sincerely.

His heart skipped a beat and felt as if it was going to burst from the mixed emotions that flowed through him right then. For a fleeting moment, she sounded like Lucy. For the briefest of moments, he could see the woman he'd vowed to love and cherish for the rest of his existence. She surfaced ever so briefly, from within the bowels of the veil that held her soul captive. He wanted to hold her, kiss her, love her and never let her go. Of course, he couldn't. If he told her the truth would it free her completely or send her deeper into the depths of the veil? If it did free her, what would happen to her now that he'd brought her back? Now it was Brandon who wished for the assistance of Maggie. She was back in Fiona's body, but she'd still know what to do.

Suddenly, he remembered the map he'd drawn of Shadow Land. If he was careful with his explanation, it just might get him out of this dilemma. He pulled it from his pocket and poured over it carefully.

"Okay," he said with a satisfied smile. "I think I have the answer."

"What is that?" she asked suspiciously.

"I took advantage of our down time and drew a map of what I could remember about Shadow Land from my aunt's book," he said.

"There was no map in the book!" her distrust was apparent.

"Sorry," he said quickly as he cleared his throat and cursed himself for his faux pas. His mind scrambled for a believable reply. "I must have learned it from my Aunt Cecil and just thought it came from the book." His brain was working double time as the words poured from his mouth. "She told me about the shadow people and their land and she drew me a map in case I was ever captured by them, so I could escape." He lowered his voice to just above a whisper, "Like she did."

"What?" Tara gasped. "Your aunt was taken by the shadow people?"

"Yes," he said as he closed his eyes as if the act would make the memory go away. He pointed to a point on the map. "Look here. If I'm not mistaken, this is the entrance to Shadow Land. Do you see right here?" His finger guided her to the spot on the map, "I'm fairly certain I know how to get us there."

"How would you know that?" she asked, suspiciously.

"Why," he prayed silently while he formulated his response, "from the stories I've been told."

The silence between them was deafening while he waited to see if she would accept his story. When she finally spoke, it was like the weight of the world was lifted from his shoulders.

"Our only other option would be to return to our time and pour through my book to see if we could find the correct incantation, correct?" she stated more than asked.

He nodded.

"That would be quite taxing on our bodies, if I remember what the book said," she continued. "I'm not eager to repeat the experience. It'd also waste a lot of time because we'd have to rest and recover before we could travel again. Plus, there isn't even a guarantee that we'd find a better incantation."

"That's right," Brandon said.

"It's a risk to follow a map that's based on childhood stories, but you've been pretty helpful so far with the information you've provided from those stories so maybe staying here and finding Shadow Land would be the wiser thing to do."

"Maybe," he agreed.

He hated lying to her like this, but he saw no other option. Later, when he had her full trust, he'd confess there was no Aunt Celia who gave him her magic book. When he was sure it would be safe to tell her, he'd admit that it was her doppelganger, Lucy, who was captured by the shadow people and escaped with his and Maggie's doppelganger, Fiona's, help. It was Fiona who shared the book with him -parts of it anyway and Lucy who'd drawn the map. For now, until he knew what the consequences for him bringing her here were he needed to continue the charade.

He grabbed Tara's arm, pulling her behind him while he dove into a large crevice between a few boulders, "Hide as best you can."

"Why?"

"In case we really are in Shadow Land. I heard something. I think someone is coming. It is best we see them before they see us," he explained.

She nodded.

They stayed as still as they could for what seemed like forever. The fog slowly lifted as time dragged on. Tara's leg was cramped and growing numb. When she saw no person or shadow she shifted it to a more comfortable position. Brandon gripped her leg so hard she had to force back a scream. She followed the direction of his stare and realized the reason behind his actions. Less than twenty feet in front of them stood three men dressed in confederate civil war uniforms. Why hadn't she seen them? They were so close. How could she miss them standing so close?

The trio hovered over a map, seemingly oblivious to their surroundings.

"Aye, Eric. I agree. 'Tis a bit of a mess," mumbled the tallest of the three. "He spoke with a thick Irish brogue. "They will be rounding the bend soon. We have to think of something fast."

A fair-haired man who looked to be around Tara's age nodded his head.

"You're right, Lance," he agreed with a rolling brogue. Tara debated if it was Irish, Scottish or Welch. "I honestly don't know what to do here. We can stand and fight, but I think we'll lose."

The third man, a youth of reddish complexion with fiery red hair to match, joined in, "I didna come to this land to die for a foolish cause. I vote run."

"I agree," replied Lance, "we should run. 'Tis not our fight and not our fault the ship landed in the shores of the losing side. I came here to build a life for meself, not lose it for the greed of others. Let them fight for their own slaves to be free or not."

"Hell, I was a slave meself back home," the red head spat out, "or darn near the likes of it."

"Well, I hope they win," Eric said with gusto. "I've been in the shoes of those darkies or close enough. I hope those confederate bastards lose and the darkies give them what for."

"Aye," Lance nodded in agreement. "Me heart goes out to the poor bastards, but for now we need to worry about our own skins and get the hell out of here."

Tara was so intrigued with what she was overhearing that she was saddened when the three soldiers scooted off into the remnants of fog. Her disappointment didn't last long. Within minutes a troop of union soldiers marched so close to their hiding place the acrid smell of their dirty, sweaty bodies assaulted her senses with a force like no other.

Grateful Brandon insisted they remain hidden after the disappearance of the confederate soldiers she nudged her body even further into the boulder's crevice in hopes of being as inconspicuous as possible.

There were a lot of soldiers.

A soldier stopped and sniffed the air.

"I smell perfume," he said. "Who's wearing a button?"

His companions joined in sniffing the scent while they inspected each other for the source, but none could be found. Tara couldn't believe her idiocy. One of the fist lessons Maggie taught her about dealing with the other side was to never wear a scent. Often times spirits would produce a perfumed scent upon their arrival and if you were wearing one yourself it would be difficult to decipher if the scent was yours or that of spirit. When she performed her toiletry in preparation for the evening, she'd donned cologne without thinking. How could she be so foolish?

"Come on, lads. Someone's wearing a button. I can smell it strong as if I had it under my own collar," the soldier growled.

"It sure is rich," agreed another.

"Yeah, and different. I ain't ever smelled the likes of it before," declared a young soldier in need of a hair comb. He drew close to a fellow soldier of equal need of toiletries attention and wrinkled his nose. "Hell, it ain't you, you, raunchy goat."

The soldier smiled sheepishly and replied, "You ain't no breath of spring either."

In her absorption and amusement of the soldier's bantering, Tara forgot herself for the briefest of moments and emitted a tiny giggle. That was all it took for them to be discovered. Wrestling and fighting against the surprisingly iron grip of her captor, she watched as Brandon was unceremoniously forced to stand next to her.

"What have we got here?" asked her captor. His victorious grin displayed a full set of rotten teeth as he focused his attention on Tara. "A woman in man's clothes, is it?"

"A mighty fine-looking woman at that, although a mite skinny," the soldier next to him volunteered as he wiped at the saliva that was dribbling from the corners of his mouth. His beady eyes took in every inch of Tara with open lust.

She cringed in fear. There had to be at least fifty men closing in on her. Fifty filthy, stinky, lust filled men. One could only guess at how long it was since they saw a woman. Should they decide to misuse her, she could expect no help from Brandon against such a number. The agonizing anticipation of what was to come was more than she could handle and darkness mercifully consumed her.

Dumbstruck, a soldier caught her fall and laid her gently on the ground.

"Hell, she may be dressed like a man, but she faints like a woman," he said with surprised disgust.

"Just like a woman," someone roared from within the crowd, "and she shall be given the respect of a woman. Am I understood?"

Brandon turned in surprised at the familiar voice. His body relaxed as he watched a tall, ruggedly handsome, auburn haired officer step from the midst of the mass of blue uniforms. When the two men laid eyes on each other their grins spread wide.

"Hell Brandon, what are ya doing here?" the soldier laughed.

"Aidan, me man. ya are a sight for sore eyes," Brandon said with a hearty chuckled and a faint Irish brogue. "Ya are the last person I expected to meet up with in these parts. Why the dickens would ya fight in a war that doesn't concern ya... and an officer no less?"

"Colonel O'Connor to ya," the man boomed with half-hearted authority as he turned to his soldiers. "This man is a long-time friend of mine. Release him at once."

As an afterthought he added, "Never mind his odd attire and his funny attempt at me brogue," he turned to Brandon and winked, "the man himself is a bit odd."

The soldiers roared with appreciation of their superior's sense of humor and released their hold on Brandon. A few soldiers muttered their reluctance about releasing Tara. They weren't happy about being denied the woman who lay at their feet taunting beauty that was far too easily seen by the cut of the masculine clothes hugging her body, but none dare disobey the order of their colonel.

"Lucky for her we're friends," Aidan muttered as his eyes followed the trim curves of Tara's limp body.

"For sure," Brandon replied, doing his best to refrain from displaying the possessive jealousy that raged within him.

After taking his time drinking in Tara's feminine curves, Aidan dismissed her as he did any object he no longer desired and focused on Brandon.

"So, the last we met 'twas in dear old Ireland. What brings ya to this neck of the woods?" he asked.

"Two reasons. First of all, I happen to have made this neck of the woods my home when I'm not traveling" Brandon explained as he shifted his speech pattern back to a southern drawl.

"Have ya now?" Aidan said with surprise. "That explains your loss of the brogue. I'd have thought ye'd be more inclined to make our homeland, your home. Why the southern drawl if ya live in the north?"

"'Twas easier to shift from the brogue to the drawl," Brandon explained.

"Ya needed to shift did ya?" Aidan asked with raised eyebrows.

"The jobs they have been sending me on required I drop the brogue," Brandon said. "Apparently they're looking for a traveler of my description from Ireland. I needed to shift things about me to keep under the radar."

"Who is she?" Aiden asked.

"It is complicated," Brandon replied as he nodded his head in her direction. "The Shadow People have her brother."

Aiden sucked in air and mused, "That's not good."

"We have come to get him back," Brandon groaned.

"Come from where?" his friend pressed with curiosity.

"The twenty-first century," Brandon replied.

"'Tis how women dress then?" Aiden exclaimed more than asked.

"Many of them, yes," Brandon said. "It's practical attire for our mission."

Aidan thought about it for a minute, "'Twill not be easy."

"Tell me something I don't already know," Brandon replied.

Aidan stood about the same height and Brandon as he slapped him on his back in a friendly gesture and beckoned him to follow.

"Let's get a drink and hash over some options," he tossed over his shoulder as he started to walk away. As an added measure, he ordered two soldiers to guard Tara with their life if need be and inform him immediately when she regained consciousness.

"You have no salts?" Brandon asked.

"I do," Aidan replied, "but I'd like some alone time to catch up. Let her come around naturally."

"That is probably for the best," Brandon agreed.

He needed time to speak with his friend about why he felt it was best not to tell her about their friendship and that they'd met many times before under various circumstances and conditions.

SEVEN

She'd awoken in the comforts of the colonel's tent in their camp about three miles east of where she fainted. Disorientated at first, the sight of Brandon sitting trussed in a chair nearby quickly brought her to her senses. Tara cautiously sought out signs of any soldiers before crawling as quietly as she could to his side and seeing what she could do about the ropes binding him.

"Leave it," he whispered. "It isn't worth angering them. The colonel seems like an amiable fellow. I'm hoping to talk him into releasing us."

She stopped pulling at the ropes, totally confused. Here they were alone and in a position to escape and he talked about chatting his way to freedom. Had he lost his mind? They knew nothing of these people. The colonel spared her a horrendous ordeal, but does that mean that he'd allow them their freedom? Brandon was clearly a Southerner, after all. She didn't want to take that chance. Shaking her head, she continued pulling on the ropes. Fortunately, whoever trussed Brandon up made sloppy knots and he was easily freed.

"Stop the nonsense, Brandon. There's no time," Tara snapped as she crawled to the entry of the tent and peeked out of the flap. She had no idea how much time lapsed, but from the position of the sun she guessed it was a few hours. Precious time is lost. After their encounter with the soldiers, Tara shuddered to think what might be happening to Dennis. Who could be holding him captive right now? What could they be doing to him?

Brandon crept up behind her and peered over her shoulder.

"Are you sure this is wise?" he whispered. His words tickled her ear, sending chills down her spine. "If we're re-captured the colonel might not be so gallant again."

She shuddered. Perhaps he was right. Maybe they were taking too great a risk by escaping. Although from what she could tell, there wasn't a soldier in sight. Escape seemed easy. Would talking their way into freedom be just as easy? She wasn't willing to take the chance.

"I'll risk it," she mumbled, more to herself than to him. She hoped she sounded more confident than she felt.

Brandon took a breath of resignation.

"Follow me," he muttered before darting out of the tent toward the nearest tree with lightning speed.

After only a moment of surprised hesitation she was hot on his heels. They darted, ducked, and hid until they were secure in the thickness of the nearby woods.

"You run like a girl," he chided once they were out of danger.

"Really, what do you suppose I do about that?" she bantered back.

Tara wrestled with guilt over their light-hearted teasing. Dennis was imprisoned somewhere by the odious shadow people. She shouldn't be laughing and teasing with this man. She should be serious, solemn, and focused on his rescue, but she couldn't help herself. Her feelings for Brandon were slowing changing from frustrated mistrust to a comfortable and undeniable attraction. Being with him made her happy, even if he hadn't won her complete trust and she couldn't shake the feeling he was hiding something. It still felt good to be free of the heaviness of captivity and even better to be teasing each other in such a light hearted way.

They discovered a path leading through the woods. Although Brandon urged they go in a different direction, Tara was determined to follow it. It wasn't long before they reached a clearing that was oddly familiar. She struggled over why she felt at home here. It wasn't until she saw an enormous black gelding grazing on the far side of the clearing that it struck her.

"This place is identical to the clearing where you and I met!" she exclaimed.

Brandon knit his brows together.

"Do you think so?" he choked out, hoping she didn't notice how uncomfortable he was.

"Not only that, but look at that horse over there. He could be King's twin," she said with wonder.

"You don't say. Why yes, I think you're right. Son-of-a-gun," Brandon said as convincingly as he could.

"Well, that makes sense. If I read the book correctly, Shadow Land began as a kind of mirror of our reality," she mused.

"Your reality isn't the civil war," he stated flatly.

"Reality of the earth plane and humans in general is what I meant," she replied.

Not willing to relinquish the safety of the trees, the couple made their way around the parameter of the clearing. As they passed near the great gelding, it picked its head up, sniffed the air, whinnied, and then resumed eating.

"It's like he recognized you or something," she said with curiosity.

"Funny, right?" Brandon replied.

He never took his eyes off the gelding until they lost sight of him -an action he was grateful Tara failed to notice.

She was shocked to discover that when they reached the opposite side of the clearing, the path resumed. This was all too familiar.

"This is really creepy when you think about it," she whispered, smiling meekly at Brandon.

"Then try not to think about it," he replied.

"I can't help it. I'm dying to see where this path leads to. If it takes us to my house then I'll be knocked down with a feather," she said with excited sincerity.

Brandon pursed his lips as he wrestled with telling Tara the truth, but before he could say anything she started gingerly down the path.

"I don't even need to guess where to go at this point," she tossed back over her shoulder. Quickening her pace, she called back, "Come on!"

"It might be advisable to lower your voice and slow your pace. Remember, we aren't in our time anymore and in case you didn't notice, I have a Southern drawl," he said just loud enough for his words to reach her ears.

Brandon's words slapped Tara into reality and she subdued her pace and body language considerably.

"I forgot," she mumbled. "It just feels so much like home."

Her curiosity was almost unbearable. They didn't have to walk far before they found themselves at the edge of the estate Tara was to inherit from her grandmother. She stopped in her tracks as they neared the house. Her run-down home that whispered of better days stood mighty and grand in all of its splendid glory. She knew in her heart her house was a beauty in its day, but had no idea of the extent. The house she owned in her time was a mere shell compared to this one. She questioned if perhaps she might be in possession of the shadow house instead of the other way around.

"Wow. I knew it was a beauty, but I never really realized just how much," she said, awestruck.

"I know," he murmured.

Although she found his comment a little odd, she decided to ignore it.

"Shall we look inside?" she asked.

Brandon knew her question was more of a statement of intention.

"Be careful," he urged as he nodded his head toward the side of the wraparound porch where several soldiers sat in quiet conversation.

"Oh, I didn't see them," she whispered with agitation. Why was it that she had such trouble seeing these people? "I find their occupancy of my house offensive."

"It isn't your house," Brandon chuckled, "not yet, anyway."

"You're right," she blushed sheepishly. After taking a moment to regain her composure, she looked around in earnest. "I wonder who owns it now."

"From the looks of things, the yanks," Brandon responded with a twinkle in his eye.

"Well," Tara retorted, "We're in the north during the civil war so that doesn't come as a surprise, but seriously do you think my great grandfather is inside? What will he say when he meets me?"

Brandon squinted quizzically at Tara.

"Are you nervous?" he asked.

Surprised by his question, she knitted her brows in quiet contemplation,

"Surprisingly, no," she said.

"The shadow people can be fierce," he whispered.

"So can real people," she whispered back.

Brandon's eyebrows raised in mild surprise by her comment.

"I'm not afraid, but I'm curious," Tara continued. "Do you think Dennis is somewhere on the property?"

"I can't be sure," Brandon mused. "I'm still not convinced we're actually in Shadow Land."

"Do you think we just stepped back in time?" she asked with a worried tone.

"I think we stepped back in time and are within distance of Shadow Land, just not in it yet," he explained. "Once we investigate the house we will know more."

"Well?" Tara looked at Brandon expectantly as she asked. "Are we going?"

"Alright," he said with resolve.

He took a deep breath and led the way across the rich pasture toward the house.

They hadn't quite made it to the fence near the stable when a commanding "halt!" stopped them in their tracks. Tara turned to find a musket pointed straight at her heart. She wondered if the bullet would have the same effect on her in there as it would in her time, but quickly decided it was best not to find out.

"Who goes there?" the soldier commanded.

"At ease, soldier, at ease," Aidan's words were like music to Tara's ears. "So, we meet again," he said as she looked her up and down with a coldness that made her shiver.

Tara flinched, remembering Brandon's warnings about what might happen if they escaped and were caught. Her body trembled visibly and she was afraid she might faint again from the trauma of anticipation. Noticing her response to his greeting, Aidan supported her as he escorted them to a small office inside the stable before she fainted on them again.

Women were such trouble.

"My goodness, ya are a fragile one," he whispered in her ear as he waived smelling salts under her nose. "Whatever are ya doin' on a venture such as this and with a man like himself?"

Although Brandon wasn't privy to Aidan's words, he was certain no good could come from allowing him such close and private interaction with Tara. Reaching forward, he pulled her disoriented body possessively to his chest while giving his old friend a warning glare. Aidan chuckled and walked behind the small, highly polished oak desk that was the focal piece of the room.

"Sit, please," his voice was smooth and confident.

Brandon guided Tara to the wooden settee that Aidan's swooping gesture pointed to. She went with him freely, wanting to be as close to him as she could.

Brandon could feel her body trembling and wished he could assure her it was for naught. Timing was everything and this wasn't the time. He prayed that when the time did come to divulge it all to her, she would understand and forgive him his lies.

"Now," Aidan's voice hinted his amusement as he addressed his captives. "If memory serves me correctly, I left ya both in a tent at camp. It appears ya didn't appreciate my hospitality." He leaned back in the chair and casually locked his hands behind his head. "So, what do I do with the two of ya?" His Irish origin was displayed in his strong voice as he tapped thoughtfully at his thick, auburn beard.

"You need do nothing with us," Tara shot forth, amazing herself with the power of the words that were coming out of her mouth.

"Do tell?" Aidan cocked an eyebrow in mild surprise.

"Careful," Brandon whispered. His friend was a kind and generous man, but he still lived and existed in a world where women weren't allowed the privileges twenty-first century women enjoyed. He wasn't altogether certain Tara's cutting tongue wouldn't bring down the wrath of even the gentlest of man in eighteen-sixty-five.

Aidan lifted his hand.

"Let the lady speak," he commanded. Leaning forward, he looked directly into Tara's eyes. "Tell me, dear lady, why would that be? Just remember that there is a war going on and the gentleman ya happen to be keeping company with is the enemy."

The piercing green eyes that burrowed from the shelter of the thick auburn brows of her captor had an unexpected effect and a wave of artificial courage swept over her.

Flushed with false empowerment, the tone of her response was sharper than intended.

"We're here to find Dennis and take him home. It has nothing to do with you or your men. We've no interest in your war," she said with a confidence that Aidan found surprising considering her penchant for fainting.

"Really?" Aidan sat back and studied her from beneath heavy eyelids.

Brandon was an adventurous man to be keeping the company of such an outstanding woman. Not only was she beautiful, but she had spunk. He chuckled to himself, wondering how long Brandon would be able to tolerate such a woman. Although it could be intriguing at first, it was bound to wear on a man after a time.

He smiled broadly at his friend and asked, "Is this true?"

Brandon looked at his shoes for the longest time before responding, "Yes," in the softest of voices.

Aidan cocked his head as if straining to hear Brandon's response.

"I beg your pardon, sir?" Aidan said with force.

"Yes, sir," Brandon spoke up.

"Who is this Dennis? Better yet, why is he here?" Aidan continued with a satisfied smirk that only Brandon could understand or appreciate.

"He's my brother and he was taken by the shadow people. That's all we know... other than the fact we're wasting time," she blurted.

Now that she had vocalized their mission, the sense of urgency to find Dennis returned and her annoyance at being detained was obvious.

"Ya have quite a woman on your hands sir," Aidan said matter-of-factly as he shifted back in his chair and rested his locked hands over his stomach. "Are ya certain ya can handle her?"

Tara gasped, outraged, "Well, I..."

"Shut up!" Brandon bellowed as he yanked her arm so hard she felt her neck snap.

Stunned into silence, she rubbed her neck and forced back the tears of hurt and shame that welled up inside of her. She had no idea what got into Brandon, but as soon as they were alone he'd hear her opinion of it.

"Alright then," Aidan said. He stood up, seemingly unruffled by Brandon's sudden aggression toward Tara, "Since ya aren't the enemy and ya care not about our war, ya shall be me guests for the night." He directed his words toward Tara, "We can see about your brother's whereabouts in the morning."

Giving Brandon a nod of approval, the colonel led them upstairs to their rooms.

Tara moaned. It was getting dark outside. She couldn't believe an entire day was wasted. She had no idea what they could be doing to Dennis this very moment. There was no time to settle in and wait until morning. For all she knew, they could be torturing him right now and he may not last until morning. They needed to find him now.

She grudgingly followed Aidan while surveying her surroundings. They were near the part of the stable where Sugar was kept. Looking back, she made note of the room that they were in. It was good to know that what was now a tack room had once been a very stately office. She did her best to burn the barn as it once was into her memory. Now that she was clear on how it should look, she fully intended to do her best to restore it to this grand state when she and Dennis returned home.

Worrying about Dennis would make the night very long. She did her best to hang onto Liam's comment that, at the present time, he wasn't in danger.

EIGHT

Tara observed her dinner companions while she sat at the long, elegantly set table and waited for dinner to be served. The view before her was amazing. Having come to the conclusion that she and Brandon were not in Shadow Land, but had stayed in the same area, but gone back to the time of the civil war, she watched in wonderment and listened with fascination almost forgetting the reason they came.

Dining in the original magnificence of her home -mixed with a potent wine and candle light- caused headiness for Tara that carried on throughout the meal. She was seated opposite Brandon with Aidan between them at the head. Although he watched her every move from the corner of his eyes, Brandon's focus never left the colonel, nor did his conversation. If Tara hadn't known better she would have thought the two well acquainted.

She fidgeted in her chair as her suspicions arose. Why would Brandon be so calm and relaxed in the presence of their Yankee captor when he was from the south and why would their captor take Brandon's word for it when he said he wasn't inter-ested in the war between the north and the south? Shouldn't he be considering Brandon a spy or something? The captain obviously enjoyed Brandon's conversations. Maybe a little too much. Surely his topics weren't that fascinating. It was as if they had a silent un-derstanding beneath a layered conversation. She was well aware that her trust levels of men dropped drastically since her tragic encounter with Dominic, but this was just too obvious to be a mere matter of her trust or lack of it. These men knew each other and, more than that... these men were friends!

****

Since the colonel was settled in the room she occupied in her own time, Tara asked to be placed in the bedroom she used as her second floor den -the very same room she and Brandon situated themselves in to perform the incantation that brought them there.

The room was exquisitely furnished with a gorgeous and undeniably expensive nineteenth century Louis XV gilded writing table and an equally beautiful Louis XV marble top dressing table with a matching gilded mirror. A tapestry bench was positioned at the foot of a modest featherbed that was suitable for one to sleep comfortably. Matching tapestry draperies surrounded the bed and adorned the windows. It was a room fit for a princess.

Tara stoked the fire in the fireplace. The snow she'd been tortured by in her time hadn't found its way to them in this time yet -for which she was thankful -but the air was still very cold and damp. She took a moment to admire the well-polished brass on the gas lights that were securely positioned on the wall. Surely the soldiers weren't the ones caring for the house. They were men of war. This house clearly received constant, loving care. So far, she'd only seen soldiers. Was any of her family in the house?

She froze at the sound of creaking outside her door. The house was full of life. She assumed her frazzled nerves were behind her reaction. Tension reached new heights when the footsteps stopped at her door. Barely breathing, she watched the handle of her door slowly turn. She berated herself for not locking it.

Relief and confusion flooded her as her resident ghost stepped into the room. Studying him closely she realized he was flesh. Was he traveling dimensions to haunt her? She just didn't understand enough about ghosts, dimensions, and shadow people to really have the answer.

"Who are you?" she asked, surprised by her calm mannerism.

"Ya come from the future, do ya not lass?" he asked cautiously.

When the old man took a few timid steps forward Tara realized that he was nervous, probably more nervous than she was.

"Yes," she replied, retaining her calm demeanor as best she could while she watched him move closer.

"I thought as much," he sighed. With a disheartened look on his face he walked to the tapestry bench and unceremoniously sat down.

"You seem disappointed," she said softly.

As if suddenly remembering her, he looked up at her and straightened his spine. "Forgive me, lass. I didn't mean to offend ya. I was hoping ya was me Lucy returning to me." The old man twisted his face in frustration. "I mean the original Lucy."

"I have no idea what you mean," she said.

"Aye, I imagine ya don't," he replied.

"Pardon me?" she said.

"Ya are the image of me Lucy. In a way ya are her because ya share her soul's memories," the old man patiently, "if ya would only remember."

Tara scowled and shook her head.

"I don't get it," she said hesitantly.

"No, no, ya wouldn't. Ya are still lost in that fog they say surrounds those who split souls," he replied. Sadness permeated his words while he witnessed Tara's dumbstruck face. The old man growled and stood up, "Good heavens, lass. Do they not teach ya anything where ya come from?"

"Why, yes... some, I guess," Tara hedged. Not only was his brogue difficult to follow, but she had absolutely no idea what he was talking about and even less idea of how to respond to him. "How did you appear to me?"

The old man poured himself another drink and tossed it down. "'Tis fine whiskey, gal, almost as good as back home." After a brief moment he continued, "I don't think they teach ya much, lass." Scratching his grey stubbly chin, he paced the floor. "There must be a way to make ya understand... to make ya remember. Let me think about it." He shook his head and waved his arms, as if limbering up for an athletic event. "Now, if me Alana was here," he leaned forward and spoke in a hushed tone, "she would make ya understand. Alana has a way with words and ideas."

"Alana?" Tara wondered if his Alana was also Mitch's Alana.

"She's one of me daughters... Lucy's sister," he stated matter-of-factly. "Lucy's brother, Angus, is with relatives in Ireland and with stay there until this crazy war ends."

She stared at the old man as if he had two heads. In fact, if he had she would have thought him no less odd than she did at this moment.

He flung his hands in frustration.

"Sit down while I try to explain," he said as he worked to calm down. "I know I'll not do as good a job as me Alana, but I'll try me best."

She listened intently to the old man's ramblings. He began with the incredulous tale of how she and his Lucy were in essence one in the same and then shifted to how he and his wife met in Ireland and fell in love. She was a southern belle. He tried his darnedest to tolerate the humid weather and the slavery that grated on every moral he possessed, but he couldn't. He moved north and to appease his wife he built this fine estate home for her. It was intended to be a replica of their southern plantation, but turned out to be far grander. Fortunately, he came from considerable wealth and his wife had an equally impressive dowry. He was able to secure one-thousand, five-hundred acres of prime woodland and start a lumber company.

Tara couldn't believe her ears. The estate started out with one-thousand and fifty acres! It made her one-hundred-twenty-five acres seem embarrassingly pale in comparison.

When she questioned the whereabouts of his wife he said nothing more than she recently passed from a disease of the lungs.

The glowing new grandfather clock that she recognized

as the majestic antique one in her time was still in its same location. It chimed the hour several times before she and the old man completed their conversation. She found her great- great grandfather to be a fascinating and amiable man. His tales were full of a love for life as he reminisced about his childhood in Ireland and how he met my great-great grandmother while she toured Europe with her family. His adventures while settling and developing the land were both exciting and captivating. It wasn't until he spoke of Lucy's disappearance that his mood changed and his eyes clouded over. Sadness radiated from him.

According to Papa, Alana was prone to be a rebel all of her life. She wasn't comfortable in her own time and place. She was born with the memories that had the potential to drive one crazy if not understood and controlled. She remembered time travel and when she was a young adult discovered a way to do it again. Although it was easier to travel to the past, Alana went to the future. She was on a mission to find the crystal key.

Time travel was something the old man found difficult to believe possible until his youngest sister, Fiona, arrived from Ireland and changed his perception of the world entirely. She was very young when he left the home and he never got to know her like he would have had he stayed in Ireland.

He discovered she was highly skilled in the ways of magic, the kind practiced in the old world. She shed light and understanding on so much. He learned how time existed only as man knows it and it exists all at once. This is why anyone who understands can pass through the shadow lines of time at will. Of course, it is easier to pass back through time since the past is already recorded in the conscious planet memories and easily connected to.

In her naivety, Alana associated with the evils of Shadow Land and was coerced into going into the future to search for the crystal key. Now, she was stuck there until she found it.

Fiona showed him how to travel into future time by way of the astral plane, thus not risking his body getting stuck in one particular location. It didn't allow him to stay and interact for any length of time, but it was the safer way to do it.

Lucy also went forward in time to prevent her sister from succeeding on her mission, but she didn't pass through the Shadows. She traveled to the future by way of a channel that was extremely risky in many ways, but offered her a stronger hold on her powers and allowed her to say a very long time. She needed time to remember her powers in order to be able to stand up to the evils that plagued her for not only the key, but the magic she possessed and also to remember where she put the key. The spell she'd cast to forget its location would have weakened enough to break it by then.

Lucy's body was placed somewhere so secret that even he was ignorant to its location. Through magic, Lucy's genetics and part of her soul were placed in the body of a future infant of the O'Shea blood line, thus creating a doppelganger. The intention was that the doppelganger would be full grown by the time Alana's visit occurred and she would also be much stronger than if Tara crossed over in the traditional time traveler method.

There was risk involved with this method. First of all, the soul is actually split between two bodies -something that only a few white enchantresses successfully mastered, his sister being one of them. Secondly, a person born anew is enveloped by the veil of forgetfulness. This veil doesn't differentiate from those who are being reincarnated and those who willingly move pieces of their soul ahead in time to stop the evils from doing their dirty work. Such was the case with Fiona and Lucy.

Tara found it all confusing and hard to believe, let alone digest and accept. She did her best to hide this from the old man. Their conversation confirmed she wasn't in Shadow Land and he wasn't a shadow person. He was simply an old widow living out his life in the nineteenth century during the trying times of war while worrying about two daughters who were both absent from his life right now. She, on the other hand was a woman quite extraordinary, a soul divided, a doppelganger. Or so he claimed.

Her head hurt from the strain of the conversation. It was all too much. She decided to prod the old man for any information on Shadow Land me might provide. That, at least, was a topic she was prepared for. He told her he hadn't known Shadow Land existed until Alana got into trouble and Lucy explained what she must do to correct things. He'd spent a great deal of time processing and trying to understand it all. It wasn't until he mastered the art of astral projecting through time that he even believed in the supernatural or underworlds. He questioned Fiona and learned Shadow Land started as an exact replica of their human world, right down to the tiniest speck of dust. The shadow people lost their connection with their human counterparts just as man lost connection with the gods who once walked amongst them. These shadow people took many different paths -from haunting and torturing humans out of anger and spite, to working with the Lord of Darkness, to fighting alongside those few shadow people who managed to maintain a small connection with their human counterpart in hopes of assuming that connection for themselves. Others became slaves or servants to demonic monsters like vampires and werewolves. All existed in Shadow Land, but most of the human race wasn't aware of it. They fight their wars and profess it is a war of righteousness for the cause not trusting problems could be solved by talking them out and negotiating. They believed war the only option because of the underlying influence of Shadow Land. Evil thrives on darkness and sorrow.

Tara listened intently. Something he was saying finally made sense.

"So, Alana is in my time dimension now?" she asked.

"I don't know for sure," the old man stated with a deep sigh, "'Tis hard to keep track of Alana's reckless wanderings. She was there ransacking the attic not that long ago. 'Twas me you saw interrupting her."

"You said she can't return until her mission is complete," she said. Keeping up with this man's words was a job in itself.

"Aye, that I did, but that doesn't mean she's still in the same time. 'Tis hard to tell with that lass," he explained. "Maybe she went further ahead in time or maybe a little further back.

She's a powerful witch in this time, but when a person travels their powers are weakened. If she had all her powers she would have found the key by now."

He looked deep into Tara's eyes and his voice grew soft, but strong. "We live in the same world, gal. We may live in different times, but we're in the same world. 'Tis different for those in Shadow Land, I don't know if I can even explain it as I've never been to Shadow Land meself. I can only repeat what Fiona and Lucy told me."

"Will they hurt Dennis?" Tara whispered.

"Aye, eventually," he replied. "'Tis their way. I'm sorry, lass."

"How will they hurt him?" She asked with hesitation.

She had no idea why she asked this question, and she sure didn't know if she wanted to know its answer, but she was compelled to ask anyway.

"I don't rightly know. The only ones I ever met who escaped Shadow Land are Fiona and Lucy," he replied.

Tara gasped in horror, "What about Alana?"

"She's never entered Shadow Land, "he explained. "She meets them here. They're everywhere, ya know. They travel in the wind. Ya can't see them because they move so fast. They slow down only to communicate with ya if they want ya to know they are there."

Tara nodded. She was familiar with the concept. Maggie mentioned something along the same line. She called it the infiltration of the laggards. Although she was still working on grasping all he told her, she was at least more at ease with the conversation.

"Of all the evils, the shadow people are the ones most connected to humans," Papa continued. "'Tis because they started out as extensions of us. They're also the ones who covet the human body and the human world the most. They want to take it over. They want to live inside our bodies. There's an old wizard who partnered with certain humans possessed by shadow people. I'm told he lives on the edge of a mountain. I suspect he's the one who persuaded me Alana to turn bad. She studied with him." The old man scowled. "I can't think of his name. Hannigan maybe, but I can't be sure," he mused as he heaved a sigh. "He gave her a crystal. It was a small crystal, but a very powerful one. It has the power to open the portal between Shadow Land and the Human world from anywhere and any era. They call this crystal the key."

The old man poured himself another shot of whiskey and tossed it down his throat before continuing.

"If the shadow people get possession of this crystal key," he said with concern, "they'll be able to enter our world no matter what the year with their powers full strength. They won't have to come through specific portals like the one in this century. There will be no need for a wizard's spell or such to help get them to the time they wish to be in with only limited abilities intact. I can't stay there long when I travel to the future, but from what I've been able to see, there's a lot in your time that the evils could use as weapons to control all of the realms."

"Can no one stop them?" Tara asked.

"There are soldiers guarding the gateway to Shadow Land to try to keep them from running' hairy scary about the lands as best they can in most of the time zones they're able to travel to," he explained. He cocked his head to the side and scowled. "Alana took the crystal key and gave it to ya... err... Lucy, but she never told Lucy what power it held. She lied and told her it belonged to their mother and asked her to hide it for safe keeping. When the evils kidnapped Lucy, she cast a spell on herself to forget its location. Sadly, she cast such a powerful spell to insure the shadow people couldn't break it that it wiped out most of her memories. She also forgot her engagement to Brandon and a few other important things." He shook his head. "When Maggie snuck into Shadow Land and recued Lucy we nursed her body, but it took longer for her mind. Not only did she put a spell on herself, but the evils did harsh things to the lass to try to get at the information. This pushed certain memories so deep that no matter what we tried, she couldn't remember them." Papa shook his head, "Alana went crazy tearing the house up looking for the crystal, but Fiona put a cloaking spell on it." He heaved a sigh before continuing, "The wizard managed to recruit Alana to travel into the future where Fiona's spell would be faded and less able to cloak the crystal key. When Lucy learned of this she had Fiona cast a spell to split her soul and place part of it in your body. Fiona did the same with her own soul so she could help ya if need be."

"I knew a Maggie O'Shea. She was much older than me," Tara said softly.

"'Twas me Fiona," he replied.

Tara focused on the fact that her doppelganger was captured by the shadow people and returned with no memory. She grimaced as she thought of what they could have done to cause the amnesia. Would they do the same to Dennis?

Papa could see Tara growing tired and decided it was time to end the conversation.

"Now, lass," he said gently, "'tis time for ya to rest up a bit,"

She still wasn't totally clear on what he said but she understood enough information to piece together and make some sense out of it. She'd hear enough to satisfy her for now. She was tired. Retiring for the night was a good idea.

The clock chimed the hour one more time.

"Let's make a deal," she said earnestly. "I came here to find my brother. If you help me find him, I'll do my best to help you get Alana back and do what I can to help close the portal the shadow people use to move between our worlds" After a short silence she asked, "Do we have a deal?"

For the briefest of seconds, the girl before him was like the enthusiastic, steadfast, wise daughter he knew and loved. His eyes teared as he replied, "Aye, we have a deal."

****

Tara peered up and down the hallway. After what she'd witnessed over dinner her trust level for Brandon was sorely dwindled. She knew in her heart of hearts that he and Aidan weren't strangers and she was sure he was keeping more from her. She couldn't take that chance on trusting him. It was better to go it alone.

Fortunately, the old man agreed to help her as much as he could.

Papa agreed to meet her at the far end of the stable with a horse. Hopefully, by then he'd have discovered something more concrete about her brother's whereabouts. He insisted she make herself less conspicuous by wearing Lucy's riding habit. It fit like it was made for her.

As she crept down the hallway, she was grateful she knew the house so well. Stopping at the bottom of the third floor level, her curiosity got the better of her and she slipped stealthily up the steps. She just had to see what it looked like in its glory days.

It was amazing. Never in her wildest dreams could she imagine the dilapidated third floor of her estate to be so breathtakingly gorgeous. Although more modestly furnished, the setting was delightfully decorated in a tasteful blend of brilliant yellow, blue, green and red. The tall oval mirror she only recently studied her reflection in glowed from a recent beeswax polish. She moved in front of it and recalled the night not so long ago when she held the lovely dress in front of her. She searched for the dress, but the room was in immaculate order and the dress was clearly not a servant's dress. The sound of someone shuffling at the far end of the narrow passage way that led to the servant's bedrooms ended her exploring and reminded her why she was there.

She quickly tip-toed to the second floor and scanned the great hall before scooting down the service stairs to the kitchen. The rich aromas of breakfast being prepared brought her senses alive and reminded her that it was hours since dinner. Sadly, she saw no way of partaking in the scrumptious looking scones, honey, thick sliced bacon, scrambled eggs and creamy porridge without bringing attention to herself. She held her stomach, shook her head and snuck past the cook.

NINE

Brandon stretched across the soft feather mattress and looked at the ceiling. This was the very same room Tara put him in whenever he was her guest. He thought about the faded disrepair that awaited the room. It was always a shame to see things go downhill and deteriorate. It was fortunate Fiona's spell worked enough to convince Tara's grandmother to will it to Tara with enough stipulations to prompt the girl to keep it and live in it. He hoped that living it would jog her memory, but the veil wove itself tight around her even her studies with Maggie weren't pulling it free. Between the veil and Lucy's forgetting spell, he wondered if she'd ever recall her life with him and the good days before Alana made a mess of it all.

Brandon met Lucy just before the onset of the war. He was immediately smitten by her beauty, poise, and charm.   He was delighted to discover she had a head on her shoulders as well. She, on the other hand, was reserved with her affections. With perseverance, he managed to break through the barriers she put between them and won her heart. It was later that he learned the cause of her hesitating was her sister Alana. Having designs on Brandon herself, Alana was immediately consumed by jealousy when she learned it was Lucy he desired. Alana convinced Lucy that Brandon wasn't to be trusted and was possibly even a confederate spy for a war that was brewing. Lucy fell for her crafty sister's ruse completely.

Once Brandon convinced Lucy that she had nothing to fear from him the love between them grew strong and fast. Brandon was devastated when Lucy returned from Shadow Land and didn't recognize him or recall the love they shared. In fact, he sometimes questioned if it was truly Lucy who returned.

When a shadow person took possession of someone, the human's personality shifted just slightly, but still remained basically the same. These subtle differences can be extremely difficult to detect since they could easily be credited to post trauma from the person's recent ordeal. They would be particularly difficult to detect in a situation such as the one with Lucy, where amnesia was involved. He expressed his concerns to Fiona and was assured that she too had thought of this possibility and had tested Lucy's blood in a way only a witch could test. Lucy was indeed their Lucy with no attachments, although no longer whole. It would take time, Fiona told him. In the meantime, they had to get possession of that crystal key before the shadow people did. Hence the drastic and dangerous action of splitting her soul.

Now neither Lucy nor Tara knew him.

Although it was good to be back, he couldn't help feeling nervous about their mission. The shadow people were a formidable lot. Bringing Tara to find and rescue Dennis put her in tremendous danger. Lucy was fortunate to have escaped them and she was a powerful enchantress. Tara still hadn't unleashed those skills and was far more vulnerable. If they were able to break Lucy, what would they do to Tara if she was caught?

There was also the fact that Lucy's body lay in state somewhere awaiting the return of her soul. He couldn't help wondering what would happen now that both bodies were in the same time and vicinity.

He should have told Tara that he was a traveler. More than that, he should have warned her about the dangers of their mission. If Dennis was where he thought he was, it would be difficult to get him back. Although Shadow Land started as the home for the shadow people, invaders from other planets and realms frequently came and infiltrated amongst them, just as they'd done to the humans on the earth plane.

There existed in Shadow Land a large portal that could be easily passed through by an experienced traveler. In order to contain the shadow people as best as possible, the portal was guarded around the clock by some of the fiercest humans. They let no one in and no one out if they could help it. Many a human and non-human died trying. Shadow Land was no longer an easy place to get in or out of.

The crystal key had the power to seal the portal to Shadow Land forever if in the hands of the right people or open it in any time dimension to the point it could never be sealed if in the hands of the wrong people. Along with the other parts of Lucy's life the amnesia also stole recollection of the key. It was believed she hid it somewhere in the great house before she was taken, but no such crystal was ever found.

It was his, Papa's, and Fiona's hope that Tara would be able to remember what Lucy couldn't about the location of the key, but the veil of forgetfulness proved too difficult for Tara to remove before Dominic made his appearance. The trauma of her ordeal set Tara's spiritual growth into a tailspin, resulting in her regressing instead of progressing. That was how Alana found her to be when she arrived. Now, the race to find the crystal was intense.

The guards of Shadow Land were particularly suspicious of all life forms because the evil of Shadow Land had the ability to take on the appearance of the life beings around them. They could and did take on the appearance of humans, animals, fowl and sea creatures. Whatever is necessary for them to do accomplish their mission. Brandon encountered them off and on in his travels and it had never been good. Fortunately, since they weren't in possession of all of their abilities he was able to get the better of them and survive. He thought that Dominic was a shadow person lurking around Tara in hopes of finding the key, but when his true nature was shown he realized that he was far worse that the ordinary evil doer. These evil doers may work for the demonic realm, but they aren't demons themselves and couldn't command creatures and elements in the manner Dominic had. He was more than likely one of Shadow Land's soldiers, sent forth to find and take possession of the coveted key by whatever means necessary.

It was getting serious.

Brandon shuddered as he recalled Dominic's eyes while he set Maggie's cottage on fire and demanded Tara's soul if he couldn't have her body. Did he know her soul would return to Lucy's body upon Tara's demise or did he assume that once she died her soul would be vulnerable for the picking? Control of the soul before it found its way back to the heavens to await reincarnation was a prize for the dark ones.

He heaved a heavy sigh. The panic he felt when he thought he'd be burned alive was acute and still surfaced when he remembered the ordeal. He was suffering post-traumatic stress syndrome and he was sure Tara was suffering the same. After all, not only had Dominic tried to kill her, but she witnessed Maggie being torn apart. It was a traumatic sight for Brandon too, but not to the extent as Tara. He knew Maggie's soul was going to return to Fiona so he kept his sorrow at the appropriate level for someone who had compassion for what happened, but didn't feel the loss.

Brandon shook his head. He couldn't think about that now. He needed to focus on Dennis. Dennis was a trooper during that entire Dominic ordeal, but being kidnapped by the shadow people so soon after it... well, Brandon shuddered to think about Dennis' suffering and state of mind. He could only hope that the small vacation his friend took rejuvenated him enough to give him strength to endure.

They say time heals all wounds. Brandon never wanted a saying to be more correct in his life. Whether he wanted to admit it or not, he had strong feelings for Tara. He needed to take control of them before it was too late. Her soul inevitably could only inhabit one body at a time. He'd brought Tara to Lucy's time and he sensed too late that it might just cost one of them their life. He loved his Lucy with all his heart, but he had allowed his heart to fall for Tara as well. He couldn't see either of them hurt at this point and he hoped he didn't have to. Should the time come where he would have to make a choice he honestly couldn't say who he'd choose.

Although Maggie left a grieving Tara behind, once Tara understood things her grief would end. That wasn't the case with Brandon. Lucy's soul took on a slightly altered personality in Tara. He assumed it was because of the amnesia she suffered since Fiona and Maggie were identical in personality. Whatever the case, he found Tara delightfully appealing and fell in love all over again. Unfortunately, it was like falling in love with two different women. He was completely torn.

He wondered if Fiona felt the pain of Maggie's death or if she left her body long before the demon wolves sunk their ferocious teeth into her tender flesh and tore her to pieces. He traveled through time with his own body in tact he could have easily perished in the fire right alongside Dennis. Tara's soul would have returned to Lucy like Maggie's did to Fiona.

He'd never actually been in one of the evildoer's camps, but he'd heard the rumors and tales about them being similar to the German concentration camps that were so abundant during the days of Adolf Hitler. That would make sense, since one of the primary leaders of the shadow people was Hitler himself.

Once he was certain Tara was out of listening range, he took the liberty of discussing the situation with Aidan before retiring to his room. Aidan had been a traveler, but unlike Brandon he didn't tolerate the sometimes-chaotic transitions that traveling involved. When he showed signs of poor health and his longevity of life was threatened, he opted to remain stationary to live out his life in the era he was born in. His attention was soon captured by the slave dilemma between the north and south and he joined in to assist with a cause he considered worthy. Brandon tolerated traveling well. Since he began his travels through time his molecular composition adjusted itself accordingly. The aging process was slowed down and although he'd still die one day he aged at a rate of one year for every ten of the normal human being. It was an occupational hazard or perk, depending upon how one looked at it. He'd watched people he loved grow old and pass away. This was a part of being a traveler that he didn't enjoy.

Brandon was part of a special assignment group that moved from dimension to dimension collecting valuable information that would help save the human realm from invasion and possible destruction from beings such as the shadow people and other evil doers of Shadow Land. Often, potentially catastrophic occurrences for other time dimensions as well as their own were avoided as a result of his reports.

He rarely moved as far ahead in time as he'd gone this last time. He'd move only far enough ahead to investigate the results of this action or that strategy, or move back in time to study and observe a strategic method that some leader performed first hand. The need to be near Lucy when Alana arrived overshadowed all else and, after great reluctance from his superiors, he was given the information to find her and shown the portal to that time dimension. Now, here he was, back home in his own time and space.

What now?

The rich aroma of breakfast brought him back to reality. He'd slept later than intended. He hoped Tara was up and ready to move. It was enough slipping past sentries without waiting for the rest of the world to awaken. They needed to leave right away.

****

When Tara arrived at their designated meeting place, there was no sign of the old man or a horse. She fought panic while she peered at a small group of soldiers gathered around a tree stump playing cards and far too absorbed in their game to notice her -for which she was grateful.

The flickering of light from the edge of the grove about fifty yards to her left caught her attention. She watched closely as the light flickered again. It was papa. He'd hidden in the grove when the soldiers came about. Now all she had to do was to figure out how to reach him without being caught. For the second time that morning she was grateful for her familiarity with the property. She managed to sneak to the old man and his ever patient horse with minimal effort.

She longed for the comfort of her own saddle and the familiar gate of Sugar as she positioned herself the best she could in the horrid excuse for a saddle secured on the unfamiliar horse's back. Papa put up quite a fight insisting she ride Tara's side saddle, but she finally won out, explaining she needed to ride in a manner she was most familiar with during such perilous times. She did her best to find her seat amidst the massive fabric of her riding habit.

She followed the barely visible path through the grove toward the land where Maggie's house was in her own time at a slow steady pace while she familiarized herself with the horse and vice versa. When she heard the pounding of horse hooves racing up behind her she spurred her mount into action, heedless of the fact that she was approaching the clearing and would lose her cover. The hood of her long woolen cape fell off her head, exposing her long, thick, auburn curls. They flowed free behind her as horse and rider ran like the wind.

****

Brandon couldn't believe it. What was Tara thinking?

He'd stumbled onto Papa as he came into the kitchen for his breakfast and papa confided in a low whisper why he'd come from the stables at such an early hour. He was adamant that Brandon follow Tara to protect her.

Papa had always made it clear that he frowned upon travelers. Maybe it was because of the tragedy in his family or maybe it was more, but he'd repeatedly expressed to all who would listen his desire to see all portals closed and traveling ceased. Because of this, he was resistant to Brandon's courtship of Lucy at first. As time passed and the old man got to know the young man he developed a respect for the work he was doing and quickly accepted him into the household.

Brandon had always thought of Papa as an intelligent and

savvy man. His shock at discovering he'd sent Tara off to Shadow Land alone was overwhelming. What was he thinking? Was the old fool even in his right mind? Papa assured him he was only playing along with Tara to help lower her guard and resistance. He'd provided her with a clumsy saddle and slow mount then rushed back to inform him so he could follow close behind her. It was obvious she still didn't remember Brandon, nor did she trust him.

Breakfast be damned, Brandon needed to catch her before she was in so deep she'd be lost. Furious with Papa, he gave him a stern glower as he bellowed for someone to find Aidan. He needed the fastest horse he could get. He needed his gelding that was pastured not far away. Aiden was quick to shout orders for his men to saddle Brandon's horse on the double and reprimanded the card players for their blunder. Brandon was both appreciative and impressed at the harmonious speed in which the soldiers obeyed their colonel. His steed stood before him, tacked and ready, in record time. He headed down the path, spurring his gelding into a smooth canter.

Papa had saddled Lucy's old sorrel that she'd had since a child. It was ready to be pastured and left mostly undisturbed. It was definitely no match for the speed of Brandon's big, muscular powerhouse. He smiled with satisfaction. He'd catch up with her in no time. When he did, she had some explaining to do.

****

Tara huddled in the recesses of a shallow cave on the side of a steep hill while she watched Brandon race past. He rode so close to her she could see the whites of his enormous gelding's eyes. They made a formidable image. Every muscle in her body froze as she watched him suddenly pull up on the reins and his horse rear and beat wildly at the air with its hooves. Why was he stopping? Had he seen her? Perspiration formed like raindrops coating her brow as she flattened her body into the folds of her hiding spot. Uncertain of her mare's disposition, she quickly removed her cape and covered its head while forcing the animal's body as close to the back of the cave as she could with her meager weight.

She wasn't certain if it was the gelding's scent or its incessant snorting that made the mare quiver. If Brandon didn't leave soon she was sure they'd be discovered. The mare was growing agitated. She held her breath as she watched Brandon calm his beautiful mount and then twist his body in semi-circles while he looked for signs of what direction to take.

He scratched his head in total perplexity. How could he have lost her? He rode the far superior steed. He thought he heard some rustling a short distance behind him and was about to check it out when something in the distance caught his attention. Heeling his horse into action, he plunged forward down the narrow path and was soon out of sight.

Tara let out air that threatened to explode her lungs with one long expulsion as she continued to lean on the mare. This time it wasn't to subdue the animal. This time it was to provide her with the support her wobbly legs couldn't provide. She rested until her body felt more like its normal, vigorous self before pulling her cape off the its head and slipping it back on. The familiar scent of horse sweat filled her nostrils as the woolen fabric wrapped around her. She missed Sugar.

The sound of footsteps crunching fallen leaves and twigs caught her attention. Flattening her body as best she could, she inched her way to the edge of the cave's opening and peered out in the direction Brandon rode.

"You sure are a sight for sore eyes!" bellowed a crisp, jovial, masculine voice somewhere behind her.

She craned her head as far as she could around the foliage dense cave entrance, but could see no one. There was something about the voice that was familiar, but she just couldn't place it.

"I'm here," the mysterious voice said.

As hard as she tried, Tara just couldn't locate the source of the voice.

"Behind you... look up," it continued.

A flash of light caught her attention and she followed it with her eyes. Easing cautiously toward it, she felt every muscle in her body as she commanded it to move with controlled motion.

"Here I am," the voice teased.

Tara strained her eyes as she looked into the leaves where the voice came from, but saw nothing out of the ordinary.

"Please, show yourself," she pleaded, "It's been a difficult few days and I'm not up to games."

"Really? How very odd," the voice replied. "That's not like you, Lucy. I never thought I'd see the day when you were not up to games."

The loud thud behind her brought Tara around full circle to look straight into the face of a handsome young man who was just a few inches taller than her. She sensed a familiarity of his broad smile that boasted perfect teeth. It spread gently across a face composed of the most perfect complexion Tara had ever seen on a man. The familiarity of his rosy cheeks as they accentuated twinkling deep brown eyes that took in every inch of her was profound.

"My, oh, my, Lucy, you're just as pretty as you were when I was forced to leave you and tend to mama five years ago. May she rest in peace," he said.

Tara stared at the young man in the rag tag confederate uniform and scowled. He spoke as if he knew her well. "I'm sorry, do I know you?" she asked, hesitantly. Why did he feel so familiar?

He scowled and scratched his head.

"I heard you were stolen away from home for a bit and you returned with no memory, but I thought it was just a tale," he said with concern. "Son-of-a-gun, it really happened." He shook his head and patted his chest. "It's me, Joshua Neely. We've been the best of friends since we were kids. No... more than that, we're secretly betrothed. That old coot father of yours was so hard headed about you and me and..." he looked at her and shrugged, "then mama traveled to Virginia to see her sister and got sick and took me away from you and the war kept me away. But I'm back and I plan to stay."

"You're wearing a confederate uniform," she said.

"That I am," he replied jovially.

"We're in the north," she said with a hint of sarcasm.

"I wrote you from Virginia about it. They hog tied me into fighting when the war started," he replied, never losing his light-hearted tone.

"Aren't you afraid of getting caught by the union solders? What about the confederate army?" she asked.

Had they met one day earlier, Tara would have never believed such a wild tale, but she absorbed enough from Papa to believe there was truth behind it. She felt drawn to Joshua like she had when she met Dominic. She forced thoughts of the demon out of her mind.

"You fought for the confederacy against your will?" she asked sympathetically.

"They came into the house and dragged me out," he explained. "They shoved a gun in my hand and made me fight. It was almost a month before they suited me up in this stinking, itchy, patch of wool. I'll be happy to be rid of it."

"Is the war over?" Tara asked. She hadn't thought so because of the union soldiers in her house, but perhaps they just hadn't received the news yet.

Joshua looked around and lowered his head toward her.

"Soon," he whispered. "I'm certain of it."

"Why are you here if the war isn't over?" Tara persisted.

She held her breath, sure she already had the answer, but wishing she was wrong.

"Promise not to hate me?" he asked and then continued without waiting for her reply. "The war was wrong from the start. Most of our regiment was massacred at a battle in Gettysburg. I ran to save myself. I lived in the woods for some time and ran into a few other stray confederates. They said the army would never be able to account of all of the fallen soldiers until long after the war's end so I decided to just keep running until I ran myself back home. I hadn't planned on finding the place crawling with Union soldiers."

"This is the north. Why wouldn't you think soldiers might be here?" Tara asked with genuine curiosity.

She hoped her tone of voice didn't display the fact that she was annoyed with Joshua for running from a fight, even though she would have probably done the same thing in his place and she would have urged Dennis do the same.

"Because, darling, I thought they'd be off fighting the south, not camped out picking their noses while the war moves past them," he said with a huff.

Tara giggled. She liked this man and could see why they might be friends. As for betrothed... well, she could even see that. Besides the fact that he was strikingly handsome, there was something very charismatic about him. It was nothing she could specifically point out, but a combination of things. Even in his rag tag uniform it was easy to see he stood a fine figure of a man. Although not much taller than she was, his broad, muscled shoulders, and straight carriage gave him the illusion of being much larger than his actual height.

"Why were you hiding? Has it anything to do with that fella on the enormous black steed who looked to be chasing someone?" Joshua asked as he peered past her for signs of Brandon.

Satisfied that he was gone, he turned his focus back to the lovely lady standing before him. He moved so close she could feel the heat from his body.

She closed her eyes and bathed in the sensation of his breath caressing her cheeks while his eyes studied every inch of her face. His alluring scent was a mixture of man, the outdoors, and horseflesh. Yes, she could easily understand why her doppelganger was betrothed to this man.

He pulled her cloak away from her body and stood back to get a better view of her.

"So with morning pinions brought to thy mouth was I

impelled…Stamped with thousand seals by night, star-clear is the bond fast held…Paragons on earth are we both of grief and joy sublime-- "Be!" Part us not a second time," he whispered and then added, "You're even lovelier than ever."

Tara had to stop the urge to swoon from the romance of the moment. He was reciting a poem by Johann Wolfgang von Goethe like in a romance book. No one talked that way anymore. Yet they did. This wasn't her era and they did talk this way back then. It had quite an effect on her. Her legs felt like rubber as she bathed in the melody of the voice belonging to the handsome man before her. All else faded under the shadow of her desire to be near him. He instigated a hint of fear and uneasiness, mixed with a flooding of peace and security along with sensual excitement in her in a way that she'd experienced only once before with Dominic.

She was so wrapped up on the moment she almost forgot her reason for being there. Remembering Dominic pulled her out of her fantasizing mode and back to reality. Shaking her head to clear it, she stepped back to put some distance between them and allow her body a bit of normalcy.

"I'm looking for someone and I was hiding from that man," she muttered, thinking it best not to let him know who she really was.

"Looking for someone and hiding from someone?" Joshua asked, expectantly. When she didn't volunteer more information he continued, "I've been watching you for some time now to make sure you were alone and it was safe to approach you. I'm a fugitive, after all." He nodded his head in the direction that Brandon rode. "I saw that fella coming up after you in haste and I saw how you hid from him. So, I ask you again, Lucy O'Shea, my love and my future wife, why are you hiding? Why are you on the run? Who are you looking for?"

She had no idea how to respond to him. If she told him the truth, would he believe her? She thought not. She took a deep breath and decided to take a chance on the partial truth.

"It's a long story, but I'm willing to tell it to you if you have time and want to listen," she said in a voice that was barely above a whisper.

"I have both," he replied, "but this isn't the place for long conversations. Come with me."

Tara allowed Joshua to collect her horse's reins and pull it behind him with one hand while he guided her with the other. She had no idea where he was taking her, but it didn't matter. She felt safe in his company and more relaxed than she'd been since she started this journey. The loud grumble of her empty stomach brought a blush to her face and a raised eyebrow from her companion.

"We'll have to see to that," he said in a deep throated voice that sent goose bumps down her body to the tips of her toes.

****

Brandon pulled his horse to a stop while his eyes scoured over every inch of the countryside. How could Tara just slip away like that? Papa clearly stated that she was barely fifteen minutes ahead of him. His mount was so much faster he should have caught up with her long ago.

He was worried. Even if she recalled the truth and began to recognize and know the people and places around her, it was a dangerous time for her to be roaming. The shadow people were looking for Lucy. She hadn't regained Lucy's magical skills. She was like defenseless prey, waiting for them to find her and take her back to the hell they call home. The longer he took looking for Tara, the more danger of her being captured by the shadow people. He saw no other option. He needed help. He needed Fiona.

He squared his shoulders for what was to come and turned his mount toward the west. Kicking his gelding into a lope, he raced across the field toward the forest's edge.

TEN

Fiona straightened her back and admired her handiwork in the enormous garden that occupied acres of land. Although pleased with the progress she made with tending the myriad of vegetables, herbs and flowers that were grown in order to keep her pantry well stocked with supplies for both food and magic, she longed for some time to simply sit on her porch with her dog at her feet and rock the day away. Memories of her life in the twenty-first century doing just that were weak, but she could still pull bits and pieces of them up if she tried hard enough.

Her recollections of her final moments in that life were the strongest. She could still feel the searing pain as Dominic's evil creatures tore her apart before her soul managed to escape Maggie's body. She could still pull the memory up with such vivid clarity.

She was grateful she'd magically shared her soul with an infant in her family lineage of the twenty-first century and gone through the process of growing up as a doppelganger rather than travel time. Had she done that, she wouldn't be standing here today to guard Lucy's dormant, lifeless body until the time her soul could be wholly reunited with it. As it was, she'd been foolish and risked a lot by going forward in time without exposing the hiding place of their dormant bodies to someone to guard. Had they been found in such a vulnerable state of being they could have easily been destroyed and her soul would have had nothing to return to. This realization only struck her upon her return. She'd not make that mistake again.

Her eyes rested on the boulder that led to the cave. It was time to check on Lucy. She always dreaded when it was time to open the magical seal and make Lucy vulnerable to passersby'. Their bodies had suffered while lying in state during Fiona's absence. Someone really should have tended to them. Luckily Fiona was able to reverse the damage to herself and Lucy, but it was imperative to regularly check and make certain all was as it should be. If she didn't keep a vigilant watch something might slip by her and Lucy's soul wouldn't be able to reconnect. Lucy would be lost to her forever.

The light was fading and her bones ached from the toils of the day. Tomorrow would be a better time to check on Lucy. She'd be fresher and stronger on the morrow. Wiping her hands on her apron, Fiona picked up her gardening tools and started back toward her cozy little cottage amidst a small grove of fruit trees. The garden occupied well over ten acres of land, making it a sizable trek home.

Picking her way through the rows and rows of aromatic herbs and vegetables, she stopped at the sight of a lone rider making its way up his long drive. He wasn't in soldier's uniform. She couldn't imagine who else would be wandering the mountains during these tumultuous times. She started across the garden again at the same pace as before. Whoever it was come calling would have to wait for her. She had no intention of rushing and risking damage to her precious plants by misplacing her large feet on one of them.

As she drew closer and was able to make out the figure walking his horse into the small corral and being quite free with her water and grain her heart skipped a beat. It was Brandon Wagner! Why had he returned? What happened? Lucy's soul still hadn't returned, so Tara had to be alive. This wasn't good at all.

Fiona wrestled with the idea of placing her soul into another new infant after Dominic's beasts destroyed the body she was using so she could be near Tara again, but she thought better of it. When her soul returned to her body she found it had atrophied to a certain degree while dormant. Because of this, she regularly attended to Lucy's body to move and manipulate it to prevent what happened to her from happening to her dear niece. She also didn't trust anyone to care for them properly or to keep their location quiet. Her brother was the only one she might remotely consider, but he was too prone to falling under Alana's spell and she couldn't risk him telling her their whereabouts. Plus, overuse of such magic never brought good results. Her only other option was to time travel, but not she was needed here to guard and care for Lucy, if something happened to her like what happened to Maggie both she and Lucy could be lost forever. So, she remained where she was and put her faith in Brandon guiding Lucy's soul down memory lane.

Now here he was and here Tara wasn't!

Fiona shook her head. It was a sad surprise to discover the veil of forgetfulness had wrapped itself around Tara with such strength she questioned if the lass would be able to break free from it. If the soul can't break free from the veil it becomes stuck in the alternate body until that body either died of natural causes or meets demise like what happened to her. In the meantime, the primary body lay dormant, waiting for the soul to return and breathe life back into it. This was a fate she prayed fervently wouldn't happen to Lucy. Although this was a risk they knowingly took, they hoped Fiona and Lucy's magic would prevent it. They weren't so lucky.

The veil proved more of a challenge for her than she anticipated, but, little by little, the magic of her ancestors helped her to chisel it away. Brandon's story of who he was and how they knew each other in the past managed to remove the remainder of it just hours before her unfortunate demise. She wondered if she hadn't died that very same night if she might have been able to pull the veil from Tara as well and the two of them find the key. Then they could have both abandoned their bodies of the future magically and returned to their original selves.

Fiona's frustration was great. Why was he brushing his horse down in the year eighteen sixty-three as if he was without a care in the world? Where was Tara? What happened to Tara?

Maggie's mind screamed the questions. She quickened her pace and increased the length of her strides, eager to reach him and hear his explanation. She was less than ten feet away from the man before he noticed her.

"What are ya doin' here?" she screeched as her long legs brought her tall, lean body toward him with the grace and speed of an adept athlete.

She cursed herself for putting off checking on Lucy. Had she done so, the crystal viewer would have told her exactly where Tara was and what was happening. This mission shouldn't have become so complicated.

"She's somewhere nearby, I hope," Brandon replied while he continued to brush the sweat off his gelding.

"What do ya mean?" Fiona bellowed. "Tell me!"

Brandon rested his head against his gelding's neck and heaved a sigh. He knew Fiona wouldn't take the news well. An angry enchantress was bad enough, but one who had the powers equal to a necromancer wasn't something he was eager to get on the wrong side of.

"B-r-a-n-d-o-n," she drawled. Her Irish brogue at its peak. "Stop dawdling and tell me what's going on."

"Can I have something to drink first?" Brandon asked meekly. His throat was parched and he knew that once he started his story, she wouldn't want to stop to fetch him a drink of any sort... if she even allowed him to stay.

Staring at the distressed man before him, Fiona read his thoughts and sighed. He had bad news to tell her and was afraid she'd throw him out into the night. This was just not good. She guided him into the house and produced a tin mug filled with sweet apple juice made fresh that morning from the bounty of her overly laden apple trees. The trees were so old that anyone, but Fiona would be astonished that they were still bearing such an abundance of round, meaty fruit. She knew that with love and attention all living things, be they plants, creatures, or even peo-ple, can perform a task much longer than expected. She cared for her orchard like she cared for everything else she possessed -with genuine love and compassion. In return, her trees provided an abundance of fruit long past the season.

Brandon was far more appreciative than most for the delectable harvest from Fiona's land. The food of the twenty-first century paled in comparison to the richness of what could be had in the nineteenth century. He'd read that it was a result of over use of the soil to the point of wearing its nutrients away only to replenish them with artificial boosters. As a traveler, he'd been exposed to food from various locations and eras. He could attest first hand to the richness of the flavors of the foods in his period over those where he'd been. He savored the sweet nectar as the tension eased from his body. The juice revived and relaxed him simultaneously as it flowed down his esophagus and into the core of his being. Powerful enchantress Fiona O'Shea may be, but she was also one of the most caring and loving women who ever walked the earth. He was no longer afraid to tell her his story.

****

Tara stood before the full-length mirror as she fixed the last of the row of tiny buttons on the front of the jacket of the royal blue walking suit Joshua produced. She was completely mesmerized by her reflection. Joshua said he'd commissioned the outfit for her just before he left for Virginia, but it arrived too late and hung in the wardrobe awaiting his return. She found his concern that it still be in fashion touching and his delight that it fit her like a glove embarrassing. The bustle at the rear of the jacket and matching over skirt provided a distinctive silhouette while the black jacket, over skirt hem, and oversized sleeves balanced off the black and white striped underskirt. The outfit was surprisingly lightweight and comfortable.

Hearing Joshua's footsteps coming down the hall, she quickly pulled on the beautifully crafted black leather boots and weaved the laces through metal eyelets and hooks that went approximately five inches up her calf. It was a tedious task, but it wouldn't do to wear her shoes from the future. Blending in was of the essence. She shrugged her shoulders and pushed her longing for sneakers out of her mind.

The soft knock on her door was followed by Joshua's timid entrance. He smiled with delight at the sight of her.

"You're still the most beautiful creature in the world! Will you marry me?" he cooed.

She giggled nervously and reached for the straw hat she selected to complete her outfit.

"Lucy...err...," she stumbled as she remembered that he thought she was Lucy, "I must have been a frequent guest to have such a vast array of clothing available."

He stepped closer and took her hand. Raising it to his lips he replied, in words just above a whisper, "We were preparing for our nuptials, my dear. You had several fittings and arranged for it all to be delivered here. This isn't such an unusual thing. It was to be your home, after all."

Her knees weakened as she reveled in the moist warmth of Joshua's lips while they lightly caressed the back of her hand. Her body felt light and her mind wispy while she struggled to bring herself back down to reality. This man had quite an effect on her. She would have to remember to keep as much distance between them as possible if she was to keep a clear head on her mission. She pulled her hand gently from his grasp and cleared her throat while she regained her composure as best she could.

"The house is pretty empty," she mused, eager to change to mood.

"I'm not really alone," he smiled. "There are the servants. They run the house as if I'm not here since I'm a rebel deserter in Yankee land."

"In your land," she added.

"Yes," Joshua sighed, "and oh how I've missed my land." He turned to her, his captivating brown eyes holding her tighter than if he'd enveloped her in his muscular arms, "I've missed you even more."

Tara grew sad. She should really confess her true identity to this sexy, virile, handsome young man who thought he was her betrothed. It didn't seem right to let him think he'd finally reunited with Lucy. She opened her mouth with the intent to confess and some unseen force refused to allow the words to come out.

"I'm sorry," she mumbled as she fought back the sudden and quite unexpected, tears that were forming, "I can't remember you," was all she could say.

Until she knew Dennis was safely away from the shadow people, it was better to let him and everyone else believe she was Lucy O'Shea with amnesia for now.

Joshua smiled affectionately and patted her forearm lightly while assuring her all would be fine. He had no doubt her memories would return to her once she spent more time with him. They occupied the remainder of the day discussing her life in hopes of jogging her memory.

Tara took a chance and confided in Joshua about shadow land and her need to rescue Dennis, explaining that he was a distant cousin who came to live with them while Joshua was away. She was relieved to discover how open Joshua was to the existence of Shadow Land. In fact, he claimed to have had an encounter with the shadow people during one of the many battles he fought.

Tara knew she should feel sympathetic about Joshua being forced to fight against his will, but upon hearing he'd experienced direct contact with the shadow people she could think of nothing else. The fact that he'd seen and interacted with a shadow person even in the slightest way gave them an edge.

As luck would have it, he knew of the location of the portal to Shadow Land. Apparently, it wasn't as big a secret as Brandon believed. He also knew of a wizard who lived in the hills near the portal who could put a spell around them to help get past the guards and protect them from discovery once through the portal.

Tara smiled. So, he believed in magic as well. Things were looking up.

What Joshua didn't tell her was his concern about her

health. Her abnormally pale complexion accentuated her shadowy and sunken eyes. He knew of only three magical healers in the area. The enchantress would recognize him immediately. The witchdoctor was a crazy old coot who'd probably try to eat them. They stood a better chance with the wizard, who worked for Balthazar on more than one occasion.

Tara couldn't believe her good fortune. They were going into Shadow Land and soon she'd take Dennis home. She had no idea how since she'd thoughtlessly left the spell in the pocket of the pants she wore back at the estate house, but she wouldn't worry about that now. There would be time for that once Dennis was safely away from Shadow Land.

They decided to get an early start in the morning. After a light meal of cold biscuits and chicken washed down with warm port they bid each other a good night and went their separate ways. She was relieved and grateful for the genteel manners Joshua displayed and the security she felt.

****

Fiona struggled to sense Tara's location, but to no avail. Her soul was in a body that belonged to a time and space far into the future. It traveled back by means of time traveling making Fiona's ability to track her weaker. It would be much easier if her soul was in its true nineteenth century body, like Brandon's was. She snarled with frustration while yanking the cotton table cloth off the thick oak table in the center of the room. She walked to the bookcase in the far end of her living area and pulled down one of her thick spell books from the roughhewn shelf and slammed it on the well-used oak table top that was stained from the many herbal concoctions she'd created on it.

Brandon winced with every movement the angry enchantress made. He didn't worry about what she might do to him because he knew she was of a good nature and would never harm him intentionally. Even so, he was filled with remorse for his folly.

When he agreed to bring Tara back in time to find Dennis it hadn't occurred to him that her soul would be in the same time as Lucy's body. It was something that Fiona had never known happen before and she had no idea what would or could occur to one or both of the bodies as a result of such a thing. They both guessed it could turn bad, but weren't completely sure.

Fiona spent the better part of the evening pouring through her books in search of information to help her understand the consequences of his actions. As she flipped through the pages of the musty, leather bound book he noticed had a peculiar group of interlocking circles on its cover, she expelled an enormous sigh combined with a groan and rested her elbows on the table top with her face buried in the palm of her hands. The room was quiet enough to hear a squirrel scurrying across the porch outside the open window. After an excruciating and interminable silence, Fiona pulled her hands away from her face and sat back, straightening her spine against the solid back of her wooden chair.

She shook her head slowly as she spoke, "I'm just not sure I have what it takes to protect them."

"What does it say?" Brandon prodded.

Fiona turned the book toward Brandon and pointed to the section she read. His face went white and his heart ceased pumping life-giving blood for a brief moment while he read the consequences of his actions.

> *As one's soul travels space and time*
> *Leaving its body tucked behind*
> *Return not in the body that is not thine,*
> *For it shall lack the endurance and strength to persevere,*
> *The ability to show that it is near,*
> *The assurance to once again return*
> *To its true body, even though it may yearn.*
> *Caution o fellow traveler of time and space*
> *Caution to remain in the perfect place*
> *For to mix and mingle forward and back*
> *May cause the soul discernment to lack*

Then lost be the eternal soul to thee
No longer may it roam joyful and free.

"Can you explain this to me?" he stammered, "I don't completely understand."

"I think ya do," Fiona murmured flatly. After presenting him with a piercing stare that bared all of the emotions she struggled to hold inside. She closed her eyes and did her best to speak in a steady tone, "Let me make it clear for ya. It states that Lucy's soul is at risk of perishing. Both bodies in the same era confuse the soul. Soon it will want to leave Tara because it senses Lucy. Since Tara is still alive and animated it may get so confused it leaves them both. If that happens, both Lucy and Tara will be lost to us. Is that clear enough?" Fiona snapped.

Brandon sat back in his chair and stared at the poem with disbelief.

"What have I done?" he gasped.

Fiona sat quietly staring at Brandon's, but not seeing him for several minutes. Just when he began to be concerned for her wellbeing she burst into animated chattering, declaring she wouldn't accept such a fate for Lucy and if she had to stay awake nonstop for the next week while she poured through the books to find the means to locate Tara and return her to the future, if she had to conjure the spirit world in search of assistance, if she had to return to Shadow Land... then so be it.

ELEVEN

Tara fidgeted with the waist of her corduroy walking suit. It was such a tedious outfit to put on and she dreaded doing it all over again, especially since the events of the last few days caught up with her and she felt abnormally tired. Keeping on the underskirt and pantalets, she positioned herself as comfortably as she could on the thick, feather mattress and did her best to sleep. Unable to accomplish total relaxation, her sleep was restless and fitful, leaving her attire in tussled disarray.

Without the assistance of an attendant, she was unable to rectify the damage done to the alignment of her clothing before Joshua offered her a quick breakfast of coffee and cold biscuits to be eaten while they walked to the stables. She did her best to tug and adjust with her free hand, while she balanced the biscuit and coffee in the other hand and followed him to the stables. Noticing her dilemma, Joshua smiled to himself, but made no offer to assist. When they reached the stable, their horses were tacked up and waiting for them. Joshua looked long and hard at her.

"You should really be wearing a riding habit, not a walking suit," he said with a scowl, "What happened to the one you were wearing when I found you?"

"It was too heavy and hot. I didn't have help getting out of this and into that even if I wanted to wear it," she stated flatly as she pulled at her bodice. "This suit feels tight."

Joshua chuckled, "Give it time. It's new. Soon you'll feel so comfortable in your clothing you'll consider them second skin."

"Humph," she puffed. "I hope so."

"Well, do your best my dearest," he replied.

Tara smiled at the handsome man's reference of familiarity. It slid across his tongue freely and because of this she grew more and more at ease with its usage.

Grateful that he'd at least heeded her request to have a gentleman's saddle placed on her mount instead of a clumsy side saddle he argued a respectable woman like herself should use she threw herself onto the horses back with minimal effort, taking in Joshua's surprised appraisal from the corner of her eye. It felt good to be riding, even if the mare she rode wasn't Sugar.

They moved carefully while Tara adjusted herself to the horse's gait and determined the most comfortable method of draping her skirts so they didn't interfere with her seat on the younger and more spirited horse Joshua provided.

Joshua was right. A riding habit would be the better choice of attire. Once satisfied she was comfortable and secure with her mount, Joshua kicked his gelding into motion and they made haste toward the western skyline. It would take them a few hours to reach the wizard's place, which wasn't far from the boundary of Shadow Land. They'd have to expend time for the traditional pleasantries Joshua explained were expected of all guests in the wizard's domain until the opportunity arose for him to state the purpose of their visit.

He felt her health needed inspection and care and then he'd request the spell to get them into Shadow Land be created. Even with them leaving at dawn, if they were fortunate enough to have everything go as planned he anticipated they wouldn't be ready to head to the portal to Shadow Land until early afternoon. With a comfortable distance between their mounts and the house, he slowed their pace to let the horses regain their stamina.

Tara took as much of the clean air into her lungs as they'd hold. It was marvelous how pure and free from pollution the atmosphere was. In her time, even the most remote location still hinted at the toxic waste that accumulated from the abuse and misuse of its population over the years.

She scowled. It was clear she'd stepped back in time to the very same geographical area that she was in when she spoke the traveling spell. After chewing on the disappointment that flooded her when she realized she and Brandon failed to place themselves into the bowels of Shadow Land she allowed herself to contemplate her conversation with the old man. Although a lot of it still didn't make sense, she believed there was validity to his story which meant her doppelganger was somewhere nearby.

She hoped that their close proximity would help her pull at Lucy's memories. She felt something familiar when she was with Joshua, but that was all. She could pull up no memories of their lifelong friendship or engagement. Hence, he was a stranger to her. Even though she wasn't in the body of the woman Joshua had fallen in love he thought she was her. She wondered if this was an illusion or if the other body was indeed a mirror of her own.

Joshua used the duration of time it took to reach the wizard's place to orientate Tara on what was allowed and disallowed once they arrived. She received the strictest instruction to remain silent until either he or the old wizard addressed her. Listening intently, she reminded herself that she was no longer in the twenty-first century and things were different here. To her surprise, this didn't upset her. In fact, the longer she remained in conversation with Joshua, the more familiar her surroundings and the era felt to her. Could it be that she was blending in with and remembering Lucy's life?

She casually inspected the man riding beside her. If they were as serious as he claimed, then one would think she would be able to at least get something. The only familiar thing about him was the sensations she experienced whenever she was near him, but she couldn't put a label on them. She assumed it was probably just the chemistry of his scent or something along that line. There was a word for it, but she just couldn't think of it.

"Pheromones," Joshua stated, matter-of-factly.

"I beg your pardon?" she replied quizzically.

"That's the word you're looking for," Joshua chuckled.

"I don't know wha..." she stopped in midsentence. It was the word. How did he know that? Was he reading her mind?

"Yes, as a matter of fact I read your mind," Joshua stated.

"I'm surprised, my love. You used to block me quite well."

"You're a telepath?" she gasped.

"Amongst other things, and not a very good one at that," he chuckled. "You're really broadcasting. I suggest you cease before we reach the wizard. He's far better at it than I am."

Tara waited for him to explain the other things, but he remained content to move in silent unison with his mount as it picked its way up the steep, rugged mountainside.

"What other things? Are you going to tell me what the other things are?" she pressed, making a mental note to monitor her thoughts more closely.

It wouldn't do for him to discover her secret before she was ready to divulge it. Maggie taught her how to block her thoughts. She just didn't think it was necessary with this man. She now knew better.

"What I'm going to do is to focus on getting up the side of this mountain without any mishaps," he replied. "I suggest you do the same."

She looked around in surprise. The terrain had changed drastically. She must have been deeper in thought than she realized because she didn't notice the shift occurring in their surroundings until it was completely different.

"We've crossed over the wizard's boundary line. This terrain discourages visitors," Joshua volunteered.

Looking behind her, she was shocked to see how far they'd climbed over such a rugged and treacherous terrain. She agreed with Joshua. Now wasn't the time for chit chat. She needed to focus completely on safely reaching the ridge that was so near and yet so far.

****

Hannigan stood at the top of the ridge and watched the two riders as they picked their way along the precarious path. The old wizard's beady eyes narrowed as the pair got close enough for him to distinguish their identities. He displayed the remnants of a questionable set of teeth when his eyes settled on the woman. He recognized her as the niece of the enchantress. He'd heard rumors she was a star student. For years the evil old wizard longed to lure her into his own tutelage. Having both sisters would be a major boon. He'd heard she traveled to another time in order to avoid those who were after the key. Did the fact that she returned mean that she had it? He scowled as he thought how foolish he'd been to place the key in Alana's care to begin with. He'd reprimanded himself repeatedly for that folly.

Fondling his waist length frizzy white beard, he watched them as they slowly made their way toward him. He didn't recognize the man accompanying her, but that didn't matter. He'd be rewarded for surrendering the girl to him. It saved him a tremendous amount of trouble. Why, just this morning he spent over an hour in deep contemplation over the right spell to use to conjure her back from the future. Had he decided upon the right spell and performed the ritual he'd have taken credit for the arrival of the pair, but, alas, he was side tracked by a rabbit in one of his traps. He'd tossed thoughts of all else to the wind and wasted no time creating the most aromatic stew. The thought of the savory liquid filled with root vegetables, herbs, and fresh rabbit bubbling away in the caldron made it difficult to keep his mind on the here and now. He shook his head and rubbed his pot belly affectionately. It would be satisfied soon enough. For now, he needed to focus on the gift that was coming so close he could see the whites of her eyes. She was a lovely young woman with looks that rivaled her sister's.

****

As they neared the ridge, Tara eyed the old wizard with curiosity. He looked like he'd stepped out of a fairy tale. His long white and incredibly fluffy beard looked soft and supple as it cascaded down the front of his torso, hugging his rounded stomach affectionately. Although not a tall man, he held his body so erect it gave the illusion he was much taller than the five-foot, six inches of his true height. The grey tufts of outlandishly wild hair, rosy cheeks, broad smile and rounded belly reminded her of Santa Clause. All he lacked was a red suit and a few reindeer.

"Santa is a myth," the wizard chuckled. "As you can see, I'm quite real."

"I forgot you read minds too," Tara said with mild irritation. She'd followed Fiona's instructions on blocking her thoughts and was disappointed it wasn't working. Joshua spoke the truth when he said the wizard was good at it.

"That I do, my dear girl. You have the power to block me if it bothers you," he said matter-of-factly before turning his attention to Joshua. "Who might you be, young man?"

"Why," Joshua looked surprised, "you don't recognize one of your old students, great wizard? It is I, Joshua Neely."

The old wizard scowled while he took in every inch of Joshua as he dismounted and stood at the head of his horse, offering the wizard a greater ease of inspection. After a long study, the wizard looked from Joshua to Tara and then back to Joshua. He'd never met this man before, but he recognized the energy. This man was a warrior for Balthazar. It was best he went along with the ruse.

"Oh yes, Joshua Neely. Now I remember you. It has been a while my boy," he said as convincingly as he could.

"Yes, sir, that it has," Joshua replied, pleased the old man caught on so quickly.

"Well, come along then," Hannigan urged. "I've a huge pot of rabbit stew waiting. We'll eat until our bellies are full and then relax for a good story."

"Yes sir, thank you," Joshua stated in a tone of voice that relayed to Tara the importance of her being patient. It was a good thing he'd prepared her for what to expect. Even armed with this information, the impatience and irritation of wasted time showed plainly in her expression.

"Why so glum, girl?" Hannigan asked as he watched the scowl consume her face. "Are you not a fan of rabbit stew?"

Realizing that she was doing exactly what Joshua warned her not to do, Tara forced her face to light up with a smile.

"I'm not sure if I like rabbit stew, sir," she said sweetly. "I've never tried it. It sounds delicious."

"Hannigan," the old wizard stated.

"Pardon me?" she replied.

"I prefer to be called by my name, which is Hannigan. I'm the Wizard Hannigan. Hannigan to you," he emphasized.

"Hannigan," she repeated.

Satisfied, Hannigan continued, "You'll love the stew. Everyone loves rabbit stew... everyone."

"I can smell it from here and it smells delicious," she agreed.

She spoke the truth. Her stomach rumbled and mouth watered from the rich, exotic aromas that swirled around the cauldron dangling over the steady flames in the large open fire pit. She wiped at the moistness around the corner of her mouth with her finger tips as inconspicuously as possible. Never had she displayed such wanton hunger. She was both surprised and embarrassed

Hannigan eyed her with his peripheral vision. It was refreshing to meet up with a young lady who wasn't concerned about the display of a healthy appetite. He detested women eating the bulk of their food in solitude and then picking like birds to fool society into thinking they owned a far daintier appetite than was true. Hannigan was sure this woman practiced nothing of the sort.

"We'll partake of it shortly, I assure you," he volunteered. "Until then, let's tend to your horses and settle you in. It's a fine thing to have visitor, a fine thing indeed."

Joshua took her reins and led the horses as he followed Hannigan. She was grateful for the moment alone. Her uncharacteristic weakness and unsteady legs surprised and concerned her. She considered herself an accomplished rider and couldn't imagine why she felt like she did after such a brief ride, even if the terrain was more challenging than what she normally rode. Perhaps it was the change of horses. This mare's gait was a great deal rougher than Sugar's and she'd had to struggle to maintain a smooth balance between rider and horse. The expenditure of energy probably caused her to feel like she did right now. Whatever the reason, she was glad for the opportunity to eat and rest.

****

Fiona scooped large chunks of root vegetables into a bowl with a well-worn tin ladle and pushed it unceremoniously across the table until it rested a few inches in front of Brandon before turning her attention to the cast iron pot that was filled three-quarters full, with a boiling, green goop that hinted of purple on the front plate of her baker's oven. She'd spent the better part of an hour in her garden collecting ingredients for the concoction. After which she loaded her arms with bits of wood and built a hot fire in the stove to bring the goop to a rapid boil that lasted twenty minutes. Her reddened face glowed with sweat that flowed freely from her pores while she held vigil over the volcanic bubbles with a thick wooden spoon.

Brandon chewed steadily as he savored the flavor of an, oversized, jagged piece of the boiled roots. He wanted to question her about the purpose of the goop and if she was able to get a sense of Tara's whereabouts. Was she safe or had she fallen prey to the shadow people? He dared not. This enchantress was furious with him. Although he was bursting with questions, he had sense enough to hold them at bay until a more appropriate opportunity surfaced. Surely Fiona wouldn't be angry much longer. He'd broken the news to her hours ago. He was certain once she was no longer required to give that pot of goop her undivided attention she would calm down and he'd question her then. For now, he thought it best to remain silent and chew, chew, chew.

She heaved a sigh as she gripped the handle of the heavy pot with her apron and pulled it off the stove. Walking carefully the few paces necessary to reach the thick, stone hearth built with stone from the quarry on the far side of her property, she placed the pot on the large flat surface and stood back. With her hands on her hips, she stared at the liquid as the bubbles slowly dissipated. When she was satisfied its temperature cooled enough, she grabbed the spoon and gently stirred in a clock wise direction while she hummed an odd sounding tune. It reminded Brandon of one of the tribal chants he witnessed in his travels, but instead of a chant it was a hum. She finished her humming and stood with her arms stretched wide over her arched back with eyes closed and nostrils flared. He didn't know which was more formidable, the deafening silence in the room or the imposing vision of the enchantress before him.

He decided it was a tie.

The air swirled around the magical woman's head, causing tendrils that escaped her long auburn braid to dance to its rhythm. The room was stifling for the briefest of moments. Fiona stood motionless while the earth moved around her. Brandon held onto the table's edge for fear he'd be swept away. Interestingly, his table and chair never moved. When it was all finished, she put her hands on her hips, cocked her head to its side and looked at him.

"Okay, now that I've finished with me task, you're next," Fiona sputtered as she stretched her body and rubbed her hand briskly at the small of her back.

Brandon was horrified. What did she mean? Could it be he wasn't to be forgiven? What type of punishment would she put him through? He'd seen so much in his travels he couldn't even allow his mind to trickle in that direction. It was overwhelming terrifying.

"What in the name of all that's holy are ya shaking for? Ya'd think ya thought I was going to stick ya in that pot or something," Fiona bellowed.

"Or something," he muttered.

"Well, I never..." Fiona sputtered as she turned back to the thick wooden table top and pulled the book closer to her. "I've no patience for ya right now. None! So, do us both a favor and think before ya mutter."

"I'm sorry," Brandon said as he bowed his head toward the plate before him. He was at a complete loss at how to act or what to say. He knew the power this woman held and could wield at her slightest whim, but he also knew her to be of strong moral character. Therefore, no matter how powerful she may be, he wasn't in any real danger. How could he be? He hadn't intentionally jeopardized Lucy. Hopefully she would take that into consideration.

"I know ya are. I take the blame for the most part. I should've told ya more about things when I remembered ya, but I didn't realize our time together would be so short. I'm sorry I didn't recognize ya at first or that ya didn't recognize me. For you it was because of me age and for me it was that confounded veil. I got most of it up to do what I needed to do, but I still struggled with some things. I remembered the magic much sooner than I did the fact that I belonged here. It wasn't until I summoned for help and ya appeared and told me who ya was that it all came clear to me. It didn't help that ya showed up at the same time as that demon Dominic. 'Twas darn confusing!"

"I can imagine," he replied. "So, what happens now?"

He waited for her response while he watched her pour over the pages of the thick, leather bound book in front of her. He knew he was pushing her patience by disturbing her concentration, but he couldn't stand another moment without some answers.

"I'm still not exactly clear on why Tara can't be here," he said humbly.

"Why is it dangerous for Tara to be here with Lucy? Is that what ya are asking me?" Fiona's tone displayed impatience mixed with irritation.

Undeterred by her display of temperament, Brandon stood his ground and replied in a firm and steady voice, "Yes."

He sucked in air as she rested her elbows on the table and buried her face in her hands. The silence in the room crushed against his chest while he waited for her response. Just when it seemed quite clear that she had no intention of answering, she pulled her face free and looked directly at him.

With a heavy sigh, she began, "As ya read, but clearly don't understand, the soul can only occupy one body at a time per era and dimension of time. For Tara to be born, I had to separate Lucy's soul from her body with magic, leaving only the slightest connection for it to return when the time came. The spell holds as long as Tara is alive or until I summon it home. Now that Tara is here in our time, her soul will sense Lucy's body and will be drawn to her because that's the body it should be in at this time."

"What will happen?" he asked timidly, ignoring the insult of her words and tone. He already knew what she was talking about. He'd clearly understood what he read. As ridiculous as it was, he somehow hoped that he was wrong and if he pressed the issue Fiona would come up with a different reality.

Fiona looked at the handsome young man before her and smiled sadly.

"I'm not absolutely certain, but my guess is it will make an attempt to leave Tara and return to Lucy," she explained patiently. "If Tara's work was done and her affairs are in order, then that's good. If the mission's not accomplished... and in this case it wasn't... then Tara's subconscious will fight for the right to keep the soul. The struggle could cause such confusion for the soul that it leaves both bodies behind and goes into the state of limbo until it is given the right to reincarnate in an entirely new body in a completely different time and place."

"It can do that?" he asked.

"Absolutely," she said with conviction. "If that happens, then we've lost both of them."

Brandon was horrified, "I had no idea when I brought her here..."

"I know ya didn't, which is why I blame meself," she said flatly as she reached over and grabbed Brandon's hand, squeezing it reassuringly. The power she possessed was undeniably portrayed in her strong grip.

He looked at the enchantress. She was beautiful in her mid-thirties. He recalled the Maggie of the future and smiled. She would age gracefully.

"Now is not the time to be speculating on my looks," Fiona snapped.

He shook his head, duly chagrined.

"Well, as long as we're on the subject of the future me, I've a curiosity that I'd like to question ya about," she said softly.

"What might that be?" he asked apprehensively.

"Since I've never traveled forward in time like ya do, I've a curiosity about it," she said.

"I had no idea you've never traveled time," he burst forth.

"I didn't say that. Listen closely to my words. I said I've never traveled forward in time," she spat.

"I see," Brandon replied, embarrassed once again by his inability to do or say anything pleasing to this woman. Filling his lungs with the brisk, fresh mountain air that was coming through the opened window nearby he asked, "What's your curiosity?"

"Does the veil affect ya at all? I mean, I know I didn't recall ya right away, but ya didn't seem to know me either," she said. "Ya didn't, correct?"

"That's correct," he responded.

"So, every time ya travel forward in time, do ya lose your memory?" Fiona asked with a concerned tone.

"I used to lose a bit now and then, but no more. I've taken to traveling quite well," he replied, thankful to have the tension in the room subside and the subject to shift from Tara's potential fate. "I didn't recognize you because I wasn't looking for a woman of considerably advanced years. I was expecting you as you're now."

Fiona contemplated his words for some time before nodding -thus dismissing the conversation. She stood up and stretched her body in a cat-like manner before walking to the opened window to observe the star clustered sky. He watched with admiration as she silently mouthed some words to the twinkling darkness before returning her attention to the goop in the cast iron pot.

****

Hannigan hovered near the fire with outstretched hands. He was grateful it hadn't yet snowed. The cold bothered him more and more these days. He longed for the youthful strength and endurance he possessed for the better part of the century. He looked closely at the sleeping couple while they sat on the floor pillows with their backs against the roughhewn walls of his cottage and their heads together. He'd drugged their stew with a powerful potion he reserved for times such as this. They should be asleep until well into the morrow. This would provide him the time he needed to find a way to pull the information from the girl with a spell.

He'd never performed a spell of this nature, especially on someone who was as skilled in magic as the enchantress's protégé was reported to be. It was important he not miss a step or it could backfire on him miserably. He would spend the next few hours in trance and ask the spirits advice on the matter. With his guests deep in sleep, he was free to go far into the otherworld for his answers if need be.

TWELVE

Tara's mouth tasted like she chewed on an old cotton rag for the majority of the night. To add to her misery, her head felt like someone slammed a hammer across her skull more than once. The room looked as out of focus as the rest of her. The faint murmur of voices in the distance sounded familiar, but she couldn't think who they belonged to nor could she understand the words.

****

Joshua's nostrils flared with rage and his eyes glowed with a wicked orange hue as he interrupted his heated conversation with the old wizard to observe Tara's stirring. The old fool obviously gave her far too potent a dosage of the potion he admitted to slipping into their stew. He'd been up and about for several hours with minimal residual effects.

"If you've damaged her in any way old man," Joshua spit from between clenched teeth, "you'll feel not only my wrath, but that of my king." He turned and looked Hannigan squarely in the eye, "I assure you old wizard that's something you don't wish for... ever."

"Don't threaten me young man. The foolishness you display is surprising. I expected better from you," Hannigan replied with calm disdain.

"You'd do well to fear me old man," Joshua spat as turned his back on the indignant wizard and made his way to Tara's side.

His touch was cool and soothing against her skin. She was so very hot. She should have known better than to have fallen asleep so close to the fire. A cool glass of water would be wonderful right now. If she could only get her wits about her so she could request one. Her tongue refused to move. The rest of her body rebelled as well. She was miserably hot, miserably parched, and unable to do a thing about it.

Hannigan moved to inspect her a little closer. His long, thick beard tickled her skin, but she was unable to move away. She wondered what purpose such a long beard served. Wizards were described in books with beards as such, but she never actually questioned the reason for the abundance of facial hair until now. For that matter, up until now she hadn't considered the fact that wizards were anything more than a funny looking character in fairy tales and their beards and long hair were simply part of the imagery effect.

As the old man drew closer, she was able to make out his concerned features from beneath her lazy eyelids. His eyes looked like beady pools of dark, misty water set a generous distance apart beneath bushy white brows that accentuated his deep creased forehead. He was clearly old, yet he radiated a youthful energy that she'd never felt from someone as aged as he. With his face just inches from hers, her senses were teased by his aromatic breath that hinted of mint and honey. Still unable to move and her vision only mildly restored with words a foreign jumble, she grew concerned. What caused her body to go on strike? She would have thought it was something the old wizard had done, but the only thing he could do would be to lace her food with some concoction and Joshua ate the same food as she did.

"Al-ja-ha-ma-dom," the old man purred as he slowly moved his hand from left to right only inches from her face. "Dom-ma-ha-hunda, dom-ma-ha-jume," he continued.

As the old wizard said his incantation a buzzing sensation spread from Tara's ear until it consumed her entire body. She could feel a ball of energy form in the base of her spine and work its way up until it reached the center of her back. From there it split and rushed down her arms all the way to her fingertips. She felt like she would explode if the energy hadn't left her body as quickly as it did. She instinctively swung her arms wide and spread her fingers to assist the energy with its exit. Marveling at the myriad of colors that shot from her fingertips, it took a moment for her to realize that she wasn't only seeing and hearing clearly, but her mobility also returned.

She had no idea what the old wizard did, but she was grateful beyond words for his doing it. Stretching in a cat-like manner she slowly stood up, bringing herself to full height. She felt slightly light-headed, but instinctively knew that would pass within a short period of time. Taking deep gulps of air, she focused her mind on grounding thoughts, something Maggie taught her early in their lessons.

Hannigan smiled with satisfaction as he watched the enchantress's star pupil display a hint of her knowledge to the others in the room. She should have known better. The potion must have affected her far more than he'd anticipated. He was delighted. This could work out quite favorably. If her mind was that loose, then obtaining the information he desired would be easy.

Joshua pushed past the old wizard and offered his arm to Tara. She took it gratefully.

"Shall we take in some of fresh air?" he asked.

"That sounds wonderful," she replied.

Hannigan scowled, but made no attempt to stop the couple as they made their way out of his wizard's cottage. He watched them stroll down the path that led to the lake. He'd take advantage of this time alone and make a fresh drawing potion; something strong enough to handle the kind of resistance a protégé of the enchantress was capable of.

Humming his odd tune, he pulled out jars that were laden with dust and cobwebs. His moment was at hand. He could feel it.

****

Fiona guided Brandon toward the narrow passage hidden so expertly behind the thick hillside brush that one would have to know its exact location in order to reach it. She'd kept this location secret from everyone except Lucy until now. It was a display of absolute trust for her to share its existence with Brandon. He vowed to prove himself worthy of such trust. The thick branches scratched at his bare skin as they groped and grabbed at the invaders. He noticed Fiona wasn't suffering such a fate and realized she'd placed a spell of protection on the passage that affected everyone, but her. Even though she selected a location that was almost impossible to find, the added protection of a spell made her rest easier at night.

He pulled his collar up as high as he could and his sleeves as low as they would go and forged his way behind her, doing his best to stifle the grunts that involuntarily escaped his lips when a branch was successful in gouging his flesh. The opening of the passage was so small he questioned whether he'd be able to fit through it. He stood back and watched as the enchantress. A woman of height and stature, it seemed doubtful she'd be able to accomplish it either, but then he remembered it was something she did on a regular basis. He watched her closely so he could emulate her actions and avoid any further injury from the unmerciful protection spell that held nature obedient to its whim.

Fiona silently moved her hand in a slow circular motion over the opening of the passage before gripping the largest bolder and pulling it back with such ease one would never guess its true weight. Looking back, she motioned for him to follow quickly. Releasing her hold on the boulder, it started to slowly roll back in position. Realizing he needed to act quickly or lose his chance and be left unprotected in the midst of the caustic brush he dove forward, landing face first on the packed dirt of the well-traveled passage just before the boulder repositioned itself in its resting place.

It was pitch black.

He lay on his stomach while he waited to see how Fiona planned on lighting the passage way. After a few moments of silence, he moved his hand around to familiarize himself with his surroundings. He fought back the claustrophobia that was threatening to overtake him. He was never comfortable in tight, closed in places. He knew he was in a passage that led to a specific destination, but the darkness gave the illusion of confinement to the point of being buried alive. He could easily see why Fiona chose such an entrance. He could think of no explorer stumbling upon the entrance that would bother with it and believe it led to anything, but his demise.

"Fiona," he whispered, "where are you?" His ears roared and beads of sweat formed across his forehead as he listed to his words thud against the hard rock interior. "Fiona, are you there?"

The air felt ominous as he waited for her reply. He hated tight spaces. Being in one as tight as this and not being able to see even an inch in front of him was overwhelming. His body grew weak from its involuntary trembling as adrenaline gushed through his veins.

"I never saw a traveler so scared of the dark. Gods forgive ya," Fiona bellowed through the darkness. "Follow my voice, brave sir. Ya will be in light soon enough."

Brandon could feel the heat of his face. He found himself actually grateful it was too dark for Fiona to see the effects of her comment. His senses having somewhat acclimated to his surroundings, he listened intently to the faint padding of Fiona's sensible shoes as she led the way deeper into the passage. Although he regained his composure to a certain degree, his legs still required assistance in supporting him. With his arms stretched out to his sides, he pushed against the walls of the narrow passageway as a means of support while his wobbly legs slowly moved him forward. He prayed fervently for the passage to be short and for space and air to greet him soon. Seeing a flickering flame ahead of him restored the strength and reserve in his body and his legs found the means to move at a faster, steadier pace. When he was finally standing next to Fiona in an airy and quite spacious cave he drew a deep breath of relief.

Looking back, he shuddered. When the time came to

leave he'd have to brave that passage once again. He decided not to think about it and turned his attention to the far side of the large, airy cave.

"'Tis important to remain calm," Fiona said in an authoritative voice that was just above a whisper. "The life that still clings to Lucy is weak and any kind of commotion could cause it to sever itself from her. That goes for emotions as well. Just stay as calm and peaceful as ya possibly can. Got it?"

He nodded.

Moving slowly, the enchantress made her way to the pillow lined stone slab where Lucy lay peacefully. The long, firelight curls that framed her face glowed in the candlelight, reflecting their rosiness onto her porcelain cheeks. Brandon wanted nothing more than to kiss her soft, supple lips and pull her into his arms. He missed his beautiful, sweet, loving, Lucy. The amnesia she'd suffered at the hands of the shadow people, followed by the tension and trauma of his interactions with Tara, took its toll on him. He thought of the things he loved about Lucy and Tara that made them unique from each other. It was then that he realized he'd begun to love Tara. Loving her wouldn't do. It was wrong in so many ways. He shook his head to clear it. Fiona had specifically said to remain calm and balanced. He'd sort his feelings out later.

"She looks like she's sleeping," he whispered.

"In a way, she is," Fiona replied.

****

Joshua paced the wizard's cottage exterior as he looked toward the stars, not really seeing them. Something was wrong with Lucy, but he couldn't put his finger on what it might be. He knew time travel had its pitfalls and repercussions. He experienced a few of them himself more than once. For someone traveling for the first time it could be doubly difficult. The more one traveled, the easier it became and the quicker the memory and faculties returned. Going into the past was far easier than going into the future. Since she was actually returning to her own time it should be a piece of cake. He didn't understand it.

When he discovered Lucy back to her time and stumbled upon her hiding in the shadows seeking refuge from Brandon's obvious pursuit, he couldn't believe his good fortune. He'd crossed paths with the traveler before. He was known for taking assignments that kept him close to his own era which was why Joshua was so surprised to discover he'd traveled to the twenty-first century, but then he shouldn't have been surprised since Lucy was there as well and Brandon was her true fiancé. Joshua's disguise in the future as Dominic served him well. He went undetected even by Brandon. Of course, Joshua would have preferred to have been allowed to finish the task of killing Brandon when they met up in the grove in the future, but Lucy's arrival interrupted him. He almost got his way when he set the cottage on fire if that pesky Spirit hadn't interfered and stripped him from the body he possessed.

What puzzled Joshua was why Lucy hid from Brandon now. A lover's spat, perhaps? He'd heard she didn't remember him when she escaped Shadow Land. She certainly played out her ruse of being Tara with him in the future. It was seeing her hiding from Brandon and discovering she still suffered amnesia that had given him the idea of claiming fiancé status himself. He couldn't risk jeopardizing asking questions that might jog her memories of Brandon just to satisfy his curiosity.

As luck would have it, even though Lucy saw Joshua from a distance several times while she was held captive in Shadow Land, she didn't recall him. Balthazar assured him that would be the case, eliminating the need for Joshua to assume a separate identity. He disliked possessing other bodies. He'd questioned the need to do so in the future, but since the enchantress had reportedly traveled there as well, they didn't want to take any changes. He never saw the enchantress -just an old woman who he assumed was of the same bloodline, but fortunately not of the same skills. Even so, with the way things turned out, he was glad he took the trouble to seize Dominic's identity even though it took time -something of which was there was little of in the race to find the key.

Now it wasn't just time he was up against, but the old wizard as well. He hadn't thought of that when he forged his way up the incredibly tedious mountainside. How foolish he was to have forgotten it was the wizard who gave the crystal key to Alana for safe keeping in the first place. Of course he'd want it back.

Well, he couldn't have it. The old coot made a mistake in trusting Alana. He had only himself to blame that it was no longer in his possession and free for the taking. The king sent him on the mission of bringing both Lucy and the key back to Shadow Land and he fully intended to complete that mission with or without Hannigan's help.

While disguised as Dominic he'd been very close to moving in with her. Had that pesky Dennis not interfered he was sure he'd have accomplished it. Once there, he planned on searching the house for the key under the ruse of remodeling. He'd almost sealed possession of her free will as well. He had only one more ritual to perform and it would have been solidified. If it hadn't been for that old crone's interference he'd be sitting pretty in Shadow Land enjoying the favors of his king instead of wrestling with an old wizard for power over an amnesiac enchantress who was unnaturally frail and disoriented. She was far more impressive in future times even though her true time and power was in the here and now.

Joshua shook his head. He didn't really understand the ways of wizards and enchantresses. He longed to be back at court with his lovely Luella at his side. She was someone he understood completely. Born of magical humans, she came from a long line of sorcerers. A day didn't pass when he didn't thank Balthazar for sealing their union. They were a good match.

He chuckled when he thought of how foolish he'd been to think he could bring Lucy back to Shadow Land as his possession. Luella would never accept a second mistress of their castle. Even so, it would have been nice to try. There was something enticing about the young enchantress even in her weakened condition. He never seemed to get enough of her. He assumed it was the enchantress blood flowing through her veins. He heard it could be so addictive it consumed a soul until it you knew not who you were. This is one of the reported reasons why an enchantress fails to find true love and marry, or so he was told. Lucy found true love, had she not? She wasn't yet a fully-fledged enchantress. Perhaps that made a difference.

His piercing dark eyes glowed with a hint of yellow as they peered through the open window. Her long, firelight curls fell softly over her shoulders as she stoked the logs in the fireplace to rejuvenate the fire that was threatening to abandon them to the night air. He closed his eyes while remembering their embraces in the future, then scoffed at his own display of weakness. He knew full well about the powers the enchantress bloodline possessed. Even so, he was surprised that he, Balthazar's superior soldier, could be affected by anything an enchantress might have to offer. He was no mere human. He wasn't even the average demon. He was a soldier of the highest rank for the great Balthazar, king of demons and lord of Shadow Land. He was a magician of sorts, as well as a seer. True, his gifts were more prominent in Shadow Land than they were here, and even less in the future, but they still worked well enough to accomplish the tasks required.

"Now that we're alone, would you mind explaining to me who you're and why you're here?" Hannigan said through the dark.

Joshua whirled around to face the old wizard.

"What?" he said with surprise.

"It's not every day I'm honored with a visit from one of Balthazar's royal soldiers. So, I ask to what do I owe this honor?" Hannigan cooed.

"You know me then," Joshua stated flatly.

"Of course," the old wizard replied.

"How?" he asked.

Hannigan said with mild amusement, "You glow with the

residue of Shadow Land."

"Really? I had no idea," Joshua said with genuine surprise. "No one has ever mentioned that to me before."

"Perhaps that's because no one has ever noticed. Don't forget I'm a wizard and no ordinary one at that," he boasted.

"Do you know who she is?" Joshua asked.

Hannigan chuckled and grinned, displaying the pathetic remnants of a once full and beautiful set of teeth.

"Indeed, I do," he said with smug satisfaction. "She's the sister I've longed to have as a student, but could never summon to my side."

"You have Alana with you," Joshua said.

"As a student yes, with me now... no," he replied.

"It's my understanding you gave Alana a crystal of great importance," Joshua said cautiously. He chose his words carefully since he was uncertain where the wizard stood when it came to Balthazar gaining possession of such a powerful device.

"A foolish move on my part," the old wizard confessed.

"Might I ask what prompted you to do such a thing?" he asked.

"Greed, my boy, greed," Hannigan retorted. "You see; I've been trying to summon Lucy to my mountain for years. That's how her sister came to me. She inadvertently intercepted my summons. That one," he nodded toward Tara, "is protected by a shield of some sort. Placed there, not doubt, by the enchantress who some consider my nemesis." The old wizard heaved a sigh, "I thought perhaps if my key came into her possession it would be powerful enough to remove the block. Lucy was to return the key to me when she became my student. I underestimated the enchantress. It's a shame. Lucy has the potential to outshine both the enchantress and myself with thaumaturgy. Odd though," he tapped his chin, "she seems quite ill equipped to be a star protégé of the great enchantress."

Joshua raised an eyebrow as he nodded in understanding. The enchantress was a wise one. She didn't waste her time on someone who wasn't worthy of her mentorship even if she was a relative. He had to believe the girl suffered the effects of time travel.

Joshua hadn't been face to face with the enchantress, but he knew the day would come. The more he learned of her, the more he looked forward to it. Conquering someone as great and powerful as this witch would be a huge feather in his cap. The news that Lucy had the potential to be even more powerful than her mentor was indeed a boon. Perhaps he'd rethink her status when he took her back to Shadow Land. Someone with her skills and abilities could be an asset to the king and a political boon to him. Luella would just have to adjust.

Hannigan watched Joshua silently while he picked at the remnants of his teeth with a sturdy piece of hay. He was able to read bits and pieces of the young warrior's guarded thoughts and they didn't sit well with him. He may be a wizard who worked for his own personal gain and not necessarily for the good of mankind, but he wasn't a solid supporter of Shadow Land. It would be tragic days for all humanity should Balthazar get his hands on the key and have a magical being as potentially talented as Lucy at his disposal to do his bidding. He must prevent this from happening at all costs, even if it meant killing her.

He shook his head and hunched his shoulders at the thought of having to kill someone he'd coveted for so long. Curse this young demon for his interference. Perhaps he should kill him and be done with it.

"So, you plan on killing me old man?" Joshua growled. "By what method might you try?"

Hannigan remained almost regal as he faced his opponent. His only hint of emotion was one raised eyebrow.

"You read minds," he said with admiration. "I should have guessed."

"Lucky for me, you didn't," Joshua snarled. "I ask again. By what method do you think you would succeed in killing me old fool?"

In an instant, his decision was made for him. If he didn't kill the warrior, the warrior was certain to kill him. He had no choice, but to act.

"By this method," Hannigan bellowed as he raised his hands toward the sky.

Thunder clapped like boulders colliding in mid-air amidst the scattering of lightning bolts of all shapes and sizes. Joshua ducked and ran for the sanctuary of a nearby thicket. Diving into its depths face first, his curses filled the air as the thicket's razor-sharp thorns assaulted his flesh.

"Do you intend to hide in that bush forever?" Hannigan asked.

He was almost amused by the actions of Balthazar's mighty warrior.

"Only until I have my wits about me so I can select my own method of killing you," Joshua called out. "I'll not take long."

Hannigan tossed his head back in a fit of laughter that caused his soft belly to jiggle in a manner Joshua found mesmerizing. The wizard was a comical sight, but he knew better than to be deceived by appearances. The man was as old as the day was long, and with every passing year he acquired more skills and powers. There was also the fact that Joshua's own powers were weakened outside of Shadow Land. He'd have to be very clever in the way he dealt with the wizard if he wanted to leave the mountain alive. Even more so if he wanted to have Lucy at his side. He peered through the brambles toward the window. She was clearly visible. A determination like none he'd experienced before surged through him. He may not be able to kill the magical old goat, but he could at least disarm him long enough to grab her and escape the mountain.

Closing his eyes, he drew in as much breath as his lungs would allow and then expelled it with all his might. The force was enough to knock Hannigan off balance long enough for him to charge him. The astonished wizard barely regained control of his footing before Joshua slammed into him. The impact sent the two men tumbling down the small hill that led to the edge of the cliff where the wizard was known to hold vigil from time to time while watching the world below. The loud crack of Hannigan's rib cage didn't go unnoticed by Joshua. Encouraged by this stroke of good luck Joshua raised his body up as high as he could and let it slam back down. He watched with satisfaction and the troublesome wizard's consciousness ebbed away.

He wished he'd brought his pets with him. They would have torn the old coot to shreds within minutes. Even if Lucy didn't recognize him she was sure to remember them. After all, it wasn't every day a human encountered an animal that possessed the head of a vicious wolf and the body of a powerful feline. It was even less common for a human to survive to tell about it. In fact, Lucy, Dennis, and that bothersome traveler were the first. Of course, they had some super-natural do-gooder helping out.

Joshua shook his head to clear it. It was dangerous to allow his thoughts to wander like that. The old wizard was a force to be reckoned with even in his wounded condition. He needed to seize the opportunity to grab Lucy and run before Hannigan summoned the strength or the magic to attack. Leaping to his feet, he rushed into the cottage, looking back only once to assure himself that the wizard was no threat.

Tara stared at Joshua's disheveled appearance while she listened to his chatter about the crazy old wizard and their need to go. She'd felt something strange about Hannigan from the moment she allowed him to pull her up the path to his cottage, but she hadn't been able to put her finger on what it was. Now, hearing the urgency in Joshua's words she forgot about identifying it and responded obediently.

She stared at her companion's back as she followed him down the path toward the collection of poles outside the small stable where he'd tethered the horses. There was a familiarity about Joshua that she was on the cusp of remembering. Unfortunately, all she could focus on now was the danger she was in. Once she was free from this mountain and safe somewhere with Joshua she could work on pulling up the memories of the relationship Lucy had with him.

Moving as quickly as she could, Tara held her hand to her temple. She felt stranger with every passing minute. Her thoughts were fading in and out. At times, she recalled her mission to save Dennis from Shadow Land clearly and other times she could barely connect with her own identity.

"Dennis," Tara gasped.

Joshua stopped short.

"What, my sweet?" he cooed.

"My brother...err cousin... I almost forgot. I must help him," Tara replied. "My mind is soft or something. I don't know what's happening. I shouldn't have come here. I'm wasting time. I need to help Dennis." Tara moved closer to Joshua and placed her hand on his chest. She could feel his heartbeat beneath the palm of her slender hand. "Will you help me?"

Placing his hand gently over hers, Joshua stared deep into her clouded eyes. Could it be she was losing her senses? Why was she asking him to join her on a mission they were already on?

"He was kidnapped and taken to Shadow Land. I must help him," she mumbled, as if hypnotized by his intense eye contact.

"We're on our way to save your cousin, my sweet," Joshua whispered. Thinking to test her state of mind he added, "You have no brother."

She shook her head.

"Why, of course I do," she stumbled backward a few steps and looked around, "but not here."

"Where my sweet?" Joshua questioned cautiously.

"In my other home..." her voice trailed off and she stared at him with tear filled eyes. "I don't know. I thought..."

He moved toward her swiftly and scooped her into his arms. There was something endearing about her vulnerability even to someone like him. It made what he was about to do a bit more tortuous, for he knew that the sweet endearing nature that was chiseling at his hardened heart would be burned away swiftly once she was placed in the service of Balthazar. It was probably just as well. He couldn't have his evilness tainted with purity. There was no room for sentiment in Shadow Land. Possessing it made one and easy target. The king would strip her of all vulnerability soon enough and all would be well.

He pulled his thoughts back to the situation at hand. He needed to get a grip on what bothered Lucy to such a degree. Grant it, he'd only observed her from a distance while she was held captive and had never had the privilege of actually interacting with her prior to his trip to the future, but he'd heard enough about her powers, skills and character to realize that she wasn't herself right now.

Burying his head deep into her thick lengths of strawberry tangles, he turned his lips so they grazed her ear as he whispered, "Tell me what you know about Shadow Land."

Tara nodded vigorously, but didn't speak.

"What do you know?" he repeated.

"I... I'm not sure. I'm trying. I can't think. My mind is mush," she sniffed back the words along with her tears. "I... I know Dennis is there." Tara pushed herself far enough away from him to allow her to look deep into his rich brown eyes while she pleaded, "Will you take me there?"

THIRTEEN

Fiona watched the shooting star make its way across the rich blue sea of the cloudless night sky while she listened to Brandon's footsteps steadily approach. They were solid steps belonging to a man of strength, determination and confidence. The brilliant moon cast his shadow past her long before his actual arrival. She regretted involving him with this mess. After all, he was just a time traveler with no magical skills to speak of. Placing him in such a risky position when she summoned him to her in the future almost cost him his life at the mercy of that demon. Was that really fair?

"You're deep in thought," Brandon said in a hushed tone. "Am I interrupting?"

"Not at all," Fiona replied. "I was just thinking about what to do next."

"I've had some thoughts of my own. If you don't mind I'd like to pass them by you," he volunteered.

Fiona looked at him long and hard with a faint smile while she wondered what a traveler might come up with that an enchantress couldn't.

He returned her look with confusion, seeing nothing in his comment that should have been amusing.

"What are your ideas?" she finally asked.

"If I understand you correctly," he said as he paced absent mindedly. "Lucy is at risk of perishing completely because she and Tara are in the same time zone. Am I correct?"

"Ya are," Fiona agreed.

"I see no other option than to return Tara to the future as quickly as possible. Then, I shall come back alone and search for

Dennis in Shadow Land," he said firmly.

"I thought of the first part myself. Returning Tara as soon as possible is a must, but ya can't go into Shadow Land alone. Ya would never return if ya did."

Brandon stopped pacing and faced Fiona, a frown consumed his face.

"It will be difficult enough to convince Tara to return to the future without Dennis even if I promise to come back and collect him myself," he said.

"Never mind the lass. She can be dealt with once we find her," Fiona grumbled. "I didn't say ya wouldn't go to Shadow Land. I said ya couldn't go into Shadow Land alone." She heaved a sigh, "I'll have to go with ya."

"Isn't it just as dangerous for you?" he asked hesitantly.

"Balthazar would like nothing more than to capture an enchantress and force her to do his bidding, "she said with a nod, "but I see no other options. Tara is fading." She closed her eyes and filled her lungs, "I can feel her fading." Fiona spoke over her shoulder as she hurried toward her humble house. "If Tara returns to the future without Dennis she'll focus only on saving him until it happens, which will block any progress in removing that veil so we can find the key and get our Lucy back."

Brandon felt a wave of dread upon Fiona's reference to Lucy's soul returning to her. It meant Tara would be no more. He found the idea crushing, but there was nothing to be done about it. Her soul could only be with one of them and Lucy owned it first. It seemed only fair and logical to allow her the life she deserved. It was just hard to think of Tara having to lose her life in order for Lucy to have it.

He followed Fiona into the aromatic kitchen and watched as she methodically packed a large leather sack with a variety of herbs. Some he recognized while others were foreign, almost sinister looking. As he watched her methodical movements his mind turned to Maggie. Now that he realized they were one in the same, he could easily see the resemblance. It's frustrating that he hadn't recognized her then until shortly before her demise.

"I had a shield around me to protect me from demons. It prevented ya from seeing the resemblances I think," Fiona stated in a matter-of-fact tone. "Plus, I was old. You said you expected me like this, not like that."

"Ha," he laughed, "there's no privacy while in your presence, is there?

"None when times are as they are my boy," she replied.

Brandon cleared his throat, "You do realize the age difference between us isn't as it was in the future, don't you?"

"I do," she chuckled.

"I'd estimate you to be in your mid-thirties at best," he said timidly, knowing it was risky to discuss a woman's age with her. "If that's the case, I'm only a few years your junior and find your reference to me as "boy" a bit disturbing. I'd like to ask you to please refrain from calling me that."

Fiona stopped packing and looked at Brandon long and hard. He was right. There wasn't a great deal of difference in their ages and she really shouldn't be addressing him as "boy". Prior to her experience in the future, she would have never dreamed of such. Apparently, not only could she recall her life in the future, but she actually had retained some of the personality traits she'd developed.

"Fair enough," she said.

"I don't recall ever seeing herbs of such a nature, dried or otherwise," Brandon said with curiosity.

"As well ya shouldn't. These herbs came from Shadow Land," she replied briskly, not looking at him.

Silence filled the air as his mind raced. Had she entered Shadow Land to get these herbs?

"I went to Shadow Land. That's correct," Fiona stated flatly. "I never said I've not been there before. I just said that 'twould be dangerous for me to go. Ya need to pay closer attention to words and the meaning behind them traveler." Securing her overstuffed sack to her back, she started for the door, "Come. There's no time to waste. Ya can tell me once again where ya lost the lass while we saddle the horses."

Brandon's face burned scarlet as her words rang in his ears. He may not wish to hear them, but they were words of truth. He did lose Tara. He had no idea how that happened, but happen it did.

****

Hannigan pulled himself to the edge of the ridge with the aid of the make shift crutch he fashioned from a branch of a young oak tree. The pain in his ribs slowed him down considerably and it took him most of the night to accomplish a task that should have only taken minutes. Now, standing and seeing what he saw he was glad he'd worked so diligently to make himself mobile and not put it off until the morning. His sense of urgency to be mobile in his wounded state instead of resting and healing was now making sense.

At first, he thought his eyes were playing tricks on him, but as the riders drew closer he was more certain than ever that the smaller bay carried on its back none other than the enchantress herself!

So, the enchantress was finally paying him a visit. He made no effort to deceive himself. There was no doubt that it wasn't he who she climbed the tumultuous mountain to reach. He wondered what reaction she'd have when she discovered her protégé was no longer with him, but in the possession of one of Balthazar's soldiers. He scowled. As much pleasure as it gave him to know the high and mighty empress was trumped by the powers of Shadow Land, he was also trumped. For that he wanted revenge.

Gloating in her face about the fact that she was the first to break the absence of their eventual meeting was probably not his best move. He braced himself for the more diplomatic, although less desirable greeting. He'd have to partner up with her if they were to get Lucy back before she was forever lost to Shadow Land. Then he'd see who got the girl. Family or not, he could teach the young woman far more than her witchy aunt, of that he was certain. She may be the most powerful enchantress in the land, but he was Hannigan the Great. He was the greatest weaver of wizardly magic known to history. The enchantress would stare into the face of her master when she set her eyes upon him.

His blood rushed through his veins with renewed vigor as he anticipated their eventual contest of skills and wondered why he hadn't initiated a meeting long ago. What difference did it make who approached who? It was the battle that mattered, the sheer contest of who bested who. It was elating and life giving. He should have sought her out long ago.

As the pair drew closer his eyes widened. This was his first time setting eyes on the famed enchantress. She was nothing like he thought. She looked quite common in fact. How very strange. Could he be mistaken? Perhaps the woman on horseback wasn't who he thought her to be. Looking closer, he spotted traces of the energy swirling around her. He couldn't mistake remnants of a magic shield. He could also see her resemblance to her young protégé. If information served him, the enchantress was the girl's aunt on her father's side. The girl favored her father while Alana favored her mother. That explained a lot about the girl's powers and Alana's lack of them.

Waving his arms in a broad swoop he forced a smile and gestured for them to complete their journey. It would do no good to show his cards now. After all, if he could see through her shield of magic, then she could most likely see through his and at this point he was in no position to face off with her. He needed time to heal his bruised and broken body, during which he could study his opponent more closely.

****

Fiona scowled as she watched the old man do his best to hide the pain his welcoming gesture caused. She heard he was young beyond his years and quite vigorous. This didn't match up with the man she spotted at the edge of the ridge. Perhaps he wasn't the wizard, but an assistant come to greet them. That would make more sense.

She adjusted the magic shield she placed around herself prior to ascending the mountain. It wouldn't serve to expose her identity at the moment. She needed time to access the situation. The stories she heard about the great wizard of the mountain had primarily depicted him as an egoist sort who coveted the title of the mightiest of wizards. He wouldn't take kindly to having an enchantress of her caliper in his presence without wanting to prove himself. She wasn't in the mood for a faceoff with an egotistical old magic maker. Time was far too precious for that. She wouldn't have come, had she seen any other option, but this was where Tara's trail led them.

Years and years of avoiding the maniac on the mountain were for naught. Here she was riding right into the den of the lion with barely enough time to prepare her defense. The simple shield was all she was able to muster on such short notice. She filled her lungs with air and expelled it slowly, hoping to regain as much composure as possible as they drew closer to the top of the ridge where the mighty wizard stood waiting like a wolf stalking its prey.

****

Brandon paced the well-trodden path behind Hannigan's cottage while he waited for Fiona to complete her meeting with the odd looking little man. He'd heard of him many times, but never had occasion to be in his company. The wizard was nothing like he'd imagined. Other than a few tribal magic men, Fiona was the only magic maker he came in contact with and she was quite normal looking. This man looked like he'd stepped off the pages of a child's story book.

The afternoon sun shone bright and the air spoke of promise of the winter that was soon to come. He recalled the cold he'd left in the future and shuddered. Although they experienced winters that could sometimes prove unbearable in the nineteenth century, the climate was colder in the future. He'd heard rumors the planet shifting its axis and a damaged ozone layer were the reasons behind the change in climate. Whatever the cause, there was no denying it was miserably cold when they left and would be the same when they returned.

His thoughts were interrupted when Fiona popped her head out of the cottage door and motioned for him to join them. He obeyed with caution. He'd always been sensitive to magical energies. The air around a magic maker could be intense. Being in a room with two of the strongest magic makers in the north could prove overwhelming. As he entered the small cottage he braced himself for the blast of chaos he suspected would assault him.

To his surprise, all was calm.

The oversized hobbit lay stretched out on the long wooden table that dominated the far side of the great hearth, its crackling fire radiated warmth to every inch of the room. His shirt was removed and his long beard rested alongside his torso, leaving his wrinkled flesh exposed. Fiona laid some large leaves soaked in a purplish solution across his rib cage, but only after she smeared a pungent paste over the angry bruises that dominated most of his chest. Calling for Brandon's assistance, she pulled the old magician's body into an upright position and had Brandon hold him steady while she bandaged her handiwork. During the entire process, Hannigan stayed surprisingly motionless.

"He's in a trance," Fiona explained in response to Brandon's unasked question. "I had no desire to hear him bellowing up a storm."

"He allowed it?" Brandon asked.

Fiona just chuckled and went about her business. Her lack of words told him more than words ever could. He stood back and looked at the enchantress with a new level of respect. How powerful she must be to be able to place a wizard of such reputed magic under a spell that would render him helpless without his permission. He gave thanks she saw fit to restrain from taking her anger over his foolishness out on him. If this powerful wizard could be turned into mush what would happen to him? He dared not even imagine.

****

Hannigan paced the cottage floor in a rage. He awoke from a deep trance to find the fire down to mere embers and the only light illuminating the great room of his cottage coming from the rich beams from the full moon through the oversized window on the north wall. He'd agreed to allow the enchantress to say a few words that would give him strength to endure the resetting of his ribcage and also speed up the healing process in general. Instead, the conniving witch put him into a deep trance. Not only was he furious, he was humiliated to have been bested like that.

Had the healing at least worked? He pulled the bandages away to inspect his injuries. There was only a faint ghost of the angry bruise remaining and his chest no longer pained him when he moved this way or that. She may have been a conniving witch, but at least she honored her word.

He'd hoped to solicit the aid of the enchantress to secure Lucy from the demon warrior. It would have been far easier with her partnership of forces, not to mention the fact that he stood a better chance of winning the girl's trust if she thought he and the enchantress were working together to protect her from harm. Then, once he had her safe within his grasp he'd show his true worth to the enchantress who relied on potions and weeds to wield her magic.

Well, now that he was almost as good as new, he didn't need her help. It was every man for himself... a race to the girl. He rubbed his hands together in anticipation of the challenge ahead of him. She was a very foolish woman to heal him.

After thinking through the maze of crafty conversation that passed between them for hours while they sized each other up, Hannigan came to the conclusion that the powerful enchantress was little more than a fairy come out of the closet. She'd be no match for him when the time came.

She was a tricky one though. He hadn't considered that. She and her bodyguard slipped off while he was in blissful recovery. He made himself vulnerable to her, true, but it was only because he was certain she wouldn't harm him. She possessed a strong sense of right, wrong, and the karma it could bring so she healed the man and then slipped off into the night before he could awaken. She was a wise woman to recognize the danger he was to her, but a foolish woman to leave him alive and well. He wouldn't have been so generous to her. Having the one and only person who could even remotely be a worthy opponent at his mercy would have been an invitation to snuff her out and eliminate the possibility of her causing him an inconvenience at a later date. Karma was a law for the weak. He spat on karma. He was the Hannigan the Great, lord of wizards and immune to all laws except those he laid down. He knew it, Balthazar knew it, and it was about time the enchantress knew it!

Slowly, his anger subsided and his mind moved toward more productive thoughts such as how to catch up with the demon warrior before he made it into Shadow Land and had his full powers at his disposal. Had the enchantress been at his side he'd have stood a better chance of battling a demon on his own turf, but without her support in battle, it would be more challenging. Once in the hands of Balthazar, Lucy wouldn't only be forced to unveil the location of his crystal key, but she'd be forced to serve him. With a young enchantress under his rule, Balthazar would have no further use for an aged old wizard such as Hannigan. He shuddered to think of his fate should that happen.

Gathering the few staples to sustain him on his trip Hannigan saddled his mule and headed down the narrow path of the mountain. Time was of the essence. Although not as comfortable a ride as his gelding, his mule was more sure footed and familiar with the hazardous short cut he intended to take.

Fiona's excruciatingly silence unnerved Brandon as he guided his horse up the narrow path behind her. They'd traveled for hours without one exchange of words. He wanted to ask where they were going and how long she expected it to take them to get there, but he dared not. In all of the years he'd known Fiona he'd never seen her in such a dark mood. It was best he remained silent and let whatever happened, happen.

The sound of a twig snapping caught his attention. Fiona's failure to react surprised him.   He slowed his horse down as his eyes combed their surroundings. There was so much to be on the lookout for. The country was in the middle of a civil war. His southern drawl could land him in trouble if he ran into anyone other than Dennis. He'd spoken with the drawl for so long he'd lost the authenticity of his Irish brogue which could also cause suspicion. An army of the north could capture him for being a traitor rebel or possibly believe him of the north and not take kindly to his wandering the north as a civilian instead of enlisting to fight for their cause. The old wizard informed them while in trance that Tara was in the hands of a demon warrior from Shadow Land. If this demon warrior was aware of their approach he could be hiding in wait for them. Then, there were the everyday cautions one displayed while traveling in mountains that were home for wolves and mountain lions, amongst other things.

The sound of a large snap followed by a thud finally caught Fiona's attention. To Brandon's surprise, she simply stopped her horse and waited. What was she waiting for? She didn't volunteer the information and he knew better than to ask. He sucked back his impatience as best he could and pulled his gelding up beside her mare.

"Come out," Fiona called out.

The air stood still and the sun beat hot on their faces while they waited for a pair of dark green and red eyes to come out of the shrub that lined the path they traveled. Brandon silently braced himself for what was to come. He had a sense of familiarity about those eyes that took time to place. Memories of the demon wolves peering through the night flashed through his mind and every nerve ending in his body stood ready for action.

The thorny leaves on the thick shrubbery lining the narrow path shook violently as the silver and grey wolf leapt from its depths and stood before Fiona.

"So, there ya are. I've been calling for ya for some time now," Fiona scolded. "Pick a friendlier beast. You're scaring me companion."

Brandon watched in amazement as the wolf raised himself onto his hind legs and then slowly transformed into an enormous hare. Brandon rubbed his eyes, as if to make certain he wasn't imagining the scene before him.

Fiona gave an exasperated sigh.

"Now, what good do ya think ya will be to us like that?" she barked. "Use your brain. This is serious business."

Brandon shook his head. Did he hear correctly? This was all too confusing.

Suddenly the hare was replaced by the figure of a boy who looked to be no older than his mid-teens. His dark, wiry hair tossed to and fro in total disarray. A deep complexion hinted of the Anglo heritage at the base of a mix of what Brandon guessed was islander and Asian. With his body as erect as a human body could possibly hold itself, he stood halfway between four and five feet tall.

"I'm very serious, milady," the young boy stated in English that spoke of the old country. "I'm at your service," he continued as he bowed low for emphasis.

"I need ya to scout ahead for me to the edge of Shadow Land. A demon warrior has captured a red headed lass and is taking her there. They must be stopped before they reach the entrance," Fiona stated boldly. "Find them and then report their location to me when ya do."

"If I find them at the entrance to Shadow Land?" he asked calmly.

"Stop them," Fiona replied in a blunt, matter-of-fact tone.

"How?" he asked.

"However," she replied. "Just keep the lass safe."

"Very good, milady," stated the boy just before his slender body transformed into one of the largest and most beautiful eagles Brandon ever laid eyes upon.

Brandon sat so still upon his horse he could have easily been mistaken for a statue. Waiting for Fiona to explain what just occurred seemed wishful as he watched her once again nudge her mare forward along the path. It was obvious she had no intention of explaining anything to him -not at this time anyway. Shrugging his shoulders, he heeled his enormous gelding just enough to signal it was time to continue their tedious trek along the narrow, mountainous path.

FOURTEEN

Flames danced around the light show of elusive sparks as Joshua put another branch he'd obtained from a seasoned fallen oak tree onto the fire. His mind raced with concern as he watched Lucy's health dissipate with every passing hour. He was baffled. She looked healthy to the naked eye. She showed no symptoms of disease yet grew weaker and weaker for no apparent reason. He'd hoped the old wizard would create a potion to heal her. Now he was faced with the dilemma of taking her to Balthazar in her weakened condition or seeking aide from an old witchdoctor who lived in the most remote depths of the mountains. He weighed the pros and cons of both and decided that it would be far more advantageous for him to deliver a healthy and vibrant young enchantress to the Lord of Shadow Land than to show up with the shell of a woman who lay snuggled beneath the woolen blankets he'd brought along.

Joshua sighed. He'd never been to the witchdoctor and only had a vague idea of where he was located. He was going to need help finding him. This would necessitate calling upon one of his pets. Normally, he wouldn't hesitate, but his fear of the girl recognizing them was acute.

Lucy moaned as she rolled around the ground in search of a more comfortable position. Her normally rosy complexion was hallowed and pale. The dark circles under her eyes hinted at the severity of the situation. Every bone in his body told him the young enchantress was dying, but why?

If he was to solicit help in finding the witchdoctor he'd better do it while she was sleeping. Looking at the sky, he searched for the location of the North Star. Once he found it he closed his eyes and focused his thoughts to project across the barrier that stood between the human world and Shadow Land. This was no easy task and his body swayed from the exertion. When he finished he walked back to the fire and sat cross-legged on the grass, close enough to stay warm, but far enough away to avoid burns from a rogue spark or two. He'd given it his all. There was nothing to do now, but wait and regain his strength for whatever powers he possessed outside of Shadow Land. With the dangers that awaited in the territory they had ahead of them, he'd need them.

Not thirty minutes later he heard Bog's familiar steps. Standing just shy of eight feet tall with skin the color of midnight, unruly black coarse hair that cascaded down his back in what looked like an attempt of braiding, and piercing green and red eyes, Bog was a formidable sight to behold. Joshua was grateful Lucy wasn't awake to witness his imposing presence.

"You summed me," Bog's deep, emotionless voice boomed.

Other than looking in Bog's direction, Joshua's body never moved from its cozy spot near the fire.

"I need you to find the witchdoctor that lives deep in these mountains. I need his exact location. Do it quickly," Joshua commanded in a firm, level tone.

"As you wish," Bog said as he bowed low and backed away until he disappeared into the deep thickets that bordered the edge of their camp.

Joshua scrutinized Lucy's sleeping body one more time before closing his eyes. Bog was the best watcher in Shadow Land. He'd accomplish his mission swiftly and efficiently, at which time he'd have to push both him and his precarious charge deep into the mountains over unfamiliar terrain to wherever the witchdoctor resided. The little quiet time he had between now and then had best be spent resting.

****

Fiona waited for Brandon's mount to drink the crisp water from the mountain stream they went out of their way to find. Using the opportunity to tune into Tara's energy, she closed her tired eyes and relaxed into the well-worn saddle she only recently re-secured on her mount. Focusing on the rhythm of her horse's breathing, Fiona's body grew lighter and lighter as she fell into an easy altered state of consciousness. Within seconds she was outside of her physical self, looking down at the picturesque scene she and Brandon made on their mounts next to the crystal blue stream of water in the untarnished wilderness. Wasting no time, she willed herself to Tara's side.

Darkness consumed her and her breathing grew labored as she sensed, more than saw, Lucy stretched out within the bowels of the cave where she so lovingly guarded her. Without warning, her vision shifted to Tara bundled up in woolen blankets as she lay by a roaring fire under the starry sky. It didn't take long for her to spot the demon warrior sitting on the opposite side of the fire in a lotus position. His eyes were closed. There was something familiar about him. Shaking her head, she reminded herself of the purpose of her vision quest and returned to the sleeping Tara. Was she still strong and vigorous? Had her soul begun to separate from her body? More importantly, were she and Brandon too late to help her?

Fiona considered the consequences of allowing Tara to die while she was in the company of a demon. Her soul hadn't brought back enough connection to Tara for her feel emotion for the lass. Her only worry was what would happen to Lucy should this happen. She looked upon Tara bundled in a blanket more as a shell that housed Lucy's soul. Realizing this, she chastised herself for being so callous. Tara shared Lucy's soul and was in a sense still Lucy, but something went astray with the spell and she developed her own unique personality. She was, therefore, not Lucy, but a separate human being with her own sense of person who loved her when she was Maggie. It was Fiona's intention from the start to call back Lucy's soul as soon as the key was found, but it was a foolish and abstract plan. After experiencing firsthand, the truth of placing souls in the future, the concept of doing nothing to help Tara seemed criminal at the very least.

The spell was to program the soul to travel back in time once Tara's body expired or Fiona invoked the spell to call it back. The soul hadn't been programmed to accommodate both bodies in the same era and geographical location. Fiona looked for a spell for such a situation, but had come up empty handed. The safest thing would be to return Tara to the future and let things play out naturally.

First, she needed to find her and get her away from that demon fella.

The sound of Brandon clearing his throat brought her back into her body in a flash. She opened her eyes and looked once again at their surroundings.

"We should probably stop for the night. Tara isn't far from here and she's resting. So should we," Fiona said while struggling with her emotions.

She thought it best not to tell Brandon how weak Tara was. There was no sense in both of them being overwrought.

Brandon nodded and looked around. They'd gone off the mountain path and forged their way into the thick of the pines in order to find water and rest for their mounts. He'd hoped to reach the mountain top before nightfall, but the going was far more tedious than anticipated. They were forced to stop often.

He was surprised at how quickly night came upon them. His mind was so occupied with matters of Tara's safety, Dennis' rescue, and making sure his horse wasn't directed toward peril, all else seemed unimportant. He worried over his attachment to Tara. He was engaged to Lucy, but Tara held a place in his heart as well, maybe more so.

It made sense that he'd be attracted to Tara. She looked like Lucy with many of the same personality traits along with a few unique ones added to the mix. What concerned him most was that he might care for Tara just a little bit more. There was a bond between them that could never be with Lucy; the bond that formed while fighting for his life next to her.

Lucy was a powerful enchantress who could have easily taken on Dominic and saved them with the wave of her hand. Tara was still vulnerable and needed his help and support. It was inevitable for him to worry and care for her as he'd never done for his beautiful fiancé. Something like that bonds people together whether they're aware of it or not. He needed to constantly remind himself that he was promised to present Lucy and she would soon be awake with her memories returned to resume their courtship.

Brandon knew all along that when the key was found Fiona intended to call Lucy's soul back to her. He'd given it little thought. Tara's was an abstract idea, not a real person. Now he'd met her. Now he'd interacted with her. Now, he'd fallen in love with her. He couldn't see her perish any more than he could see Lucy perish. He couldn't choose between them. There had to be another way. There just had to be.

Fiona pointed to the east, "If we go this way a bit, we'll find a clearing suitable for camp."

"You've been here before?" he recognized his foolishness only after the words had slid off his tongue.

She shot him a look of impatience as she urged her horse forward. She needed to be alone for a few minutes to give herself time to digest what she discovered when she connected with Tara and make some sense of it all. Brandon's words of stupidity gave her just that opening.

****

Bog stood at the edge of the witchdoctor's property, grateful to have found a thick oak trunk to hide his bulk. He'd been forced to step-down his vibration in order to cross through the magical force field the old witch placed around his cottage. Because of this, he was now visible to the naked eye. This wasn't advisable when out of Shadow Land and something he rarely did in general. He enjoyed the anonymity of invisibility.

The sun was just peeking through the forest's rooftop, filtering where it could through the dense foliage that tried to fence him in. He could see life stirring inside the rustic cottage in the distance. He wanted to move closer, but didn't dare. He couldn't risk detection. It was no secret that witchdoctors found watchers a delectable fare. This was why he was so stunned to have been sent on such a mission. It must be of great importance for Joshua to risk losing Bog to the cannibal witchdoctor. He assumed it had to do with the dying woman resting near the fire. He had no idea who she was, but she must be of great value to either Joshua or the king.

He studied the small rustic cottage through squinted eyes. The oval shaped door creaked open and an old man the height of a young child stepped out into the morning light. He looked fragile with sagging, leathery, and incredibly wrinkled skin that looked like it belonged to a rhinoceros. If Bog didn't know better, he'd have questioned the old man's humanity, but human he was -and a mean human at that.

He stood quietly in the shadows while the old man walked to the well and drew a bucket of water to wash with. Bog marveled at the way his loose skin slid around his slight frame under his vigorous scrubbing. His brows knit together in disbelief as he watched the old man lift the folds of skin resting around his middle and wash between them. He'd never seen a human with this much excess flesh before. The magic man stretched his arms above his head while he slowly grew until he was large enough to accommodate all of the excess flesh he'd been vigorously scrubbing and it was taught against his frame. Bog estimated he added two feet, if not more, to his height.

Having completed his morning wash ritual, the witchdoctor set about selecting twigs for the fire pit that glowed with the remnants of the roaring flames it sported the night before. He neared the part of the clearing lined by the trees harboring Bog and stopped to sniff the air. Cocking his head, he listened for the sounds of whomever or whatever the unusual scent belonged to.

Recognizing his peril, Bog slowly moved deeper into the

woods, never taking his eyes off the witchdoctor. If he was spotted it could mean his demise. Bog may be fast and clever, but he was no match for the human wielding magic with the power and efficiency of a wizard. He was almost to the path leading to safety when the wizard spotted his large frame moving from one tree to another.

The chase was on.

****

Tara sat up and studied her surroundings. Where was she? Her mind was heavily fogged, making concentration difficult. Her surroundings spun like she was drunk. The setting felt familiar, but she couldn't place it. Was she still back in time? Where was Brandon? Wasn't he stoking the fire not too long ago? The sound of footsteps approaching caught her attention. She turned and squint her eyes against the piercing morning sunlight that silhouetted Joshua's handsome frame. Joshua, yes, it was Joshua who tended the fire. Now she remembered.

After effort and patience, her eyes adjusted to the morning light and the world stopped twirling enough for her to focus on her companion. He truly was a vision of beauty. His dark hair accentuated his deep set, mesmerizing eyes. His richly tanned complexion accentuated his perfectly straight nose and prominent cheekbones framing well-shaped lips, like one might see on a chiseled work of art. She could see no flaw when she looked at Joshua, none at all.

She suddenly found herself comparing his looks to Brandon's. Interestingly, they both shared the same swarthy complexion that came from being out of doors on a regular basis. They both had thick, dark hair. Both had striking facial features. Yet, there was something haunting about Joshua that she didn't feel when she was with Brandon. At first, she thought it was the animal attraction he spurred whenever he came too near. There was an underlying something that nagged at her whenever he looked at her, spoke to her, or came near her. She battled between the desire to run away or run into his arms.

Noticing her staring at him, Joshua flashed a smile that displayed his perfectly straight and brilliantly white teeth. Her eyes settled on his lips spreading taught in an irresistible manner. If she wasn't so exhausted, she would have thrown caution to the wind and run into his arms, but just the thought made her want to lie down and sleep, sleep, sleep.

Joshua frowned as he watched Tara close her eyes and fall back into a deep, coma-like slumber. He needed help and he needed it now. Where was Bog? He should have been back by now. He wasn't certain of the exact whereabouts of the old witchdoctor, but he knew they were in the general vicinity of his residence. There was an element of risk sending Bog to locate him. The man was a cannibal. Bog was top in his profession and Joshua had no doubt he'd steer clear of his clutches and report his whereabouts without having been seen. Besides, Bog wasn't human. He was a watcher -a creature created by Balthazar to act as his eyes and move from world to world reporting what he witnessed.

After almost losing his life while successfully completing one of Balthazar's riskier assignments, he was gifted Bog. It was a very prestigious and coveted gift that made him the envy of his peers. He thought about the instructions Balthazar gave him for working with and caring for his new watcher and froze. He'd forgotten witchdoctors found watchers delectable fare. He could very well have sent his prize possession into the lion's pit, never to return!

He wanted to kick himself. He should have remembered that very important factor and sent someone else. He wondered why Bog didn't remind him of it. He shook his head. Bog was the best in the business, he reassured himself. If anyone could get past that witchdoctor undetected it would be him. He had to believe that.

A groan caught his attention and he watched Lucy struggle to roll her body onto its side. He sniffed the air with disgust. The smell of death was all around her. Soon she'd be worthless to him. He growled. He wanted to bring back the coveted enchantress, not just her soul. Balthazar would be most displeased. Where was Bog? By the look and scent of Lucy, he guessed he had less than a week before she expired.

His mind raced to come up with an alternative method of locating the old witchdoctor. Since he'd never actually met the old coot he had no idea of his skill level and at what point in Lucy's decline it would be too late for the old man to help. He dared not wait longer than an hour more for Bog's return. Time was far too precious.

****

His lungs ached as he pumped more air into them, calling upon all his strength to find more stamina and speed. How could such an old man find the where-with-all to out run him? Bog was almost out of steam. The only thing that stopped him from dropping to the ground and succumbing to the sheer exhaustion that vied to consume every ounce of his fabricated being was that he knew the moment he stopped he'd be at the mercy of a cannibalistic maniac. Why did Joshua send him on such a fool hardy mission? He thought his master was proud and pleased to be one of the few in possession of a watcher. Why did he risk losing him?

The sun was high in the sky. Its brilliant rays weaved their way through the heavily laden branches of the dense forest. Bog estimated it was about noon. He'd been running for hours. Although it was a cool day, the heat from the sun's rays accentuated the heat produced by exertion and his ebony skin was drenched with sweat. It was revoltingly uncomfortable. The sound of running water reached his ears and he headed for it. Perhaps he could lose the old man by running in the water. If nothing else, he'd at least be able to cool off and rinse the nasty sweat from his body.

Encouraged by this new hope, he reached down deep and summoned the strength he needed to sprint forward. The terrain he needed to cover to reach the water was far more treacherous than the path he'd been running all this time. He assumed it was made by creatures of the forest who knew the easiest places to walk and traveled it often. The thick bed of the natural debris on the forest's floor camouflaged potential pitfalls. He did his best to maintain his footing and moved with steadfast speed through the ever thickening foliage.

With a sigh of relief, he dove into the depths of the pool of cool water at the base of a water fall. The roar of the water tumbling from a height of sixty feet or more was almost enough to drown out the wails of frustration that poured forth from the old man's mouth as he paced the water's edge. Could it be the old witchdoctor couldn't swim?

****

Fiona raised her hand, signaling Brandon to stop behind her. He was so engrossed in his thoughts that his powerful gelding nearly climbed the back of her mare, causing quite a raucous from the mare and a dark scowl from Fiona. Duly chagrined, Brandon knew better than to ask the question that pounded against his pursed lips. Why were they stopping? What did she see or hear?

He looked around. The forest seemed still to him. In fact, now that he thought about it the forest was really still... abnormally still. She put her finger to lips her while she gingerly dismounted. Tossing her mare's reins to him she quietly made her way into the thicket until she was no longer visible. He sat in the deafening silence while he waited and watched for the enchantress to return.

The horses were getting progressively restless, yet he could see no reason for it. He twisted in the saddle and searched his surroundings while he struggled to keep them calm. It was difficult enough to gentle his powerful mount without having the added burden of a spooked, rider-less horse at the opposite end of the extra set of reins he clutched.

His mouth fell open when he found himself staring in disbelief at the enormous man who appeared out of nowhere before them. Standing about eight feet in height, his ebony skin glistened with tiny droplets of excess water spilling from the soaked wiry hair flying wild and free as I cascaded in what was left of a braid down the length of his back. The darkness of his complexion accentuated the green-red of his piercing eyes. The thick nose that sat off centered on his wide face ended just above a mouth that was lined with thick lips resembling a blow fish. He couldn't recall when he'd seen an uglier person.

Since he'd been exposed to the world of magic and time travel, he'd also been exposed to an array of creatures that resembled humans, but weren't in the human family. He sensed one might be in front of him now.

His gelding reared and pawed at the air as Bog slowly approached them. Brandon did his best to calm the horses while frantically looking for Fiona. Of all times to be missing, he could really use the aide of her magic right now. He had no idea what this thing was or what it wanted, but it sure didn't look friendly. If it came to combat between them, he was no match and he carried no weapon to support him.

Bog almost reached them when he stopped, closed his eyes and cocked his head to the side while listening intently. With a heavy sigh, he turned away from Brandon and looked off into the distance. To his dismay, the old witchdoctor was moving steadily through the forest in his direction. He was far too tired to continue. He considered tossing the human off the gelding that looked to be of a size that would be able to carry him, but after seeing how unruly it was he questioned his ability to ride it. Watchers weren't known for their riding ability.

There was nothing more to do. He could go no further.

"Help me," he gasped as he fell to the ground.

"What's wrong? Help you how?" Brandon asked as he dismounted and inched closer to Bog.

As he drew nearer, Brandon was more certain than ever that he was in the presence of something supernatural but it seemed harmless enough and had asked for his help. If he'd learned nothing else from all he'd seen and experienced in his travels, he'd learned that it was best not to ignore a plea for help no matter what type of creature uttered it.

Bog looked up at Brandon with resignation.

"Kill me before the witchdoctor catches up with me, please," he begged. "I don't wish to be his meal for the day."

witchdoctor! Brandon's mind screamed. He knew all too well the perils that awaited an encounter with a witchdoctor. They were known for their cannibalistic ways.

"Can you get up?" he asked. "I need you to get on a horse." He looked back at the mare and sighed, "On my horse, I think."

With Brandon's assistance, Bog struggled onto the back of the reluctant gelding. Brandon did his best to reassure the horses and calm them until they had grown more accustomed to Bog's scent before leaping onto Fiona's mare and spurring it into action. Bog expressed his dismay over his inability to ride well, resulting in Brandon grabbing the reins of his enormous gelding and pulling it behind Fiona's mare. He hoped with all his might that the powerful gelding would restrain from barreling over the top of his less muscular mount.

Fiona stayed hidden in the bushes while she watched Brandon race past her pulling the giant black horse with its giant black rider and sighed. She'd deliberately avoided the part of the woods where the witchdoctor dwelled. It was just bad luck to run across him out of his own area and on the hunt. Just bad luck indeed.

She'd encountered this old fool once before, many years ago when she was under the tutelage of her aunt Millie who was a powerful enchantress in her own right. The witchdoctor was in his prime then and a formidable opponent. The battle drained Millie of her strength for many months following, forcing her to go into retreat until she was once again able to protect herself against those who might wish to do her harm. For an enchantress, that was many. To prove to the world that you can best an enchantress was a fine feather in one's cap.

Fiona often wondered why the world of magic need be so

competitive. It seemed to her that if they all came together for a common cause, each bringing with them their own unique knowledge and abilities, they'd have a wonderful world. Instead, her world was ruled by magicians consumed by ego and envy. She'd never understand it.

Her eyes narrowed as the witchdoctor drew closer. So far, her presence escaped his preoccupied senses as he focused in the direction Brandon and the oversized watcher rode. She took advantage of the time allowed to size him up. He still sported a thick magic shield indicating that he hadn't weakened in that department. Unlike Hannigan, she doubted he'd be as easy to fool. No, she was sure she'd be forced into battle with this evil spell bender. She had no doubt it would be a battle to the death.

Reaching into her pocket, she pulled out a small leather pouch and loosened its drawstring. Cupping her hand, she dropped the herbs into her palm and moved them around with her index finger while she softly whispered, "Ma chema mai departe de putere de la varste si ia-o in mine. Nu ma umple. Maestrul i."

After filling her lungs with air, she blew slowly and lightly on the herbs until there was no more air to expel from her lungs. Closing her eyes, she popped the herbs into her mouth. She did her best to down them without the assistance of water as quickly as she could, before filling her lungs in a slow, controlled manner. After a few moments of silence, Fiona opened her eyes and looked around. This was odd. She felt no different. Although she never had the need to consume these herbs before and had kept them on her person just in case she should ever encounter a situation such as this, she studied their effects quite closely and was certain she should have experienced a surging of energy after ingesting them. Yet, she felt nothing.

She regretted having to re-attune her magic since returning to her body. Prior to sending her soul into the future she'd have easy done the spell without the need of herbal assistance. That time would come again, but for now she still needed some help.

She went over the words of the incantation carefully in her head trying to detect a mistake in the pronunciation or order in which it was spoken, but could find no fault in the words, the way she spoke them, or the order in which she placed them. There had to be another reason for their lack of potency. Had she kept them in the pouch for too long a period? She thought not. This was a mystery.

Suddenly, the world was black.

****

Brandon gently reined in Fiona's mare. He patiently coaxed her from a full gallop into a fast walk while he looked around for signs of the witchdoctor. Bog did the same. Although the two had only just met, there was an unspoken sense of comradeship formed the minute Brandon responded to Bog's plea for help. Loyalty was a treasured character of a watcher and Brandon's kindness had won his loyalty.

Having spent a great deal of time in the human realm, Bog's Shadow Land identity had blended with the vibrations of humanity, altering the pure sinister from which Balthazar created him. There had once been a time when he'd have rewarded Brandon's kindness by snapping his neck and taking his soul back to Shadow Land, but he wasn't the same Bog who Balthazar created centuries ago. Venturing into the human realm on countless missions while doing Joshua's bidding left traces of humanity's light upon him. As a result, he'd developed a conscience, albeit a small one.

"It looks like we lost him," Bog said breathlessly. The exertion of riding the giant gelding took what little strength remained.

"Might we stop for a small rest?" he asked. "I'm exhausted."

Brandon reined in his horse and hopped off. Holding the

mare's reins in one hand, he grabbed his gelding's bridle with the other and nodded for Bog to dismount.

"How far had you run in your escape?" Brandon asked.

"Miles," Bog replied as he hopped off the gelding. "At one point, I was on a well-trodden path that led down the mountain. Then I heard water and shifted course in hopes of losing him in the water. He apparently can't swim. I almost did, but he summoned an enormous turtle with a great deal of speed to stand upon. So, I resume fleeing on solid ground."

"How did you come upon him to begin with?" Brandon asked. "It is my understanding he lives deep within the bowels of these mountains. I can't imagine you would deliberately seek him out."

Bog knit his brows together. Brandon's words were correct. It was common knowledge the witchdoctor lived in these hills, therefore they were avoided. Someone traveling them would almost certainly be discovered. He'd have to either plead ignorance, hoping to be believed, or confess he was a watcher for a demon solder. Neither explanation sat well on his tongue. After taking a brief moment to size up his companion, he decided to plead ignorance until he discovered the man's reason for being in the very same woods with the convenience of a spare horse at his side.

"You probably realized I'm not from this world," Bog began. "Because of this, I didn't know."

Fearful that he might not like the answer, Brandon hesitated before asking, "Do I want to know where you come from?"

"That depends," Bog said with a shrug.

"On what," Brandon said.

His voice was just above a whisper. Every muscle in his body coiled, ready for the unexpected. If his companion was from where he suspected, he was far darker than his skin.

"On whether or not you're curious about where I'm from, or if you just feel obligated to question me on it because I brought it up," Bog stated in a cool, relaxed manner.

A sense of relief swept over Brandon as he realized he'd

just been given an out to a possible very unpleasant topic.

"As curious as I may be, I wouldn't wish to trouble you with having to tell the tale when you have already expressed your exhaustion," he said with relief in his voice. "Let's rest now and discuss topics of this nature at a later time, shall we? I believe I see a clearing up ahead. Perhaps we'll find water for the horses and a solid boulder or two for ourselves. I too could use a good rest."

Bog nodded and followed Brandon toward the small clearing.

"Do you know much about the old coot chasing you?" Brandon asked over his shoulder.

"I came upon his little cottage in the woods and watched him morph from this tiny man with sagging skin to what you saw chasing me. It was very magical and quite disturbing," Bog replied. He was pleased to be able to tell the truth to his new companion to whom he owed his life.

"I'm not surprised," Brandon replied, "since he's a witch-doctor of the worst repute. He's a loner and a cannibal from what I hear. He's quite dangerous."

"Even if he hadn't given me chase, I'd have feared him. There was something about him even more than the metamorphosis that I witnessed. He stunk of wickedness," Bog explained in a thoughtful tone.

Although he'd known who Joshua sent him to find and he was aware of the danger and risk involved, he hadn't been aware of the full extent of the witchdoctor's might. Had he known this, he might not have taken on the task. Of course, resisting an assignment for Joshua was equally dangerous. Defiance of any form would never be tolerated and would warrant punishment, possibly even death.

Having found the clearing with a cool stream and several invitingly broad flat-topped boulders, Bog settled his body onto the nearest boulder. He savored its smooth, sun-warmed surface as he watched Brandon lead the horses to the narrow, free flowing mountain stream. He could use a drink and would join the horses as soon he'd rested a bit. He couldn't recall ever feeling such exhaustion, but then he'd never been forced to run for his life. The physical exertion combined with the emotional stress was exhausting.

Although he may have looked preoccupied with the care of their horses, Brandon was still acutely aware of Bog's every move. He was relieved to see the black giant lay across a big flat boulder and fall into a deep slumber. He needed time to think. Where had Fiona gone? Why did she disappear like that? Did the old witchdoctor find her? If so, was she alright? Had she known what was about to happen? Was that why she took off so quickly? Nothing made sense.

****

Her arms ached to the extreme. They felt far too weak to do much struggling against the coarse rope that cut into her wrists and imprisoned her hands snuggly behind her back. Closing her eyes to the pain, Fiona flattened her ear against a rough floorboard to try to hear if her captor was somewhere in the room. It was pitch black and impossible to see even an inch in front of her. She could be surrounded by others or totally alone, it was difficult to tell. She guessed it was the latter. She assumed her captor was the old witchdoctor, but she wasn't certain. Whoever it was came upon her from behind with lightning speed. Only a creature made of magic or someone who was extremely adept at magic could accomplish it successfully without her awareness of his presence in plenty of time. If she hadn't been so preoccupied with those herbs she wouldn't be in this situation right now.

She thought of Brandon's foolishness in helping that dark watcher escape the witchdoctor. It was clearly created in the bowels of Shadow Land and not to be trusted.

Her head pounded and it felt like she might be bleeding at the nape of her neck. The blow was precariously close to the delicate part of her neck. She was grateful to be alive. What she didn't understand was why the herbs and spell hadn't kept her guarded from something like this happening. The sound of feet shuffling along the floor boards caught her attention. Had some-one entered the room or been there all along? Is it the witchdoctor or another evil fiend?

"So my magical friend, are you ready to become soup?" chuckled the voice through the darkness. "It's a shame that old crone that mentored you wasn't with you. Eating her would give me double the pleasure."

FIFTEEN

Her life force was ebbing away, making even that simple task of breathing an excruciating chore. Joshua aided her in sitting beneath the gnarled apple tree. Its rough bark cut into her back. Feeling the pain somehow reminded her she was still alive so she made no move to adjust her position. He was off searching for more firewood. She hadn't paid attention to the time, but it seemed like he should have been back by now. It would be dark soon. The last thing she wanted was to be alone in the wilds of the woods at night. She was completely defenseless against a myriad of predators that roamed the darkness. She hoped he'd return soon.

Tara!

Tara heard the voice so clearly that she swore the woman stood nearby. She turned her head quickly from left to right while she searched for its source.

'Tara, can you hear me!'

The voice echoed through her head. She wished her head was clearer so she could tell who the voice belonged to. It had a vague resemblance to Maggie's voice. Was Maggie trying to reach her from the spirit world?

Joshua returned with an arm load of firewood just as she was contemplating calling for Liam. It was the first she thought to do so and she wasn't even sure he'd be able to reach her while she was back in time, but it was worth a try. Of course, with Joshua so close, she abandoned the idea.

Tara!

"Did you hear that?" Tara struggled with the words, finding her vocal chords reluctant to respond.

"What, dearest? Did I hear what?" Joshua soothed.

"Someone's calling my name. It was loud," She said as she shook her head. "You didn't hear anything?"

Joshua approached her crouched body and gently took her hands.

Pulling her carefully to her feet, he said, "No darling, I heard nothing except the howling of a few wolves in the distance. Now, let's get you closer to the fire and under the lean-to I made of some fine pine branches. I caught a fat rabbit for a stew that will be ready soon. I dug up some roots and wild mushrooms so our meal should be tasty, but even if it isn't I want you to promise to eat every bite that I give you. Tomorrow we enter Shadow Land and you will need all your strength for the journey."

Tara nodded and followed him willingly. The mere mention of the rabbit stew, no matter what it tasted like, pulled her attention to the fact that she hadn't eaten in quite some time and she was very hungry.

After helping her settle into the make-shift quarters he'd created, Joshua set forth building a larger fire to insure it would last through the night. It would be dark soon and although the howling sounded far off, he didn't trust the creatures of the night in this realm. They weren't as responsive to his commands as those of Shadow Land. Looking at the brilliant full moon, he questioned if it was even wolves they were hearing.

He pulled tin bowls from his pack and dished out a fair amount of the surprisingly aromatic stew for her. Realizing he'd forgotten the eating utensils from the inner zippered compartment of the bag, he set the bowl down in front of her and moved back to the bag.

The faint sound of twigs breaking under the weight of someone or something caught his attention. He turned to focus in the direction of the sounds and searched the darkening tree line. He saw nothing. After waiting a little longer for more noises that would key him into the exact location of whatever wandered in the thick brush, he grabbed the spoons and moved back to his ward. Grateful for the attention, she smiled weakly as she gripped the spoon with her trembling hand.

With poor dexterity and extreme effort Tara did her best to transfer the evening's fare from the bowl to her mouth, chew, and then swallow. She accomplished it far better than she'd expected, with only a small amount of it spilling onto her chin or lap. Not only was it the most delicious stew she could remember eating, she felt mildly rejuvenated after cleaning her bowl. Satiated and relaxed and feeling a little more like herself, she snuggled into the bedding Joshua arranged to provide her as much comfort as possible.

"What time do we leave?" she asked quietly.

"At first light," Joshua replied.

"How long will it take to reach Shadow Land?" she continued.

"Hopefully, we'll arrive at the portal late morning," he said.

"The portal?" she asked as a tug of nagging familiarity consumed her.

"The opening," Joshua explained, "the doorway into Shadow Land. I'd hoped to have some help getting us past the guards from the wizard, but it looks like we're on our own."

The talk about Shadow Land brought memories of her purpose and mission flooding back. Every minute Dennis spent in Shadow Land brought him closer to the time when his life would no longer be his. She knew this. She didn't know how she knew this, but she knew.

Studying her carefully in the dusky light, Joshua looked for signs that the potion he placed in her bowl was taking effect. He needed her to be travel worthy if they were to get past the guards at the portal of Shadow Land. He'd rummaged through one of Luella's potion books one boring afternoon. Although difficult to decipher, he managed to understand a few of the recipes -the energy potion being one of them. If all went well, Lucy would have superior strength and stamina, at least until they were safely within the boundary of Shadow Land. Then, he'd see.

"How are you feeling?" he asked warily.

"Remarkably rejuvenated," she replied. "I think I need to get your rabbit stew recipe."

He smiled.

"I shall record it for you. Now, do your best to sleep. Morning comes all too early in these woods," he said.

"They do have an odd feel to them," Tara remarked, more to herself than to him.

"That's because we're near the boundary of Shadow Land," he offered. Tomorrow it will feel even odder as we cross dimensions. That's why you need as much strength and stamina as your body can muster. Now, please go to sleep."

Tara smiled warmly at the man who was her doppelganger's love and protector as she snuggled deeper beneath her wool blanket and closed her eyes. It took no time at all for sleep to come.

The howling in the distance grew louder.

Joshua looked up at the moon as it peeked through the dusky haze. It was full. This wasn't good. Outside the boundary of Shadow Land his powers were considerably diminished. If they came across a lycanthrope or even a hum-wolf now, he might not be able to defend them. Snuggling beneath the piece of canvas he used to substitute the wool blanket he forfeited to his half dead companion he surveyed the tree line as best he could. He looked at the fire and scowled. It could draw attention, but there was nothing to be done about it. The fire had to be. With luck, they'd pass the night undiscovered. He closed his eyes. Where was Bog?

****

Bog paced the open space of the small clearing, careful to keep his distance from Brandon's sleeping body. Brandon fell into a deep slumber almost immediately after they set up camp for the night. The watcher was torn. He should be returning to Joshua with his report on the witchdoctor, but if he did so it would mean leaving Brandon alone and vulnerable in the night. He wasn't certain of their exact location, but he knew they were in close proximity to the boundary of Shadow Land. He could feel the energy of his homeland coursing through his veins. Camping for the night in such close proximity to the boundary wasn't the wisest thing to do. Rogue creatures of indescribable natures roamed the area. It wasn't a safe place for humans and shadow people alike. The sound of howling in the distance caught his attention. He knew that sound. It wasn't a wolf -not a normal wolf, anyway.

His pacing grew more aggressive as he struggled with what to do. He belonged to Joshua and he needed to return. He could feel Joshua pulling on him, willing him back to him, reinforcing his inherent dark nature. It was difficult to resist.

His sleeping companion certainly made a tempting target. Was that fair? After all, the human did save him from the clutches of the old witchdoctor and the unthinkable fate that would follow. He liked the man. He liked his energy, his mannerisms, and his kindness. He displayed qualities that went beyond that of a normal human. He wondered what would happen if he resisted Joshua and remained with Brandon and let him live.

The howling grew closer.

Bog puffed his body to full height and width. He'd made a decision. He'd stay with Brandon through the night. He owed him that much. Once the creatures of the night receded from the morning's rays he'd reconsider what to do. For tonight he'd stand guard and kill anything that tried to harm his new friend. He just hoped the old witchdoctor wasn't one of those things.

****

The salty excess of sweat dripping down her forehead assaulted Fiona's eyes with slow deliberation. The pain in her leg surpassed the pain in her arms. When the old man tried to plunge his blade into her flesh she managed to kick him back with only a small slash to her shin before placing a shield of magic around her body. She wasn't sure how long she could maintain the shield while in this state. He was almost as powerful as she was. As her strength faded, so did her magic. Soon they'd be equally matched.

****

The snarl echoed into the dark night as the creature slowly circled Bog. They were a short distance from the fire where Brandon lay peacefully sleeping. Much more noise from the beast and Brandon was sure to have his slumber interrupted. This wouldn't do.

Bog wasn't yet ready to divulge his true identity to his new companion. If he was to awaken and witness what was about to occur, Bog's origin would be painfully clear. He hadn't had enough time to study the human well enough to know how he'd react to such information.

After a quick glance in Brandon's direction, Bog focused on the hum-wolf before him. A cousin to the werewolf, it was a cross between a human and a wolf... never shifting from one to the other, always staying the same. Its human torso was thick with fur and it had the head of a fierce wolf. It was baring its powerful fangs at Bog while its long, talon-like fingers stretched dangerously near the watcher's throat. Bog jumped back with lightning speed and positioned himself behind the beast while the creature of abomination shook its head in bewilderment.

The hum-wolf was a ferocious opponent, but couldn't match the wit and speed of a watcher. It was only seconds before Bog was plowing a heavy oak branch into the beast's skull. The impact sounded like distant thunder. Bog's chest heaved while he balanced his breathing. He stood over the creature and absorbed the true idiocy of his former opponent before grabbing him by an ankle and twirling its limp body so rapidly the two became nothing more than a blur. When he finally stopped twirling, the creature was gone.

"Where did it go?" Brandon whispered.

Startled, Bog swung his breathless body in Brandon's direction.

"I didn't know you were awake," Bog blurted.

"You were busy," Brandon replied casually as he sat up and

stretched his legs away from the fire. "Where did you send it?"

"To No Man's Land," Bog replied.

"I've heard of that, but I have no idea where it is," Brandon said matter-of-factly.

"It rests between the layers of reality. It comes from no-where and leads to nowhere. Once you enter it, you can't return," Bog stated.

"You returned," Brandon said softly.

"I," Bog explained, "never entered it. I'm strong. I stood on the edge and tossed it through the portal."

Brandon looked at Bog in silence for what seemed like hours to the nervous watcher, but was really only a few seconds before saying "Good" and repositioned himself for sleep.

Bog stood in quiet contemplation. His companion was a complicated human. He clearly had no powers of his own yet nothing of the magical realm fazed him.

Brandon watched through lowered lids as Bog settle himself against a large boulder that was close enough to the fire to offer a little warmth.

"You're a watcher, I think," Brandon stated matter-of-factly.

"What makes you say that?" Bog asked, trying to hide his surprise.

"I'm not sure. Your speed of movement, I guess," Brandon replied.

"Only watchers have speed?" Bog asked.

"If you're not a watcher, what are you?" Brandon persisted.

Bog's mind raced. Was this a trap? The man sounded calm, but was it just a ruse? How did he know about watchers? Maybe he was magical and just so good at disguising the fact that he even fooled a watcher.

"I ask again. If you're not a watcher, what are you?" Brandon demanded. This time his tone wasn't as balanced.

The distinct agitation in Brandon's voice relaxed Bog. This was an emotion he was very familiar with. This was an emotion that provided manna to many of the inhabitants of Shadow Land. If Brandon was truly magical, he'd not expel such energy so freely in front of someone he suspected to have come from Shadow Land.

"I repeat my question. Is it only watchers who have speed?" Bog blurted with confidence.

"So, we're going to play that game?" Brandon asked with mild impatience.

He'd woken up in time to see Bog face off the oddest creature he'd set eyes on since he'd faced off the demon wolves at Tara's future home. Those creatures had the body of a feline and the head of a wolf. The creature he just witnessed disappear at the hands of Bog looked like a combination of wolf and human. He'd seen a werewolf. The creature was different than a werewolf. What was it?

Deciding that pulling the identity of the beast from Bog would probably be easier than pulling his own identity from him, Brandon changed tactics.

"The creature wasn't a werewolf. What was it?" he asked.

"It's a cousin, of sorts," Bog explained, relieved to have the focus taken from him. "It is called a hum-wolf... half human and half wolf."

"And it comes from...?" Brandon pressed.

"The boundary between here and Shadow Land," Bog explained.

"We're close then?" Brandon asked.

"Very close." Bog replied.

Brandon scowled. He'd never been this close to the boundary before, but he was all too familiar with the risks and dangers it entailed. He was annoyed with the way things were going. Where was Fiona? If he'd arrived at the boundary so quickly then surely so had Tara. She could even be beyond it by now. He needed to find Fiona.

"Where were you headed when we met up?" Bog questioned.

After a brief hesitation, Brandon sucked in air until his lungs were full and spoke as he expelled it.

"Shadow Land," he said bluntly.

"Hmm," Bog hummed between pursed lips. This bit of information came as a surprise to him. "May I ask why?"

"You're from there, are you not?" Brandon responded.

He was hesitant to explain his reasoning to Bog or anyone.

Divulging their true identity to a human was something that was forbidden for watchers. Bog never really understood the actual reason for this rule. He heard a myriad of rumors that included the claim that humans could compel watchers to do their bidding and that humans considered watchers to be a delectable dinner fare. He'd hoped to avoid exposing himself to Brandon and simply part with a handshake and a thank-you. It was obvious now that he wouldn't get that wish.

Looking at Brandon long and hard, Bog gambled and replied, "Yes, I'm from there and yes, I'm a watcher."

SIXTEEN

The sun was persistent as it wove its brilliant golden rays through the thick netting formed by the tree tops and warming the ground around Tara enough to ease the damp frigidity of the blanket of morning's dew. Joshua stood up and stretched the kinks out to his long legs and narrow waist torso while Tara admired him from beneath half-closed eyelids. Sensing her eyes on him, he looked at her and smiled.

"Good morning, sleepy head," he whispered in a sultry voice that had a seductive effect. "How are you feeling today?"

He recalled how well this manner of speaking worked on her in the future when he was Dominic and was pleased it was still having the effect he wanted on her now.

She closed her eyes tightly while she struggled to control her fickle body. How did she feel today? She felt like jumping up, running into his arms and kissing him silly. That's how she felt today. Tara felt her face redden when she realized she hadn't guarded her thoughts.

Joshua moved toward her, stopping so close she could feel the heat of his breath on her flushed cheeks. His long, slender fingers gently brushed a lock of hair from her temple and she shudder with delight. This was the first she felt the warmth of a man's loving touch in a long time. It felt wonderful. She hadn't realized how rigid her muscles were until they eased under his caress. A brief shadow was cast over her as the thought of Dominic passed through her mind, but within no time it disappeared and she was once again focusing on enjoying the touch of the man who mistook her for his fiancé. The odd thing was that even though they were from different centuries and had never met, his touch felt very familiar.

After a light breakfast of cold stew from the night before, they cleaned up camp and he helped her onto her horse. She seemed ill at ease in her riding habit. Joshua chuckled at how quickly she'd become accustomed to the clothing of the twenty-first century. He was certain she preferred wearing the comfortable pair of jeans and bulky Irish wool sweater she favored when she'd entertained him as Dominic. He couldn't blame her. Women's clothing of the nineteenth century was incredibly cumbersome in comparison.

Tara sat tall and straight in her saddle. Her ease on the back of her mount clearly displayed her skilled horsemanship. Joshua took a moment to take in how robust she looked. He should have used the potion earlier. If he had, then perhaps they would have already crossed through the portal to Shadow Land and he'd be back in the arms of his lovely Luella. Although he found Lucy's beauty pleasing to look at his bond with Luella was solid. He could never forsake her for another woman. She gave him no reason to think about such things.

Time wasn't measured the same in Shadow Land as it was in the human realm. One distinct difference was the aging process slowed considerably in Shadow Land. Luella was almost a century old and looked a mere quarter of that. Her thick, dark tresses flowed down her back, almost to her knees, and glistened with health and vitality. The rosiness in her porcelain cheeks completed her youthful doll-like appearance. Her touch had the power to drive him mad. No, there was no replacement for Luella. She was one of a kind and he was grateful she loved him.

He had to admit that it would be something to see his love's reaction when he returned with the young enchantress. Although he saw nothing to indicate her powers during their journey, he'd seen her in action once before during her brief captivity in Shadow Land and was sure she would create a formidable opponent for his own lovely and very sinister sorceress should they ever go head to head.

Joshua thought back at the time when he'd stood at the edge of the courtyard and witnessed the torment the crowd poured onto Lucy and how easily she thwarted it. They threw everything from energy balls to rocks at the fiery creature and all she did was raise her hand and spur them away. Her power certainly took Balthazar by surprise, which was why she managed to escape. It would be different now. Balthazar would be prepared for her. The fact that she suffered from amnesia was an unexpected boon. With the exception of her waning health, it was pleasingly easy to bring her on the journey. Her desire to enter Shadow Land on her own volition was a bonus he hadn't counted on. Whoever captured Dennis did him a huge favor in more ways than one.

Although Dennis' presence in Shadow Land made his quest for Lucy's return to Balthazar far easier than he imagined, that wasn't the reason he was so pleased to discover his capture. Dennis played a heavy role in the destruction of Dominic. I proved an experience he'd never wish to repeat and could never forget. He was still trying to figure out how they managed to summon a divine being powerful enough to destroy him and his pets. It puzzled him daily. Even Luella was uncertain of how such a feat was accomplished. Divine Beings weren't that easy to summon.

He intended to pull this information out of Dennis before he killed him. Perhaps he'd burn him to the stake so he could feel the flames of hell against his skin like Joshua felt during the destruction of Dominic's body. It took time and a considerable amount of ministering from Luella to return his singed dark soul back to normalcy. If she hadn't been such a powerful sorceress he'd probably have truly perished from the ordeal. Dennis would pay for his part in it. Dennis would pay, Lucy would pay and then he'd find that time traveler and give him his as well.

Joshua had just nudged his mount into motion when he spotted Bog coming out of the tree line a short distance away. He commanded Lucy to stay where she was as he spurred his horse in Bog's direction.

Bog had some explaining to do.

Tara watched Joshua leave with mild curiosity. She saw nothing on the edge of the grove that would cause him to leave so quickly, but then her spurt of energy had already dissipated and she was once again feeling weak and tired. Saddened by the reversal she didn't bother to pursue Joshua's whereabouts with her eyes. Instead, she closed them to reserve her energy.

****

Her connection was with Tara's soul not Brandon's, but since Tara wasn't responding to her telepathic messages Fiona saw no other option than to try to reach Brandon. With any luck, he'd be receptive and listen. She prayed there was enough strength left in her to do what needed to be done. Communicating telepathically with someone who she hadn't formed a connection with prior to the communication was something Fiona had only done once before and she did it badly. Of course, she was much younger then and less skilled. It should be easier and more effective now. It had to be. Her life depended on it.

The old goat of a witchdoctor left the shack during the night and hadn't yet returned. He was killing time waiting for her magic to weaken by foraging for roots and wild herbs for the soup he planned on making with her flesh as its main ingredient.

Tiny slivers of sunshine filtered through the cracks of the wide planked walls, alerting her to the dawn of a new day. She listened intently for sounds of life. The gurgling of her empty stomach pierced the eerie quiet of her dark habitat. Her eyes were a little more accustomed to the darkness, making it easier to make out shapes around the room. The flecks of light filtering in added just enough for her to get a clearer scope of her surroundings.

The room was cramped and cluttered and stunk of rot, body odor, and death. She could make out a small pile of bones in the far corner beneath the only window.

The binding holding her captive made it impossible for her to do anything other than roll toward the pile of bones. The act caused searing pain in her arms and brought tears to her eyes. She ignored the pain as best she could and with slow laborious deliberation she managed to position herself so she could fumble through the bones until she found one that was brittle enough to break.

Pushing the bone against the floor boards, she leaned as much of her weight against it as she could until she heard the snap she sought. Feeling the break, she let out a gust of exasperated air. She'd hoped to produce an edge that was sharp enough to saw through the bindings, but the edge of this bone would be smoothed from the friction in no time. Sucking in enough air to generate a renewed gust of energy, she did her best to feel the bones in the pile while she searched for a more suitable one for her needs. When her fingers fondled what felt like the femur bone of a large animal, she smiled. Not only was it dry and brittle, but it was thick enough to snap in the jagged manner she sought.

The extended length of the bone created a more difficulty than she expected, but she eventually heard the snap she struggled so hard to achieve. After what seemed like hours -and probably was- she managed to fray her bindings to a point where they were thin enough to tug free.

Her arms moved slowly at first while she waited for the blood to regain full circulation in them and complete feeling to come back. Her fingers fumbled at the bindings around her ankles. She was successful in freeing herself only after multiple failed attempts.

Standing on long, lean, shaky legs, she wiped the sweat from her face with her hands and stood in place while her body rebalanced itself. She used this time to close her eyes and scope the property for signs of the witchdoctor. She allowed herself to float out of her body to the top of the roof where she could get a clear vision of the land. It looked peaceful and uninhabited. Moving beyond the door that held her prisoner, she scoped the rest of the cottage. There was no sign of him.

Returning to her body, she briefly focused on grounding

herself before waving her arm in a circular motion over her head. Within seconds her body was its normal, healthy, strong, youthful self. She found the door unlocked. The old man obviously hadn't expected her to free herself. She intended on leaving immediately, but couldn't resist the rows and rows of herbs, animal parts, and jars of multi-colored liquids that sat neatly on roughhewn shelves along the wall. Some she recognized as common herbs for even more common remedies, but others were completely foreign to her.

Her eyes slowly combed the contents of the jars as she moved from shelf to shelf. When she came upon a jar that looked particularly interesting, she'd remove it carefully from its designated spot and inspected it closely.

It was when she removed a jar of thick green, gooey looking liquid that she spotted the dust laden book hidden behind it. Setting the jar down on the table while being careful not to crack it or spill any of the foreign contents she exercised equal care pulling the book from its hiding spot. Spotting a rickety looking, roughhewn chair in the far corner of the room she pulled it closer to the window and sat down to briefly scan through the book.

Over an hour passed before she closed the book and sat up, stretching her long torso in a cat-like manner. She looked out across the green. The sun reflected off the lush, emerald grass from an angle that indicated it was nearing noon.

There was still no sign of the witchdoctor. Realizing her good fortune at his extended absence and her folly for lingering to study his magical recipes, she tucked the ancient leather-bound book under her arm and headed out the door. Her luck couldn't possibly last much longer. He'd be returning soon and although she was free and would be ready for him there was no guarantee that she would be the victor. He was a skilled and knowledgeable witchdoctor and they were on his property. That fact alone gave him the advantage. If he'd perfected even a fraction of the spells and conjures on the musty, leather-bound pages, he'd be a force to reckon with. She had no desire to stick around and see who'd best who.

Moving quickly across the green, she made it to the trees just before his small frame meandered down the path balancing a long pole sporting several rabbits on one end and a sack bulging with roots and herbs on the other over his left shoulder.

She debated what to do. Should she run as fast as she could and hope he didn't decide to chase her or should she stand her ground and see what may come and fight if need be? The scream of outrage that echoed off the hillsides surrounding the little valley he called home told her all she needed to know. He discovered her escape and wasn't about to let his prize catch go that easily.

Within seconds the old witchdoctor was outside his rustic house sniffing the air for her scent. She closed her eyes and pulled on the magic of the property. As she did so her body grew translucent, blending with the forest foliage. She diminished her human scent by absorbing the scent of the evergreens. Frustrated, he slammed his fist into his other hand and stomped around in a circle, chanting in a language Fiona wasn't familiar with. Her eyes grew wide with astonished wonder as she saw his small, spindly body almost double in size. She now understood how he managed to drag her to his hut. Pushing his powerful legs into motion, the witchdoctor started across the green with a speed that both surprised and amazed Fiona. Her mind reeled on what to do. He was heading right for her! Moving further back into the thickness of the forest, she pulled some branches in front of her, hoping that this would be enough to complete the camouflage. She would know soon enough. He was almost in front of her. Holding her breath, she watched as he stopped just feet away and searched the ground for her tracks. He tilted his head back and sniffed the air.

A frustrated snarl exposed jagged teeth filed to a point, something cannibals did to help tear their meat off bones better. Between the razor teeth and the bone projecting through his nose, he certainly did look sinister. Her lungs felt like they'd explode in seconds and she started to feel light headed. If the old coot didn't move away soon, she'd have no choice than to expose herself by expelling the stagnant air. It was either that or pass out, at which point she'd certainly be left to his merciless whim. The world started to fade before the old man finally gave up and returned to his humble abode.

Fiona waited until he was well out of ear shot before she allowed her lungs to slowly empty. She sucked in a new, refreshing supply as quietly as she was able. After a few good gulps of cool, clean air, her body stabilized.

She was tired. The effort to maintain invisibility and scent free while struggling to keep from breathing was great. She wanted to take the time to recover, but knew staying this close to the old man's cottage was asking for trouble. She needed to move on. She needed to find Brandon and the horses and then Tara.

Mustering up as much stamina as she could, she surprised herself with the power and speed her legs displayed as she darted along the well-worn path that she was certain was used to bring her here. Leaping over fallen trees with the grace of a gazelle, she covered the significant amount of ground back to the spot where she was captured. Stopping only briefly to catch her breath, Fiona found the horse's tracks and headed off at a steady jog in their direction. She wanted to get just a little closer before reaching out to Brandon telepathically.

****

Bog was gone when Brandon awoke and now he had to decide what to do. The horses stood peacefully grazing, side by side. The remains of the fire still sported a few embers that looked strong enough to revive. He grabbed a few of the twigs Bog thoughtfully collected before he departed and smiled. He'd never spent time with a watcher and his knowledge about them was minimal, but he'd heard many tales. Bog seemed nothing like what a dark watcher was supposed to be like.

Although he'd hesitated telling Brandon about himself and his mission, he eventually came forth with the truth. He also spent the night with him without trying to bind him up to drag back to Shadow Land.

Brandon knew Fiona used a watcher on occasion. In fact, he was certain it was a watcher who was sent ahead of them to look for Tara. How different that little creature seemed from the enormous Bog.

There was still a bit of wild turkey Bog provided for dinner the night before. Brandon skewered it on a stick and held it over the fire to warm. He salivated at the aromatic juices coming to life as the flames danced just beneath it. As he stared, mesmerized, into the flames he heard Fiona's voice. It didn't enter through his ears, but more through his temples.

Brandon!

He turned quickly, but saw no one. Standing up, he strained his eyes to look as deep into the trees as he could. There was no sign of Fiona.

Brandon!

He heard her again.

Shaking his head, he decided he was so distraught over losing her that he was now hearing her voice in his head. He forced himself to return to the matter at hand. His turkey was dangerously close to burning and his stomach was growling. Whatever was going on in his head would have to wait. He needed to assure he had the strength and stamina for what the day held. This meant he needed to sustain it with this turkey and he'd rather not consume burned meat.

He looked around for the jug of water Bog pulled from Fiona's mare. There should still be enough in it to make some pine tea to help wash down the turkey, something he'd managed to acquire a taste for and actually enjoyed. He placed his tin cup at the edge of the fire and sprinkled a few pine needles in it before adding water. The cup was small so it wouldn't take long for the water to reach the right temperature.

Chewing slowly on the sizzling meat, he thought of Fiona. Was she still alive? Where could she have gone on foot? Maybe he should return to the spot where they parted and see if he could pick up a sign of her whereabouts. If he did, would he encounter the witchdoctor again?

Brandon! Listen!

Fiona's voice echoed so loud in his head it caused him to jump up and look around. She sounded close, but he saw no sign of her.

"Where are you?" he shouted.

Brandon! Listen!

Fiona's voice grew louder.

"Where are you?" Brandon shouted again, more frustrated. "I hear you, but I can't see you!"

Come back.

He may not have been able to see her, but the message was clear enough. Without hesitation, he kicked dirt onto the fire and quickly packed his few belongings. Within minutes he was in the saddle and heading back in the direction he'd come, pulling Fiona's horse behind him. Although tempted to push the horses, he decided to take his time so their strength would be available should he need to outrun the witchdoctor or some sort of boundary predator. He'd traveled only a few miles when he spotted Fiona walking down the path.

"What a relief!" he yelled as he spurred his horse onward.

Her mare needed no coaxing when she recognized her mistress up ahead and almost bypassed Brandon and his enormous gelding in her effort to reach Fiona. Noticing the bond between Fiona and her mare, Brandon thought back on the bond Tara and her mare had. Although he'd always appreciated and valued his gelding and there was most definitely a bond between them, it paled next to the one these women possessed with their beasts. He decided it was an enchantress thing.

"Am I happy to see you," he said sincerely as he pulled his gelding up next to the mare.

"And I you," she replied as she swung herself effortlessly into the saddle.

"Where did you go? It has been quite an adventure in your absence," Brandon stated hesitantly. He wasn't sure what to tell her and what to keep to himself.

"Same here, but now is not the time to discuss it," she urged. "I fear for Tara. She's so weak that she's no longer connected to me. We must hurry or 'twill soon be too late."

Just then an eagle flew overhead screeching until it disappeared into the trees. Fiona recognized it as her watcher. He'd found Tara too late. Her worst fears had come true.

SEVENTEEN

She felt like she was floating or things were floating around her, she couldn't tell which. Tara held her fingertips to her temples in hopes that the mild pressure she applied would help her equilibrium, but it didn't. She heard, rather than saw the large dark cloaked figure before her. Where was Joshua? He'd whispered something in her ear, but she couldn't recall what it was. Did he say they'd arrived? Arrived where? Oh, yes. They'd arrived in Shadow Land and he needed to go. Where did he need to go? Oh yes, he was going to see his beloved Luella. Wasn't Lucy supposed to be his beloved? Didn't he think she was Lucy?

"Stand straight in the presence of our Lord and Master!" bellowed the guard as he cracked a small whip across her back.

Tara screamed in pain and fell to her knees. Even if the whip hadn't been used she was certain she'd have fallen to her knees anyway. Her legs were like rubber and her body was dangerously weak.

"Get up!" barked the head guard as he pulled his whip back in preparation for another strike.

"Leave her!" Balthazar bellowed, as he moved across the platform with regal grace to seat himself in the oversized gilded thrown that awaited him.

Tara could barely make out the features of the man before her as she wavered back and forth. She guessed it would be only a matter of seconds before she fainted.

She was right.

Balthazar stood up and looked down at her crumpled body with disgust.

"What have you brought me?" he asked with distaste.

"This is the young enchantress, milord," his guard replied.

Balthazar scowled.

"This isn't the enchantress you fool!" he barked.

The guard looked closely at Tara's slumped body with horror. Since he'd never seen her himself, he'd foolishly taken Joshua's word that this was the young enchantress. Just wait until he caught up with that scoundrel!

"Where is Joshua?" Balthazar spat between clenched teeth.

"I'm not certain, milord," the guard stammered. "Shall I send for him?"

"What do you think?" the dark lord bellowed.

"Yes, milord," he said as he half-bowed, half-cringed his way out of the room.

As the room scrambled to life, the dark lord's roamed over Tara as he inspected her more carefully. She certainly was the image of the young enchantress. Had he not held the young enchantress prisoner for almost a month and become familiar with her light, he might have even believed this was indeed Lucy O'Shea, niece and star protégé of the great and powerful Fiona O'Shea. Looking closely, he hesitated. Could it be? Was he looking at a doppelganger? Impossible! He'd have known if one existed. A doppelganger of someone such as the young enchantress could prove quite valuable. Yes, indeed. This might not be such a bad thing after all.

He ordered her lifeless body to be taken to the slave quarters along with instructions for the old witchdoctor to be summoned. He was to revive her, not eat her. The next time he laid eyes on the girl he expected her to be pert, chipper and full of life. If not, then the witchdoctor beware!

****

Adam cringed as he received his orders. He'd only just

earned the position of palace guard and he already wished he was back on the farm with his mother and two brothers. Since he'd arrived at the dark lord's palace and been appointed his position not even a month earlier, he'd experienced nothing, but hardship and peril. Now, he was ordered to leave the safety of Shadow Land to summon the witchdoctor who lived just beyond the boundary.

He wore the crest of Balthazar's kingdom and hoped that it would be recognized by the old man. Not everyone who approached the sinister man of magic returned to Shadow Land. Adam had no desire to become someone's dinner.

He was no stranger to the boundary, which was the main reason he was selected for the task. He was a skinner born on the human side of the boundary where his family resided and worked on a farm. They walked as humans by day and roamed as canine by night, often wandering and hunting the boundary. Tired of living in deception amongst people he despised, he'd packed his meager belongings and bid his family good-bye. Having heard of the riches and lifestyle that awaited the servants of the palace of Balthazar and having an innate longing to explore Shadow Land and meet the great Lord of the underworld, he'd snuck through the portal.

He'd encountered significant perils along the way, from beasts of nondescript form to his less than amiable cousin, the hum-wolf. He'd encountered them all. When he was just at the edge of the portal to Shadow Land he faced a small pack of creatures of great oddity, having the head of a wolf and the body of a powerful cat he'd questioned his wisdom in leaving his home.

After putting him through a few grueling tests that included proving he was an adept skinner who could change on demand, Balthazar's guards determined him worthy of entering. For someone to have actually passed through their guard and earned respect and friendship was a rarity indeed. Of course, he also had to get past the human guards, although that wasn't nearly as difficult as rumors led him to believe.

And now, not long after he'd made the perilous journey

through the boundary, he must once again brave it. Once in the company of the witchdoctor, he'd be safe. For no one dared challenge the crazy old magical coot. Unfortunately, he must first reach him and convince him that he was a messenger from the dark lord and not dinner. He decided to change to canine, thinking it would be easier to retrace his steps with the use of smell.

He'd been ordered to secure the young enchantress's doppelganger in one of the slave shacks before starting his journey. It really shouldn't have been his duty, but one of the first lessons he learned upon arrival was that the head guard was incredibly lazy and would farm whatever tasks he could out to his underlings. One of the second lessons he learned was that to complain about such disbursement of duty would lead to ill-favor in the headmaster's eyes; something no guard wanted. Earning ill-favor could easily lead to an assignment that could lead to death. He hoped that wasn't the case with him. He'd foolishly spoken up when he first arrived about being given the task of midnight portal patrol when he was supposed to be a palace guard. It earned him ten lashes for insubordination and an extra week of patrol. He'd been careful with his wordage after that. Even so, could he have unwittingly said something that was construed as a complaint?

He signaled a servant to assist him in carrying the limp woman to the slave quarters. The sooner he got on his way, the better.

****

Dennis paced the wooden planked floorboards of the small cottage that was his prison. He had no idea where he was, how he'd gotten there, or how long he'd been there. If it weren't for a tiny, heavily leaded window he wouldn't even know when it was night or day. The last thing he recalled was walking toward the stable to care for Sugar. He'd almost reached the door when everything went black. The next thing he knew he was stripped naked and locked in this smelly little hovel. Clothing made of coarse woven wool was shoved through the door not long after he awoke. They were ill fitting and severely outdated.

He'd tried to get someone to respond to his questions, but after a time he realized they were mute. Now he paced while he waited to discover the identity of his kidnappers, the purpose behind his kidnapping, and the fate awaiting him. From the few times he was able to steal a glance beyond the open door of his hovel, he deduced was in the encampment of some backward cult. They lacked all modern amenities. It was as if the village stepped out of the nineteenth century.

He strained his memories, trying to remember doing business with or interacting in any way with someone who might be a member of a cult of this nature and what he might have done to induce his abduction. He could think of nothing.

The thick, uneven lead glass window distorted and blurred images which was why he questioned if he really saw the limp form of his sister being carried into the cottage next to his. He shook his head and tried to get a better look through the thick, murky glass.

His attention was pulled away from the activity of the cottage next to his when the door swung. An ebony skinned man bent his body to enter through the doorway. His complexion looked remarkably smooth and supple. It was the perfect accent for his tall, slender physique. His movements were graceful as his bare feet glided across the planked flooring with a tray holding the mid-day meal.

"You're new. What happened to my old caretaker?" Dennis asked, even though he knew he'd get no answer.

"I'll be your caretaker now, Mr. Dennis," said an elegant voice with a hint of accent said just above a whisper. "My name is Eiflethropally. You may call me Eif, if you wish."

Stunned by the fact that he was getting a response, it took Dennis a moment to gather his wits about him. He'd finally get some answers.

"Tell me where I am. Better yet, why I'm here?" he asked

eagerly. "I'm not a wealthy man, so there's little ransom for you. You must have me mistaken with someone else. I'd have clarified things earlier, but everyone around me is mute."

"You're Dennis O'Shea from the twenty-first century?" Eif asked.

"What do you mean from the twenty-first century?" Dennis asked with genuine confusion. "Where am I?"

"There is no mistake," Eif said firmly. "I shall return within the half hour and I expect your plate to be clean. We don't tolerate waste here. Am I clear?"

Dennis nodded in silent bewilderment.

Satisfied, Eif gave a slight bow and left the room.

"Wait!" he called out. "What do you mean by twenty-first century! I don't understand."

When he got no response, he leaned his body against the door in frustration.

The loud click of the key in the lock echoed off the walls as Dennis stared at the bowl of thick, hearty stew and freshly baked rolls. The one thing he had to admit about his captors was that although they kept him locked up and isolated, they fed him well. A culinary expert could produce nothing greater.

The rich aroma of the blend of the stew, warm rolls and dark roasted coffee encouraged the juices in his stomach to come to life. He was hungry. With nothing more to do, he sat down to enjoy his mid-day fare. He'd barely sopped the last of the broth from the bowl with his roll before his eyes grew heavy. He gulped down the last of his coffee and made his way to the cot. Within a matter of a few seconds, he was fast asleep.

****

Adam crept through the tree laden grounds that made up the boundary between Shadow Land and the human realm. The air was thick and heaving, making breathing laborious at best. The energies of the boundary had the potential to cripple, if not kill the unsuspecting. It was especially dangerous in the center, half-way between Shadow Land and the human realm where the transition was at its peak.

Most humans weren't even aware the boundary existed. They went about their daily business completely oblivious to the fact that there was more than their supercilious reality. Of course, they believed in a Supreme Being, but they couldn't agree on this being's identity or purpose. Because of their ostentatious ignorance, a great number of things slipped passed them while they floundered through their days, oblivious to the depth of the true reality.

There was, however, a small populous in the human realm that was aware of alternate realms. This group consisted of the highly evolved spiritualists and pagans. It was these people who posed a threat for the continued growth and expansion of Shadow Land. It was these people who he'd grown to admire yet despise while living in the human realm. They were crafty and manipulative and sometimes lethal.

The old witchdoctor lived in the human realm, but his audacious mannerisms brought him into the boundary where he discovered the portal to Shadow Land and entered with little effort and absolutely no fear. He stood boldly before Balthazar and challenged him for the right to come and go. Adam heard many rumors about what that challenge was and what occurred, but they were only rumors. No one knew for sure because Balthazar and the old witch stayed behind closed doors for days before emerging bonded and amiable.

The witchdoctor came and went as he pleased, weaving his magic wherever he went. Balthazar was amused by him whenever he entered Shadow Land. Even the occasional killing of one of his subjects to appease the fierce magic man's cannibalistic cravings didn't disturb the great leader. It was an odd relationship that no one in Shadow Land understood and no one dared question.

The sound of twigs snapping underfoot caught his attention. He still hadn't shifted into his canine form. His human form

sported certain attributes that weren't available through his canine form, such as speaking to the guards at the portal and presenting them with his pass which sported the seal of the royal
palace. Ducking behind a nearby boulder, he peered from behind
it in the direction of the sound. This part of the boundary harbored the most bestial and malevolent creatures imaginable.

If it weren't for the snapping sound the creature could
have easily passed Adam undetected. Although only a few yards
separated them in distance, the foliage was so dense it made visibility of more than a few feet away nearly impossible.

Upon closer study, Adam could detect at least two, possibly three creatures coming his way. Beads of sweat coated his
neck while he waited for them to pass, barely breathing for fear
of making a sound. As luck would have it, they stopped, just feet
away from him. He flattened his body as best he could against the
smooth, hard surface of the boulder. Its height required he twist
at an angle he found incredibly uncomfortable and he wondered
just how long he'd be able to maintain this position.

"I think we should rest the horses for a spell," said a tall,
slender woman with a long fiery braid down her back.

Adam recognized the lilt in her speech as Irish. The hair
on the back of his neck stood on end. An Irish woman braving
the boundary near the portal of Shadow Land could only be one
person. The enchantress!

His heart pounded as he wrestled with a mixture of excitement, confusion, and fear. He'd dreamt of being in the company of the infamous enchantress often since joining Balthazar's
service. She was often the topic of conversation in many a circle.
Never more so than since Joshua returned with the doppelganger
of her niece. Now, here he was just feet away from her.

Blood to rush through his veins, his heart beat wildly,
and his mind raced. He'd been sent to bring back the witchdoctor. What if he brought back the enchantress instead? How would
that affect his status in Balthazar's court? He saw how glorious
Joshua's return was even after Balthazar discovered he hadn't

brought back a doppelganger instead of the true young enchantress. If he returned with the real thing, he was sure he'd receive the highest reward.

Since it appeared the enchantress was already on her way to Shadow Land, he merely had to turn into his canine form and accompany her through the portal and then take the credit for getting her there. It would be her word against his. Who would believe the enchantress would ever do such a foolish thing as enter Shadow Land by her own volition?

He thanked the gods of the underworld such a boon. Things were looking up! Transitioning into his canine identity, he leapt from behind the boulder and headed toward the riders.

Brandon stared in disbelief.

"Is that a dog?" he asked. "What the devil is a dog doing in these parts?"

"The devil exactly," Fiona replied. "Trust no one, nothing. Understand?"

Brandon nodded while he watched the dog limp toward them. He had to be one of the finest looking collies he'd ever laid eyes on.

"Have you seen such a fine-looking collie since you left Ireland?" he asked.

Fiona squinted in Adam's direction.

"I can't say as I have. Even so, heads up," she replied.

"He's limping. I think he's hurt," Brandon mused.

"It could be a ploy," she hissed.

EIGHTEEN

Luella stormed out of the bedroom. Joshua was acting very strange. He was far too preoccupied for a man just returned from a lengthy assignment. Rumor had it the young woman he brought back was the young enchantress' doppelganger. Rumor also had it that the girl was under the impression she and Joshua were engaged to be married. How did she get such an idea? Could that rogue of a lover of hers played such a role while he was away?

Although furious with Joshua, it wasn't the reason for her rampage now. Once again Balthazar overlooked her prowess as a sorceress and sent for that decaying old man. Why would he favor a witchdoctor over a powerful sorceress? It was an insult.

She was a young girl when her mother, Elspeth, brought her through the boundary to Shadow Land. It was a bold move on her part. A bold move that paid off.

Born human, Luella was the daughter of a powerful sorceress who felt her abilities were wasted. She wanted a far greater challenge than what she encountered from the villagers who came to her for a remedy here and a remedy there. When she discovered the portal to Shadow Land, she boldly passed through it and presented herself and her services to Balthazar. Taken by her beauty, Balthazar made her his palace sorceress as well as his head mistress. Luella was raised within the palace walls, enjoying all the luxuries and privileges of a princess.

A human living in Shadow Land walked a perilous line. Knowing her looks and her hold over Balthazar would eventually fade, Elspeth taught everything she knew to Luella. Her daughter's best chance for survival rested within her knowledge and skill as a sorceress.

As she witnessed her mother's eventual decline from favor, Luella kept her warnings in the forefront of her mind and studied magic every possible moment. Palace life was all she knew. She had no memories of the human realm and no desire to live in exile amongst shadow people and mystical beings. She wanted to remain in the familiar surroundings where she grew up. When the fateful day came and Balthazar exiled Elspeth from the palace, forcing her to return to the human realm or spend the rest of her days as a cast off in Shadow Land, Luella was fully grown and thoroughly prepared to step into her mother's shoes as palace sorceress and Balthazar's mistress. To her disappointment, surprise, and dismay, she wasn't appointed the position of palace sorceress and was vehemently rejected as mistress. Instead, she was forced to stand by and watch the old witchdoctor receive the honor of court magician and the very sultry daughter of one of the palace attendees replaced her aged mother.

To add to her insult, the old coot of a magician could come and go as he pleased. This was a luxury her mother never knew. On the few occasions that they did leave the palace unescorted, it was in the night and in secret.

Cast out alongside her mother, they scrambled for safe harbor within the walls of Shadow Land. Her mother, after many failed attempts to persuade her to accompany her back through the boundary, finally set off alone. Luella was uncertain if the woman made it or not.

Fortunately for Luella, her beauty was of such depth that she won the heart and protection of Balthazar's most revered and handsome soldiers, Joshua. Although the luxuries he provided for her fell short of those of the palace, they were in no way modest.

She found she really didn't miss palace life. The freedom Joshua allowed her far outweighed any luxury she lacked. She'd never feared her position in his household or his heart until he returned from the future, having failed at obtaining the crystal key or the young enchantress who hid it.

There was something different about him. She feared the

enchantress may have put a love spell on him. More than once she found him calling the woman's name in his sleep. To top things off it reached her ears that he returned with her doppelganger who had the audacity to inform anyone who'd listen she was betrothed to Joshua. This was a rumor that better have no credence to it!

The outrage of another woman claiming her man acted as a perfect cover-up and excuse for her rage over the summons of the old witchdoctor. Discovering the enchantress' doppelganger was held in the slave quarters, she stormed off to release some of her pent-up anger on the woman. She might even conjure a few warts for the whore's nose while she was there!

Fury spurred her away from the luxury she knew so well and into the humble quarters of the slaves. Although rough in style and manner the buildings and environment looked surprisingly neat and clean. Balthazar demanded cleanliness and order around him at all times, even in the homes of his slaves. He despised poverty and filth so much that he considered them a weapon and used them as one of the horrors he bestowed upon his prey in other realms.

In her haste, she'd neglected to obtain the exact location of the cottage. Now, looking around, she saw no one with the ability of speech to ask. With the mind-set that a slave should be seen and not heard, along with his desire to keep gossip amongst the slaves at a minimum, Balthazar ordered speech capabilities removed when the slave was captured. Only the few who advisors felt loyal and placed in charge of the others were allowed to maintain their speech capabilities.

Luella heard stories about the methods used to remove the speech from the captive slaves. Balthazar left these things up to the head guard, a vicious creature with no heart. Stories ran rampant of the torture he incorporated in the procedure for his own pleasure, from cutting out tongues to the surgical removal of the vocal cords using no anesthesia. No one seemed to mind his methods. They were in Shadow Land after all and the slaves were mere humans.

The eyes that followed her made her skin crawl. She may

be a sorceress and under the protection of Balthazar's top soldier, but she was still a human in a realm where humans were regarded as the lowest of low. Venturing this far from the safety of her nucleus meant she was also far away from her protector. Did these people know her to be the sorceress? If they tried to harm her they'd quickly find out.

It was a little more difficult to spot the energy of a human around the cottages, since the entire slave community was made up of them, but she eventually decided on a cottage to enter. With a flick of her fingers, the lock clicked and the door swung open.

Dennis stared at the raven-haired beauty with mild disbelief. This had to be a dream. The only women who walked through his door were dark skinned, haggard and mute women who came to tend to the washing of his body, clothing, and bedding. He shook his head in disbelief and squint his eyes against the brilliant sky that encased her goddess-like silhouette. Never has he set eyes on such a beauty. This had to be a dream.

"Well," she almost whispered in a rich sultry voice, "what have we here?"

Luella gracefully entered the small one room hut and closed the door behind her. With the flick of her wrist, the lock latched and she was alone with the handsome auburn haired human before her. Having seen very few humans who weren't black skinned with hair as black as hers, she took a moment to take in his striking features. His pale skin sported small freckles that were almost faded from the lack of sun. She imagined his thick shaggy hair combed smooth and the stubble that detracted from his chiseled chin removed. Underneath the rubble he was quite handsome. With minimal effort, she closed the distance between them. Several inches shorter than he, she looked up at him with deep brown eyes that bore right through him and laid her hand on his chest.

"You're strong like a warrior," she purred.

"I guess," he mumbled, still not certain if he was in a dream or reality had taken a turn for the better.

"You guess? What does this mean?" Luella asked with a

scowl.

Looking more closely, she inspected the clothing he'd been allowed to wear again after he'd developed an unsightly rash from the fabric of the clothes they'd provided. They were unusual looking. His speech was unusual as well. It wasn't just the phrase he used, but the way he pronounced his words. He was different. From a place that was far different than any she knew.

"Where are you from?" she asked warily.

"Manhattan," he replied.

"I've haven't heard of this place," she scowled.

"Where am I?" he asked.

Luella stared at him briefly before replying with great impatience.

"Shadow Land, of course," she said with pride.

"I can't say I've heard of it," Dennis replied, trying not to sound flippant.

"Everyone has heard of Shadow Land," Luella retorted.

"Everyone's heard of Manhattan," he said flippantly.

"You have an odd way of speaking," she preened her words as she slowly circled him, "and your dress is very strange."

Remembering that in this village -wherever it may be- he was the odd one for dress and speech, Dennis remained still. Dream or not, he had no desire to enter into a battle of wits with this goddess of beauty.

"You're human, aren't you?" Luella asked with accentuated concern.

Perhaps she made a mistake and barged into the quarters of someone not from the human realm. After all, the stench of human flesh was everywhere. It would be easy to get confused.

"What else would I be?" he asked.

"How very odd," she mused.

Suddenly bored, she looked around the small hovel and wrinkled her nose. Although neat and tidy, it lacked the rich, warm, and inviting appeal that she was accustomed to.

"How can you live here?" she asked without thinking.

"My condo's being remodeled," he replied, not altogether

sure why he was so flippant with her.

Luella shot him a stern look before walking to the window.

"I should have asked what house she was in," she muttered. "I have no wish to go from door to door inspecting the contents of each shack looking for her."

Dennis stood silent while he struggled with the overwhelming urge to ask who this lovely creature was looking for. It was obviously a woman. He was aware of only one female hostage in his circle of huts. She was in the hut next door. Should he tell her?

"What are you thinking, my handsome lion?" she purred as she moved back in front of him and stroked his cheek.

"How remarkably beautiful you're," he replied.

"I know," she whispered in his ear before nibbling at its lobe. "You're unusually handsome. You rival my Joshua with your body of iron and your striking good looks. Your face is strong and framed with a mane like a lion." Her voice stayed soft and breathy as she traced his chin with the tip of her tongue while making her way to his other ear, sending shivers of sensual delight through him. "Of course, you're fair and he's dark," she breathed into his ear.

Without warning Dennis pulled her into his arms and kissed her with an urgency difficult to describe. When he did, something happened inside of her that she couldn't explain. It was like the world exploded.

Never before had Luella experienced such a thing and she was unsure what to make of it. Joshua was her lover and protector yet she wanted nothing more than to remain in this prisoner's arms and never be free. She pulled away. This was dangerous. If Joshua discovered her indiscretion, it could mean death for them both.

"What is your name?" she panted.

"Dennis" he managed as he gulped in air to help him regain his composure.

"We shall meet again, I'm certain," she said as she backed away and headed for the door.

****

Luella sought every opportunity and excuse she could to sneak back into the hut of her handsome prisoner. All thoughts of the woman and Joshua fell to the wayside. After much grilling, she concluded Dennis wasn't a sorcerer. He was simply a human who she had a strong physical attraction to and quite a bit in common. Each visit she managed to achieve uncovered yet another idea, habit, or pleasure they agreed upon whole heartedly. They grew to be friends as well as lovers.

He told her about his home. It sounded strange and different in an exciting sort of way. Some of the things he talked about, like the car and the airplane, sounded so farfetched she questioned whether he'd spun a tale to amuse her. She could believe it if the world was inhabited by magical creatures, but humans? Really.

Whatever was behind his stories, she found him fascinating. If she hadn't known better, she would have thought she'd fallen in love with him, but love was a luxury she never experienced. A luxury one couldn't experience. Not in Shadow Land. Balthazar forbade such an emotion.

She quickly forgot about visiting the girl's cottage. She knew Joshua made repeated visits and stayed a considerable length of time. Surprisingly she didn't care. In fact, there were times when she would visit Dennis at the same time Joshua was with the doppelganger next door. She would watch his strong physique come and go through the thick, uneven window pane. She'd feared discovery at one point when he walked toward Dennis' shack. Her heart stuck in her throat and its pounding pierced her eardrums while she frantically tried to think of what to do to save them from his wrath. Then, as the dark gods would have it, Eif approached Joshua and spent a considerable time huddled with him in conversation... after which the two took off together. Luella couldn't recall ever feeling such relief. She may be a powerful sorceress, but she wasn't up to battling all of Shadow Land, and that's what would happen should Joshua or Balthazar unleash their wrath on her.

When they finally got around to discussing Shadow Land, Dennis was shocked to discover he'd been teleported back in time and into a different dimension. Although confused about the how and why of it all, it certainly explained their clothing and living conditions.

Luella's description of Shadow Land sent cold shivers down his spine, especially when she confessed she had no idea why he'd been brought there. It seemed odd, since he'd been left basically on his own since he arrived. She promised to do a little snooping to see if she could get some answers.

As he watched her leave after a very satisfying and lengthy visit his eyes settled on the hut next door. With the exception of Eif bringing him his food and Luella's visits, the only other attention he received was the occasional visit from the slaves for his washings. Yet, the shack next door was incredibly active. He wondered who the young woman was and why she commanded so much attention.

****

Joshua pushed his chair away from the long mahogany dining table. The light from the candelabra bounced off the highly polished beeswax surface onto the brilliant silver platters that were still heavily laden with wild boar, an assortment of roasted root vegetables and a platter of rosemary potatoes. Stretching his legs out to full length before him, he casually leaned back in the chair and tipped his wine goblet to his lips. He savored the smooth, woody taste of the liquid as it slid over his tongue to the back of his throat.

Luella looked at her longtime lover through heavy lids while she played at finishing the rich creamy pudding in front of her. There was no denying his striking good looks. Although his family migrated from Russia to Shadow Land centuries ago and his lineage resided there long enough for them to shed their humanity and take on the attributes of extended mortality, he still retained his human appearance. This was why he was often chosen for missions in the human realm and why Luella was so attracted to him.

Even though she abhorred humans -as all longtime residents of Shadow Land did- she found their looks far more appealing than that of a true Shadow Land native. The Shadow Land native had the shape and some human attributes, but also distinct differences, such as their deep-set eyes resting within dark, almost bruised looking hollow wells or their sunken cheekbones and grayish skin tone. Their hands were long and bony with extended fingers, as were their feet. Just as Luella found the native Shadow Land people unappealing, so they found Luella and Joshua's looks to be just as repulsive. Since she had no desire to mix with the other species that made Shadow Land their home -such as vampires, werewolves and aliens from dark planets- Luella was fortunate to have caught the eye of Joshua. He'd literally been her salvation.

The heaviness of guilt over seeing Dennis since she was so beholding to Joshua hovered over her. This was a new twist she couldn't say she enjoyed. It had to be some minute remnant of her human side surfacing. Residents of Shadow Land never felt guilt. It was a foreign emotion, just like love. She pushed it back to the recesses of her being where it belonged. Buried alongside the few memories she still had of her life before Shadow Land.

"You look deep in thought, my dear," Joshua said as he laid his head back and inspected the candelabra and took a long, slow drag from the cigar he'd just lit. "What makes you so somber?"

Feeling like a child caught with her hand in the cookie jar, she looked up with a start.

"Nothing," she replied, hesitantly.

"Do you expect me to believe that?" he questioned. "Tell... why have you been frequenting the slave quarters?"

Joshua's thoughts went to the doppelganger. Had Luella

been searching for her?

"I'm searching for that bitch you brought back," she replied with as much jealousy in her voice as she could muster.

"You have not found her?" Joshua laughed.

He was thoroughly amused by the jealously he'd known would come forth from his lovely Luella even while he traveled back to Shadow Land with the doppelganger in tow. He was only surprised that it hadn't surfaced immediately.

"No," she spat.

"No?" he repeated with surprise.

"That place stinks of humans. I wandered into the hut of some disgusting male prisoner today," she spat.

Luella held her breath. By the look on Joshua's face, he was aware of Dennis' presence. She hoped he wouldn't probe her further about her visit to the slave quarters. Keeping secrets from him was almost impossible. She questioned her wisdom at admitting it to begin with. In her defense, if she was to find out why Dennis was captured and brought there she needed to bring him up in conversation. She did her best to look as disinterested as possible while she continued her probe.

"That horrid weasel had the audacity to question me about where he was and why he was here. I hope Balthazar mutes him," she said with a scowl, hoping her tone and words were convincing.

"Oh, he has greater plans than just muting, my dear," Joshua preened. "That poor excuse of a man was nothing more than a decoy for Balthazar to spur the enchantress to return from the future to save him. You see, he poses as her brother in the future. To me he's far more than that. He's a swine who played a pivotal role in my failure while there," he scowled, "as well as the demise of the body I possessed. I've petitioned Balthazar and when I get his approval, I'll kill that filthy pig with my own hands... after I torture him, of course."

He held his hands around an imaginary neck and shook them vehemently for emphasis. It was then that Luella realized she loved Dennis. The thought of Joshua taking his life and depriving her of one moment with him filled her with unfamiliar panic.

Her mind raced.

She had to stop it somehow.

****

There wasn't a star in the sky and the clouds were so thick and heavy the moonbeams didn't stand a chance of getting past them to illuminate the night. The clicking of the lock on his door echoed through the silence of his. Unable to identify who entered, Dennis held his breath and stared into the blackness that enveloped him. Now that he knew where he was and the perils that existed outside the sanctuary of his four walls he found it difficult to relax enough to fall into a deep sleep. He was captured for a reason and that reason couldn't have been a good one. Perhaps ignoring him and making him wait like they had was part of their torture method. Had they discovered he'd started spending time in bliss while in the arms of their sorceress?

Was this the beginning of his end?

The warm hand over his mouth startled him and his body responded with a panicked struggle. Whoever held him down was forced to use brute strength to subdue him. If he was going to be tortured and killed in a manner that he'd learned was common through his conversations with Luella or if they were to cut out his tongue or seize his vocal cords to silence him forever, he fully intended to make it as difficult as possible for them.

"Stop it," Luella hissed softly in his ear. "Stop struggling or you'll alert the guards," she whispered in the harshest tone she could muster.

She waited to be certain he understood and was calm before removing a grip so firm Dennis would have sworn it belonged to a man.

"I had no idea you had such strength," he whispered as he gulped in much needed air.

"You'd be surprised at my many talents," she replied.

"I guess so," he said with admiration.

"I've learned of your plight and it isn't good," Luella said softly.

"I figured as much," he said flatly.

"I'm going to get you out of here," she whispered before pressing her soft, supple lips to his and kissing him briefly. "We must go while we have the chance."

Dennis pulled back and shook his head as the impact of her words struck him. Was she going to help him escape from this place? He couldn't believe his ears. Suddenly sober and very, very awake, he pushed passed her and swung his feet to the floor.

"I can't see a thing," he whispered. "How are you able to manage?"

"I've a sort of night vision, my love," she replied.

"Thank God for that," he whispered happily.

Although Luella found the fact that he'd thank one god for her abilities, she said nothing. Now wasn't the time for conversation. They needed to make their escape before the effects of the sleeping potion she slipped into the guard's wine wore off. Grabbing Dennis' hand, she guided him out of the hut. The cool night air was in stark contrast to the thick, stale, hothouse he'd lived in since his capture. His body shivered involuntarily.

It was far easier to see now that he was out of the confines of the light-less room and he kept up with her easily. As they moved behind the hut next to him, the sound of a woman's moaning stopped him. It was a sad, agonizing sound, but that wasn't what caught his attention. There was something familiar about the voice, something he recognized.

"Wait!" he hissed. His urgent whisper caught Luella off guard and she stumbled to a stop. "Who are they holding in there?"

"I don't know," Luella moaned, annoyed with the interruption.

She wasn't certain, but she suspected the doppelganger

was within those walls.

Dennis listened again as another agonizing moan. It made the hair stand on his head. Not so much for its sound, but for the familiarity of the voice making it.

"I want to see who's in there. The voice sounds like... like..." he couldn't even say it aloud and prayed he was wrong.

"We have to go," she urged in a harsh whisper as she grabbed his arm to pull him along.

"I can't," he snapped as he resisted her grip. "I have to see who's in here first. If she's not who I think she is we'll go, but I have to see."

Luella took a deep breath. She hadn't counted on this and had no plan of action for it. She considered abandoning him and saving herself. The guards would arouse soon and if she was caught she'd be hanged, or burned, or tortured until she died. With an exasperated expulsion of air to emphasize how unhappy she was, she flicked her hand and the thick, lead glass window swung open.

"Look then, but be quick about it," she hissed.

Dennis ignored Luella's obvious irritation and popped his head through the small opening.

"Tara? Tara, is that you?" he whispered.

The faintest response reached his ears.

"Dennis?" Tara said weakly.

The validation that his sister was behind those walls -and none too well at that- caused his adrenaline to pump so heavily through his veins that his chest pained with every beat of his heart. If Tara uttered anything else it didn't get past the roaring in his ears, nor did the pleas coming from Luella as he hoisted himself through the small opening of which he was lucky to fit. He hit the floorboards with a loud thump that caused everyone to hold their breath while they waited to see if the guard's heard. After a few tense moments he stood up and felt his way to her cot. His eyes were a little more accustomed to the night and he was able to make out her pale silhouette. Her long, firelight hair lay matted against her breast and her breathing was noticeably shallow.

"What's happened?" he asked as he stroked her head gently.

"Dennis? Is that you?" she asked weakly. "I came to rescue you from the shadow people, but I'm not well."

"What's wrong?" he asked worriedly.

"I don't really know. I teleported with Brandon and little by little I've gotten weaker and weaker. I think I need to go home. I'll be alright once I'm home," she replied.

Scooping her frail frame into his arms he headed for the door. He hadn't picked her up in many years, but he was certain she should have weighed more.

"Luella," he barked in a hushed tone, "Open the door."

"No!" she replied. "We can't take her."

"I'm not leaving without her," he said stubbornly.

Even though his sister lost weight, the forced break from his regime at the gym had taken its toll and his muscles weren't as strong as they'd normally be. He felt the strain on his arms. He was just about to lay her back on her cot when the lock clanked and the door slowly swung open.

He stared at the voluptuous figure of Luella as she stood in the doorway and smiled.

"Thank you," he whispered with heartfelt emotion.

"Let's get going," Luella grunted.

She had no desire to drag a half dead woman with them. The journey would be treacherous enough without the added burden.

Without another word, Dennis shifted Tara over his shoulder to make it easier for him to move as quickly as possible while he followed Luella. She moved with the speed and grace of a gazelle as she guided them out of the slave quarters and along the edge of the village to the portal, never stopping for as much as a second until they reached their destination.

Hiding behind a large out building, Brandon set Tara on the ground, flexed his muscles, and caught his wind while Luella studied the situation with the guards. They were changing shifts.

She hadn't counted on that.

"Dennis?" Tara murmured.

Luella flew with lightning speed to Tara's side and clamped her hand over her mouth. Tara tried to struggle, but was too weak. Using her eyes, facial expressions and her hands, Luella made it clear to Dennis that either Tara stayed totally silent or she would see to it that the woman never uttered a sound again. Although outraged at her threat to his sister, he understood her reasoning. The guards were close and any type of sound could cause their discovery.

Although she abhorred the idea of waiting for the guards to finish their switch over, she knew no other alternative. She had just enough twilight dust for two guards. If she tried to divide it amongst all four, its power would be ineffective for their needs. She pulled a pocket watch from the folds of her skirt and checked the dial. The sleeping potion she slipped the guards in the slave quarters would wear off in a matter of minutes. They were cutting it close. Heaving a sigh, she motioned for Dennis to relax, indicating as best she could that they needed to wait out the changing of the guard. Dennis nodded and pulled Tara to him. He assumed Luella induced her fainting spell. If so, it was probably a wise course of action, since Tara could have easily become a detriment to their escape in her condition.

The next few minutes seemed like eternity. It wasn't until the guards finally parted ways and the two beginning their shift settled into their posts that Dennis and Luella breathed relief. Nodding her head for him to pick up his sister, Luella pulled out her powder and led the way for their escape through the portal.

****

Joshua hadn't visited Tara in several days. The fact that she wasn't the real enchantress didn't bother him. Balthazar saw the magic that was locked within her and it pleased him. She may not be Lucy O'Shea, but Tara O'Shea still had the family magic buried within her and as soon as that witchdoctor brought her back to life Balthazar intended to make full use of it. This was a definite boon for Joshua.

The potion he'd given her on their journey to Shadow Land wore off and her decline was rapid. For a while, she was well enough for him to visited in the afternoons. Now she once again smelled of decay. He found it repulsive and he wondered if she'd last until the magic doc arrived. He had no intention of continuing the visits until after she was treated and the stench was gone.

He thought about how robust and vibrant she'd been while in the future. She'd captured him body and soul to the point of his seriously considering taking her into his protection as Luella's second. He still might if she survived.

With Tara no longer in the forefront of his mind, his thoughts returned to Luella. She was in one of her moods of late. He hadn't bothered about it. In fact, he'd expected it when he returned with the lovely doppelganger in tow, but now it was time to pull her out of her state of mind and assure her she was still his number one. He stretched his arm across the immense feather mattress in search for her supple body. His hand patted and searched in frustration. Where could she be?

Sitting up, he growled at the darkness that swept the room. It was difficult to see his hand in front of his face. Fumbling for the oil lamp, he almost knocked it over. He felt around for the match sticks. They weren't in their usual place. She knew better than to move them! What was she thinking? The woman was with him long enough to know he insisted on things being where they belonged. Order was imperative. She'd better have a good explanation or it was the lash for her.

The light tapping on the front door was barely audible. Scowling, he grabbed the coverlet off the bed and wrapped it around himself before stumbling to the door. Yelping over a stubbed toe, he flung the door open. The light from the lantern the guard held hurt his eyes and he turned his head away.

"What is it?" he growled.

NINETEEN

Adam lay by the fire with his head resting on his paws. Things weren't going well. The enchantress was sharp and suspicious. Instead of accepting him as a cute and cuddly collie that wandered into the boundary and was in need of human assistance she suspected him of being exactly what he was, a creature of the dark in disguise. He'd been laying low in an effort to gain her trust and convince her otherwise. He should have returned to Shadow Land with the witchdoctor in tow by now. If he couldn't get the enchantress to soften soon, he'd have to abandon the idea of glory and fetch the witchdoctor. He really hoped it wouldn't come to that. At least here, in the company of the enchantress and her companion, his life wasn't at risk. He wanted to keep it that way. Delaying much longer would also put him in jeopardy with Balthazar. Any way he looked at it, getting the enchantress to enter Shadow Land with him was imperative.

"How long do you plan on hanging out here?" Brandon asked, openly frustrated.

"As long as we need to," Fiona replied, doing her best to mask the irritation she felt with the situation. "We're in the heart of the boundary so we need to take things slow and easy. One wrong move could prove fatal."

"Wouldn't it be safer to be mobile rather than sitting here like easy game?" he asked hesitantly.

"We're safe within the circle I cast. Nothing evil can get in or out," she explained.

"Really?" Brandon looked around. Nothing looked different to him. "I can't see a thing."

"Exactly," she huffed.

This wasn't good news for Adam. He was very much aware of how powerful the magic circle of protection was and she was right, nothing of evil persuasion could get in or out unless she spoke them in or out. This would be a problem if he wasn't able to get her to trust him.

Fiona watched the collie's body language when she spoke of the magic ring. Did she detect a reaction? Did he understand their conversation? She wasn't sure, but she suspected it. In the beginning, she thought he might be a dark creature in disguise to fool them into letting him get closer to them, but after inaction on his end she felt she might be wrong.

She decided to lay some bait. If he was something other than a dog, this would prove it. Sliding next to Brandon, she pulled out a sack from the saddle bag she hadn't touched since they began their trip. Untying the leather strap that secured the sack she reached in and pulled out a small vile.

"Hand me some of that meat from the fire, will ya?" she said to Brandon.

Confused, but knowing better than to speak, Brandon pulled off a small chunk of the venison that was roasting over the fire pit. Since it had only recently been skewered and balanced over the flames, it was still cool to the touch and therefore, easy to remove. As he handed the meat to Fiona, his curiosity got the better of him.

"Can I ask what you're doing?" he said.

"I think 'tis time to find out the truth about this dog. I want to move on, but I won't make a move with that beast at me heels unless I can be certain he's really a dog," she said as she soaked the meat in the liquid from the vile. "This here should do the trick."

"What is it?" he asked.

"Poison," she replied. "The way I figure it, if this is a creature in disguise it understands every word we say. That means he heard me say this meat is poisoned. It is tasteless and odorless poison, so the only way he'd know the meat could kill him is if he's not a dog and understands me words."

"So, you're planning on feeding this bad meat to the dog and if he eats it and dies you know he was the real thing?" Brandon asked incredulously.

"That's right," she replied.

"Isn't that a little extreme?" he asked in earnest.

"Beasts from Shadow Land are tricky devils. We can't be traveling with one. Trust me," she said.

"I do," Brandon sighed.

He knew Fiona wouldn't do such a thing to a creature if it wasn't a matter of life or death. Even so, he felt bad for the poor dog.

Adam's mind raced. What a cunning witch! She knew he wouldn't want to eat the meat if it meant certain death, but if he refused it she'd likely kill him anyway. No matter how he looked at it, he was doomed.

"Here boy," Fiona called as she held out the meat for Adam to take.

The moment had arrived. He'd reached a fork in the road and choices had to be made. Was he to die by poison or in battle against an opponent who'd surely win? Would dying at her hands be as horrid as the stories he'd heard? Would she strip him of his flesh while he cried for mercy and skewer him over a fire to die a slow, painful death? He shuddered at the thought. It was certainly something the witchdoctor would do. Was she as evil? He couldn't take the chance.

As he accepted the venison she held out to him and swallowed quickly, he prayed death would be swift and merciful. Almost immediately his head grew light and the world grew hazy. He needed to lie down. Softness surrounded him. Smiling inside, he praised himself for making the right choice. He felt no pain. Only bliss. Death wasn't so bad after all.

"Well, are you satisfied?" Brandon's tone was scolding.

"Yep," Fiona replied. "I could have sworn he was a skinner." Straightening up she stretched her back and shook the kinks out of her legs. "We'll be heading out first thing in the morning.

That meat should be done enough to eat in a few hours. I think I'll just head to bed and eat in the morning, but ya go ahead and feed yourself. Ya look a might skinny." Fiona chuckled to herself as she made her way to her sleeping roll.

"What about the dog?" Brandon had no desire to stare at a dead collie all night long.

"'Twas only a sleeping potion. He'll be right as rain in the morning," she tossed over her shoulder as she positioned herself for sleep.

Brandon smiled. What a clever woman she was. He'd never really taken the time to get to know her since his schedule was demanding and she was a reclusive sort. Lucy always spoke highly of her and now, after being with her during this time of crisis –as well as the crisis in the future- he could understand why. She clearly loved Lucy, but she didn't let that cloud her head. Her skills far exceeded any enchantress, common witch, wizard or witchdoctor he'd ever encountered yet she spent the majority of their time in this place studying the old book she'd pilfered from the witchdoctor's cottage. Humility, power, love, kindness and good looks... she was actually a mighty good catch.

Surprised and uncomfortable with the direction his thoughts were roaming, Brandon stood up and stretched his limbs.

"I think I won't eat just yet. The meat will make nice fare to breakfast on in the morning." He moved the meat to a part of the fire that offered less intense heat so they wouldn't wake up to burnt mead and headed over to his bedding. He vigorously shook out the bugs and debris that collected during his absence and settled his tired body down. He was never one for camping out like this and the fact that the ground was icy cold didn't help. He looked forward to the time when he was once again in a soft warm bed.

"I guess I should be thankful it isn't snowing like it is back in the future," he muttered.

Although he much preferred the time and era of his birth

he had to admit that there were a few things about the future he enjoyed and missed. Their sophisticated heating systems and bedding were amongst them.

Fiona watched her companion while he prepared his bedding. She never took the time to get to know him. Of course, the fact that Lucy adored him enough to be betrothed spoke considerably about his character. Even so, it was actually nice to get to know him first hand, even if it was under such circumstances. He'd proven to be strong and steadfast -something she never would have expected from a traveler. In truth, Fiona knew very little about travelers. Since they weren't of the magical realm, her books contained minimal information. She'd met only a few and they weren't from her era. Brandon was, in fact, the only traveler she ever met who'd actually been born in her era and grew up only a few miles from her home town in Ireland. He'd traded his Irish brogue for a southern drawl, but she could still pick up a syllable or two pronounced in her native tongue.

"What brought ya to this country?" she asked softly.

Surprised by her question, he responded without thinking. "The war," he said.

Fiona sat up, confused.

"The war is only recent," she offered. "Did ya know about it in advance?"

"Not the Civil War. I meant the war with Shadow Land," he explained. "The main portal to many dimensions from Shadow Land is nearby. They enter our realm through it and then travel time to the era they desire. I basically came to the front line."

"Ya come and go. I didn't realize a traveler played such a role in the war," she said. "How can ya when ya are here and there all of the time?"

Brandon chuckled at Fiona's perception of his life. He'd never really thought about how it looked to others, mainly because very few knew of his traveling.

"Being here and there, as you put it, is how I play my part in the war," he explained. "By traveling to the future I can get a better idea of how certain actions we're considering will work out and if they're unfavorable I report back and a new strategy is created."

"That makes sense," Fiona replied. "What about traveling back in time? How could that help with the war?"

Brandon felt she tested him more than questioned him. Surely, a woman as wise as she already knew the answers to these questions. Even so, he responded readily.

"It is sometimes advantageous for me to study the actions of the past and their outcomes to advise on future actions. After all, not everything in history was recorded for us to know," he said.

"How true, how very true," Fiona agreed. "Do ya know why the portal to Shadow Land is most easily traveled in this era? Why not in Roman times or in the future? Why now?"

Brandon stared at Fiona for a moment before responding.

"Now is the time when magic is the strongest in these parts. The reason is something I don't know. I just know that to be the case," he said. "This magic enhances the portal. The magic of this land will fade with time and the portal will shrink and move to a more advantageous time and location... providing the evils don't get their hands on the crystal key before then."

"I see," Fiona mused. Rolling on her side, she propped herself onto her elbow and cradled her cheek in the palm of her hand. "Tell me a little about meself when I was in the future."

"You mean; you don't remember?" Brandon was stunned.

"Bits and pieces, but not the whole of it," she replied.

"I didn't realize that," he said.

"I was surprised as well. It was me first experience being reborn and sharing a soul," she explained. "'Twas far more complex than I ever imagined. It took me years to break through the veil of forgetfulness and remember me magic, and even then, I didn't recall all of it. That's something I never had to deal with when I traveled like ya do. I underestimated the veil's hold on a soul. I couldn't remember all I needed to remember until ya broke the veil away by telling me all about things. Of course, that was just before me body was torn to pieces. If I had remembered before then we might have the key by now."

"You were pretty effective as you were," he said admiringly.

"I was old when ya met me and still had not developed one third of the skills I have today. 'Tis shameful," she spat.

"Don't be so hard on yourself," he said soothingly. "You really did help Tara a lot. She loved you then like Lucy loves you now, maybe more. I don't know what she would have done if you hadn't been there to help save her from Dominic. That goes for me and Dennis too. We all hold a huge load of gratitude for you."

"'Twas not me who saved ya from the demon, they killed me. Remember?" she said.

"It's a memory that I wish I could forget, but will carry with me always," he sighed, "but, you did hold us together and kept us calm. It got pretty wild in there once you were killed."

"What happened?" she asked.

"Tara went a little crazy when she saw you being torn to bits," he said. He stopped quickly when he saw Fiona shudder visibly at the mention of her demise. "Do you want me to continue?"

She nodded.

"Then I got a little crazy when Dominic set fire to the house and suggested we all shoot ourselves," he chuckled. "Come to think of it, the only one who stayed fairly balanced during the ordeal was Dennis. He was a trooper."

"He was a decent lad from what I recall," she mused.

"I think it was his steadfast support the brought Tara around from the trauma enough to think to call on her spirit guide," he said.

Fiona knit her brows together.

"I met him when I left me body. He was with several other spirits who were watching the whole thing. I remember scolding him for not helping and he said that he couldn't interfere until called upon. Liam... I think he said his name was Liam," she said.

"That sounds right," he mused. He drew a deep breath, "She shouted for him and then pouf, the fire went out and Dominic was gone and there was the greatest sense of peace in the air." He was silent for a minute and then continued, "There's a lot about what occurred in the future that makes me sad. One of the biggest things is the fact that Lucy's soul doesn't remember me either. Neither Tara or Lucy remembers me."

"That hurts," she said sympathetically. "We know why Lucy can't remember ya and having experienced the veil first hand I can understand why Tara doesn't remember ya, especially when her soul was stripped of your memory of ya before we did all that."

"It was gut wrenching to watch the woman I'm betrothed to have an affair with another man, demon or not, while she spurned me and treated me like a stranger," he said softly.

"She's not the woman ya are betrothed to. Ya must keep that in mind," Fiona scolded. "The woman ya are betrothed to lays in wait in the cave, safe and snug. We're on our way to rescue Tara who is a person all her own, but a person who carries deep within her the soul of our Lucy as well as the memories." She looked at Brandon sympathetically, "I know 'tis a difficult thing to comprehend. 'Tis even complicated for me and I'm the one who made it all happen, but know this... Although the Tara we seek is not the Lucy ya love and will marry one day, she's the one in possession of the life force that our dear Lucy relies upon and if we don't save her, they both may perish. Of that ya can be certain."

The sound of heavy running caught their attention and they sat up to see what it could be. From what Brandon could tell, it was either a couple of two legged creatures or one four legged creatures that was wounded because its gait didn't match. If he was a betting man, he'd have chosen the first.

Fiona moved stealthily to her bag and pulled out a pistol. Brandon did the same.

The boundary was a formidable place to be in and even though she placed them in a circle of protection, there were a few creatures of the night that had the power to penetrate it. Vampires and lycanthropes were amongst them because they had the ability to jump high enough to get over the ring. From the sounds of things, they might be about to have a faceoff with one of them.

As the clambering grew closer, she realized that whatever or whoever it was headed straight for them. In a few more seconds they'd reach the boundaries of her circle and one of two things would happen. They would be either shocked and propelled backward, or they would leap right over its rim and land in the center.

The loud boom of a body slamming into the barrier told Fiona what she needed to know. She stood up and took one of the torches they placed around the fire to contribute to their lighting and walked to the edge of the circle. Holding the torch high to illuminate as much as she could, she gasped despairingly as she watched a woman with raven colored hair bending over an unconscious Tara who was in the arms of a young man who was also unconscious.

"Brandon, come quick!" she bellowed as she raised her hand and created an opening to go through.

With lightning speed, Brandon was on his feet and at her side. He stared with equal disbelief at the trio before him.

"I don't recognize the woman, but the unconscious man with his arms around Tara is Dennis," Brandon muttered.

"I thought as much," Fiona murmured as she moved cautiously forward.

Seeing Fiona and Brandon approach, Luella stood up and maintained a stance that was common of a sorceress who was under attack. Brandon remembered Maggie did the same on more than one occasion. It was easy to see why. Often times the energy that shot out from a magical being was powerful enough to knock them over. Standing with their feet planted shoulder wide apart and knees slightly bowed gave them the extra balance needed to withstand such a blow. This stance also gave a strong indication to the powers and abilities the woman possessed. She obviously could be a formidable opponent.

"No need to be defending yourself against us, lass," Fiona

said. "Since ya are running in the opposite direction from that place of rot and scurvy I'm assuming ya are rescuing these folks. Ya may be of evil persuasion, but since we're here to fetch them back home we won't harm the one who brought them to us."

Luella fought the desire to strike out and attack the woman whose words attacked her home. How dare she call Shadow Land a place of scurvy? She eyed the woman's aura and noticed a magical shield around her that would be difficult -but not impossible- to penetrate or remove. She was far too tired to battle so she let the comment slide, but if the whore dared make such comment again...

Ignoring Luella's thoughts that shouted into the night, Fiona hunched down over Tara and Dennis and studied their vitals. Dennis was just knocked unconscious from the blow of the shield. No real harm was done and he should be coming around shortly. Tara, on the other hand, was barely hanging onto life.

"I slammed into the shield and he slammed into me," Luella explained. "He was carrying her."

"Help me get them by the fire," Fiona barked. Pointing to Tara, she added, "Her first. He's fine and just needs time to come out of it. She's in serious condition." Looking directly at Luella, she asked, "What happened to her?"

Luella thought about the question for a moment and realized that she really didn't know the answer.

"She was that way when Joshua brought her back to the village. I never questioned it," she replied.

"Well," Fiona placed her hands on her hips and sighed. "If I had an idea what went on, I'd be better equipped to deal with it."

"I wish I could help you, but I never laid eyes on her until Dennis passed by the hut and insisted on dragging her along," Luella said impatiently. "Apparently, she's his sister."

"Aye, that she is and a very dear girl, to be sure," Fiona replied.

Brandon listened to the women conversing while he did his best to make Tara comfortable. His emotions were torn. He knew she wasn't Lucy. He knew she was Tara and she mistrusted him and ran away from him at the first opportunity. Even so, there was a part of his heart that cared deeply for her... that loved her. Seeing her like this tore at the very depths of his being. After all her trials, it couldn't end for her like this. What made it worse was the fact that he knew it was his fault. Had he not brought her back in time, she would still be healthy, robust and full of life. Thinking of the trauma he'd created in this beautiful young woman's life caused him extreme heartache and shame. He'd never forgive himself. How could he expect her to?

Being left to her own devices, Luella watched as she warmed herself by the fire. She was bone tired and would have loved to just lay down on one of the vacant bed rolls she spotted. They were situated close enough for the flames to warm the occupants, but far enough away that the heat and smoke weren't detrimental to their lungs. She scowled when she spotted the skinner in canine guise sleeping opposite her. Skinners weren't well thought of in the magical realm. Even their cousins, the hum-wolf, frowned upon them. It was obvious the woman was a witch of significant status and the man had an energy around him that spoke of dimensional travel. They made an unusual pair, but even so, she found it very odd that they would be traveling with the likes of a skinner.

Her eyes narrowed as the collie's lids fluttered open and it looked directly at her. It didn't take long for recognition set in. Without a moment's hesitation, he was up on his feet and running for his life. Since Fiona hadn't thought to close the opening to the circle of protection after bringing them in, he made a quick and easy escape.

"Where's he off to, I wonder," Brandon mused, more to himself than anyone else.

"Skinners are an unpredictable bunch," Luella said with a shrug.

Taken aback by her comment and the fact that he'd managed to fool them, Fiona and Brandon locked eyes. Nothing in the boundary was as it appeared to be and they'd do well to remember it.

TWENTY

Things were serious. Tara was clearly dying. To add to this dilemma, they were in the company of a sorceress who'd been raised in Shadow Land and had been living under the protection of Joshua who one of Balthazar's most prized and powerful soldiers.

After spending time with Fiona, Luella's defenses slowly lowered and she responded readily to the woman's questions. It was obvious Fiona was a woman with only the best intent for Dennis and his sister. Since she risked everything, including her life, to see Dennis to safety she saw the advantage in teaming up with her ideas, powers and skills.

"So, enchantress, I'm at your disposal," Luella offered.

"Aye, as I am you," Fiona replied with a sincerity that tugged at something deep inside the other woman.

"Can I ask ya how ya came to be living in Shadow Land?" Fiona asked. "Much of ya has changed, but I can still see that ya are human."

Surprised at the woman's boldness, Luella chewed on her words before answering. It was obvious she couldn't get away with lying and for some crazy reason it mattered to her what the enchantress thought of both her and her mother. She decided to tell the truth and hope for the best.

"My mother was a beautiful woman with a heart. She spent her younger years aspiring to be a powerful enchantress, but somewhere along the path she took a different direction and turned to sorcery instead. She was good at it," Luella said.

Fiona nodded that she understood. There was a fine line

between good magic performed by an enchantress and evil magic wielded by sorcery. There were occasions when she was called upon to wield just such, but it was always in defense against the dark side, never against good.

"One day when I was quite young," Luella continued, "she packed up a few meager belongings and told me we were going to seek our fame and fortune in another land. She brought me through the boundary, killing anything that stood in her way with her magic and walked boldly through the portal to Shadow Land as if she was queen. Balthazar was so impressed with her fearlessness and so taken by her beauty that he immediately placed her in the position of palace sorceress and head mistress." Luella sighed, "I was raised within those palace walls and enjoyed my life immensely until..."

Fiona remained quiet while she watched a myriad of emotions consume the raven-haired beauty. She could easily see why Dennis fell for the young woman. Not only was she lovely to look at, but under that evil exterior remained bits and pieces of the innocence and gentleness of a good-hearted human. Her true self hadn't been lost, simply buried and conditioned.

"Until the day Balthazar tired of her and cast her out," Luella continued. "He threw us away like trash." Her eyes welled up with tears that she quickly wiped away, hoping they hadn't been noticed. "Mother returned to the human realm, although I know not where. As for me, well I don't remember my life in the human realm. I was such a young girl when we left. Shadow Land was all I knew. Fortunately, Joshua found me appealing enough to take me under his protection. If he hadn't, I can't even imagine my fate."

A chill ran down Fiona's back every time Luella mentioned Joshua. She was aware he was the demon soldier who had seduced Tara into entering Shadow Land, but it was more than that. She decided to dig a little deeper.

"Tell me a little about this Joshua," Fiona said in a gentle, but commanding tone.

"Really?" Luella asked with surprise.

To have the enchantress interested in a soldier of Balthazar was unusual, but then this entire experience was unusual. Shrugging her shoulders, she obliged Fiona with as much information about her former lover and protector as she could remember. When she got to the part of explaining that Joshua had gone into the future and disguised himself in the body of a human named Dominic in order to lure Tara into giving him the thaumaturgic key, but failed in accomplishing this task, Fiona's blood froze. Her ears roared with the flow of her own adrenaline, making it difficult to hear the rest of Luella's tale of Joshua's plans for Dennis' demise.

"So, we meet again, devil man, or soon will," Fiona growled ferociously. "This time I'll be ready for ya!"

Luella looked confused, but said nothing.

"Fiona! Something's wrong," Brandon shouted as he held Tara's head in his lap and stroked her long auburn tresses. "Her breathing is too shallow."

Scowling, Fiona jumped from the cool, moss covered boulder she'd settled on while conversing with the young sorceress and leapt to Tara's side. Feeling her pulse both in her neck and in her wrist, she placed her cheek near her mouth to feel the power of her breathing. Brandon was right. Her breathing was far too shallow.

"We need to get out of here and back to my cottage so I can give her proper care," Fiona urged.

"Is there time?" Luella asked, fully aware that Tara hung on to only minutes of life.

"I don't know for sure, but what I do know is that we can do nothing for her here. I need supplies that I just don't have here and I'm sure ya didn't bring with ya," Fiona lamented.

"I brought nothing accept my wand and a small sack with a few of the basics. I didn't have much time to pack, plus I didn't want to be weighted down." Luella explained. "Had I known we were bringing a half dead woman with us perhaps I'd have packed differently."

Although Fiona scowled at Luella's last comment, she

understood her frustration. Having to bring Tara along certainly slowed them down. If he wasn't already on their trail, Joshua soon would be. No one double crossed a soldier of Balthazar and lived to tell about it. Luella's love for Dennis must be powerful. Otherwise, she'd never cross Joshua to save him. It was a lucky factor for Tara. Without Luella's help, it was clear Fiona and Brandon would have arrived too late. Even now, it still might be.

Fiona had an idea.

"How are ya at teleporting?" she asked.

"Who me?" Luella asked.

"Have ya ever done it?" Brandon joined in.

"Once, a long time ago," Luella replied reluctantly.

Fiona stroked her chin. "Do ya think ya could do it now?"

"Possibly," she said. "Where do you want me to go? I'm not familiar with the world outside of Shadow Land."

"Could ya follow me?" Fiona asked.

Luella thought about it for a moment before nodding her head.

"Good." Fiona smiled with relief. "Now, I have to ask one more thing of ya. Do ya think ya can teleport Dennis and yourself?"

"Oh," Luella sighed.

Her heart jumped. She wasn't even certain she could successfully teleport herself and now this woman asked her to teleport both herself and the man she loved. She didn't want to take the risk. Sadly, she shook her head.

"I can take him," Brandon volunteered.

Fiona completely forgot they had a traveler in their midst. He could take them all with much greater ease than they could take themselves. With him at the helm they were guaranteed to all end up in the same place.

Fiona reached over and grabbed Brandon's arm while she shot him a look of gratitude.

"Thank the gods that we're blessed with the presence of a seasoned traveler. Do ya think ya can get us all there safely?" she asked.

"Absolutely," Brandon said with conviction.

"What do we need to do?" This time it was Luella who took charge. "Tell me, and I'll see that it's done."

"Well," Brandon said as he looked around. "It will be easier to take you from one spot to another in the same time dimension than it would to go forward or backward, but even so we'll need to make sure your bodies are devoid of anything that might choke or restrain you in any way. The twirling can be pretty intense and sometimes objects like a necklace will wrap around so tight you can choke to death. Also, pockets need to be empty and," he looked at the full skirts of the women, "we'll need to tie your skirts down around your legs in some way."

"Done," exclaimed Luella and she set to work doing just that. "What about the horses?"

"Hmm," Fiona pondered, "I had not thought of them."

"I don't think it's wise to teleport them at the same time as we teleport, but I can come back for them," Brandon said.

Fiona's eyes lit up.

"This man was truly a gift!" she exclaimed. "'Tis a plan then."

"'Tis a plan," Brandon agreed, happy to be useful.

"A plan," Luella piped in as she smoothed the hair from Dennis' forehead.

"With any luck, he'll stay out until we're back at the cottage," Fiona said as she watched Luella's loving hands caress his temples.

"That would probably be for the best," Brandon joined in. "Tara had a pretty bad time of it, but we came back in time not just from one place to another."

"Even so, I agree it would be for the best," Luella sighed. "Should we do something as a precautionary insurance?"

"'Tis a good idea," Fiona replied.

Luella nodded and reached into the folds of her skirt. Pulling out her wand, she waived it slowly over Dennis' body, impressing Fiona with the ease in which she encased him with her magic shield.

Moving to Tara, Fiona did the same, but without a wand. This time Luella was impressed.

"Now, if everyone doesn't mind, I think it might be a good idea if we were to bind ourselves to each other. I've only teleported a group of people from one location to another a few times in my career as a traveler and both times I lost things on the way. I'd hate to lose a passenger," Brandon stated timidly. He wasn't sure how an enchantress and a sorceress would feel about being bound together.

Fiona looked long and hard at Luella while she studied the woman's reaction to Brandon's request. Once satisfied there would be no resistance given, she nodded her agreement.

****

Adam hovered in the shrubs that edged the woods surrounding the clearing while he studied the witchdoctor from a distance. He was still uncertain as to the safest approach. If he did it incorrectly, he could end up as the main course. He cursed the arrival of the sorceress. If she hadn't shown up he'd be back in Shadow Land earning the favor of Balthazar as he presented the enchantress and her companion by now. It was incredible luck that he hadn't died from the poison she laced the meat with. The dark gods must want him to succeed. It was that knowledge that gave him the renewed courage to continue on his quest. He was destined for great things; of this he was certain.

Still in canine form since four legs gave him much greater speed to outrun two legs, he picked up his ears and sniffed the air when the front door of the little cottage opened and the old magic man came out. The iron kettle he carried emitted the most tantalizing aroma. The glands in his mouth activated and saliva flowed from his jaw line.

If he waited until the witchdoctor ate he stood a better

chance of not being a meal himself. There was no denying if he chose to remain a canine his wait would be torturous. Should he revert to human form? The realization struck him that either way he'd be tortured by the aromatic fumes the light breeze wafted his way. It was hours since he'd eaten. He was hungry. He decided to stay as he was.

Time passed slowly while he suffered the aromas and view before him. The witchdoctor ate at an agonizing slow pace while reveling in the pleasures of his food. It was as if he knew he had an audience and made the best of it, licking his fingers and rolling the bones around in his mouth while he sucked out all of the nutritious marrow. The urge to pounce forward and start devouring the old man's fare was incredibly strong. Adam prayed to the dark gods for the strength to restrain himself.

When the magic man was finally finished he leaned back in a rickety looking chair and rubbed his belly. Now was the time. Moving stealthily across the green, he warily approached, stopping far enough away to have a good head start should his instincts be wrong.

"I wondered when you'd come out from behind that bush." the witchdoctor said while picking the meat from between his teeth with a twig. He never looked in Adam's direction as he spoke.

Adam sucked in air, completely shocked he'd been aware of his presence the entire time.

"You're a skinner, are you not?" he asked.

Adam nodded.

"Then shift back, will you? I never did like dogs," he said.

Not certain if it was a trap, Adam hesitated. What if the witchdoctor was baiting him? He'd stopped far enough away to outrun him as a canine with four legs, but as a human with only two... well, he wasn't sure. He knew all too well the transformation the witchdoctor was able to make and the speed that transformation provided. Deciding not to trust him, he shook his head.

"Listen you mangy mutt. If you don't do as I say, I'll turn

you into a rodent and send you off into a pack of your own and you won't have to worry about me devouring you. I have no doubt your flea-bitten relatives would consider you a fine meal. What do you think?" He tapped his chin thoughtfully, "A woodchuck? A squirrel? I know... a rat!"

Adam hesitated just a moment longer while he weighed the truth to the magic man's words. Deciding he meant his threat he saw no other choice, but to transform into his human identity. He did it with extreme reluctance.

Normally he'd return to the place of transformation to retrieve his clothes, but in this instance, that was miles away. He stood, cold and as naked as the day he was born under the scrutiny of the old witchdoctor's piercing eyes.

"You have nothing to worry about here," the old man laughed. "You're as scrawny as a road chicken. There is no benefit in making you my dinner. I'd leave the table hungry."

Adam silently thanked the dark gods, once again.

"Tell me," the magic man grunted as he shifted to a more comfortable position in his chair, "what is it Balthazar desires of me this time?"

Adam was amazed at the witchdoctor's perception. He'd only seen him at the palace once or twice and that was from the depths of a crowded room. Surely, he hadn't been recognized. Adam's mind raced. Should he tell him of Balthazar's plan to have him return to Shadow Land to bring life into the doppelganger and leave it at that? Or, should he go one step further and admit he'd witnessed the doppelganger being tended to at the campfire of the enchantress. Would the witchdoctor seek her out at the camp site and then take her back to Shadow Land or would he just turn his back on the situation and consider it too much trouble?

If he turned his back and Adam returned to Shadow Land without him, it meant Adam's hide. It wouldn't matter that the doppelganger was no longer in the village. It would only matter that he'd failed to complete his mission.

He decided to risk it and tell all.

The magic man listened, showing no emotion. When Adam

finally finished his story, he stood up and walked into the small cottage.

Adam moaned openly. He shouldn't have gambled like that. The dark gods were on his side up until now. Had they abandoned him? Was he left in a position of having to return to Shadow Land and accept his punishment or wander the human realm for the rest of his life, never happy, always alone?

He was cold. Night was upon them and the already cool temperature dropped even more. If he didn't find clothes soon he'd freeze to death. He decided to return to canine form. At least then he'd have fur to protect him. He was about to make the transition when the old witchdoctor came out of the little cottage wearing his traveling gear. Adam spotted what looked like clothing draped over one of his arms. He fervently hoped they were for him.

They were.

"I can't have you freezing to death before you show me where that camp is and I sure don't want to be traveling with a flea-bitten mutt," the witchdoctor said as he tossed the clothes at Adam's feet. "Put these on and be quick about it. It'll be dark soon and I want to cover as much ground as I can before darkness makes it harder to travel."

****

Joshua mounted his horse and turned to survey his men. He had a small party. It would be easier to search that way, plus it was all he could convince Balthazar to allow him. Luella's little stunt cost him dearly in the eyes of the king who had cast Luella out several years ago. If not for Joshua, the woman would have been long gone and not around to cause such trouble. It was imperative that Joshua retrieve the doppelganger. Balthazar made that perfectly clear. He'd also made no secret as to what awaited Joshua if he failed.

He growled as he thought of the punishment he planned for Luella when he caught up with her. She'd beg for death before he was done with her. It was a pity. She'd pleasured him greatly. No matter. Once the witchdoctor arrived and worked his magic on Tara, he'd take her as his mistress and Luella would be a wiped from his memory.

He thought about the fact that the Tara was a doppelganger instead of the real thing. It made more sense why she didn't pick up on his identity when he appeared in the body of Dominic. A true enchantress who'd already spent time in Shadow Land would have recognized the energy around him. It also explained why she lacked in the magic arena.

It was a boon for Joshua that Tara wasn't the true target for Balthazar, but the decoy to lead the target to him. Once he'd finished with her, Joshua planned on petitioning to have possession of her. In his mind Luella was already replaced.

TWENTY-ONE

The world was spinning and she needed it to stop. Her head hurt and her eyes burned. Everything was blurry. What was happening? Dennis. Did she dream he carried her off? It certainly felt real. Make the spinning stop. Everything moved too fast. Her stomach was queasy. She would vomit if the spinning didn't stop!

****

Fiona stood over Tara as Brandon laid her on the cowhide covered sofa in the great room of her quaint country cottage. Tara's long, shapely torso stretched from one end to the other. It was as if the sofa was created just for her.

Fiona marveled over every inch of the young woman's body. This was the first she'd seen Tara. The lass was an exact replica of Lucy. If Fiona hadn't known better, she might easily be fooled herself. It was easy to see why Brandon was so crushed when she didn't remember him. Had this girl lived in the same era as Lucy, she would have been considered a doppelganger, but since she was a creation of Fiona's handiwork and harbored the same soul that belonged to Lucy she was nothing short of a marvel. Could she be called a doppelganger? Since doppelganger meant a look alike, then yes... but she was so much more than that. She was, in reality, a product of magic mixed with nature.

"Do you think she'll remember you?" Brandon asked Fiona.

"She never knew me. She knew a future me. Maggie was well beyond the years I am now. I see no reason for her to recognize me," Fiona replied, "which means I'll have to earn her trust."

"Do you remember her?" he whispered.

"Only a little," she sighed. "As time goes on I remember less and less."

"You loved her," he said.

"I guess I did, but now I don't know the lass. She's a stranger that looks like Lucy," Fiona said with a sigh of sadness.

Brandon sighed.

"She not only forgot me, she doesn't trust me, "he reminded the enchantress. "She ran away from me, remember?"

"'Tis good her brother is here," Fiona stated flatly.

Her mind whirled about what possible action she could take to bring the young woman back to life. She gave her a bit of worm wort Luella happened to have in her pocket, but so far there was no sign of life returning to her.

Without warning Tara placed her hand to her forehead. She could hear people talking. Who were they? Did someone say Maggie? Maggie was dead.

She was going to vomit.

The vomit projected quite a distance out of Tara's mouth. It was as if she had a pump in her stomach working hard. Luella wrinkled her nose in disgust while the other three scrambled to make certain Tara didn't choke on it. When the heaving subsided, Fiona handed Dennis a bowl of warm water and a clean cloth and directed him to clean his sister up while she got a bucket of water and a large rag and set to cleaning up the floor. She heaved an enormous sigh relief and gratitude when she realized that her sofa escaped the onslaught with only the minutest amount settling on it.

"Tara, its Dennis. Tara," Dennis cooed as he wiped the vomit from her chin.

"Wi.... Wi...," she whispered.

"Brandon! Quick! Get me that big blue jar off the shelf in the kitchen," Fiona barked, excited by the signs of life from Tara.

"Did you hear her? Brandon, Fiona, did you hear her? I think she knows I'm here," Dennis bellowed with excitement.

"Yes, I did," Fiona replied.

Her mind was already whirling on what to do next. She managed to revive Tara, but not enough. Something more needed to be done. Remembering something she read in the book she stole from the witchdoctor, she ran to it and flipped the pages. If memory served her correctly, the solution to what was happening was within these pages.

Tara's mind whirled. Was she hearing correctly? Were Dennis and Brandon together in the same room? Why couldn't she see them? Her eyes refused to open, but her ears were functioning just fine. She could hear everything. And smell... she could smell the herbs in the room. It was such a lovely, aromatic smell that reminded her of the times she visited Maggie's house in the grove. She smiled at the thought.

"Look, look, she's smiling!" Dennis could hardly contain his excitement.

Luella walked up behind Dennis and studied the woman on the sofa. With her life force returning, so was her beauty. She really was a looker. She understood why Joshua was so taken with her.

Feeling Luella's hand on his shoulder, Dennis looked up.

"Do you see?" he asked. "She's smiling!"

"Yes my darling. I see. It certainly does look like she's smiling," she replied.

The excitement in the room stirred something deep within her. It was an indefinable sensation, something she felt was familiar yet buried so deep that it was years since she felt it. Possibly before she entered Shadow Land? Yes, definitely before she entered Shadow Land.

Tiny tears trickled down Luella's cheeks and she scowled while she quickly wiped them. She scoped the room to see if anyone noticed. What was this? What was happening to her? Whatever it was, she wanted it to stop! She was Luella, the great sorceress of Shadow Land. She didn't cry! She needed to take her mind of things.

Walking over to the table where Fiona was rapidly setting out herbs, she commanded, "Let me help."

Fiona stopped and looked Luella in the eye. After a moment of silence, their eyes continually locked, she nodded.

"I found a spell in this book that I stole from the witchdoctor that will bring her back to life," Fiona stated matter-of-factly. "I've never done it. I could use your help."

"You stole from the witch....," Luella caught herself.

She had no idea when or how Fiona managed to get into the witchdoctor's private domicile and steal from him, but it certainly put her in a new category in the sorceress' eyes. The enchantress was full of surprises. Very impressive. As for the spell, she knew it well, which was why she was so infuriated when Balthazar sent for the witchdoctor instead of calling for her when she was just a few doors away. Now she was being asked to help with that very same spell.

The joke is on you Balthazar, she thought with delight. A just payback, is it not?

"I know the spell. I can do it," Luella said matter-of-factly.

A gust of air flooded from Fiona's lungs and her legs threatened to collapse. All of the tension her body held dissipated at once and threw her off guard.

Seeing Fiona swaying, Brandon rushed to her side and grabbed her waist, "Whoa, are you okay?"

"Yes," Fiona replied in a voice that was just above a whisper. "I guess the relief threw me a bit off balance." Turning to Luella, she asked, "Are ya sure?"

"Oh yes. I've done it many times. I can do it," Luella said proudly.

"Gods be thanked," Fiona exclaimed. "What do ya need, lass? What can I do to help?"

Without a moment's hesitation, Luella rattled off the supplies she required in order to perform the spell. Fiona was overjoyed as she cross referenced some of them with the pages of the witchdoctor's book and found them to be a perfect match.

After lighting the herbs, she placed in a small cast iron cauldron and making sure they smoked heavily and then ordering everyone -including Fiona- to stand clear, Luella stood over Tara's body and spoke her incantation.

Fiona stood in the corner and compared Luella's words to those on the pages of the spell book. She marveled over the ease that the sorceress performed a spell that looked incredibly complicated.

"Omra-ordela-tumutra-odayyyyyy," Luella chanted over and over again while she weaved her hands into a pattern in the air over Tara's chest.

The smoke from the burning herbs intensified and visibility around Luella and Tara was almost impossible.

The sound of Tara coughing and gasping for air permeated the room. Luella's chanting grew stronger and more forceful. Then, there was silence.

No one moved.

Luella placed one hand over Tara's eyes and another over her heart.

"Rise," bellowed the sorceress.

The smoke cleared as fast as it appeared, allowing the others to see that Luella was already looking at a beautifully vibrant and alert Tara sitting quietly on the sofa. Gasping with relief, Dennis rushed forward and fell to his knees. Cradling her legs in his arms, he laid his head in her lap and allowed his fears to release in the form of tears.

Tara caressed her brother's head, lovingly.

"You're safe!" she said with wonder.

Dennis popped his head up with surprise.

"Me?" he replied with surprise.

Her incredulous statement brought chuckles throughout the room.

"I don't understand the humor," Tara admitted.

"She wouldn't," Luella interjected. "Part of the spell is to make them forget certain things. All that she'll remember is what happened the day she arrived or thereafter, before she became... err... ill."

"I was ill?" Tara questioned.

"You were very ill, but you're fine now and that's all that matters," Dennis exclaimed.

"Really? I don't... hmmm... I feel fine," Tara mused aloud.

"'Tis wonderful dear," Fiona said. Her voice was smooth and gentle as she set the witchdoctor's book down and walked forward.

Tara looked at Fiona with confusion. There was something familiar about her,

"Have we met?" Tara asked.

Looking around the room, she noticed a familiarity about it as well. It resembled Maggie's little cottage. It had the same smell, the same feel, even the same layout. "Where am I?"

"Ya are in me home and ya are most welcome," Fiona replied.

"Your home?" Tara looked around. "It looks so familiar."

"Aye, it would at that," Fiona chuckled.

Tara sucked in air at the shock of the woman's comment. She sounded just like Maggie!

"Tara, do you remember me?" Brandon asked as he stepped forward.

Tara sunk back into the sofa.

"Of course I do, Brandon," she said with reluctance. "How did you find me? Did these people help you?"

"Why did you run away from me like that?" Brandon asked.

He knew there were more important matters to tend to, but he just couldn't resist asking her.

"You know why," she replied.

His heart grew heavy as he said, "You don't trust me."

"Should I?" she asked.

"Yes, ya should," Fiona interjected.

"Yes, you should," Dennis added. "Brandon played a vital role in our salvation. If it weren't for him, we would be in the boundary fighting off Joshua or some other demon creature... maybe even the witchdoctor." He turned to Luella, "You said you thought the skinner was on his way to fetch him, right?"

Luella closed her eyes and nodded her head.

"Skinner? What's a skinner?" Tara asked.

"'Tis a shape shifter," Fiona explained.

Luella expanded on Fiona's explanation, "It is the cousin to the hum-wolf, which is part human, part wolf. The hum-wolf always looks the same. The skinner can shift from human to animal at will. This particular one happened to live in Shadow Land. I knew him. He was assigned the task of bringing the witchdoctor to Shadow Land so he could do for you what I just did."

She couldn't help puffing her chest out with self-importance. She'd performed a miracle, after all.

Tara saw Luella for the first time. She looked the woman over carefully. Her rich, gleaming, thick raven tresses fell well below a waist that couldn't have been more than twenty inches in diameter. Her narrow waist accentuated the round, fullness of her ripe breasts and perfect hips. Full, naturally ruby lips and rosy cheeks against porcelain skin brought out the depth of her sky-blue eyes. She was every man's dream of the ideal woman. Tara was duly intimidated. She locked eyes with Luella. They were mesmerizing. There was something mysterious and intimidating about her. The fact that she knew a, what was it called... a skinner... didn't sit well with her.

Tara's look of surprise was barely concealed when her brother walked up behind the raven-haired beauty and put his arm around her in a manner that spoke of familiarity. Luella smiled, laid her head against his chest and patted his hand affectionately while never releasing Tara's eyes.

"Have we met?" Tara asked, finally regaining her senses.

"Not officially," Luella replied.

Did Tara detect a hint of humor in her tone? She looked accusingly at Dennis. Who was this woman and why fondled her so affectionately?

"Let me introduce the loves of my life to each other. Tara, this is Luella. Luella... Tara," Dennis volunteered.

Although shocked at Dennis' admission, Tara did her best to maintain composure and etiquette. She smiled the warmest smile she could muster and extended her hand to Luella who took it with equal warmth. The sensation that shot up Tara's arm when their hands clasped stunned her, but she did her best to disguise her surprise. She hoped she succeeded.

Brandon stepped forward pulling Fiona gently behind him.

"This special lady may also feel familiar to you," he began. "You knew her at an older age in at different time, but never-the-less, you knew her. Allow me to introduce Fiona O'Shea. You knew her as Maggie."

Brandon couldn't tell who gasped the loudest at his introduction, Tara or Dennis. Both were equally surprised.

"You never told me that," Dennis gaped.

"You never asked," Brandon chuckled. The stunned looks on both sibling faces made him instantly regret his joke. "That was in poor taste. I'm sorry."

Fiona stepped forward.

"Why don't I make us a big pot of tea and we can all get to know each other a little better." She looked from person to person and added, "We have a lot to discuss."

Brandon stepped forward and asked, "Do you need me here while you explain? I should go back for the horses before Joshua or anyone else gets to them first."

Fiona hesitated. She would have preferred to have everyone present, but Brandon had a point. The longer they waited to go back for the horses the riskier it became.

She nodded and said, "I'd have preferred ya stayed, but ya are right. Go, but please hurry."

"Do you want company?" Luella asked anxiously.

She was suddenly uncomfortable with the emotions that were circulating the room. They were having a powerful effect on her. She wanted time to clear her head.

"It could be dangerous," Brandon admitted. "You felt how we swirled during the transport. I don't know what will happen with two horses. I've never transported multiple animals before."

"All the more reason you need me with you," Luella replied. "I can hold one and you hold the other."

"She's right," Fiona stated in a tone that seemed more command than statement.

Dennis sighed. It was settled. Luella would return to the boundary with Brandon. He wasn't sure how he felt about that. He knew she was a sorceress and very capable of taking care of herself. In fact, she was better equipped to do so than he, but even so, his male instinct was to protect her and keep her safe, something he couldn't do if he stayed behind. He looked from Tara to Luella and then back to Tara. He wanted to go, but he knew he needed to stay.

Sensing his dilemma Fiona laid her hand on his arm.

"We left the horses behind in the first place because it was dangerous to combine humans with them in the transport," she said softly. "It would seem foolish for a bunch of humans to return to bring them here."

"I see your point," Dennis sighed. He pulled Luella close and kissed her moist lips passionately, heedless of the audience they had. "Stay safe," he whispered and he hugged her close.

Those unfamiliar tears threatened her again and Luella pulled away a little more forcefully than intended. She was aware of his surprise, but she didn't care. Her need to be free from the suffocating emotions of the room overpowered all else.

"Let's go," she barked.

Dennis' eyes told of his confusion as he watched Luella stand next to Brandon. The two held hands, closed their eyes, and disappeared into a swirling wind tunnel.

Tara watched in awe.

They arrived about a quarter mile off their mark, but that turned out to be a good thing. Luella could smell the stench of the witchdoctor. He was in the area and probably at their camp site.

She knew that if she could smell him, then he could also smell her. Grabbing a plant that resembled skunk cabbage, she rubbed it all over herself and bade Brandon do the same. Disgusted and certain he'd vomit from the stench, he obliged. He wondering if the horses would even let them near them smelling like skunk.

Moving with the stealth of a mountain cat, Luella led Brandon along the rocky ledge that lined the clearing where they camped. The skunk cabbage did the trick and for all appearances it seemed that their presence went undetected by the witchdoctor. They watched as he inspected the area. He kicked over rocks and dug his hands into the soil, holding clumps of it close to his nose for inspection.

"They're not gone long," he stated, more to himself than to Adam. "They left their horses behind. That can be for only one reason. They thought them too difficult to take through the portal." Smiling to himself he added, "They were correct."

Slapping his hands together to shed as much of the dirt from them as he could, he began walking, "Come boy. If we hurry, we can catch them before they reach the portal and we can take the credit for their arrival."

Adam shook his head. That was exactly what he'd wanted. Now, the witchdoctor would get all of the glory.

Brandon and Luella watched in silence as the witchdoctor and the young man, who Luella knew to be the skinner named Adam, walked directly beneath them and onto the path that led deep into the woods. When they were out of sight and Brandon started to stand up, she grabbed him and yanked him back down with remarkable force. Shaking her head, she silently mouthed that they needed to wait to make sure he was truly gone. Realizing her wisdom, he sat back on his heels. After what seemed like hours -but was in fact only minutes- she was satisfied and motioned him to follow her.

The horses reacted to their stench just as Brandon suspected. Collecting them was no easy task. When they managed to finally have them in place, he began the transport, eager to be free from the oppressive energies of the boundary.

Luella, on the other hand, was sad to say good-bye. Her life would never be the same. She knew it. She accepted it. She created this situation by her own actions, but had she done the right thing? She was human, true, but she'd lived in Shadow Land for so long, could she survive in the human realm?

Time would tell.

****

Joshua arrived at the camp just in time to see Luella, Brandon and their horses swirl into a wind tunnel and disappear. He felt the blood in his veins heat with anger until his body felt on fire. This was the ultimate insult! He'd thought she left with that mortal, Dennis. That was bad enough, but to cast him aside for the very traveler who participated in his demise while in the future, well, she would pay. Brandon would pay. Dennis would pay. Tara would also pay, but differently. Once Balthazar was done with her, she'd be his slave for as long as he chose. The way he felt right now that would be a very, very long time.

Closing his eyes, he focused on Tara. Her life force flowed again. Good, that made her easier to track.

TWENTY-TWO

She'd witnessed and learned so much over the past months that the incredulous story she was hearing made perfect sense. Tara was full of emotion as she listened to Fiona's speech pattern and watched her body language. There was no denying the resemblance. Dennis, on the other hand, hadn't spent the hours in study of the mystical arts like Tara and he required a more in-depth explanation. Even with all that had happened he had a difficult time grasping things.

"Never mind," Tara said as she patted her brother's hand. "It'll all make sense someday."

"How are ya feeling, truly?" Fiona asked Tara.

"I feel fantastic," she replied. "It's nothing like when I first arrived. I was off from the minute we...err... landed and I grew progressively weaker. Except for, let me think, there was a time when I felt a little more like myself, but I can't put my finger on just when it was."

Realizing the risk in encouraging Tara to remember the time when she was in Joshua's grasp, Fiona quickly changed the subject.

"Ya could be her twin, ya know," Fiona said warmly. "I wonder if I was such a close match."

Tara studied Fiona closely. She was younger by at least thirty years, but there was a very strong resemblance. She did her best to add years to Fiona's facial expression and a few pounds to her physique and nodded.

"Yes, I can see it," Tara said with delight. "I think if we were able to get our hands on some photos of Maggie in her younger years we'd have a pretty good match."

"At least I got something right," Fiona said with a smile.

Tara frowned.

"You're being far too hard on yourself, Fiona," she said lovingly. "From all you taught me and all I remember from reading and even what I know instinctively, the veil of forgetfulness is potent. Not to mention the friction created by Balthazar while babies come to life. I think that it was a miracle you managed as well as you did. Think about it. We both found our way to the right house in the right area at about the same time. Then we found each other and made friends and I became your student. I think that if Dominic hadn't shown up and thrown a monkey wrench in it all, we would have succeeded."

"A monkey wrench?" Fiona said with confusion.

"Sorry, I forgot. That's a term you enjoyed in the future. It means to mess things up," Tara chuckled.

"Oh," Fiona laughed.

Tara grew somber when she asked, "You don't remember the future, do you?"

"Some," Fiona replied, "but not much." She shrugged her shoulders, "'Tis probably for the best."

"I loved you," Tara muttered.

"I loved ya too. That much I do remember," she lied for she barely remembered Tara. Standing up and stretching in a catlike manner, Fiona added, "Now, if ya will all excuse me, I'd like to check on me Lucy."

"Can I join you?" Tara stood up in anticipation.

"And me?" Dennis joined in.

Fiona studied the siblings closely, uncertain what to do. With the exception of Brandon, Lucy's resting place was kept secret. The more people who knew of it, the more dangerous her situation became.

"I'm not sure about that," Fiona shook her head. "I have kept her safe because I have kept her resting place a secret."

"She's me, isn't she? If she's not then she's my great aunt who I look exactly like," Tara's voice expressed her need to go with Fiona.

Hesitating and insecure about her decision, Fiona nodded and motioned for them to follow. As they reached the door, she stopped short.

"I want to explain something to ya both and I hope ya take this the right way," Fiona said. "Although ya are me blood and I know and love ya as one would their blood, the body that lies in that cave is the body of me niece and protégé in this lifetime and I know and love her more. If one hint of her whereabouts is leaked from either one of your lips ya will live to regret, it. Have I made meself clear?"

Tara and Dennis nodded in shocked unison.

Although startled at Fiona's threat, Tara could understand the reasoning behind it. Instead of being hurt or upset, it made her love the Irish enchantress even more.

Although the sun shone brilliant in the sky, the entrance and long tunnel that led to Lucy's resting place was pitch black. Tara squeezed Dennis' hand in an effort to hold back her panic as they listened carefully for Fiona's footsteps to lead them in the right direction.

Dennis fought back a horrific case of claustrophobia as he felt the stone tunnel get smaller and smaller. Thankfully, just as he thought he'd lose control and panic they reached the opening of a very large and roomy cave. He watched Fiona move across the cool, well-trodden dirt floor with the torch she lit while he waited for his nerves to settle down. Fiona lit two more torches and the cave came alive. His mouth fell open while he watched his sister slowly approach the lifeless body of a woman who could easily be her! With the exception of the hair style, one could tell no difference between the two. It made him uneasy and he backed himself as tightly as he could against the stone wall. Were it not for the fact that he'd have had to brave the pitch black tunnel alone, he'd have fled the cave.

"She looks dead," he whispered.

"She's not dead. She's just waiting for her soul to be returned to her," Fiona whispered lovingly as she patted Lucy's cheeks lovingly. "If you look closely, you can see she still breathes."

Tara drew close to the body of her double and lowered her face to within a half-inch of her nose. The faintest of breath tickled her cheek. Standing with a start, she looked at Fiona.

"Can I touch her?" she asked timidly.

Fiona scowled, but nodded her okay. She wasn't sure about the confusion the soul these two women shared would experience with them both in the cave. It was something she hadn't considered when she brought them with her; having only considered the secrecy of the cave at the time. Now, seeing Tara standing over Lucy, she questioned her wisdom in allowing them to join her. In fact, bringing Tara to her home may have even been wrong, since she had no idea how powerful the spell Luella cast was or if it would last. She intended on sending Tara back to the future as quickly as possible so risk of the soul's confusion would cease. Instead, she foolishly brought her here. Her stupidity could mean the death of both girls. Perhaps allowing Tara to touch Lucy wasn't such a good idea after all.

She jumped forward to try to grab Tara's arm and stop her, but was too late. The damage was done. As Tara laid her hand on her sleeping double's cheek a strange pulling sensation wracked at her chest. She doubled over as a searing pain pierced through her.

"What's happening?" she cried. "My heart... my heart feels like its stopping."

Dennis leapt forward, concern for his sister overpowering the fear that had temporarily ripped his senses. "Tara!" he shouted as he scooped her in his arms just before her legs gave out and her body slumped.

Fiona stood horrified by the scene in front of her. What had she done? This couldn't be happening! Her eyes moved to Lucy just as the young woman's chest heaved and her body gave an enormous jerk.

"Gods preserve us," she yelped, "what have I done?"

Slapping her hands to her cheeks she watched in horror at the bodies of both Tara and Lucy as they twisted and writhed in obvious agony.

"Fiona, help!" Dennis cried. It was clear his panic was getting the better of him.

After her own brief moment of panic, Fiona managed to pull it together enough to once again take charge.

"Dennis, ya are going to have to go back to the house and get a few things for me." When he didn't respond she continued, "Dennis, are ya listening?"

Dennis slowly raised his eyes from his sister. His face was flooded with tears. "Yes," he squeaked.

"Good. When ya get there, I want ya to bring back me leather pouch, a jug of water and the witchdoctor's book. Can ya do that?" she asked.

He was too numb to do much more than nod.

Fiona grabbed Tara from his arms and laid her gently onto the floor.

"Get going then! Time is against us!" she barked as she set forth aligning Tara's body as closely with Lucy's body as she could.

She wished for another table so they would be level with each other, but would have to make do with things the way they were.

Dennis never noticed the darkness, nor did he feel panic from the cramped tunnel as he raced down it as best he could. He was too consumed with panic of a different sort.

****

After tethering the horses in Fiona's small barn and seeing to their wellbeing, Brandon followed Luella into the cottage. It was empty. They split up. Luella checked the small rooms that branched off the great room while Brandon checked the grounds.

There was no one in sight. Where could they have gone?

Brandon was just about to go back inside when he spotted Dennis running wildly toward him. Barely able to breathe, it took Dennis a little longer than everyone would have liked to get his story out, but he finally managed.

Luella was livid. How could an enchantress be so foolish? She stomped around Fiona's great room. Her anger was barely concealed. It was Brandon who came to Fiona's defense.

"Let's not forget that this isn't something Fiona is adept at. She has never performed that spell. Perhaps if she was warned about the consequences, she might have been more careful."

"Oh," Luella spun on him, "so now it is I who is to blame?"

Brandon instantly regretted his words. Angering a sorceress who was raised in Shadow Land wasn't the wisest thing to do.

Realizing the situation, Dennis stepped in.

"He didn't mean that, honey, did you?" he said as he looked directly at Brandon. Brandon shook his head to confirm just that. "You see? You misunderstood."

"Well, then explain it to me please, because, from where I stand, it sounded like a clean-cut accusation!" Luella hissed.

Dennis' mind reeled. This couldn't be happening. His sister lay writhing on the floor of a cave next to her body double and all these two could do was argue.

"Please," he begged. "Please stop. I need you... we need you to keep your heads and work together. Tara's life is on the line here."

"Yes," Luella's chest heaved and her breathing was erratic as she struggled with emotions that were foreign to her, "it is."

"Please," Dennis grabbed her hands and held them close to his chest. "Please," he whispered, "help."

She was overwhelmed with the emotion that flooded forth. Tears that she struggled to subdue gushed forth like a dam unleashed. Nodding her head vigorously, she grabbed a few things from Fiona's supply, added them to the supply list Dennis recited and ran out of the door.

Dennis and Brandon followed close at her heels. Both men were duly impressed by the speed the woman possessed. As they neared the entrance to the cave, Dennis stopped. Fiona made a big issue about his not divulging the location of the cave. He was at a loss as what to do.

"Why have we stopped?" Luella barked. "We don't have a lot of time. Where is she?" she asked, spinning around looking for some sort of sign.

"I don't know what to do. Fiona didn't want to show the spot to me or Tara. She threatened us about telling anyone else. I don't know how she'll react to my bringing two more," Dennis admitted.

Brandon pushed past Dennis and barked over his shoulder, "She's already shown it to me. Come on. We don't have time for this. We'll worry about Fiona and her secrets later."

After taking a brief second to digest the realization that someone other than he and Tara saw the hiding place, he kicked his body into motion and caught up with Luella, who was close at Brandon's heels.

Brandon had forgotten about how suffocating and black the tunnel was and was relieved to finally reach the cave. He stumbled into the open space and made directly for Tara.

"How is she?" he asked with the same sense of urgency that Fiona felt.

"Which one?" Fiona asked accusingly.

Taken aback by her comment, Brandon stopped.

"Both," he said quickly.

He had to admit to himself that he was asking about Tara. He looked long and hard at them both. He had feelings for them both. They both had qualities that were similar, yet separate. Why would he worry about one and not the other? He reasoned it was because it was Tara who was his comrade through a tremendous amount of peril. There was a unique bond between them, a bond that couldn't be explained. It had to be experienced. He knew that Tara felt it too. She was just still too clouded with trauma and suspicions to identify it.

"They're both in jeopardy," Fiona continued. "Did ya bring the supplies?"

"I have them," Luella volunteered as she leapt from the darkness of the tunnel. She'd experienced dark, tight and airless tunnels in her early days as a student of her mother's, but this one had to have been one of the worst.

Fiona looked at the sorceress with surprise and then relief. She settled her eyes on Dennis long enough to give a smile of thanks before motioning Luella to her side.

Dennis' body relaxed. He was grateful to have done the right thing. He felt confident that the combination of the powers of an enchantress and a sorceress was a winning one. The two magic women put their heads together and had a plan of action in no time. Luella refrained from scolding Fiona, aware that enchantress had reprimanded herself enough.

Fiona stood at Lucy's head and Luella knelt at Tara's head. In unison, they held their hands in the air and spoke an incantation. As they repeated it over and over again, they reached such synchronicity that their voices sounded as one. When the women stopped the cave was so quiet Dennis was certain he could hear the bugs walking on the walls before his ears started to roar from the stress and anticipation. It had to work. It just had to work.

The blood on Brandon's knuckles surprised him. He had no idea he'd clenched his teeth against them until the relief of seeing Luella helping Tara up prompted him to pull his fist from his mouth.

"Steady," Luella urged. "Go slow."

"What happened?" Tara's voice was shaky.

"Why don't we get out of here and I'll explain it to you," Luella urged.

One by one they filed back into the stifling blackness that led to the outer world. Only Fiona stayed behind. She stood at the head of her beloved Lucy while the tears rolled down her cheeks. Looking at the young woman's long lashes as they rested against her pale cheeks she sighed.

"I'm so sorry lass. What a stupid, stupid thing I did. 'Twas lucky the sorceress was here." Fiona emitted a sarcastic chuckle, "A sorceress from Shadow Land had to come to the aide of the almighty enchantress. How do ya like that?" She stoked Lucy's lifeless cheek and kissed it gently. "'Twill all work out me darling girl. It may not have worked like we hoped, but at least we got your future self-back living again. I'll figure out the rest. Not to worry. I promise. I'll figure out the rest."

When she was satisfied that all was well once again with her charge, she extinguished the torches and entered the passage. She was grateful for the night vision the gods blessed her with. It was a birthright that was handed down from generation to generation. Lucy had it too. She hadn't had time to get to know Tara to discover what traits she shared with Lucy, shared other than looks and soul.

TWENTY-THREE

"The doppelganger is an exact double of a person. They're an extension of the person, but there's a difference. Here, read this," Luella said as she pushed the open book in front of Dennis and pointed to a paragraph. "I was never good at explaining things. I'd make a horrible teacher."

Dennis focused on the words.

"A ghostly double of a living person, especially one that haunts its fleshly counterpart," he read.

"I'll admit that even though that's the true definition of a doppelganger, little by little the meaning has turned toward a label for a person's twin or double. So, in a sense, you're her doppelganger and she's yours, but, in truth, you're not. Especially since you're both sharing the same soul. I've never heard of doppelgangers sharing the same soul," Luella said.

"If her soul is attached to me, what happens to her?" Tara asked timidly. She wanted to know, but was afraid of the answer.

"She'll be fine," Fiona piped in as she entered the little house. "She's fine and she'll be fine. Not to worry."

Tara expelled the air she didn't know she was holding in and smiled.

"That's good news," she said.

"And you?" Fiona asked as she laid the back of her hand on Tara's cheek. "Are ya fine?"

Without thinking, Tara grabbed Fiona's hand and held it against her flesh for a brief moment before kissing it lightly and releasing it.

"I'm perfectly fine. Thank you," Tara replied.

Surprised by Tara's actions, Fiona smiled warmly and

walked to the fireplace where an iron tea kettle filled with piping hot water hung near flames that danced excitedly.

"I keep a never-ending pot of soup simmering," Fiona informed the room. "I think I'd like a bowl and a cup of tea. Would anyone like to join me?"

Since it was quite some time since anyone had eaten, they all readily agreed. It soon became a joyous event. Each person was assigned a task, from getting more wood from the woodpile for the fireplace to stirring the soup heating on the pot belly stove to setting the table with some of the loveliest china Tara had ever seen. Smiles and laughter were abundant.

"Can I ask you something?" Tara's words were soft as she spooned a large chunk of carrot into her mouth, chewing quickly so that she could continue.

"What's that, love?" Fiona replied.

"Why was Lucy's soul sent to my body in the future? Can you tell me or is that against the rules?" she asked.

"Well," Fiona mused, "I don't rightly know if it is against the rules, but I seem to have been breaking rules much worse than this along the way, so I'm going to tell ya."

Pleased with the woman's response, Tara and the others perked up to listen.

"Well," Fiona began, "it started with that fool sister and her nonsense." Turning to Tara, she continued, "Lucy has a sister. Her name is Alana and she's nothing like either one of ya, my dear."

"I know. We've met," Tara replied.

"You have?" Dennis interjected.

"She's marrying Mark," Tara said flatly.

"What? She's from here?" Dennis roared.

"It's a long story that I'll be happy to tell you later, okay?" Tara looked at Fiona, "I'm sorry. Please continue."

"Well, the sisters were both me students, but Alana was jealous of Lucy. Lucy was a far better student. She was me star student in fact and a powerful witch. 'Tis a shame ya remember so little. All her memories are in her soul if ya could just unlock them."

Tara looked down at her hands, suddenly embarrassed about her inability to remember.

"Now don't be letting that get to ya," Fiona said soothingly. "I had a dickens of a time with that veil meself! I've a newfound respect for those who manage to shed it completely. Anyway, Alana hooked up with a wizard who lives on the mountain side. He's not one hundred percent evil, but he's not all that good either. He and I rarely agree." Fiona took a sip of her tea before continuing, "He was in possession of a thaumaturgic crystal stone that's a magical key. If in the right hands it has the power to control the portal between our realm and Shadow Land no matter what century of past or future. Balthazar - he's the evil dark lord," she said as she looked at Luella, nodded and smiled, "heard about the thaumaturgic crystal and now he wants it. That crazy Alana gave the crystal to Lucy without telling the truth about how she came by it or what it was for. She asked Lucy to keep it secret from everyone, including me. She claimed it would destroy me if I got my hands on it."

Tara gasped, "Is that true?"

Luella laughed and interjected, "Hardly. If an enchantress touches the stone, it is bound to serve good just like if a sorcerer touches the stone it is bound to serve evil."

"Exactly," Fiona agreed. "Alana decided to walk on the side of evil. From what I understand she intended to take it to Balthazar herself after she programmed it to respond to her and only her, but the wizard who gave it to her to protect for him decided he wanted it back. The foolish chit thought that if she placed it in Lucy's hands it would throw him off and give her the time she needed to discover the right spell to cast." Fiona shook her head, "My powerful Lucy held that stone in her hand, felt its connection to evil and cast the evil out, binding the stone to her. Without realizing it she cast the spell her idiot sister was searching for. Like I said, she's me star pupil," Fiona said with pride.

"So, what did she do with the stone after that?" Tara asked impatiently. There was something she couldn't explain stirring within her and she felt certain it was connected to the stone.

"That's the million-dollar question," Fiona replied. "Balthazar discovered Lucy was in possession of the key and he ordered her kidnapped and taken to him. In order to keep the key safe, she cast a spell that caused her to forget its whereabouts. Unfortunately, by the time Balthazar was through with trying to force her to remember she forgot a lot of other stuff too. She remembered me alright, and most of her magic, but she forgot the whereabouts of the key, she forgot the spell she'd cast to make her forget its whereabouts and she forgot who her pa was. She even forgot that charming man over there." Fiona pointed to Brandon, who nodded and smiled sadly. "He's the love of her life and her betrothed, my dear."

Tara gasped.

"One story at a time," Fiona continued with a smile. "We'll get to that one soon enough." Sipping once on her tea she scowled, "Bah, me tea is cold. These dishes are lovely, but they don't keep things hot. I much prefer me old mug. Anyway, Lucy and I did some scrying for the key, but spell was too strong and the connection was lost. We even tried to astral travel to the time when she hid it."

"Really?" Brandon exclaimed.

"I never thought of asking ya. We should have asked ya. I had no idea ya was so gifted as a traveler," Fiona said apologetically as she smiled in Brandon's direction. Heaving a sigh, she continued, "We were unsuccessful. So when we learned of Alana's travel to the future we came up with this scheme to place ourselves in new bodies in the future with the intention of finding the key before Alana. It being far enough after this lifetime, the spell she cast would have weakened and have little effect. What we hadn't counted on was the veil of forgetfulness."

"Wow. You cast a spell on yourself. I heard Joshua had brought a human witch into the village who cast a spell on herself to make her forget, but I thought it was a bunch of rubbish. It was true! I've never met a witch who had the nerve to do such a dangerous thing," Luella said.

"Joshua?" Tara was puzzled. The name sounded familiar. Who was he? She should know him.

"Yes, Joshua. He's the one who brought you back to Shadow Land. He thought you were Lucy with amnesia so he convinced you he was your fiancé," Luella spat. She was angrier at him than her, "Since you're who you're and things were the way they were, you believed him."

"I remember. Yes, I remember. I believed him because he felt so familiar," Tara said as she strained her mind to try to understand why she felt like she knew a man she'd never met.

"He felt familiar to you because he was," Luella explained. After capturing the attention of everyone at the table, she continued, "Joshua was sent to the future to get you and the key back. They thought that, since Lucy were the lover of a time traveler, he'd teleported her there. It never dawned on anyone that Lucy would cast a spell for her soul to be reborn like she did. Thinking you were Lucy and knowing she'd been a captive of Shadow Land and may have seen him on occasion he assumed a completely different identity. He went from this dark haired stud to a blonde haired god." Luella laughed, "He'd never allow himself to be plain. Not with that ego." She took a moment to look at each face before continuing. "You killed the body he occupied, but you didn't kill him. You see, we do something similar to what you did to revive the soul, but I think we do it better." Luella looked at Fiona while making her statement.

Fiona sucked in air at Luella's egoist comment, but nodded her agreement. This wasn't a time for an enchantress and a sorceress, both well matched in skills, to start bickering. Besides, Luella was right, they did do it better than she did. She could hardly call herself skilled at it.

"Perhaps we can discuss your methods at a later time," Fiona said gently.

"It would be my pleasure," Luella stated, doing her best to sound earnest. These people were, after all, a vital part of her new existence and she wanted to fit in and be liked. If sharing a few Shadow Land secrets was all it took then the dark gods be praised.

Dennis jumped into the conversation.

"I know the story," he said with pride. "She told me enough of it when she helped us escape." Turning to Tara, he continued, "Sis, Joshua and that demon fella, Dominic, are one in the same. That's why he felt so familiar to you."

Tara half screamed and half wailed at the realization that she once again fell prey to Dominic.

Apathetic to Tara's distress, Luella continued, "If I hadn't gotten you out of there when I did, Joshua would have killed Dennis and then petitioned Balthazar to turn you over to be his slave, amongst other things."

Tara could listen no more. Pushing her chair away from the table with such force it almost toppled over, she leapt up and ran outside. She needed to be alone, away from the woman from Shadow Land, away from the memories of Dominic, Joshua, and all that had happened.

"Tara!" Dennis shouted as he followed, but still remaining far enough away to allow her the sensation of space that he knew his sister always required when she was genuinely upset.

Her chest heaved with emotions that threatened to pour forth in a torrent.

"I just need a moment," she shouted back at him. "Just a moment, please."

Brandon stood next to Dennis with a look of concern.

"Do you think she's heard more than she can handle?" he asked.

"She'll be alright," Dennis replied, "but I have to admit it was a lot for me so I can only imagine how it hit her."

"Yeah," Brandon agreed.

****

Morning came and Tara still sat beneath the apple tree at the far edge of Fiona's garden. Fiona paced the porch, stopping on occasion to shade her eyes from the brilliant sun and inspect the young woman's position.

"That there is a trait she brought with her from Lucy," Fiona observed. "She can sit and sit and sit so perfectly still for hours... days I'd bet." She turned to Brandon who'd eased himself into a sturdy rocking chair next to her. "'Tis a sign of a skilled witch, ya know."

"No, I didn't know," he replied

"Well, now ya do." Fiona smiled. "I hate to interrupt her, but I think ya should be getting her back to the future. 'Tis not safe to keep her here."

"I don't know if it is all that safe keeping her in the future either. Especially without you," Brandon replied.

"That as it may be, she can't stay, I have me Lucy to think about as well as Tara. If she stays and dies, then Lucy could die too."

"If she goes back to the future and dies?" Brandon asked, already knowing the answer.

"Then Lucy comes alive again. Like I did," she said flatly.

"I see," he mused uncomfortably.

Fiona stood in front of Brandon and looked him in the eye.

"Your Lucy is here and she loves you very much and we'll find a way to make her remember that," Fiona said as she nodded her head toward Tara. "Tara is not Lucy. She's a messed-up woman who mistrusts ya and has even less memories about ya than Lucy. I think ya need to re-evaluate your loyalties my man."

"I love them both. I can't help it. They both carry those qualities that I fell in love with, and they both have such unique and endearing qualities of their own." Brandon moaned.

"Well, if ya love them both, then it seems to me ya would want to do what's best for them both. That would be to separate them before harm comes and ya lose them both," Fiona scolded.

"You're right. You're very, very right," Brandon admitted with a sigh. He stood up and gently grabbed Fiona's shoulders. "I just wish you were coming back to the future with us."

"I can't leave Lucy unattended," she said softly. "Ya know that I can't and the time has passed to put my soul in a newborn again."

"I know," he sighed.

"Of course," Fiona added, "If ya need me for a moment or two, I could probably slip in and out. A day or two at a time is all."

Brandon gave her a quick hug and said, "A day or two it is then, but only if we need you."

"Only if ya need me," Fiona gave one last look in Tara's direction and then focused her attention to the matter at hand. "What do you say we collect the love birds from inside and set to getting these people back to where they belong?"

"My assignment is not over. I should return as well," Brandon volunteered.

"Very well, we'll send ya there too," she said.

"Do you think Luella will like it in the future?" he asked thoughtfully.

"I can't say, but she'll not stand a chance if she remains here. She'll be better off there, I think," she said.

"You're probably right," Brandon replied. He started to walk toward the door, then stopped and turned, "Can I ask you something?"

"That depends upon the question," Fiona said warily.

Brandon chuckled.

"This is more a general question," he explained. "I'm trying to understand why it would be safer from Shadow Land in the future than now. I mean, they can teleport and come after her and even open the portal there if they're strong enough so why would Leona be safer in the future, rather than now?"

"I can understand your perplexity and I'll do me best to

explain a very complication thing. Ya see, the strength of the grasp that Shadow Land has on an individual depends upon the era they were born into. In other words, if I teleported to the future, the grasp that someone from Shadow Land had on me wouldn't be a strong as it would have if someone came through the portal of that era or teleported to that era and came after me there. As we both know, the portal in the future isn't as easy to pass through as it is today. Now, mind ya, no matter what time era one is in, Shadow Land inhabitants can mess with ya, but, never as strong as in the time that ya belong in."

"So then, Tara would actually be in greater danger from Shadow Land in the future?" Brandon voiced his concern.

"Yes and no. Yes, because it is her true birth time, but because Balthazar thinks she has teleported from here so he won't know he has the power he truly has," she replied.

"I don't know. That sounds pretty risky to me," he said.

"Risky or not, it has to be," Fiona said as she grabbed Brandon's collar and pulled his face close to hers. "Let me make meself perfectly clear. Get her away from me Lucy and help her find that key before trouble starts. Do it!"

Brandon looked into Fiona's hardened eyes with amazement. How could she be so insensitive to the dangers that awaited Tara? This seemed so out of character for her. He had no words to respond so he waited for her to release his collar, adjusted it, and walked inside.

Fiona sighed. She struggled within herself. She understood Brandon's fears and hesitations about returning Tara to the future, but if he didn't then both lasses would perish. She felt as if she was choosing one over the other. In a way she was, but she saw no other solution to the problem. Tara must go back to the future. She should never have come in the first place. This was all a big mess. A great big mess!

As she stomped across the porch, releasing as much frustration through her gait as she could on her way to fetch Tara, she stopped short. Were her eyes playing tricks on her? What were those creatures sneaking up behind the lass? Were they wolves? No, wait, they looked more like cats... no wolves. Oh, she just couldn't tell. They were too far away and her eyes weren't able to focus on them clearly. She may not be close enough to identify what they were, but she was absolutely sure they were stalking the lass. Running into the house, she grabbed her rifle from its holder over the fireplace and a small bag of shot.

"What's wrong?" Brandon barked as he followed her outside. Looking off into the distance he moaned, "Oh no."

"Ya know what they are?" Fiona asked in surprise.

"So do you... or you did. You shot a crap load of them just before they tore you to shreds," Brandon replied.

"Oh no, not demon wolves!" Fiona wailed.

Running as fast as she could, she started in Tara's direction, waiving her hands wildly over her head and shouting in an effort to attract them away from her. Tara stood up and looked at her with confusion. Fiona's efforts weren't in vein. The demon wolves abandoned their focus on Tara and started for her. She counted four. Did she have enough shot? Balancing her rifle against her shoulder, she placed the leader in her sights and fired. It yelped and exploded into pieces. Stunned, it took her a moment to regain her composure, reload the rifle and aim it once again. Their cat bodies made them fast and sleek while their wolf-like heads sported jaws that could crush a bone with one bite. They're getting mighty close. She needed to work faster or they would succeed in really killing her this time. She felt the bullet whizzing past her head long before she heard the sound of the shot being fired. Within seconds a demon creature was exploding. She had no idea who was behind her firing away, but now wasn't the time to find out. She aimed at the third demon wolf, shot and missed. Her heart pounded and her sweat coated her palms. Her fingers fumbled as she struggled to reload once again. Bang! Another shot whizzed past her, hitting its mark. There was one monster left. She somehow managed to reload and fire. This time she hit her mark.

All was quiet.

It was then that the adrenaline that fueled her through the ordeal ceased to flow and she was suddenly exhausted. Her legs were shaking and no longer able to hold her. As she fell to the ground she stared in disbelief as she watched Joshua ride quickly out of the grove of trees, scoop Tara onto his horse with him and ride off. It happened so quickly it seemed surreal.

"She'll be fine. For a while anyway," Luella said as she ran to help Fiona stand. "We have bigger problems."

By the time Fiona regained composure, Dennis and Brandon were also at her side. Brandon still had his fire arm in his hand.

"Joshua has her," Fiona groaned.

"Yes, I saw," Brandon replied. His voice was filled with frustrated anguish.

"We have to go after her!" Dennis shouted.

As he started to run in the direction Joshua took Tara, Luella grabbed his arm and held him steadfast.

"We have other problems to deal with," she said firmly. "I spotted the witchdoctor lurking in those trees."

"Get in the house, now!" Fiona roared as she propelled her body as fast as she could toward her home. She couldn't risk the witchdoctor entering and having access to her supplies.

She was on the porch when she spotted him dancing and laughing at the edge of the clearing. It was as if he didn't have a care in the world. She stopped at the doorway and peered in. She didn't trust that he hadn't already been inside and planted a trap. Why else would he be gloating like he was?

"Don't enter!" She barked as she held her hand in the air as a signal for them to stop. "There may be a trap."

Luella closed her eyes and scanned the perimeter of the house. She was very familiar with the witchdoctor's energy and would be able to detect its residue if he'd entered. She found nothing that would indicate he had.

"I don't sense that he came this far," she stated.

"Then, why do you think he's gloating like that?" Fiona

asked as she nodded her head in his direction.

Luella looked closer and scowled.

"He isn't gloating he's doing his war dance," she explained. "I've seen him do it before. He's summoning help from the underworld."

"Lord have mercy," Dennis moaned.

"Oh, it gets better," Brandon whispered to Dennis. "Do you see those shadows in the trees?"

Dennis strained his eyes and shook his head. As hard as he tried, he could see nothing.

"Look closer, they move with the wind," Brandon persisted. "We call them shadows in the wind. Can you see them, the dark wavy figures that sway and blend with the trees?"

After listening to Brandon's more distinctive description, Dennis tried again. This time he was able to see what the man was talking about. There, swirling around the trees was the faintest trace of ghostly shadows. Had he not been told otherwise, he'd have just considered it the wind weaving its way through the trees, carrying with it particles of soil or something.

"I see," he whispered. "What are they?"

"They're the watchers of Shadow Land. They weave their way through the human realm and report back to Balthazar."

"Yes," added Luella, "and they'll report back to him our location. So, my dears, if the witchdoctor doesn't kill us, Balthazar will."

"Not if I can help it!" Fiona bellowed as she headed for her supplies. Grabbing a thick leather-bound book from the shelf that Brandon recognized as the book Maggie gifted to Tara in the future, she flipped through the pages until she found what she was looking for. "It's been a long time since I've cast this spell."

"Let me help." Luella stepped forward.

Fiona locked eyes with Luella before asking, "Do you understand what may happen?"

Luella nodded.

"Well, I don't," Dennis barked.

His nerves were frazzled and he had no idea what was happening, but from the way Fiona looked into Luella's eyes, he expected what could happen wasn't good.

"Someone explain to me what might happen." When no one spoke he added, "Now!"

Startled by his sudden outburst, Luella spoke up.

"It's quite simple, really." she soothed. "I can handle it."

"Handle what?" Dennis persisted.

"Well, you see," she said nervously, "I was raised on black magic. What Fiona does is white magic. Its energy is different. There's nothing to worry about."

"Don't lie to him," Brandon commanded. "I know better." Turning to Fiona he asked, "Isn't it that when a black witch performs white magic without first going through the cleansing process, the white magic could turn on her and kill her? It is true, correct?"

"Ya are correct," Fiona said softly.

"What?" Dennis screeched. "Are you kidding me? You did the spells for Tara."

"Those spells walk the line of good and evil, they aren't pure white magic," Fiona said firmly. "We call spells that can be used by the white and the dark, grey magic."

"I can handle it," Luella insisted.

"What if you can't," Dennis demanded. "What then?"

"I will," Luella coaxed. "I will. Trust me."

"No! No! I can't lose you. No!" Dennis insisted.

It was clear to everyone in the room that Dennis had reached the peak of his level of tolerance. Brandon could understand. He was almost there himself.

"I can do this alone, Luella. There's no need for ya to take such a risk," Fiona stated in a tone designed to bring calm into a room that had exploded with emotion.

"I can handle it," Luella insisted once again.

"Yes, but he can't," Fiona said gently as she nodded her head toward Dennis. "For his sake, please let me do this alone."

Folding her arms across her chest, Luella let out a small "humph" and walked to the sofa. By the time she reached it she was already calm and beckoned Dennis to join her. She needed to remember he wasn't a part of the world of magic. They went through a lot. It was only natural he'd be concerned. She smiled. Actually, it was kind of sweet. Dennis eased himself down beside her. He was both traumatized and exhausted. He hoped Luella knew what she what she was saying when she said Tara would be safe for a while.

"Don't worry," Luella cooed, "Balthazar wants to use your sister to lure Lucy to him, but, ultimately, he wants the mighty enchantress over there. He won't harm her while he thinks Lucy will come, followed by Fiona. We have time to do something. Try to relax."

"What about Joshua? You said..." Dennis began.

"Yes, darling, I'll admit there is a small concern about Joshua," she agreed, "but, it is small. As long as Tara keeps her head he won't harm her. He wouldn't dare. Not until he's granted possession of her from the dark lord. Of course that won't happen until Balthazar realizes that Lucy and the enchantress aren't coming."

"It looks like he has his army set and is getting ready to attack," Brandon barked as he looked out the window.

Fiona ran to Brandon's side. Dennis tried to follow, but Luella held him back, explaining there was nothing he could do about it and, therefore, no reason for him to upset himself even more by looking. She reminded him that evil fed on fear and if he wasn't careful he'd be fueling the enemy with his. After mild resistance, he settled back and reveled in her soothing touch.

"Well, gods preserve us. He's dumber that I thought," Fiona chuckled.

"Dumb?" Brandon said incredulously, "You call a field full of soldiers dumb?"

"Yep," Fiona stated flatly as she moved back to her supply corner and selected a few jars from the shelf.

Brandon looked at the field beyond the garden and shook his head. He had no idea why Fiona would think that several dozen confederate soldiers would be considered dumb. They looked mighty formidable from where he stood, especially since they were all fully armed and ready for combat. Fiona was magical, but who was to say these solders weren't as well? After all, they were summoned by a witchdoctor.

"Luella," Fiona asked while she filled a few jars with a liquid mixture she just created. "Would ya say that killing a zombie was difficult?"

Luella threw her head back and laughed, "Hardly."

"Would ya say that killing a zombie required good magic?" Fiona continued.

"Oh no, zombies are the scurvy of creation. They're fair game for both white and black magicians."

"Well then, my black magic friend, are ya up for a little sport?" Fiona chuckled.

"You have to be kidding me!" Luella exclaimed as she jumped up and ran to the window. "Do you mean to tell me that idiot old man summoned zombies?"

"Yep," Fiona replied.

Luella threw her head back and roared with laughter and said, "Is he stupid?"

"Yep," Fiona chuckled.

Dennis ran to the window and looked out, "The fields are loaded with them."

"Back away from the window, my love. Zombies can hypnotize someone who isn't magical. I need you to help me so please, back away before you're worthless," Luella barked.

Brandon looked past Dennis to Fiona, wondering why she didn't take care to give him the same warning. When she closed her eyes and shook her head ever so slightly, he knew that it was just a ruse Luella used to keep Dennis calm.

Luella bounced her way to Fiona like an eager child.

"What have you got for us to use?" she asked while rubbing her hands together in anticipation.

"Well," Fiona said with a hint of amusement, "I mixed some baneberry juice with the blood of a bat and the powder of dried calabar beans."

Luella nodded her head. "Pretty good, pretty good, but bat's blood is used in black magic, not white. Do you mean you...?"

"Yes, I'm able to do both when need be," Fiona interjected.

"Very impressive," Luella murmured, more to herself than to anyone else in the room.   "It's lucky Balthazar never got his hands on you,"

"'Tis lucky indeed. Also, me Lucy," Fiona said, "I can see the magic in Tara. She could be a powerful witch just on the memories alone if we could get that shield of forgetfulness to lift. 'Tis luck Balthazar didn't realize that she too has gone through the initiation into both white and black magic."

"That's rare," Luella breathed, completely in awe.

"Yes, but 'tis necessary at times to be able to pull on both sides even if ya are working for the good," Fiona explained, "'Tis the balance of things and all."

"I agree," Brandon piped in. "In my travels, I've seen many situations where the dark side was conquered by itself. I can see where it would come in handy to be able to wield both white and black magic."

"Indeed," Fiona replied. Filling her lungs with air and pushing it out quickly, she grabbed a few bottles of the liquid and handed them to Luella. "Are ya ready for a little target practice?"

Luella giggled and nodded.

"Let me help," Dennis started to grab a jar.

"No!" Luella and Fiona burst out, simultaneously.

Stunned, Dennis stopped in mid-air, just before his hand touched the jar.

"Ya aren't magic," Fiona explained, "Touching the jar could kill ya."

Dennis' hands shot up over his head and he backed off.

Beads of sweat formed on his forehead as the realization of how close he'd just come to death set in.

"What can I do?" Brandon asked.

Fiona looked at Brandon long and hard.

"There are some cast iron tongues hanging on the wall," she said. "Both of ya grab a set and grip the jars with them and pile them onto the porch for us, will ya?"

"You only made a few jars," Brandon voiced.

"Really?" Fiona replied. Brandon thought he caught a hint of amused twinkle in her eye as he followed her look to the table where she'd prepared a few jars of the liquid. There were dozens of them stacked neatly on top of each other! He looked from Fiona to Luella and then back to Fiona, making no attempt to hide his confusion.

Luella shrugged her shoulders, flashed him a grin and headed out onto the porch.

"Come on, old man, this has been a long time coming!" Luella bellowed, "Show me what you got!"

TWENTY-FOUR

Her backside hurt from being forced to balance on the pommel of the military saddle. The musky scent of Joshua's skin that she'd found so alluring in the past repulsed her now. She seethed inwardly as the reality of everything that occurred set in and the memories came forth. As his arm tightened around her waist and her body stiffened, the saddle irritated her all the more. She didn't care. He'd fooled her twice. There would be no third time.

Her mind raced with what to do. She was no longer disoriented and weak, but did he realize that? Perhaps it would be in her best interest not to let him see that she was well and healthy. At least until she could figure out a plan of action. As much as it repulsed her to do so, she leaned into him and feigned fainting. His hand came up to stroke her hair and her nostrils filled with his scent. She felt repulse and it took considerable effort to maintain control to hide it. He slowed his horse down to a gentle walk, which gave her a chance to get a better idea of where they were.

The horse plodded through the forest for about an hour before they reached a small clearing that contained the remnants of a campsite. She willed her body to remain limp while he pulled her off the horse and laid her down on a blanket he'd stretched out beforehand.

Tara watched from beneath closed lids as Joshua tossed a few twigs into a stone lined fire pit and worked at getting a fire going. Once satisfied, he pulled a few potatoes out of a saddle roll and tossed them onto the edge of the fire. Taking a long, solid stick, he covered the potatoes with burning coals from the fire before pulling out a small iron pot and filling it with water from his canteen. Dropping a few tea leaves into the water, he set the pot on the stones surrounding the fire.

Sensing he was about to look up at her, Tara closed her eyes all the way and took a deep sigh to camouflage her body adjustment from one of tenseness to that of a sleeping woman. She could feel him standing over her, staring at her, watching her every movement. She prayed he wasn't astute enough to see that she was faking it.

He wasn't.

Too fearful to open her eyes, she listened intently as he pulled his rifle from its holder and walked off into the forest. She stayed still, listening to the quiet for several minutes before opening her eyes to look around. He was obviously off looking for game to finish off the meal he was preparing. With any luck, he'd have to hunt a little for it and she'd have time to figure out how to escape. With the return of her life force so came the return of many of her memories. Perhaps it was because she'd lain next to Lucy when her life force was being reinstated within her by magic or perhaps not. Whatever the reason, her body felt invigorated and her mind was sharp. She closed her eyes as images of open spell books floated before her. They were flying so fast that she couldn't see what was written on the pages. Taking a deep breath, she willed them to slow down long enough for her to read the clean, hand written pages. It was a binding spell. Reading on, she realized that it utilized words and energies only. There were no herbs or liquids to gather. As she read on, the memories of her casting this spell on the guards of Shadow Land came forth.

But, she never....

It was like a light bulb went off in her head. She was a modern-day version of the nineteenth century woman who lay in wait in the secluded cave. This meant that deep within her were the memories of the life that woman led. Everything she felt, saw, experienced was recorded in her memory bank and she was in possession of that bank.

"How good were you?" she mused out loud.

Good enough to take care of this swine.

Tara's head spun around while she looked for the source of the woman's voice, but she could see no one. She got the sense she knew the voice, but couldn't place it.

"Where are you?" she asked.

I am within you.

Tara scowled. Now wasn't the time for riddles. Joshua could return at any moment.

"I don't understand and I don't have time for fun and games. Show yourself," she demanded.

You see me every day when you look in the mirror and you laid beside me where I rest in wait. I am you as you're me.

"Lucy?" she gasped.

The very same.

"How?" she asked.

When Fiona and the sorceress worked their spell, it bound us to our soul so well that I'm able to feel and hear you. I still have a connection to our soul, you know. I need it in order for it to return to me when the time comes.

"You mean, when I die?" she said hesitantly.

Yes, when you die.

"But..." she began.

Now is not the time to discuss this. We must cast the spell on Joshua, he's returning. It will take both of us to do it. He's powerful demon.

"What do we do?" Tara started to feel a tinge of panic at the thought of Joshua returning and her opportunity to flee leaving. "Maybe I should just run."

He'll catch you.

"Then, what?" she asked with a little less patience than she planned.

Focus on the words, the voice said calmly. *Close your eyes, pull up the spell once again and read the words aloud. We must say them in unison three consecutive times. Do it now!*

Tara closed her eyes, but the book wouldn't appear.

You're allowing your emotions to interfere, the voice remained calm, but firm. *Relax. Stop worrying about him returning and focus.*

She took a deep breath, willed her body to relax, and focused on visualizing the spell she'd witnessed earlier.

"I've got it," she announced.

Okay, now. Say it with me.

Their voices sounded mismatched at first, but neither let it stop them. Little by little they joined in cadence until they were speaking the words as one. It was similar to what happened in the cave with Fiona and the Sorceress. Similar, but not the same for in the cave dark magic and light worked in unison. Here, two forces from the same source were joining together to create one powerhouse to be reckoned with.

Joshua's horse reared as it approached the campsite. His struggle to subdue it caused him to miss the fact that Tara was standing tall and strong with her arms raised high and her hair flowing even though there was no wind. Her eyes glowed bright yellow as she pointed in his direction, never ceasing the chant that came from her lips with a vengeance. Beams of light shot from her finger tips and wound around his torso, restricting his every move. He struggled to break free, but the harder he struggled, the tighter the binds became.

"I can't breathe," he groaned as the binds continued to tighten around him.

"Good!" Tara shouted. Her voice sounded foreign to her. "Now you die evil demon!"

This wasn't her speaking! Of that she knew. It was also not her wielding her hands in the air and bringing down thunderous lightning bolts to obliterate his body. She didn't fight it. She simply stepped aside and watched as the demon that caused her so much heartache was obliterated before her very eyes.

She felt no remorse.

****

Fiona and Luella dispensed of the witchdoctor's army of zombies with minimal effort. It took a little more effort on Luella's part to destroy the witchdoctor, but Fiona didn't interfere. She sensed the need within the sorceress to perform this task on her own. When all was quiet, the foursome immediately set out to find Tara. The sound of thunder up ahead caught all of their attention.

Brandon pulled his enormous gelding to a stop and waited for the others to pull up beside him.

"Was that thunder?" he asked as he looked at the clear blue sky with confusion.

"Aye, it was, but not ordinary thunder," Fiona said. "'Tis the thunder of magic."

A loud explosion permeated their surroundings. The trees swayed against the gust of air that followed. Then all was silent. A flock of crows flew overhead in a cluster that gave the appearance of a large, black hole.

"A demon was killed," Luella breathed.

"Tara," Fiona whispered.

"Tara?" Dennis asked. "Do you think Tara did this?"

"You mean Tara killed Joshua?" Brandon asked with disbelief.

"Not just Tara," Fiona said as she looked Dennis in the eye. Spurring her horse into a lope she shouted back, "Lucy helped."

The others followed Fiona as she gave her mare freedom for speed and trusted her to know where to go. She could hear the pounding of the hoofs behind her. They were close behind and probably doing the same thing with their mounts.

The path was rocky and more than once Dennis thought his horse was going to fall. Not the most experienced rider, he held tight to the pommel with one hand and a fist full of mane at the horse's wither in his other hand as horse and rider soared over fallen logs and darted around boulders. He barely gripped the reins while he allowed his mount to keep up with the other horses. The ground flew beneath him. His only wish was to keep his seat until they reached their destination. His teeth felt like they were about to be jostled out of his mouth long before they reached the small clearing where Tara stood motionless, surrounded by black liquid.

Fiona sucked in her breath when she saw Tara's dilemma.

"Stay there, lass! Don't move!" she bellowed.

Luella reined up beside Fiona and also made a loud noise as she sucked in air. Tara stood on a boulder, but the black liquid was rising.

"Balthazar!" Luella said with disgust.

"What is it?" Tara cried. "I don't know what it is, but I know enough not to walk in it."

"Good! Stay there," Brandon shouted.

He'd seen this liquid once before when he'd traveled back to medieval times. It was the blood of darkness and would consume any living creature that made the fateful mistake of stepping into it.

"What is it?" Dennis asked, thunderstruck by the sight before him.

Not only was there a thick black menacing looking liquid surrounding the stone Tara stood on, but all around its perimeter lay the remains of small animals and something else.

"'Tis the magic of the dark lord," Fiona said with disgust. "He must have attached it to the demon soldier. It activated when he was destroyed."

"Yes," Luella groaned, "and if we don't do something soon it will resurrect Joshua."

"No!' Tara exclaimed. The mere thought of Joshua coming back to life sent icy chills down her spine. "No! Do something!"

"I'm thinking, me dear," Fiona said gently. "Don't panic. There is nothing to be accomplished by panicking."

Memories of Maggie flooded back to Tara. That was a saying Maggie used often. Her eyes welled with tears. She missed her dear friend. She missed her so much. Of course, the woman before her was an earlier version of that woman, but she wasn't that woman. She wasn't her Maggie. She wondered if Fiona felt the same way about her.

Noticing Tara's tear-filled eyes, Luella mistook them for tears of fear and did her best to soothe her.

"Don't worry, Tara," Luella assured her. "None of us want that evil bastard to come back to life."

Dennis looked at Luella with surprise, but said nothing. As he digested her words his heart warmed from the realization that Luella really was telling the truth when she told him she never cared for Joshua. He was just all she knew. It wasn't until she met Dennis that she understood the difference between tolerance and true love. Luella loved Dennis and it felt right and good. Now all he needed to do was get her and his sister safely back to the twenty-first century.

Easier said than done.

"Have ya ever dealt with the likes of this before?" Fiona's question to Luella brought Dennis' attention back to the matter at hand.

"I haven't," Luella replied, her voice filled with regret, "but between the two of us we should be able to think of something."

"You need to think fast," Brandon pointed to a spot in the muck. "Do you see it bubbling? That has to mean something and I doubt it is good."

"No," Luella sighed. "No, it certainly isn't good. It is Joshua gathering himself together. He will be whole again soon."

"Gods preserve us. What to do? What to do?" Fiona spoke more to herself than to the others.

"I might have an idea," Brandon volunteered. All eyes were on him as he nudged his gelding into a position that would allow him to face both Fiona and Luella. He not only wanted their full attention, but he wanted to be able to see Luella's face when he spoke. She was only recently a runaway from Shadow Land and had been this demon's lover. Did she really mean it when she claimed she didn't want him to resurrect? If she didn't, his idea wouldn't work and there was no time to waste on failed attempts.

Whatever they did, it had to work and it had to work at first try.

"What is it?" Fiona asked.

She had to admit she was curious about what type of solution a traveler would come up with when two witches couldn't put their heads together and think of one.

"Well," Brandon took a deep breath to steady his words. "What about reversing the spell you did in the cave when you brought Tara back? Could you change a few words to reverse its effect?"

Luella and Fiona sat frozen in their saddles.

"That would work, wouldn't it?" Dennis piped in. When neither woman replied, he asked more insistently, "Wouldn't it?"

"Yes, it would," boomed a voice from deep within Tara that resembled her voice, but was slightly different. Fiona threw her hand to her mouth and stared at the young woman standing on the rock. There was a haze around her, an almost transparent form of her Lucy hovering over Tara. "Lucy," she declared in a hushed tone of wonder and awe.

"What's happening?" Dennis was confused by the vision he saw and the voice he heard. "Is she alright?"

"It is Lucy," Brandon explained. In all of his travels he'd never encountered anything like what was happening. "She's working through your sister."

The only one who didn't seem surprised was Luella, who was exposed to double soul disbursement many times while in the tutelage of her mother. The soul is so connected to both bodies that when one body is in trouble or need, the other one feels it and can come through. Sometimes, if one body is weaker than the other, the stronger body literally takes over the mechanics of the other body, and no one is the wiser, but in this case both Lucy and Tara were of equal strength and in cooperation with each other. It was also the reason Lucy could only hover in Tara's aura, instead of occupying her body.

"I agree. It should work," Luella said in a voice that was loud enough and firm enough to pull everyone's attention away from Tara."

"Do you know what is happening?" Fiona asked in a low, steady tone.

"I do and I'll be more than happy to explain when we have time. Right now, I think we better re-word the spell and do it fast," Luella said.

"Look!" Dennis exploded. The bubbles that Brandon had pointed out were almost double in size and quantity. "I think out time's running out."

"Lucy and I know the spell. We can say it with you," Tara insisted.

"Yes, lass, good idea," Fiona's tone was proud and pleased.

Fiona and Luella dismounted and surrendered their horses' reins to the men. Standing on the edge of the thick bubbling liquid, the three women quickly bounced a few suggestions for changes in the spell off each other. When they were all in agreement, they positioned themselves to form a triangle and chanted.

Brandon nudged his horse next to Dennis' and grabbed its bridle to redirect it away from the scene before them.

"I can't explain it, but I get a strong feeling we shouldn't be witnessing this. I say we ride off a little ways and give these ladies their space."

Dennis hesitated briefly before nodding and nudging his horse to follow Brandon's. He was immediately grateful for the suggestion when the horses reared and balked from fear of the unfamiliar and potent energy that swirled around them. It was all the men could do to subdue their mounts and stay seated in their saddles. Little by little the voices of the three women blended and became as one as they chanted the words that would end Joshua's life forever.

"This has to work," Dennis mutter urgently.

"It will," Brandon said with confidence. "I can feel it. It will work." He gave a little chuckle. "Balthazar is going to be hopping mad about this one."

"And that's funny?" Dennis stated in surprise.

"No, not funny, but poetic," Brandon replied.

Dennis thought about it for a moment.

"You're right. It is, isn't it?" he said with a smirk.

"It s-u-r-r-r-r-e is," Brandon said as turned in time to see the bubbles disappear, followed by the goop.

Dennis stared at the ground around his sister. There was no sign of the black liquid that once threatened to consume her and bring back the demon that caused so much agony for everyone.

"Wow," whispered Dennis and Brandon simultaneously.

"I agree," Luella chuckled as she took her horse's reins from Dennis and mounted.

Fiona walked closer to Tara and stared at the almost transparent figure that hovered over the body of its double.

"Hello, Lass," she said quietly.

"Hello auntie," Tara's silhouette giggled. "This was an adventure, was it not?"

Fiona shook her head and smiled, "Ya do love an adventure."

"That I do," Lucy chuckled.

"What now?" Fiona asked.

"I return to the cave and wait," Lucy replied.

"I'll come to check on ya just as soon as things are sorted out and settled down," Fiona assured her.

"I know you will," Lucy said with confidence. After a brief moment of silence, she added, "You need to send her away, auntie. I can feel my soul's confusion. All will be well as long as you send her away."

"Not to worry, lass. I intend to," Fiona assured her.

Tara listened to her double's conversation with her enchantress aunt and sighed. She had no idea that traveling through time to rescue Dennis would cause so much trouble for so many people. Although she still would have done something to get Dennis back from Shadow Land, she may have done it differently had she realized the peril she placed herself and her double in. For that, she was sorry.

She could feel Lucy's energy pulling away from her. She felt lighter, freer. She hadn't realized until her double had left how occupied her body had become. Even though she stayed primarily in her aura, she still entered her enough to use her vocal cords and influence her body movements in order to perform the spells correctly.

Sadness swept over Tara when she realized that Lucy was gone. She was connected only briefly, but it was a powerful connect that she knew she would remember. She wanted to know more about Lucy. She wasn't ready to be separated from her.

Fiona wiped the moistness from her eyes while she watched her niece fade into nothingness. Seeing her animated after such a long time made her realize how much she missed her. It wasn't supposed to turn out like this. They were both supposed to be lying in wait for their souls to be returned together once the key was found. No one had considered the fact that one of them might return earlier than planned. No one expected Balthazar to send one of his soldiers after them and certainly no one ever expected the veil of forgetfulness to have been so difficult to lift.

Now, Fiona watched over her lovely niece's body while she waited for her to come back to life and prayed it would be before she, herself, died.

"I miss you," she whispered shortly after Lucy disappeared.

"I miss you too," Tara replied.

Both women knew who the other one was really talking to.

****

It was evening before they settled themselves down to discuss their next move. Dennis was eager to return to his own time. He'd lost track of how long it was since he'd taken that fateful walk to the stable to feed Sugar, but it felt like years. He wanted to go home, have a hot shower, a change of clean clothes and a hamburger and French fries.

Brandon, on the other hand dragged his heels. He dreaded the thought of returning Tara back to a time when she would be in her element and likely revert back to mistrusting him. He knew it had to be done, but he was in no hurry to do it. The moon had risen and the night air was crisp when he walked out onto the porch to think. They were pressuring him to transport everyone back. He felt the strain of the tension that his resistance added to their already stressful day.

Tara watched him leave the room and waited a few moments before following him out. She walked over to his left and stood on the edge of the porch to get a good view of the night sky.

"It's beautiful, isn't it?" she asked as she hugged her arms close to her body.

"Are you cold?" Brandon looked around for a wrap or blanket that someone may have tossed across the back of the chair, but there was nothing to offer her for warmth.

"Maggie always kept a wrap draped over the back of her rocker on the porch," she chuckled. "Looks like that's a habit she develops in the future."

"No, she does the same here, but for some reason it's gone," he said.

"Well, with all the coming and going around here I can understand how it could be misplaced," She rubbed her arms briskly and then stomped her feet. "I'll be fine."

"You don't look like you will be fine. Maybe you should go back inside," he said.

Tara slipped him a coy look, "Are you trying to get rid of me, sir?"

"N...no, absolutely not. I just thought...." he stammered.

Tara threw her head back and laughed heartily.

"You really are an easy target," she said.

Brandon lowered his head to hide his embarrassment.

"Thanks," he mumbled.

"I meant no harm Brandon," she said as she slid her hand

on his arm.

The warmth of her hand bore right through the wool fabric of his long sleeves, sending shivers of delight throughout his body.

"I came out here because I wanted to speak with you in private about a few things. Is that alright?" she asked.

"Why of course," He berated himself for sounding like a school boy.

"Can we walk?" she asked.

"Maybe a short way," he said. "It probably wouldn't be the best idea to wander too far."

"You're probably right," she sighed. "It's such a lovely night for a walk. What a shame, but it can't be helped."

As she started off the porch, she extended her hand to him and motioned him to follow. He did so willingly. When he caught up with her she looked at him teasingly.

"Since we're in an era of chivalry, would you mind if I held your arm? I know it's silly, but I've always wanted to walk in the moonlight on the arm of a chivalrous male and now I have my chance," she said softly.

Brandon couldn't help tossing his head back in laughter. This was the Tara he'd grown to know in the future and it was the Tara he loved. He'd missed her witty nature. He was happy to discover it hadn't been lost amidst the trauma that she endured.

He extended the crook of his arm, bowed and said, "May I ma'am?"

"You may," she chuckled as she slid her hand in place. "What fun!"

They walked in silence, each deep in thought. Having Tara on his arm like this brought back memories of the nights, not that long ago, when he walked arm in arm with Lucy. They were romantic, pleasurable nights. It was under the light of a brilliant full moon, similar to the one they were presently experiencing, that he confessed his love to her and asked her to marry him. Guilt welled up within him as he realized that this was the first time he'd thought about Lucy in that way since he met the woman who now walked at his side. He loved Lucy and he'd never take away his offer of marriage, so why was he so attached to Tara? He couldn't explain it.

Tara took her time before speaking. She wanted to word her sentences carefully so that they came out the way she intended them to.

"I think this is far enough. Any further from the house and we may be risking things. We don't know what else may be lurking about," Brandon said as he positioned himself to face her, yet still making it so that she could comfortably leave her hand in the crook of his arm if she so chose.

Tara looked back at the house. She was surprised to discover they'd moved much further from it than she intended, so deep in thought were they both.

"You're right." she agreed.

Taking a deep breath, she looked up at his steel grey eyes. He really was a handsome man. He was very rugged and virile looking with a charismatic softness that offset it.

"I'd like to ask you about Lucy. Would you mind terribly?" Tara asked, holding her breath while she waited for his response.

"No. I don't mind. Ask away. If I can answer, I will," he replied softly.

"Fiona tells me you two are to be married. Is this true?" she asked.

"We're betrothed, but she doesn't remember me now," he explained.

"Oh," Tara hesitated then continued, "When?"

"When?" he replied. "What do you mean? When did I propose to her or when are we to be wed?"

"Both?" she hesitated, not certain if she overstepped with such questions. She looked at him closely. He didn't seem to be upset, yet he was certainly taking his time answering. "Maybe I overstepped. I'm sorry."

"No, no you're fine. It is just a difficult topic for me," he sighed. "I proposed to her under a moon that was similar to this in a spot just on the other side of the garden only days before she was kidnapped by Balthazar." He pointed to the area. Tara smiled. It sounded so romantic. She wished she could remember it. "As for when we're to be married... we had no date set. There wasn't time to make one before her memory was gone. I thought we would marry after she returned from the future. You see, I was kept in the dark about their plans and was led to believe, as was everyone not privy to their true plans that she time traveled. Of course, since I do the same I thought nothing of it until I met you in the future and you didn't have a clue who I was, nor did Fiona, for that matter. Fiona had aged so that I didn't recognize her either. It was confusing."

"It must have been," Tara said in a voice filled with compassion. "I'm sorry."

Brandon chuckled, "It certainly was nothing to fault you with. It just would have been a lot easier for all concerned if I was privy to what was truly going on instead of having to piece it together."

"I have to die before she can come back," Tara said softly.

"This is true," he said sadly.

Tara watched his facial muscles move as he wrestled with his emotions. This was obviously a difficult conversation for him. Even so, she couldn't stop.

"I have something that's been bothering me since I discovered you're a traveler," Tara continued. She locked eyes with him and asked, "Why did you stay in the cabin with us when you could have easily traveled out? Why did you risk dying like that?"

He moved so that he was square in front of her and held her shoulders, gently, but firmly before saying, "I'm going to ask you to please listen to what I have to say before you make a comment one way or the other. Will you?"

Surprised by his sudden change in mood, she nodded.

Brandon took a deep breath to settle his nerves and summoned some courage. He closed his eyes. He was about to bare his heart to this woman and he didn't want to see her reaction until he was finished. Otherwise, if she wasn't responding favorably, he may not be able to finish. For reasons he couldn't explain it was important for him to have his say.

"I remember when I first started to travel," he began, "My mind didn't seem to retain as much as it does now. It was because of this that I accepted the fact that you didn't know me when we met in the grove. As for Maggie, she was a much older woman who wore entirely different attire than what I can ever recall seeing Fiona in or even imagine she would wear and I didn't recognize her for quite some time. I'd asked to be sent to the future to follow you since you were looking for the key and that's a concern of ours as well. In essence, I truly was on assignment for the organization that I work for. We do our best to head off some of the chaos that Balthazar and his cronies in Shadow Land are forever sending our way. By traveling back and forth through time, I can gauge whether the tactics we choose will be effective or not. When I slipped you that note in the restaurant to meet me the following afternoon, I intended on discussing all this with you, but then I was wounded and while I was laid up Dominic managed to slip in and consume your every thought." He stopped for a moment and opened his eyes to see if Tara was alright with his reference of her affair with Dominic. When he saw no change in her expression, he continued, "I decided to take a different tactic and allow you to get to know me again. It was my earnest hope that the love Lucy and I shared would jog the memory that was buried so deep in your memories. I had no idea you were a doppelganger. I truly thought you were my Lucy. When we were in that house and I thought you were going to die, I couldn't bear the thought of living on without you. So, I stayed."

"Wow, you really do love her," she mused.

"Yes, I do, but," he took her hands in his, "this may sound odd or even fickle, but I love you too." Tara opened her mouth to speak and he raised his hand as a signal for her to stop. "I know what you're going to say, but hear me out. I love you. Not because you're her double, but because of you. You carry within you, bits and pieces of Lucy -which is what attracted me to you in the beginning- but you also have bits and pieces that belong to you and you alone and it is those parts of you that have captured my heart. I'm a man with a dilemma. You see, I love Lucy, but I love you just a little bit more. I don't want you to die, but I also don't want Lucy to lie lifeless in that cave. I know Fiona is wrestling with the same issues. She's more disciplined than I am and is willing to let you return for the good of all, but I'm not. Once you're back in your own era and Shadow Land is now aware of you, I fear they will continue to seek you out. It is suicide for you to return where you don't have the protection you have here and I want no part of it." He heaved a sigh, "There, I have said my peace."

"Yes, you have," Tara said in a voice that was barely above a whisper.

Softly, gently, she placed her hand on the back of his neck and pulled him to her. Her warm, moist lips against his sent flames of burning passion through him. It was a tender kiss yet a remarkable one. It spoke the words that neither one could say. It spoke of sorrow, loss, fear, but also of tenderness and love. It was the most complete kiss Brandon had ever experienced and felt he'd ever experience again.

While sitting under that tree thinking she realized she'd developed undeniable feelings for this man. Perhaps they were rooted from her memories of Lucy's love or perhaps they were emotions of her own. She didn't know and she didn't care. For right now, all that mattered was that she was in love with him. They under the moonlight in one of the most romantic settings she could imagine and he held her in a way that radiated his love. He loved her, she loved him, and it felt right. She'd think about all else another time.

****

"I know what you two were up to," Fiona whispered in Brandon's ear. "Do ya think that was such a smart thing to do?"

"It was probably a dumb thing to do, but," he said as looked her square in the eye, "if I had to do things all over again, I wouldn't change a thing. I love her."

"What about Lucy?" Fiona asked.

"I love her too. It's complicated," he said.

"Of that ya can be sure," Fiona spat as she stomped off to the garden.

The moonlight offered plenty of light to pick the fresh herbs she needed for a spell she was working on in secret. It was easy to get her actions past everyone except Luella, who had an insatiable curiosity about her every move -or perhaps it just seemed that way because she tried so hard to pull this off undetected in an environment where privacy was impossible.

She couldn't blame Brandon for the way he felt. She too had a heart that was softened by Tara. The girl had many redeeming qualities all her own. It was easy to see why he loved her. In her own way, she loved her too, but she loved Lucy more and if she wasn't able to perfect this spell and had to make a choice, then the decision was already made. She didn't mention her plans to anyone since she wasn't certain she would be successful and didn't want to raise anyone's hopes.

While studying the old witchdoctor's book she stumbled upon a spell that, if she could pull it off, would allow both Lucy and Tara to live at the same time. This would solve everyone's problems except Brandon's. He would still have to choose.

Tara's footsteps approaching caught her attention and she stood up from her picking.

"Can I speak with you a moment?" Tara asked.

"Certainly, lass. What is it?" Fiona asked.

"The crystal Lucy hid. If you had it in your possession, would you be able to seal the portal?" she asked.

"Yes, and no," Fiona replied. "I can close the portal in the era that I'm from, but not in other eras. But this is one of the stronger portals so it would be good to get it closed," Fiona replied.

"I see. So, if you have the key, you can close the portal for when exactly?" she continued.

"For one-hundred years before I was born and one-hundred years after I'm born, no more, no less," Fiona said.

"One-hundred years after you're born. Hmmm. That won't reach the twenty-first century," Tara mused.

"No lass. I'm sorry. 'Twould not," Fiona heaved a sigh.

"Is there a portal there?" Tara asked.

"Not yet... None that I'm aware of, but it really doesn't matter since we have no idea where me darling Lucy hid the key," Fiona sighed.

"So how would they get to the future to find me like Brandon fears if the portal here was closed and there isn't one in my time yet?" Tara persisted.

"They would find the nearest one and teleport," Fiona replied, clearly confused by her persistence.

They stayed in silence for a few minutes before Tara spoke again.

"I remember where she put it," Tara said softly.

Fiona stood up with a start and stared in disbelief, "How?"

Tara shrugged.

"I'm not sure exactly," she replied. "It just came to me after Brandon and I... err... took a walk."

"I see," Fiona mused. "The sharing you and Brandon did during your walk must have triggered your connection. Me Lucy truly does love him, ya know."

Tara looked away, suddenly ashamed of her actions. She was the one to initiate things with Brandon. It was she who kissed him with such passion that he'd have had to be made of stone to not respond. What had gotten into her? Even if she did have feelings for him, he was engaged to be married. She betrayed her double in the worst of ways and she was very, very ashamed.

Fiona studied her closely. She truly was a lovely woman, as lovely as her Lucy. There was something about her here in the moonlight that was so very familiar. It wasn't an action or expression that Lucy would have, but it was familiar all the same.

"Is something wrong?" Tara asked, noticing how the woman studied her.

"No," Fiona shook her head, "'Twas just that, ya seem so familiar."

"Maybe, just like I'm remembering things, so are you," Tara said. "Maggie and I were very close. She left me everything she owned in her will."

"Did I now?" Fiona chuckled. "And did I've much to leave?"

"That depends upon what you hold dear. You left me your house and its contents and a tidy sum of money plus your land, but what's worth more to me than any of is the book you entrusted in my care, the Book of Secrets."

Fiona gasped, "Ya have the Book of Secrets?"

Tara nodded.

"It's the dearest thing I possess because when I hold it I feel close to you again," she said with noticeable emotion.

Tears welled up in Fiona's eyes while she listened to Tara talk about the Maggie she knew and loved. Memories flooded her mind. She saw herself sitting opposite Tara in a restaurant, laughing and eating. She saw herself teaching Tara in a room that looked to be a shabby version of her brother's house. She saw herself sitting on her porch with her collie enjoying the evening sky. She saw herself as Maggie of the future.

"What was me collie's name?" she whispered, tears sliding down her cheeks.

"Angus," Tara said softly.

"Ha, after me troublesome nephew," she chuckled. "I remember ya, lass. I remember our love," Fiona said gently.

"Oh Maggie, I miss you so!" Tara cried softly as she threw herself into Fiona's wide stretched arms.

"There, there, lass," Fiona cooed, "not to worry. Not to worry."

"You always said that," Tara sniffed as she wiped at the tears in her eyes and chuckled.

Fiona threw her head back in laughter. Tara was right. She always did say that. Her laughter was infectious and soon Tara joined her. When they finally settled down, Fiona held Tara by the shoulders, arm's length away, looked at her squarely and said, "I have a plan."

****

Tara's stomach reeled as she sat on the ground at the edge of lawn belonging to the ancestral house she inherited in the far away future. She disliked traveling and looked forward to the time when it was no longer required of her. She had no idea how Brandon could do it so often and not seem to mind. She wondered even more how he managed to keep the contents of his stomach intact after transport. She lost her contents every time.

"It would have been nice if you had placed us inside the house," she whispered as she watched a handful of soldiers strolling on the wrap-around-porch. "How are we supposed to get past the soldiers?"

"You're not the best of travelers. Between your noisy entrances and the way you like to mark your entry with a bit of vomit, I thought it might be a little safer to arrive away from the house," Brandon teased. "It is, after all, occupied by union soldiers."

"You have a point," Tara sighed, "but now we have to figure out how to get into the house without being detected."

"We walk in," Brandon stated as he stood up and started forward.

"Wait!" Tara pulled at his arm, "Don't be crazy. There are dozens of soldiers in that house."

Brandon stopped and looked at her hesitantly.

"There's something that you should know. I couldn't tell you before because you didn't know that I was a traveler and you were already suspicious of me and I knew no way to explain it. Colonel O'Connor is a friend of mine. He and I go way back," he admitted with trepidation.

Tara was dumbfounded.

"Do you mean to tell me that the whole capture thing was

a ruse?" she gasped. She could feel her blood boiling in her veins. "I knew it. Deep down inside I knew you were friends by the way you talked and acted at dinner."

Brandon lowered his head and nodded.

"I didn't know how to tell you. You distrusted me already. How could I explain to you that I have a good friend who fights in the civil war?" he asked.

He had a point and Tara knew it. She grunted a few times for emphasis to her case and then decided to let it drop. He was right.

"So, then we walk in," she stated flatly as she walked past him proud and tall.

Brandon caught up with her and smiled. She certainly was a fine specimen of a woman.

They were almost to the porch before a solder shouted for them to halt. Holding them at gunpoint, he directed them into the room that Tara used as a study and told them to sit while he fetched the colonel. With a threatening glower, he closed the door and turned the lock.

Chuckling to himself, Brandon lifted the lid from Aidan's cigar box and helped himself. Soon its rich aroma permeated the air. Tara inhaled deeply. She loved the smell of cigars and at one time even considered taking up smoking them.

"Well, ya still have no manners, but at least ya had the decency to change your dress so I'm not left having to explain your odd appearance to me men," Aidan said as he strode into the room. Tara was surprised she didn't hear the door unlock. "Ma'am," he stated in a calm manner, as if he wasn't in the least surprised to see that she was still in Brandon's company. "'Tis a fine thing to lay eyes on your beauty once more." Looking at Brandon he jested, "What such a lovely lady sees in your mug is beyond me."

"You suppose she should be wagging behind you?" Brandon chuckled.

"Aye, that's right. She could do worse," Aidan laughed, "In fact, she did!"

Tara smiled while she watched the two men shake hands, hug, ruffle each other's hair, and pat each other on the back. The room was filled with male bonding for the better part of a quarter hour before they relaxed enough to get down to the reason Brandon and Tara had come.

Aidan listened quietly until they had finished their story. The room went silent while Tara and Brandon waited for him to light a cigar and puff on it a few times before speaking.

"'Your Papa would like to see ya before ya go, Miss O'Shea," he stated. "Stay for dinner, speak with him. Then, by all means, take your stone and have a safe journey," he leaned forward, "and, remember, ya will always have a friend in Aidan O'Connor. If ya need me, just call."

Tara raised a brow, but said nothing.

"Just for the record," Brandon whispered, "he's a retired traveler. So there's some truth to his statement. If you need him, he will come."

Tara looked at Aidan with new appreciation and said, "Thank you, colonel."

The rest of the evening passed with no mishaps.

Tara spent a few quiet hours in the company of her double's father, trying her best to be as good a companion as Lucy would have been. Dinner had to have been one of the most delightful experiences she ever had, in any era.

Aidan and Brandon proved to be incredibly funny men. They told good jokes and not so good jokes, shared stories about their travels through time and stories about their battle with Shadow Land. Aidan explained why he decided to retire from traveling and head up an army in the civil war and why he chose the United States over his homeland of Ireland. Brandon shared a little bit more about himself, giving Tara a deeper glimpse into his soul and making her fall in love with him just a little bit deeper. It was a night she wished could last forever.

With their bellies full and the hour late, Tara excused herself and made for the room three doors down from the one she stayed in the night she first arrived. It was where the stone was hidden. Pulling back the thick woolen carpet covering a great majority of the wide floor boards, she pushed in a variety of locations until she felt one give. Looking around for something to pry it up with, she grabbed the poker from the fireplace and wedged it between two boards. With a loud squeak that echoed through the room the board lifted far enough for her to finish prying it with her hands. It was no easy task.

Her brow was coated with perspiration while she reached hesitantly into the darkness and felt around. Knowing that rodents roamed the walls, she hoped that the stone was the only thing her fingers came in touch with. Finally, her fingers folded themselves around a smooth, cool stone. It was the crystal. Pulling it out, she held it high into the light that the lamp she set on a nearby table emitted and marveled over its beauty. It held within it the colors of the rainbow. They moved and swayed with the direction she turned it. It was so beautiful that, for a brief moment, she was tempted to keep it for herself. With a sigh of resignation, she tucked it into the folds of her skirt and set about putting the room back in order. When she was satisfied that all was as it was when she entered, she looked around and realized that, in the future, this room is fully carpeted. Although she did her best to restore the house to its original beauty, she was doing it room by room and she hadn't yet started on this room. She took a moment to burn the memory of what it should look like in her mind before closing the door behind her and heading back to the dining room. Now that she had the stone in her possession, she wanted to get back to Fiona as quickly as possible, even if it did mean vomiting up her delicious, undigested, meal.

That's exactly what she did.

Thankfully, Brandon had the good grace to place them at the edge of the lawn, far enough away so Tara's ritual would go unnoticed. He stroked her hair while she emptied the contents of her stomach and did his best to ease her suffering.

"Only one more time and you will be done with all of this.

Only one more time and you will be home," he assured her.

"Oh no, I have to do this again!" Tara moaned her despair.

"Yes, my darling, but just one more time. Then it will all be over," he whispered affectionately.

She'd lied to him. She had to. Otherwise he'd never take her home and she knew that it was necessary for her to go back, for many different reasons.

Fiona's footsteps in the night were soft, but still audible. She asked Brandon to excuse them while she had a small chat with Tara. He agreed to meet them at the house and left graciously.

"Did you get it, Lass?" she whispered.

"Yes, Fiona, I have it." Tara stood up and reached in her pocket. Looking down at the vomit only recently purged from her body, she wrinkled her nose.

"Can we step away from here?" she asked.

"Gladly," Fiona chuckled.

"I lied and told Brandon that he misunderstood and that you would be able to close the portal to Shadow Land in the future now that you have the crystal so he has no need to worry about me," Tara said as she handed the stone to Fiona.

Fiona looked at Brandon making his way onto the porch of her cozy cottage. She did her best to hide her surprise before grabbing Tara's hand firmly in hers and looking deep into her eyes. "That's alright lass," she said in a voice that she hoped disguised her anguish. "I'll find a solution to all of this. I promise."

"I know you will," Tara said with a smile.

"Are ya ready to go home?" Fiona asked.

Tara closed her eyes and nodded. "It's time."

****

"I wasn't going to say anything, but now I will. I'm working on a way to have them both be able to live at the same time. If that happens, you will have to choose," Fiona whispered.

"I don't have to choose now," he replied as he hugged her

good-bye.

"No, not now," she replied before planting a kiss on his cheek and rigorously patting his back.

They'd said their good-byes. There was nothing more for Fiona to do except step back and watch Brandon, Tara, Dennis and Luella hold hands while the whirlwind consumed them until they were no more.

A SNEAK PEEK AT DREAM LOVE

ONE

"Have you ever opened your door to find a this absolutely gorgeous, hunky, specimen of a man standing on the other side? I've dreamt just that repeatedly to the point I'm frustrated with myself for not having a depth of imagination to move beyond this dream guy -pun intended- and into something more substantial. I mean, all he does is stand there with a sexy smirk on his face. Night after night I see myself in this cozy little log cabin. There's an enormous fieldstone fireplace dominating the room. The warmth from its roaring fire permeates every crack and crevice of the small building. Either there's no electricity, or it's gone out for some reason because I'm sitting curled up in an overstuffed, tweed covered club chair reading a book by lantern light. I can't see the title of the book, but, by the look of the cover, I'd guess it's a romance novel.

"I feel pretty content and peaceful. Then it happens. There's a loud knock on the door. I quietly put my book down and unfold myself out of the chair to go answer the door. When I open the door, he's standing there just as bold as you please. He's tall, dark, handsome and super hunky. There's a smirk on his face and firelight in his eyes... Then I wake up."

I shifted uncomfortably in the chair while watching Dr. Mokena write in a notebook. After a long, uncomfortable silence, in which the good doctor never once looked my way, I cleared my throat in an exaggerated manner.

"How long have you had this reoccurring dream?" the slender, middle aged doctor asked with a patient smile.

I studied the platinum blonde opposite me for a considerable length of time before answering. Noting, for the first time, how the woman's brown eyes reflected a similar light to the man in my dreams, I wondered if that's where I got the inspiration to add that trait to him.

"They started shortly after I started seeing you," I replied.

"Why, that was months ago," the doctor said with surprise.

"It feels like forever," I moaned. "In the beginning, I found them exciting. Now, I just wish I could move further with them, or dream of something else. It's like 'Groundhog Day' nightly."

The good doctor surprised me with, "Are you currently dating?"

"Are you insinuating that I'm fantasizing about this hunk because I lack a boyfriend?" I asked indignantly.

"The mind is a complex thing. I'm simply looking for a direction in which to search for the reason behind your dreams," she explained. "I don't understand why you waited so long to mention them."

"I was sent here by my boss for work related issues," I said as I did my best to control my irritation. "It's a routine thing we all have to go through periodically. My dreams don't pertain to work."

"Being a software designer for a gaming company the size of Playtronics can be stressful," she mused.

"Hence the mandatory visits to the shrink every so often," I blurted.

"As well as the invasion of your sleep with dreams that could very well be your mind trying to tell you about a new game," she added.

"I don't deal with erotic software," I complained.

"Does a hunky man equate to erotic?" she asked with raised brow. Feeling embarrassingly self-conscious, I lowered my gaze and shook my head. "I believe there is something far deeper going on than just you dreaming about a man you may or may not desire. I'd like to explore this further."

"My sessions are up," I protested.

"I'd like to continue them," she added.

"Is this a mandatory thing?" I asked while raising my own brow in a manner similar to the way she'd just raised hers.

"You know it isn't," she said with exasperation.

"I'll think about it," I said as I stood to make my leave.

"This may be your last session, but your time isn't up yet," she said commandingly. "Sit."

I looked at my watch and scowled as I plopped my backside back down onto the chair while looking at the clock on the wall, "Three minutes. Are you serious?"

"A lot can be said in three minutes," she said briskly.

"Such as?" I asked.

She looked at her wrist watch and wrote something in her notebook while speaking without looking up at me, "I'd like you to attend a weekend retreat the week after next."

"If I don't?" I asked boldly as I stood back up.

"Let's not find out, okay?" she said gently.

After locking eyes with my stubborn therapist, I slumped my shoulders and muttered, "E-mail the directions to me."

"I'll do one better," she said with a broad smile. "I'll pick you up and drive you there myself."

With a rapid shake of my head, I did my best to verbally dissuade the good doctor from doing me the service of taxying me to her retreat, but to no avail. By the time I left her office, my heart was heavy with apprehension. I assumed it was because I disliked baring my belly to anyone in the way she insisted I do with her, but a deep nagging in the pit of my stomach suggested it just might be something more than that. Fitful nights occupied by the same dream and stressful work deadlines left me feeling incapable of resisting her insistence to attend her weekend retreat. Who knows... a retreat just might be the ticket to cure my insomnia and shattered nerves.

As I stepped out of the four-story brick building that housed the office of the good Dr. Mokena, I was greeted by my overly anxious friend, Chris.

"Damn girl," Chris said as she matched her step with mine while walking as far from that place as possible, "what did she do, make you run the gamut? I've been out here for ages."

"I couldn't get her to relinquish one precious minute of her time," I spat. "I need a drink."

"Roger's waiting for us back at the office," Chris said quietly.

"I need a drink," I said again.

She must have picked up on the sense of urgency I felt because she nodded and then stepped onto the curb to hail a cab.

"Mickey's sound good?" she asked.

"Perfect," I replied.

Mickey's Pub was a small Irish bar that was only a ten-minute cab ride from work and fairly centrally located between the homes of me and my circle of friends. We met there so often it easily could be labeled our hangout. As we entered the dusky interior, my nostrils flared with the familiar scent of booze, polished wood, cleaning solution, and body odor.

"Gertrude Hitchcock, as I live and breathe," came a deep voice from the shadows. "After all these years, can my eyes be deceiving me?"

I turned to look into a pair of deep-set eyes that I never expected to have to look into again. Their rich blue-black hue accentuated the natural evilness that plagued me all through school. The oversized nose on the square face that was scarred by adolescent acne rested at an angle, as a result of being broken by the wide board I swung with that very intention when I was in junior high.

"No one calls me Gertrude anymore, Jackal," I said, emphasizing the immature nick name I'd given Jack Adams long ago.

"Who's this, Gertie?" Chris asked.

"Gertie?" he said with disdain.

"He's an old pain in the ass come back to haunt me," I grumbled as I made my way to the bar.

"I came to attend the funeral," Jack said as he kept pace at my heels like a mad dog. "You weren't at the wake. Does that mean you won't be at the funeral?"

My body tensed as I listened to his taunting tone. The last thing I wanted was for evil Jack Adams to know that I had no idea who died that we'd both know.

"Who died?" Chris asked. She was clearly still trying to make sense of what was happening.

"Why not ask her?" Jack snarled.

"Jim Beam on the rocks," I said to the bartender that I'd never seen before. "Make it four fingers."

With a raise of a brow and a broad smile, the unfamiliar bartender went to work.

"Gertie?" Chris said questioningly.

The last thing I needed was to be taunted by my high school nemesis. My nerves were incapable of dealing with the stress. I placed elbows on the bar and buried my face in my hands.

"Feigning remorse?" Jack sneered.

"Bart," I said as I groaned into my hands.

Jack's comment about my feigning remorse over the death of someone we both knew was the only clue I needed to realize the deceased was my ex-fiancé, Bart Matthews.

"Your ex-fiancé, Bart?" Chris gasped.

"I can't believe you couldn't muster up enough decency to pay your respects," Jack said.

"Leave us," I snapped as I whirled around to give the full effect of my glower, "or I'll rip that ugly nose right off your face instead of simply breaking it."

"Still a bitch," he said as he crept back into the shadows.

"Don't forget it," I said threateningly.

"Who the hell is that and is Bart really dead?" Chris whispered as she took a sip of my whiskey.

I motioned for the bartender to prepare the identical drink for my friend while I proceeded to explain my painful history with both Bart Matthews and Jack Adams.

I was never a popular girl while growing up in the small

town in Upstate New York. My body was too skinny, my hair too curly, my teeth were too crooked, and my brain was too smart. Diet, exercise, a good beautician, and an outrageously expensive orthodontist took care of the cosmetic tragedies. Surrounding myself with geeks who equaled, if not bested me, took care of the braininess.

Jack was the school bully who plagued me throughout school simply because he could. Bart was his friend -although, at the time, I couldn't understand why- who took pity on me when I was fifteen and stood up to Jack when he took my books and tried to toss them down the sewer manhole. Back then, it took very little kindness to win me over. Needless to say, after that one heroic act from Bart, I was head over heels in love.

Of course, it wasn't reciprocated.

It wasn't until I'd gone through my transformation from ugly duckling to swan and was home, during my last year of college, for the holidays and bumped into him at a party before Bart paid me much notice. By then, I was no stranger to relationships, but the memories and gratitude of his simple act of kindness lured me in. It got serious fairly quickly. By summer we were engaged.

We moved in with each other after I graduated. That was the beginning of our end. The shine quickly wore off the penny. I soon discovered a side of Bart that he'd kept hidden from me. He wasn't as evil as his best buddy, Jack, but he could still be cruel. He justified his behavior by pointing out that his abusiveness was directed toward animals instead of people. When I told Bart that I couldn't marry such a sadist, he fabricated a story about my preferring girls over men and he just wasn't into such things. His family and friends -which was most of the town- believed him and cursed me for leading him on. It was a mess.

With the town being as small as it was, and with Bart's family having such a strong foothold in said town, I decided to not only move out of the apartment I shared with Bart, but I moved right out of town. The home of a college friend in the Queens borough of New York City was only a train ride away, so I headed there. I picked up a job in a game store, took an occasional train back to visit my parents on my days off, and saved as much money as I could to help fund a small studio to move into.

Little by little I gained my footing in the big city. After what seemed like a thousand interviews, I landed a job at Playtronics. Eventually, with the help of my skills, work ethics, and credentials, I climbed the corporate ladder until I'd reached the very prestigious and stressful position of software designer. That was three years ago.

So much of my life had changed in those three short years that I rarely, if ever, looked back at those pre-Playtronics days. On the rare occasions when the memories surfaced, I'd quickly kick them out. That, and the fact that I hadn't been in contact with my parents in a while, was why I had no clue that Bart was killed in an automobile accident a few days earlier.

"Correct me if I'm wrong," Chris said after downing her second four fingers of Jim Beam, "but doesn't it seem a bit odd to run into this character who claims to be back from wherever he's back from to attend a funeral of a guy who's supposedly lying in a funeral home a good eighty miles from here?"

I was so absorbed in walking down memory lane with Chris that it completely went over my head, but she was right. It was just too coincidental running into evil Jack Adams in an Irish pub in the middle of Queens like this.

"So, you caught me," Jack smirked as he stepped back out of the shadows.

By now I'd had enough to drink that I could officially call myself drunk. I did my best to focus on him, but in truth, he was little more than a blur.

"I don't want to catch you," I slurred. "I just want you to go away."

"I know you don't believe this, but Bart did love you and I'm sure he'd want you to attend his funeral," Jack said quietly. "That's all I came to say." As he started to walk away he stopped and added, "Think long and hard. Once he's buried you can't take back your actions. Could you really live with yourself knowing you didn't attend his funeral?"

"How did you find me?" I asked.

"I'm a bounty hunter," he replied. "Finding people is what I do."

"That figures," I giggled as I leaned into Chris.

"You might want to think about slowing down," Jack warned.

"Go away you evil beast," I spat.

"Yea, go away," Chris chimed.

"I think I should stick around to make sure you get home okay," he said firmly.

"Since when did you become chivalrous?" I said with surprise.

"I've never seen you like this, that's all," Jack replied.

"You don't know me, evil one," I hissed. "be gone with you!" I waved my hand as if to shoo him away.

"Let me call you a cab," he insisted.

"Listen, buddy," Chris snarled. "Take the hint and get lost."

"May I be of assistance?" asked a tall, slender man in an Armani suit from the opposite end of the bar.

"Mind your business," Jack snarled.

"It's difficult to mind much of anything while these two women are continually asking you to leave them alone," the man replied as he started toward us.

Even in my drunken stupor I couldn't help responding to the electric sensuality he had about him. A closer look told me that he wasn't as slender as I'd originally thought. In fact, he looked to be well muscled beneath the expertly-tailored virgin wool. His short brown hair was cut in a style that neatly framed strong facial features possessing a European influence. Brilliant honey-brown eyes were set evenly below perfectly shaped brows. They danced with humor as if he was enjoying my reaction to his hot, sexy self.

I heard Chris' sharp intake of breath and knew that

I wasn't the only one affected by this man. Even the bartender stood perfectly still. It was only Jack who seemed oblivious to the magnitude of this man's presence.

"Let me call you a cab," Jack insisted once again.

This time he made the mistake of grabbing my upper arm and trying to pull me away from the bar.

"I have no idea why you're so determined to suddenly play the chivalrous knight, Jack Adams, but kindly find some other female to play it with. It's too late for me," I spat. "Now let go of me."

The visible vice grip that the dark-haired stranger placed on Jack's wrist weakened him to the point he could no longer hold onto my arm. It was an intense and sobering moment for Jack and all who witnessed it.

"She said leave her alone," he said in a calm, steely tone. "I suggest you do so."

"You look familiar," I managed as I watched Jack slink away. "Can I buy you a drink?"

"Another time, perhaps," he said as he motioned to the bartender to clear our glasses away.

"I wasn't finished," I protested as I grabbed the remains of my drink and tossed it down my throat.

"I think he's trying to tell us we're drunk," Chris giggled.

"Are we?" I asked with genuine curiosity before the world spun around me and disappeared.

TWO

The ringing of the telephone was magnified by the pounding headache that was all consuming. I stretched my body as best I could on the sofa that I could only assume belonged to Chris and placed my hands over my forehead.

"Answer the phone," I groaned as I slowly opened my eyes and tried to bring the world into focus. "How much did I drink?" I asked no one in particular, while I fought down the vomit that was trying to force its way up my esophagus.

"Clearly more than you can handle," said the oh so familiar voice of Dr. Mokena.

"What are you doing here?" I groaned.

"I live here," she said in a flat tone.

Perhaps I just heard it as flat because of my all-consuming headache.

I tried to sit up, but the pain was so excruciating I was sure I'd lose the battle with the vomit.

"I'm sick," I said matter-of-factly.

"I'm not surprised," she said. "I'll get you some Alka Seltzer. It will help with both your stomach and head."

"I need something really strong for my head," I urged.

"I doubt your stomach would tolerate anything else. Just trust me and drink the Alka Seltzer for now," she said.

She was right. As I slowly sipped on the bubbly medicine, my stomach settled down and my headache reduced to a more tolerable level.

"Where's Chris?" I asked as I slowly looked around the room. "Where am I?"

"You're in my apartment," she explained.

"That's right, you already said that... I think," I mused aloud. "I've no clue how I got here."

"I brought you here. I happened to be passing that quaint little Irish pub you imbibed in and when I saw them struggling with you and your friend, I offered to help. Neither of you were in any condition to tell me where you lived so I brought you home with me," Dr. Mokena said in a low voice. "Your friend is on the sofa in my den."

"You know where I live," I protested as I struggled to sit straight up.

"I have your address on file in my office. I certainly don't carry it around with me in the event I stumble upon your drunken backside on the streets of Queens," she said briskly.

"I need to go home," I said as I stood on shaky legs.

"Who is Bart?" she asked.

"He's an old boyfriend," I replied sadly. "He's dead." After a moment, I added, "We were engaged once."

"I see," she said thoughtfully. "Is that the reason for your drunken fest?"

"I don't know," I said with frustration. "I went there with Chris to have a drink or two to unwind. Out of nowhere comes this guy from my childhood. He bullied me from the time I entered kindergarten until I graduated. He's a real son-of -a-bitch. For some crazy reason he decided to look me up to tell me Bart died and he tried to act chivalrous when he saw I drank too much. It got messy."

"Why would it get messy?" she asked.

"I didn't want him near me, let alone aiding me," I admitted. "Somehow, amidst all the arguing, remembering past hurts, and frustration over the fact he wouldn't disappear, I drank too much."

"Which of the men helping you was Jack?" she asked.

"There was more than one?" I gasped.

"There were several men hovered around you when I

stopped the cab," she admitted. "I didn't like the look of things. That's why I stopped."

"It was pretty stupid of us to get so smashed. The only male I knew in that bar was the creep from my past and he can hardly be trusted. I'd never seen the bartender before if he was one of the men helping," I said.

"There was a man with a crooked nose and acne scarred face, a man in an expensive suit," she said as she counted on her fingers, "and I believe the other was the bartender."

"I guess I owe you a huge thank you," I sighed.

"Attending my retreat will do," she chuckled.

"What's it for again?" I asked.

"Trust me. It's important for you to be there," she assured me.

"Gertie!" Chris shouted with an agonized tone from the other room. "Where the hell are we?"

The apartment was one of six in a quaint brownstone on the east side of Queens. Although not overly large, it provided plenty of room for a single, professional looking for a place to nest and get away from it all. The room I was in was an open living space where she'd set up the living room and dining area. When I saw Chris come out of what looked to be the second bedroom, it was clear the doctor had turned it into a small den for when she brought her work home with her.

"I need to pee," Chris whined as she jiggled in place.

"It's the door at the end of the hall," the good doctor said patiently. She looked at me for a moment before adding, "What aren't you telling me?"

"I'm not sure," I replied. "It's just that... that guy in the suit... he looked familiar, but I can't place where I saw him or how I know him."

"Did he say you knew each other?" she asked.

"He never even said his name," I said thoughtfully. "He just came over to help get rid of Jack."

"It must have been messy to attract a stranger to act as

your hero," she said with a grin.

"My head hurts like a bitch," Chris grumbled as she returned from the bathroom. "Oh, hello," she said as she focused on Dr. Mokena. "Thanks for putting us up."

"You remember?" I said with surprise.

"She was less under the weather than you, although still dangerously out of it," Dr. Mokena explained.

"Yea," Chris admitted. "I remember bits and pieces, but not everything. It's like someone slipped something in our drinks or something."

"Do you think?" I said eagerly. "Not that I'd want that to happen, but it makes more sense than us drinking ourselves into stupors like that."

"I'm trying to remember how many drinks we actually had," Chris mused.

"I can settle this very easily," Dr. Mokena said. "I have a friend who works in a lab. We can get her to draw a little blood and test it."

"I don't know if we need to go to all that trouble," I said warily.

"I think I'd rather just go home," Chris added.

"Okay," the doctor said as she threw her hands in the air with exasperation. "If you feel you don't need to find out if it's safe to drink there again, then skip the blood test."

I bit my lower lip while I debated what to do. I really did just want to go home, but the doctor was right. Neither Chris or I knew that bartender. What if he was in cohorts with some underground trafficking racket and drugged us. Maybe that handsome guy was there to whisk us off to market and Jack foiled his plans. Maybe he was trying to get rid of Jack for his own personal gain instead of for ours.

"She's right," I said to Chris. "We really should get that blood work done before our systems clear out."

"I feel so bad," Chris said.

"Drink some Alka Seltzer," I offered. "It helped calm me

down." I turned to the doctor and asked, "Do you have more?"

She smiled, nodded, and headed for the kitchen to prepare a glass for Chris. Within a few minutes after drinking it down, not only had the color returned to her cheeks, but she was claiming hunger. I still hadn't reached that point, which was a good thing since the doctor preferred we wait until after our blood was drawn to eat something.

The lab was within walking distance, which was good. It gave Chris and me a chance to walk off some of the negative effects from the night before. I smiled to myself as I listened to Chris chatter away with Dr. Mokena about everything and anything. It wasn't until she brought up the topic of Bart and the funeral that I noticeably scowled and asked her to change the subject.

Of course, that wasn't about to happen. Not with my therapist in the mix. She poked and prodded until she pulled as much information about Bart and my former relationship with him as she could, mindless of the fact that Chris was hanging onto every juicy tidbit divulged. It wasn't that I minded having my good friend listen in. I had nothing to hide on the subject. It's just a personality quirk of mine. I'm not comfortable telling all... to anyone.

It was decided that, for closure purposes, I would attend the funeral. Chris offered to join me and I readily agreed. When I called my parents to tell them I was coming and for what purpose, they made a watered-down attempt to dissuade me. I'm sure they were battling the mixed emotions of wanting to see me after such a long gap and wanting to protect me from the venomous talk of Bart's family. I told them I was bringing my best friend from work as a shield and assured them I'd be fine. By the time our conversation ended, we were all excited about my coming, regardless of the reason.

THREE

I won't say that I didn't feel a sense of loss from Bert's death. We were engaged once, after all. Even though it ended badly, I loved him once. It's just that the thought of sitting within the confines of the church amongst the 'Gertie haters' was more than either I or Chris wanted to endure. We decided to forgo the church and catch up with the funeral proceedings at the cemetery. I was surprised to see how intimate a crowd it was that gathered around the open grave. I stood close enough to hear the eulogy, but far enough away as not to intrude on what appeared to be a tight-knit gathering. My ever-supportive friend stayed glued to my side, gripping my elbow at times whenever someone from the group would look our way.

I smiled to myself when I remembered the time Bert accused me of being a lesbian. Chris' intent on shielding me from the mourners could easily be interpreted as the actions of a lover. Just one more thing to fuel their fire.

When the service was over, we scurried to leave before the other attendees could get close enough to offer a snide comment or two.

"Gertrude, dear, wait up!" called Eliza Matthews as she hurried toward us. I looked at the woman dressed in black with curiosity. The last we'd spoken, she reiterated the fact that she believed Bart's accusations of my being a lesbian and thought that I was a horrid person for deceiving him in such a way. Hearing her call me 'dear' completely threw me. "Please, dear," she said breathlessly as she caught up with us. "Just one moment of your time."

"I'm sorry for your loss, Mrs. Matthews," I said softly.

"Thank you," she said as she dabbed at the corner of her eye with a tissue. "I just wanted to thank you for attending today. I know it would have meant a lot to my son."

I was unsure how to handle this unexpected comment, so I simply mumbled, "Thank you."

"I'd like you and your friend to come back to the house for something to eat," she said hopefully. "Will you do that?" I looked from Chris, to Eliza, and then back to Chris again. She shrugged her acceptance of the idea, so I nodded that we'd come. "Excellent," she said with satisfaction. "Where's your car?"

"I don't own a car," I said flatly.

"How did you get here?" she asked.

"We walked," Chris offered politely.

"Across town?" she gasped.

With a hint of a smile on her face, my friend proceeded to explain that we lived in the very large borough of Queens where people walked far greater distances than the few miles we'd ventured to attend the funeral as it was cheaper, and often faster, than taking a cab or driving a car.

"It won't take us long to get to your home," I said firmly. "Our legs are strong."

"Nonsense," she sputtered. "You'll ride with me. Charles! Make room in the car for these two young ladies!"

Without waiting for our reply, she scurried off to the rather large Lincoln. Quick to comply with her request, her husband, Charles, stood waiting with its back door open. I looked at Chris with raised brow while she good naturedly nudged me into motion. It seemed we avoided the confines of the church only to suffer those of the car and then their modest Cape style home.

"I'm so glad you came," Eliza reiterated when we were all settled in the car and headed toward her house. "I simply hate the way things ended." She looked at Chris and gave a slight smile. "I'm Eliza Matthews."

"I'm Chris Benning," Chris said sweetly. "Gertie and I work together."

"How nice," Eliza mused. "Do you live together too?"

It was clear that she still believed the accusations about my sexual preferences. I smiled as I watched the myriad of emotions flash over her face when my friend proceeded to tell her that I lived alone and she lived with her boyfriend who she hoped would soon propose marriage. It wasn't necessary for Chris to divulge so much information to a perfect stranger. I knew she did this specifically to shatter the rumors about me and I was grateful. Had I truly been a lesbian -or even bi-sexual- I would have held my head up high and proudly admitted it. It was the fact that I disliked false rumors spread about me, no matter what the topic, that agitated me so. Chris knew this about me, for which I was grateful.

Considering the small group at the cemetery, I was surprised to see the number of cars outside the Matthew's residence. It seemed the attendees did just the opposite from Chris and me. They attended the church and avoided the cemetery. Considering the primitive fear that a good deal of society has where cemeteries are concerned, I understood their reasoning. I may not have agreed with it, but I understood it.

The living room and dining room of the fourteen hundred square foot house were packed with friends and family. There was a large variety of food laid out on the dining room table; ranging from lasagna and a few casseroles to potato salad and deviled eggs. Considerations were made for vegetarians and carnivores alike.

I was incredibly uncomfortable as I inched my way through the sea of strangers. Except for Jack Adams – who leaned against the wall in the corner of the room glowering at me- the Matthews, and Chris, I didn't know a soul.

"Who are these people?" Chris whispered as she stood next to me filling her plate with potato salad and cold cuts.

"Your guess is as good as mine," I replied. "We're on fairly even ground in this one."

"It's weird," she said with a slight shudder.

"It's a funeral," I reminded her. "They're rarely filled with joy and pleasantries."

"Just the same, let's eat and do the nicey- nicey thing with the Matthews and then get the hell out of here," she urged.

"You don't have to ask me twice," I sighed. "I don't know why I allowed Dr. Mokena to talk me into this to begin with."

"It seems to have brought some joy to his mother," Chris observed.

I lifted my eyes from the impressive array of food to look for Eliza Matthew's upon Chris' mention of her and stopped short when my eyes locked with those of one of the handsomest men I'd ever laid eyes on in my entire life. My body tingled unnaturally from head to toe from the somehow familiar intense look he gave me. Propriety called for me to look away- this was a funeral, after all, not a pick up joint- but I couldn't get my eyes to obey. It was as if they had a mind of their own as they shamelessly drank in every delicious inch of his six-foot plus frame.

I almost dropped my plate when he politely, but boldly elbowed his way to me.

"Hello," he said in a rich baritone voice that matched the rest of him just fine. "I'm Marcus. Marc for short. You're the ex-fiancé, right?"

"You're the guy from the bar," Chris gasped.

"Touché," he chuckled softly.

"What are you doing here?" she asked with an impolite bluntness that surprised me.

It was the very same question that occupied my mind so someone needed to ask it. Since I seemed to be stuck on stupid from the sheer nearness of him, that responsibility fell on Chris. I just wished she'd been a bit more diplomatic with her tone since I seriously doubted he was stalking us.

"I'm paying respects to some very close friends," he replied patiently. "How about you?"

My face reddened at the mere question. How callous it would sound if I told the truth about how my therapist felt it would be good for me to have closure from such a bad situation by attending the funeral of the person at the root of that situation and then I decided to stay for a few eats afterward. Just thinking it shamed me.

"Are you from here?" Chris demanded.

"Chris," I hissed.

"I find it odd that he just happened to be at the bar the other night and then he's here," she shrugged.

"It is a little odd," I muttered.

"Actually, it was intentional," Marc offered. "I was there for Jack."

"I'm not sure I follow," I said hesitantly.

"In case you haven't noticed, he's a bit off," Marc whispered as he tapped his pointer finger against his temple. "I was warned that he intended to seek you out and harass you, so I followed him."

"Who warned you?" Chris asked suspiciously.

"Eliza Matthews," he said.

"Jack was always a bully, but I never knew him to be crazy," I said thoughtfully.

"You know about the brain tumor he suffered five years ago, right?" Marc asked. At my rapid intake of air, he added. "I guess not." He lowered his head so that he was speaking close to my ear. I could feel the heat of his breath as he said, "The operation saved his life, but left him a bit touched."

I shuddered at the sensation of his hot breath against my flesh. Ripples of sheer delight traveled my body. I closed my eyes to revel in them. It was then that I realized that if you replaced the expertly tailored suit with a denim shirt and jeans, the same tall, dark, hunky stranger who haunted my dreams was the very same tall, dark, hunky stranger whose deep, breathy, voice caressed me in a way that could only be described as erotic.

The temptation to shout that I knew him from my dreams was great, but the realization of how crazy I'd sound prevented me from acting upon it. I did, however, step back to put some distance between his sexy energy and my overheated body so that I could better gather my wits about me. If he noticed my sudden retreat, he made no mention of it as Eliza approached and formally introduced him as the owner of the town's lodge and campgrounds.

It was difficult to visualize this man who stood before me dressed and looking like a GQ model operating the local campgrounds. I could, however, easily imagine him in being just that when he was dressed in the casual, manly attire he sported in my dreams.

If I said it didn't bother me that I'd somehow managed to conjure up a real live person -that I'd never laid eyes on before in my entire life- to fantasize about in my dreams, I'd be lying. It both troubled and creeped me out. For the first time since I'd started seeing Dr. Mokena, I was actually eager for an appointment. Someone needed to help me make sense of this.

When I was able to get a word in amidst Chris and Eliza Matthew's babbling, I queried the handsome man of my dreams as much as I could about himself. I learned that, although he looked to be in his late twenties, he was actually in his early forties. He was single and moved east from Montana the year before. He bought the lodge and adjoining campgrounds almost immediately.

Upon hearing this, I decided that perhaps I'd seen him in passing during one of my visits to my parents and immediately abandoned the idea for the emergency session I planned on booking with Dr. Mokena as soon as I returned home.

Rather than us enduring a long, drawn out event, the time passed quickly and pleasurably. We were so entertained by our new friend that before we knew it, it was early evening and the mourners were filing out of the quaint little Cape while giving one final note of sympathy to Eliza and Charles Matthews. Marc wouldn't hear of us calling a cab to return us to my parent's house and -with Eliza's backing- insisted on driving us himself. By now we'd spent enough time with him, watched his interactions with other guests, and learned sufficient information to feel comfortable accepting his offer.

When Chris eagerly slid into the front seat of his SUV, I chuckled and pushed my slender five-foot-three-inch frame into the back. I was glad I'd worn slacks instead of a skirt since getting up into vehicles the height of an SUV or a truck were never a graceful event for my small frame and short legs. As I adjusted myself into the seat, I noticed a slight grin lighting up Marc's handsome features as he monitored my progress through the rear-view mirror.

"All set?" he asked when I'd completed wrestling with the seat belt.

"You bet," I said with a giggle that I haven't a clue the reason for.

The streets of small town USA were fairly empty as he maneuvered the SUV with the confidence of someone who spent a great deal of time behind the wheel. Within the matter of minutes, we were outside my home giving him our thanks and saying our goodbyes.

As I opened the door to slide out of the vehicle, he reached over and gently laid his hand on my shoulder. Shards of electricity permeated every inch of me. It felt so amazing, I couldn't help sigh with pleasure.

"Have lunch with me tomorrow?" he asked.

"Both of us?" I asked softly as I looked at Chris who had already exited the car.

"Just you," he said with a grin.

"Sorry," I said with obvious regret, "she's my guest. It wouldn't be right."

"I didn't realize," he said thoughtfully. "My apologies. Please, will you both be my guests for lunch tomorrow?"

He said it loud enough for Chris to hear. The delight in her eager acceptance overpowered the nagging in my gut and I nodded my agreement.

"What time do you want us there?" I asked.

"I'll pick you up around noon," he said as he released my arm and turned back to face the wheel. "Sound good?"

"We can take a cab or borrow my parent's car," I offered.

"That's up to you, but I need to run a few errands in the morning so I'll be out anyway," he said non-chalantly.

"You're like our own personal driver," Chris giggled.

"Yes ma'am," he said with a smile and a nod.

"We'll be ready," I said with a roll of my eyes as I slid out of the door and positioned myself next to Chris.

"Until tomorrow, then," he said with a wave as he pulled the SUV away from the curve.

Chris slid her hand through the crook of my arm and guided me up the walk to my parent's house.

"Wowza, wowza, what a looker," she mused.

"You certainly were taken with him," I snickered.

"Come on," she grumbled. "Are you going to try to tell me you didn't think he was the hottest thing you'd set eyes on since... I don't know when?"

"Since the other night at the bar?" I chuckled.

"I was too drunk to really appreciate his hotness," she said with a grin.

"He's a breath taker, for sure," I agreed.

"The question is... Is he a keeper?" Chris added.

"What about Tom?" I asked with surprise.

"Not for me, silly. For you. It's time you got back into the game," she said.

"I didn't know I was out of the game," I pouted.

"I've met the guys you've been dating," Chris pointed out. "No comparison."

"I believe it would be difficult for any man to hold up against that one," I said.

"You like him, don't you?" she asked.

"I don't know him," I replied.

"You know enough," she said.

"For lunch or maybe even dinner, but don't start planning my wedding quite yet, okay?" I said.

"Can I plan the engagement party?" she giggled.

****

Don't miss out on the rest of the story. Get your copy of DREAM LOVE from your favorite bookseller

ABOUT THE AUTHOR

Eileen Sheehan lives in her native upstate New York where she enjoys the beauty of the Southern Tier countryside with her two muses, Justin -a Maine-Coon cat and Jackson – an adorable miniature schnauzer.

A prolific writer, Eileen began her writing career as a free-lance writer for periodical magazines and newspapers. Then, she tried her hand at screenplay writing. Her screenplay, "When East Meets West" was a finalist in the 2001 International Independent Film and Video Festival at Madison Square Gardens, New York, New York. Finally finding her niche in novel writing, she lets her imagination lose with new adult/paranormal romance/thrillers with the author name of Eileen Sheehan. She creates historical romances (and plans on writing contemporary romances at some point) with the author name of Ailene Frances. (Frances is her middle name and Ailene is just another way of spelling Eileen!). Seeing how far out of the box she could stretch, she crafted an alternative romance-tragedy with the author name of E. F. Sheehan and has a few self-help books under her work name of Lena Sheehan.

An incurable romantic, she has a love affair with at least one character... one book at a time.

Visit her online at: http://www.sheehan-author.info

Email: contact@sheehan-author.info and sign up to be a part of the readers she emails with notifications of upcoming titles and events. She even offers occasional free books on this site, so be sure to check it out!

OTHER BOOKS BY EILEEN SHEEHAN

VAMPIRE WITCH TRILOGY
Vampire Witch
[Book one]
Vampire Queen
[Book two']
Kings and Queens
[Book three]

THE TUGURLAN SLAYER CHRONICLES
Vampire Iniquity
[Book One]
The Cure
(Book Two)
Vampires and Werewolves
(Book Three)

Dark Escape
{Book One]

-STAND ALONE NOVELS-
The Vampire, The Handler, and Me
For Love of a Vampire
The Princess and the Vampire King
Dream Love

Shadow Love

***

Books by Ailene Frances
Love Misunderstood
Paper Widow

****

Books by E. F. Sheehan
Toast with Jelly